I0582168

THE POOL OF AESLIN

THE POOL OF AESLIN
THE ERWAIN TRILOGY

MARIAH STILLBROOK

ALSO BY MARIAH STILLBROOK

In The Pines

The Lost Erwain

Hall of Shadows

This is a work of fiction. All of the characters, organizations, and events portrayed in this novel are either products of the author's imagination or are used fictitiously.

Published in the United States by Creative James Media.

THE POOL OF AESLIN. Copyright © 2025 by Mariah Stillbrook. All rights reserved. Printed in the United States of America. For information, address Creative James Media, 9150 Fort Smallwood Road, Pasadena, MD 21122.

www.creativejamesmedia.com

978-1-956183-05-4 (trade paperback)

First U.S. Edition 2025

For Liv.

Toby Koehaias stared out into the endless rows of knights. Around their necks hung the symbol of their kingdom—a white, star-like flower. Their jaws were chiseled from stone, their expressions hard, their eyes empty; but these weren't the characteristics of all the knights in their kingdom, just the ones molded under his uncle's regime. He'd been watching it spread since the moment he'd been delivered to the throne that he was next in line to sit upon, and it was happening exactly like his mother had said it would. It was the new Aeronian way. Serve not just your king, but your race.

Toby wondered as he stared out into the endless formation —were these the sons of Danka, the elfin King of the North who died many ages ago, or were they the descendants of Danka's brother, Lanake—the king who ruled the South. Lanake's soul was said to have been absorbed first by the Bahadicaras, or the age of darkness. And Toby believed this theory wholly, for the gruel of souls that embodied that dark cloud would have first fed upon its greatest enemies. That was why they began feeding off the gods in the first place, because they knew if they could get them out of the way there would be absolutely nothing to stop them.

The Bahadicaras had done their job well, ridding the world of those embedded with the brightest light. Lanake's descendants were now few and far between. Still, Toby had been able to find enough of these souls to build up to the task his mother had sent him forward to carry out. And the faeries, well, there were a few bad seeds like the recently deceased Helene Voss, non-believers of the cause, but for the most part convincing them to join had been effortless, especially considering that it was one of their own who had the potential to end this political and spiritual catastrophe.

Toby narrowed his eyes as these thoughts sauntered through his mind. Where was it the loyalties of these knights had belonged before bleeding their hearts for the new regime? For not just their own ruler, the King of Anemone, but for his uncle. He wasn't just here on the king's orders; he had wanted to come and train these knights, to train them to be mindless drones like every other soul touched by King Loral's influence, but not because he believed in the new order. Quite the opposite. As he played his part, he was searching for traces of the true spirit. Souls moving at higher frequencies—energy with strong vibrations. Because when the Bahadicaras came through, they fed on these true spirits first, sparing only a handful.

Over the years the sons of Lanake had regrown their population. *True spirits*, falling from the sky like stars, into bodies. But darkness had still managed to leave its mark. Fireflies didn't glow in the night very often anymore, for it was dangerous to do so. Still, they existed, and it was Toby's job to find all that were left and bring them together.

He grasped the chain around his neck, feeling his mother's magic swirl around inside the silver vial. It was created specifically for him seconds before she took her last breath.

The battle he was about to engage in had nothing to do with these soldiers before him; all they were to him were pawns. Mobile statues who could be taken out just as easily as they had been molded together. But if there was even one son of Lanake mixed in with these sons of Danka, then it would make what was to happen next just that much easier.

Toby lifted his sword into the air. Scanning the army before him, he began to shout the word that would begin the faux battle they had been practicing for all week; but just as he opened his mouth, he caught a whiff of cinnamon, and *her* voice once more filtered into his ears from out of nowhere.

I fear I am not the girl you left. Is it for the better, or have I lost myself completely...?

He half lowered his sword and peered over his shoulder.

"Makayla?" He whispered the name so quietly that not even an insect flying by would have been able to hear it.

He had been hearing her now and again for several days. It was like a letter written to him in verses, sent to him in invisible bottles that floated through an imaginary ocean, from her world into his.

I miss you. Come back to me, Toby. Rescue me from this blank sheet of paper... help me define these unknown words.

An elf stationed just behind Sir Toby, on a horse rather similar in appearance to Petal, shuffled forward and leaned into his superior.

"Sir? Are you all right?"

Toby shook the haunting voice from his ears and refocused his gaze back onto the knight. "Yes, of course. I'm sorry, just a bit dazed today."

"It's been a long week, sir, but the king has requested your resurgence back into Garlandia. You only need to get through this practice, then you may depart."

Toby's ears perked up. "When did my uncle send word of this?"

3

"Just this morning, sir. We were going to wait until we were finished with the training to tell you, but you seemed as though you could use some encouraging news."

Toby nodded at the elf. "Yes Melbourne, that is exactly what I needed to hear. Thank you."

Toby faced the Knights of Anemone once more. His uncle wasn't requesting his presence so that he could praise his nephew. Toby knew that King Loral didn't trust him. His mother had warned him that no matter how well he played his part, her brother would never trust any being who had come from her loins. And he was right to feel that way. Still, Toby needed to get back—to be there when Makayla returned—for when she did, she would not be coming back to the kingdom she left. It had only been a few weeks but in that short time Garlandia had already been shoved under a dark cloud. The storm had been moving in for ages and it had finally struck with force.

Toby lifted his chest and pulled out his sword, holding it before his eyes. In it he saw her, she who he had pledged his real allegiance to. "For my queen, my everlasting heart," he whispered, before raising his sword into the air.

He prepared to give his final order before freeing himself from this place, but just as he was about to do so he heard Petal whisper, "Three rows back, Sir Toby, and to the right."

Toby paused, his gaze landing on the knight in question. Immediately he knew his horse had been right. For there, amongst all the sons of Danka was but one daughter of Lanake. The knight's eyes, the lone she-elf in a throng of males, were glued to the ones inside Toby's sword. The eyes of Makayla Wood—the next true queen of not just Garlandia, but of this world.

The white sheet of paper before me was blank, but only as far as appearances go. Inside the fibers of what made that parchment were vibrations like that of an instrument played for an entire auditorium with but one audience member.

I laid my cheek against the blank page as though it were Toby's skin. I more than missed him; without him I was broken. What I wouldn't have given just to have the pain in my side stitched—the tear I'd never known existed before I'd seen his face.

Even though it had been weeks of waiting, and every single minute felt like another lifetime, enough had happened to help me understand that the life I had always known as Makayla Wood's was over. And it wasn't even about the fact that I was an Erwain faery; it was the impending doom I felt every night as I tried to coerce myself into falling asleep, and every morning when I woke. I remember that first moment of finding myself in Garlandia—how something just felt off. Though it was the most magical place I'd ever set foot in, and the colors were as vibrant as a sanctuary filled with every flower hybrid known to man, there was still something missing. It was lackluster . . . faded. And now that shadow of foreboding tension had leaked into the human world.

My adoptive parents had of course been sent away to some weird world I'd never heard of, but at least I knew they were safe; and as for my friends, Cee-Cee and Jeremy, who King Loral now knew of because they had visited me in my homeland, I hadn't allowed them to leave my sight since the morning after I'd woken up with the realization that I was walking around with the mark of Titania on the tip of my wand. That, and the incredibly obvious emergence of several elves in our neighborhood. Not the brightest of spies. Sure, they were dressed as solicitors, handymen, and city workers, but on more than one occasion I'd seen a wand sticking out from a pair of overalls, and they weren't very good about 'playing it cool.' I'd even sighted a couple of them standing across the street, staring up at my bedroom window. Of course, as soon as I'd opened it and stared back, they'd jumped around and nervously began running in the opposite direction.

Maude and Tanker had been by but once to check in. Their visit had lasted about the length of an Ardeen faerie's attention span, and incidentally, they'd been dressed in matching renaissance dresses. Tanker had even managed to stuff his corset. When I'd initially tried to bring up the mark at the end of my wand, they'd quite literally freaked out and demanded *not* to know. It was weird, but so were they.

My faery parents had only lingered—very nervously I might add—long enough in the house of Wood to squeeze my wings in a little too tight with their embrace, and for Maude to drop into my hands a leather-bound book. At first, I thought it was a journal, but as she quickly explained, it was much more than that.

"It's my personal Book of Shadows. Every spell I've ever written or worked through is represented in those pages. I think it will help you, Lala, as you practice."

I was more than appreciative to receive the spell book, but their very overstated hesitance at being in this world at all had proved to only make me more nervous.

"Thank you," I'd said, hugging the book into my chest, feeling my birth mother's energy residing in every particle. Then, trying to revisit the matter of my wand, I held it out and began to question for the second time, "Are you sure I can't show you what I've found—"

"NO!" both Tanker and Maude had shouted, their wings wrapping around their bodies like cocoons, their hands held out before them and their eyes crammed shut. It was truly the most bizarre reaction I could've ever imagined. And here I'd thought they'd have been happy.

"*Okay* then," I'd retorted with a side eye roll, shaking away my wand. "Well, when will I see you guys again? I haven't heard a thing from Toby."

They'd very slowly unfolded their wings from around their bodies then shot one another suspicious looks.

"Well, Lala—" Maude started.

"I believe that when the time comes, you shall know," Tanker replied, crossing his arms over his chest.

I just gawked at him. "Okay, what's going on?"

Again, they'd shared an uncomfortable look.

Tanker, trying to appear as though his stitching wasn't coming apart, replied in a voice about an octave too high. "Nothing. You should know that everything is unfolding as it's always been meant to do. Now then, we've overstayed our time here—"

"You've literally just POPPED into my house."

"Yes well," Maude said, her voice getting more and more

jittery by the second, her eyes flitting to the windows anxiously. "Lots to do elsewhere—we must be off!"

"Elsewhere? Like out of Garland—"

But they'd never let me finish. They'd lunged forward, hugging me much too tight yet again, then made out with a loud exploding noise, leaving purple and blue glitter to fall to the floor. In retrospect, I was never happier than to have the gift of Maude's personal spell book, but it wasn't a gift as much as a tool for survival. Even though they thought themselves great 'critics' of the theatre, neither one of them had ever been very good at acting. Something was wrong in Garlandia, more so than when I'd left.

Presently, I lifted my cheek from the blank sheet of paper that laid beneath me, a strip of purple hair falling into my eyes. It was a constant reminder that I'd already exhausted years from my life trying to save it from my aunt's death wish.

"Hey," Jeremy said, lifting his head from his pillow.

I let out a slow, jagged breath. "Hey," I returned.

It had been one long sleepover for almost a month now, but if it wasn't for Jeremy and Cee-Cee I might've contracted the nervous habit of pulling out my hair, strand by sparkly strand. "Go back to bed," I whispered.

"What are you doing?" he asked, his eyes still closed.

"Can't sleep. Just working out some spells I found in this book Maude sent."

Jeremy struggled to look at me through the darkness. "Have you found a way to fix my ears?"

I pressed my lips together and smiled. "Not yet. But don't worry about it, it will help you blend in once we are back in Garlandia."

If I took them there, that was. I still wasn't entirely sure which was the safer option.

"Sure," he said. "Your wings look really pretty against the

moonlight by the way." And then his pointy ears hit the pillow, and he fell instantly back to sleep.

That had been my bad. I'd been messing around with morphing. I knew I wasn't ready to do anything like Maude and Tanker were capable of, not without accessing my soul for magic, and I already had more purple in my hair than I enjoyed. But morphing seemed to me like a very practical bit of sorcery to have under my belt. With it, I could learn to disguise myself, or others, like Tanker and Maude had done for much of my life; for it had been the two of them, poised as birds, perched on the branch just outside my bedroom window growing up. I'd figured that much out from page thirty-six of Maude's spell book. On that page she'd drawn a red-feathered bird and written a few lines of a morphing spell.

Since I'd been getting along fairly well with changing the color of Cee-Cee's hair to an all-around pink, I'd thought it was a good time to try something a bit more difficult. So, I'd made Jeremy's ears pointy and now he looked like any other elf in Garlandia; there was just one problem, I hadn't figured out how to undo either spell yet.

I placed the end of my wand against the plain sheet of paper. I'd been conducting a spell I'd found on page eighty-four of the weathered leather-bound book Maude had given me. Unlike my birth parents, her personal collection of enchantments showed its age with its yellow and brown pages, and it smelled of Cedar and acorns. It was over a thousand years old.

Maude had insisted it wasn't a diary, but every carefully crafted spell was highlighted by a story. The more I read, the more I felt I knew my birth mother in a way nobody else ever would. The spell I'd been practicing that night had been titled, "Heart to Heart: To Call Mine Lover Whilst He is Away."

After reading the brief entry written about the spell, I

learned that shortly after Maude and Tanker met, my grandfather had forbidden Maude to see my father ever again. But before she disobeyed him entirely, causing him to disown her—which there was plenty more to read about throughout the book—she created a spell so that my father could hear what she had to say, no matter how far apart they were. I knew as soon as I read it, I had to use it.

All I'd needed to recreate the enchantment was a piece of paper, my wand, the scent or taste of my lover, milk, honey, and a bit of my own scent. I'd already learned from a previous entry that my scent was affiliated with my dust. Apparently, it smelled different to everyone, and so if this worked, Toby would know it was me.

Dipping the end of my wand into the small bowl of combined ingredients, I then placed it against the paper.

Come find me, Toby, my love—my king. It is far too quiet here, and with too many eyes seeing. Find a way to speak to me, to let me know you can hear me.

My magic ink sank into the paper and after it was gone there was nothing left but a blank page. Cee-Cee snorted in her sleep while Jeremy whimpered something about a talking snail. I sighed at the sight of them—what I wouldn't give to be one of them right now. Funny that the one thing I'd veered away from my entire life, the daily workings of the average teenage kid, was now my one desire. An experience that was nowhere near a remote possibility anymore.

I stared up at the moon one more time before crawling outside my bedroom window and curling up against the tree, ensuring that the two pointy-eared morons posing as Jehovah's Witnesses (dumb enough to pitch a tent in my front yard) saw me. I wanted them to know that I was onto them, like the black spots on a ladybug's back—just like Helene would've said.

My head fell back against the trunk of the tree. I had to

wonder what had happened to Helene's soul. A lot of the statues I'd seen in Garlandia felt haunted, as though their essence was still there, imprisoned in stone forever. Would that be her, too? Was my aunt eternally damned into a frozen state, buried beneath the roots of an illegal tree? I shouldn't have cared, for if she'd had her way, I would be nothing more than a smothered insect. But I did care, and I worried about it . . . a lot.

I fell asleep at some point, my thoughts stirring around what was going to happen next, an anxiety I had been living with for weeks. When I awoke again my skin was tingling, but not because I was residing alongside the summer heat. It was a different kind of warmth, like one that comes with certain forms of magic.

I sat up slowly, my wings stretching out by my sides, and my spine against the trunk of the tree. My bedroom window was still open, and levitating between it and where I sat was a blue orb.

"What is that?" I whispered, leaning forward, my wings steadying me from toppling over the branch as my wand appeared in my hand.

As I stared at the glowing ball, it began to grow—the heat emanating from its center enveloping me. It continued to increase in size, hypnotizing me with its warmth and comfort. It wasn't until I realized it had grown around me—that I was inside it—that I began to regain my focus, and panic set in. But by that point it was too late. Everything became white, and then the world turned off.

Before all this happened to me, back when I was still no ordinary teenager but in control of my own future, I never would have been the kind of girl to open her eyes after blacking out to find that she was sitting in what could only be described as a *dive bar*. I may have become accustomed to the wings extended behind my back, and I daresay I was even proud of them nowadays; but finding myself situated in the back of a noisy bar, my legs rudely suctioned to a red vinyl booth—sticky from what I hoped was dried beer—I was reminded of the girl I had been just over a month ago. And when I looked down to find that I was wearing tattered lace tights, red pumps, a jean skirt that could have been spray painted onto my body, and a faded black T-shirt with the neck and arms ripped off, I was not amused.

I reached for the silver napkin holder in the middle of the table and pulled it up to my face, immediately growling at what I saw in its reflection. I had electric blue eye shadow in the place where there was usually none, and my red and purple-streaked hair was permed and as frizzy as a lion's mane.

"Can I get you something to drink?"

I looked up to find a waitress dressed similarly to me, except her hair was short and shaved on one side, and she had a chain running from a ring in her nose through one in her lip. As she stared down at me, a rude expression tattooed onto her face, I had an epiphany.

"Oh, dear god," I said out loud.

I knew where I was. As I scanned the walls, littered with magazine cutouts of rock bands and movie stars, and as I listened to the music streaming out from bulky black speakers hung in the corners of the walls—the same music my adopted father liked to listen to while working late into the night—I remembered hearing my parents speak of such a place and time.

"What year is this?"

The waitress chomped on her bright pink bubble gum. "1985, duh."

"Right." I stared at myself one more time in the reflection

of the napkin holder before putting it down. "Um, do you have any specials?"

The waitress blew a bright pink bubble and let it pop around her mouth. "What's with the wings? Are you guys in some kind of band or something?"

"Guys?" I asked.

And just then I heard it—the one voice I had been waiting to hear for weeks. "Yes, actually." Light shone from my pores as soon as I saw him. My king. Pointy ears and all. He stepped out from behind the booth, dressed in leather pants and a bright red T-shirt. My palms got sweaty the second I laid eyes on him. "We've smashed our way through England and now we're getting ready to tour the states." Sliding into the booth, wrapping an arm around my shoulders, and winking at me, he said to the waitress, "We'll take a pitcher of beer, please."

"I.D.'s," the waitress stated, her mouth still moving like a cow chewing on a piece of grass.

"Oh, right." Toby reached into his back pocket like he was pulling out his wallet, but brought out his wand instead, zapping the waitress so quickly that no one would have noticed even if they were staring in our direction.

The waitress looked confused for a mere second, but just as quickly nodded her head and made off in the direction of the bar.

Once we were alone, I didn't waste a second with my interrogation. "Toby? What the—where are we?"

He removed his arm from around my shoulder and framed my face with his hands. "You called for me. I answered." He looked at what I was wearing, and I caught an interesting scent coming from him that drew me to believe he was feeling excited all the sudden. "You look rather interesting this way." He smirked, then pressed his lips into mine, his hand coming down, wrapping around my thigh. I sighed, the familiar ginger taste sending an impulse to my brain, causing me to fall apart in his arms.

When he pulled away, I bit the side of my lip and touched it lightly with the tip of my finger. My flesh was still tingling. "Is this real right now? I mean, I suppose I could be dreaming . . ."

The waitress returned with our beer, splashing it all over the table in the process.

"I assure you, Miss Makayla, that you're quite awake." Toby grabbed the pitcher and began pouring each of us a glass.

A wicked flashback of what had happened the last time I drank alcohol returned to me, and I put my hand up. "I'm good."

"Relax. You can't have wine, but faeries love beer. Actually, they love whiskey, but that'll get you sauced, and I need your full attention. Now go ahead, look around—see anyone you might know?"

I turned my cheek at him before popping my head up out of the booth, touring the small establishment with my eyes. There weren't a lot of people in there, probably ten others. A man and woman at one side of the bar, both wearing pastel sweaters the color of taffy, shoulder pads included. A group of girls in one corner and a table of guys in the other. The guys, all dressed in black leather—all of them wearing black eyeliner —were sending flirtatious looks towards the group of girls, and the receiving party seemed gracious.

"I don't recognize anyone here."

"Look harder." Toby sipped on his beer and sat back in his seat.

"To be honest, I really don't know that many humans outside my work. I mean, these people would be my mom and dad's age now—oh my god!" I clapped a hand over my mouth and looked over at Toby, who was smirking. "Is that my dad?"

Toby closed his eyes and nodded his head. "Doesn't he look fetching?"

I gawked at my adoptive father. He was dressed from head to toe in black leather, and his hair was dyed blue at the tips, gelled into spikes. On his hands, driving gloves. If one of the dudes out of *West Side Story* had been made over by a unicorn —that's what he looked like.

"What a nerd!" I exclaimed, beginning to laugh. "How is this possible?"

Still grinning from ear to ear, Toby explained, "We are in one of his memories; I swiped it from him last I saw you. Thought we might need an impartial place to meet and neither one of us can be tracked here."

"How can we be inside of another person's memory?"

"Easy, it's a copy of a scene. We have all the players and the set, but it's already happened."

I pointed to his ears, and to my wings. "And I assume it doesn't matter that we are just being ourselves."

"Like I said, this is a slice of life that has already happened. These people are simply copied memories, and as soon as I make it go away, they will too. Their present selves will not be affected at all."

I peeked over at my adoptive father once more. This was going to be hard to keep to myself. Turning back to Toby, I changed gears, too eager to find out what I'd been missing all these weeks. "Where have you been?"

"My uncle sent me to Anemone. I'm supposed to be on my way back right now."

"Have you heard from Tanker and Maude at all?" My concern was visibly forming into wrinkles over my forehead.

"I'm afraid I have not, and I would assume you wouldn't be asking if you had."

"No, not for while anyway," I admitted quietly. Pulling my

beer under my nose, I took one sniff of it, winced, then pushed it away.

"Here," Toby said, tapping the glass with his wand. Immediately the color of the beer deepened, and little brown balls floated along the top of the beverage.

"What did you do to it?" I asked, pulling it under my nose again, but this time it actually smelled good.

"Orange and clove. That's how faeries drink their brew."

I took a reluctant sip and was immediately pleased. "Oh yeah, that's good."

"I'm glad you like it, because you might need it for what I have to tell you."

I set down the beer. "And what is that? Oh my god, you *have* heard something about them—my faery parents. Are they okay?"

Toby's eyes sharpened. "I am sure they are, and no, I really haven't heard a peep from them. But if my suspicions are correct, they've already fled."

Bracing myself, I asked, "Fled? Why would they need to leave? Toby, what's going on?"

He let out a ragged breath. "He's getting ready for something . . . my uncle. For years he's been biding his time, laying low. He never attacked because he didn't have the knowledge of how large the rebel army actually was, and he didn't want to strike until he felt he had enough force."

"Rebel army?" It wasn't the first time I'd heard it mentioned.

"Those who have been preparing," he explained. "But King Loral has been doing the same. He believes he has the alliances of both Lauslin and Anemone, therefore he is under the impression that his army has tripled."

"You say that as though he is mistaken."

"That's because he is."

I felt a small shift in my stomach. "And why is he suddenly

on all fours? What has he learned, or what does he expect is coming for him?"

"I think you already know the answer to that," Toby answered, relaxing his eyebrows.

My gut grew heavy. King Loral knew, he knew about the ghost I carried. A name one couldn't even say out loud without being turned into stone. What would he do to me when he found out that I for sure carried Titania's spirit?

"And do *you* know what he's learned?" I already knew he did.

"Makayla . . ." His eyes were tracing the star embedded into my wing. "Have you—"

Unable to handle the suspense of holding it in any longer, I pulled out my wand and whispered the magical word under my breath that would bring light to its end. Within seconds Toby's gaze was glued to the star encased in a diamond.

"And so it is," he muttered, the reflection of the star sparkling in his irises.

Slowly, allowing the mark of Titania to fade away, I whispered, "Goddess wings." Because he had said something to that effect when we'd first met.

His gaze moved back to meet mine and he whispered, "Yes."

Lowering my wand, I muttered the question I'd been pondering over for nights on end, ever since I'd come across this glaring truth. It was something I didn't want to believe, but the way Toby and I had connected, as if suddenly and overnight—I couldn't help but wonder. "Toby, you call me your queen—"

"Because you are."

"I have to know, is it me you have fallen in love with, or is it her—the old queen?"

His eyes immediately became cross, and he jumped on the

question as if it were poison. "Of course, it is *you* I love, Makayla! How could you even insinuate such a thing?"

I studied him, the defeated expression he wore. I couldn't tell if it was ignorance, or this stupid, irrational love that I had for him, but I chose to believe him. My heart fluttered and I gripped my wand tightly in my hands, staring into my lap. "You can't blame a girl for asking. I've got the spirit of a vengeful queen attached to me. It's sort of a lot to live up to."

Grasping my chin, forcing me look up at him, he said intently, "This is why I love you Makayla Wood. For only you could feel lackluster after being seen as a match by Titania herself."

I furrowed my brow. "Seen as a match?"

"Yes. Don't you understand? She hitchhiked back into this world via *your* soul because she saw in you a warrior that she had not seen for many, many years. This is why my uncle fears you. This is why he wants you gone."

My eyes grew. "So, this army he's created, or thinks he has —it's all for me?"

Toby laid a hand over my leg. "Essentially yes. Though it's the rebels he's hungry to defeat as well, those who have been preparing for this moment for longer than you or I have been in these bodies."

"The rebels . . ." My gaze was dancing out over the table. "Who are they?"

Toby was quiet for a moment. When next he spoke, his words were heavy. "This is the moment, Makayla, where I tell you everything. But I need to know that you are ready. For once you know, you will no longer be the girl you were when I first met you."

Suddenly I felt a satisfying shift inside, like a key fitting nicely into a lock, or perhaps more like a blade sliding into the ribs of my enemy, piercing his heart. I knew just then that *for sure* my lost childhood wasn't for nothing.

"Toby, you may think I've been a child up until now, but the unfortunate truth is that I have never been one. Maybe someday, a very long time from now, I will understand the youth I've encountered in others, but as far as my past and current life, I wasn't bred for play. I was born to fight."

Toby's stare locked perfectly into mine, and as he dissected the thick layers of centuries old stories that made up my soul, he gave the slightest of nods. "All right, then. Let's have a story, shall we? Or a nightmare, more like."

"All this started many years ago, but as for my involvement, I have been working undercover while playing the part of one of King Loral's knights ever since I was deposited into his kingdom—building a guard to keep *you* safe. Knights, my love, have been swearing in under your name since the moment you were born."

My lips quivered as I stifled the questions coming to the surface like aquarium fish during feeding time.

Toby pulled two necklaces up from where they had been concealed by his shirt. Two chains, each with a vial hanging from the end. One of them I recognized, the silver one, but the other one he'd pulled away from his neck was new.

"My mother, Daphne was her name, she was the only one Titania trusted."

"Your mother knew Titania?" I could barely stand it. The seal was breaking over the secrets that had been suffocating me since these wings erupted from my backside.

Toby looked down at the vial in his hands. It was a clear bottle filled with what appeared to be pine needles, colored rocks, and bits of moss. "Yes, Titania was like the mother my mother never really got to know. I think, though, that for you to understand what I am about to tell you, we need to start from the beginning. Before you or I were even a thought in our parents' minds. Back when our souls danced as pure energy, in the ether. You see, Makayla, I lied to you when we first met. When you asked if my mother told me bedtime stories, my answer to you was no. In fact, she did, and where it ends, your destiny begins." He looked up at me, and as the words began to pour from his mouth, a long-awaited breath fell from my lips.

"A long time ago Garlandia was filled with all sorts of creatures, more so than there are now . . . and it was free. It was the darkness that changed everything.

"The cult was known as the Bahidicaras." He pronounced the name with the same accent he'd used once before—when he'd said the name of the place where he'd been born. "It means bad village. It started in another world, and those who witnessed it grow into the mayhem it became say it rolled in from all corners like a reverse explosion. That it came down from the sky like the darkest of storm clouds, transforming into a solid mass of negativity, flowing through the lands like a mixture of tar and lava. It didn't terrorize those in its path because it took the souls of those in front of it before they had a chance to feel apprehensive . . . it took everything."

"Who were they, these cultists?" I asked, my brows crossed in concentration.

"Elves, witches, even fey, but by the time they got to Garlandia they were unrecognizable. What they were when they arrived were nothing more than true monsters. And they didn't just consume souls, they dug deeper than that. Before their end came, they were completely out of control. In their search for power, they began to reap the essence of the Earth and all its worlds—it, they, began to feed from the gods. It was because of this that Titania existed at all. The deities began sending their offspring into flesh and blood to fight off the Bahidicaras.

"Titania had been sent to fulfill a single quest: to aid in the war. The cult was not of Garlandia, but that didn't mean there weren't copycat creatures of every variety beginning to come out of the shadows in the land where you and I met.

"Titania, along with an armed guard, fought against the infection that was starting to grow around the Garlandian castle. She conquered anyone who crossed her path with a sword given to her by her cousin Avalon, a daughter of the sea; a gift that was rumored to have found Titania only after Avalon was sent back into the arms of the gods."

I furrowed a brow, but Toby kept rambling on before I could dwell on that part of the retelling.

"As you might have guessed, Titania met Anthony during the war. His father, the King of Garlandia didn't survive the fight, leaving Anthony next in line for the crown."

This time I couldn't stop my tongue from thrusting. "You said this terrible cult formed in a different world, so what drew the Bahidicaras to Garlandia in the first place? Were they passing through or did they arrive intentionally?"

"They were not just passing through. The assumptions were that they were there to end Titania. She was killing off new sects of those in support of the cult and though they were working from different corners of the earth—from separate worlds—Titania posed a threat to their way of life.

"Regardless of whether it was truly Titania who drew them to our land, they never actually got the chance to face her. In fact, as the story goes, their evil rebounded and the cloud of their existence evaporated before Titania even had a chance to swing her sword in their direction."

I scratched my left brow. "But Garlandia hasn't been free for years."

"Just wait, my queen." He sipped from his brew then went

on with his tale. "After the cult and the impressionist sects had all supposedly been taken care of, Anthony became the new king of Garlandia, and Titania became his queen; in fact, she was the first faery to wear the crown of the land. But as you may already know, their reign did not last long. They were found three days after their coronation and binding of souls, dead in the dungeons. King Anthony's neck was sliced open, and Titania's heart had been impaled. Between their two bodies, written in the faery queen's handwriting, in her husband's blood, were the words, 'Our love was an abomination—my mother's heart has been broken.'"

"No way," I blurted out. "Titania killed him, and then herself? But that's not right at all—she found me because she's been out for revenge."

"Makayla, I never said it's how it truly happened. I said that's how they found them."

"Were there any witnesses?"

He shook his head. "There were prisoners in nearby cells who heard the commotion, but nobody saw anything. No one really knows what happened down there."

"Well, it seems obvious to me. King Loral had to have been involved."

Toby sighed. "My uncle was nowhere near the castle when it happened. He was out searching for my mother, who had run away on Titania's orders just days before this happened. There were countless knights with him that could corroborate his story, and unfortunately the queen and king had a very public fight in front of the castle the same day my mother went missing."

The tip of my finger had found my teeth, and I was biting down over my nail. "What was their fight about?"

"Most of it was bickering so low that it was inaudible, but it was the last bit that caught the attention of every creature in ear's distance from them. Titania threatened Anthony, her words reverberating forever in the minds of her citizens that if he could not see reason, death would find him. That his sister going missing had everything to do with insurance." He paused. "People began to speculate that she'd done something with my mother. Rumors that only began to germinate and spread after her and Anthony were found dead. Obviously, the rumors, whether they were spread by the ones responsible for the deaths of the queen and king, aided in the story that had been written around their bodies in blood."

My gaze focused on the vial in Toby's hand as I verbalized my thoughts. "But she couldn't have been the one who killed them. Not only do you have your mother's account of how it went down, but it's written. I—I read it. Titania's last words were that she would be back for justice—to avenge her death." I looked up at Toby. "What she was saying couldn't have been meant as a threat, and somebody had to have heard her real last words in order for them to be written."

It was his turn to look confused. "Where are you getting your information?"

"From a book," I said. Namely the mythology book I'd found in my human parent's library. The same book that had led me to realize the importance of what was occurring at the tip of my wand.

"Interesting," Toby speculated.

"Why do you say that?"

"Because the king had every bit of literature pertaining to Titania destroyed as soon as he was crowned. If you truly had such a book, the only way it could've gotten there was if it had first come from a safe land." Assessing my confusion, he clarified, "There are places in every world—like rooms inside of secret passageways. They are often only accessible by passwords, or some bit of magic no one knows about. The king would not be able to reach these places, even with his twisted enchantments."

"Do you know anyone who lives in these safe lands?"

He parted his lips and deviated his jaw to the right. "Not personally, but I know of those living there." He was contemplative for another moment before he motioned to my beer. "Are you going to drink that?" I shook my head, and he pulled it towards him. Whispering over the glass, he turned the beer into water. He then began to uncork the vial, but just before he prepped for what was next, he paused. "Whoever put that book there wanted you to remember who you were."

"And who do you suppose that was?"

"Tanker."

"Tanker?" I questioned. "But how would *he* have been able to get the book? Unless he knew where one of these places was." I stopped myself. I'd been reading my birth mother's book of shadows for weeks—the answers were right there. "Do the rebels you've been talking about—do they live in these safe lands?"

Toby nodded.

I thought back to that awful tree where I'd been chained down in its basement, then back to some of my Aunt Helene's last words. "Toby, my grandfather is the leader of L.O.A.R. Did you know that?"

Again, he nodded.

"When Maude first met Tanker, my grandfather forbade them from knowing one another, and when my parents married, he disowned my mother. I read somewhere in the book she gave me that when I was born Tanker left to give word to my grandfather, which means he would have known how to get into the safe land. He *could* have brought back such a book . . ."

"You are quick, my queen, but brace yourself, for there is much more to hear." He shook the contents of the vial in his hands, returning to his explanation. "Before she died, Titania gave something of importance to my mother. She communicated that she had seen a darkness coming for her, something related to the Bahidicaras—"

"You've already implied that the Bahidicaras were taken care of."

Toby tilted his head towards his shoulder. "The faery queen said something *like* the Bahidicaras were after her. She could have meant something just as evil. Either way, she was aware that her end was near. She told my mother to run far into the hills, to barter whatever it was she'd given her for her safety and to make sure the object stayed within the bounds of Garlandia. She also instructed her to never come back." His eyes ran distant for a moment, and when he spoke again, he did so with an accent, relaying his mother's message. "'For who comes to lead us will not be of this world anymore, but her heart will be stronger for it. It is your job, my son, to help her remember her roots, to deliver the message from the first queen—to keep her safe until the end.'"

I dragged my teeth over my bottom lip. "Your mother said this?"

"Yes. And the day she died she told me that when the time came, when darkness gave up its hiding spot, we would be led by this faery—by you. And that's, unfortunately, where my knowledge ends. She couldn't tell me everything before she was killed, for she couldn't risk King Loral finding a way to get the information from me. I was given bits and pieces and promised a clue to where the secrets lay to undo her brother when the time was right."

My eyes fell to what was in his hands. "Is that a clue— from your mother?"

Toby uncorked the glass vial. "Yes, the first one. Gwen delivered this to me just before I sent her off with Naomi and Philip. My mother left specific instructions for her to retrieve it only after she'd seen you."

Just as Toby was about to upend the vial, I laid my hand

down over the table in an effort to pause his actions. "Titania was able to see her end coming. Did she not see how this would all end—how *we* would end?"

Toby gave me a searching look. "I think even the offspring of the gods and goddesses have their limitations. She didn't know you yet, Makayla Wood, but she knew you would exist for her." He held my gaze for at least three breaths. "Does this make sense to you?"

I waited four breaths. "Ish."

He managed a smirk. "You and your human verbiage."

I flicked my brows to the ceiling. "You and your wonky accent."

Toby shook his head in amusement then returned to his task. The contents of the vial fell into the water, dissolving as though they were made of sugar.

"My mother saw what Titania allowed her to see, and she often told me that the only way to kill the virus that had infected my uncle and then Garlandia was to hit him with the only thing he couldn't seem to understand."

"And what is that?"

Toby's eyes flickered from what was brewing inside the glass up to my eyes. "The way your heart beats when you are close to me. My uncle no longer knows what that feels like."

I sucked in an all too quick breath. "He doesn't understand love."

Toby nodded as the water swirling around in the glass started to fizzle. Only seconds later a voice began to stir from the magic brewing in the pint-sized vessel. It was repeating itself, like a scratched record playing a small bit of a song over and over.

". . . the Pool of Aeslin . . . all you need is the key . . . It's in the Pool of Aeslin . . . all you need is the key . . . It's in the Pool of Aeslin . . . all you need is the key . . ."

"Mother," Toby whispered, staring into the evaporating

water as the voice faded away, repeating the same words until there was nothing left in the glass.

"What is the Pool of Aeslin?" I asked.

"I don't know," he whispered.

"All you need is the key." My eyes rose to meet his. "Is the sword the key? You said Titania gave your mother something to barter. And you'd mentioned she had in her possession a sword given to her by her cousin—"

"No." Then, taking a step back he stated, "The sword has been missing ever since Titania was found dead. But no, a child would not be able to run away with a sword like that, not even an elfin child." Toby's eyes grew wide, then almost immediately they shrunk back down as he collapsed against the back of the booth. "It's impossible," he muttered.

"What?" I leaned in close to him. "Do you know what it means?"

He continued to stare at the empty glass. "The key . . . Of course. Titania must have given my mother a secret stone to trade for her safety, and from that stone a key was made. It all fits together so well."

"Toby, you are going to have to speak more plainly. I don't understand—"

"Secret stones, Makayla, like the one I made you. Once their secrets are revealed they become runes, and runes are nothing more than keys."

"Wait a second," I mused. Runes I knew of. I even had a few in my possession because I had created a little treat that had persuaded the gnomes to trade their precious valuable stones for muddy ice-cream.

Toby continued to speak as I tried to sort out the pieces before me. "What we would need is not just any rune, but an ancient one; and it may still be in the form of a secret stone for all we know. There is an entire country out there. How are we to find one tiny little rune?"

"Hang on," I repeated, my hand in the air. "We have to assume that your mother would have thought this out, that she would have traded it to someone who would have made sure it stayed in the kingdom."

Toby remained quiet, listening.

"Do you have *any* idea how she fled?" I asked. "She was so young, after all. If we can figure out the path she took then that could help."

Toby shook his head. "She most likely would've used a gnome, but there are so many other ways." He stared at the ceiling. "I've no idea."

I released my bottom lip from the hold my teeth had over it. "I need to get back to Garlandia," I said.

His gaze centered on me. "Do you know something?"

"No . . . but I may have a place to start."

He took a deep breath. "Makayla, there is no way to sugar coat this. When you go back it's not going to be the same."

I thought of Tanker and Maude, the expression on their faces last I'd seen them. "I figured." Then, allowing my thoughts to deviate in another direction, I asked, "Why hasn't Loral brought me in yet? He knows where I am."

"Exactly. It doesn't matter if you are in his world or not, he's got his junkies all over you—except for right now." He paused, tracing his finger over the tabletop. "There's no better place to hide than a memory." Again, he took a moment before returning his attention to mine. "I believe he is waiting for you to make the first move, to declare to him and everyone else that *you* carry Titania's mark."

"And as soon as I do this, he will pounce?"

"Most likely," Toby answered. "That is why it is very important for you to keep your wand out of sight. Do not use magic out of doors, and do not show that mark to *anyone* until the moment is right. You don't know who you can trust. King Loral has been busy taking down those living in the forest one by one, just as he's taken those directly from their homes surrounding the castle. He is still ignorant of what he's up against and is therefore taking down any creature who is liable to put up a fight."

"He's absolutely evil," I muttered.

"He's given away part of his soul. Everyday could be our last day before he strikes. All we can do is play along, to act as though we do not fear him, because Makayla, that is all he has. That and whatever spell he's used to guard himself against dying; but if we succeed, his days are numbered."

His hand appeared in mine, and I let my eyes drift up to meet his. I was thinking of 17 Serendipity Lane, of how quiet it must be inside; of Helene's expression last I saw her, and of how it would be permanently stuck onto her stone face.

"You said you received my messages, right?" I asked.

"Your messages?"

"When nobody came for me, when I didn't see you for weeks, I found a way to reach you. Did you hear me?"

Toby's face softened, his blue eyes growing deeper. "Yes, my queen. I heard every word."

"Then you must know, I'm not the girl you left. To be honest, I don't exactly know who I am, or who I'm venturing towards being, but I do know one thing. I am not afraid of King Loral."

Toby was silent for a moment, looking from me to the borrowed scene around us. When he returned his gaze to mine, he lifted the strip of purple attached to my head and felt it between his fingers. "Your magic is getting more refined, and it appears you've learned to manage it. I think you have reason to be unafraid, Miss Makayla Wood of the Erwain descent. And I think my uncle has every reason to fear you."

I leaned in and pressed my lips against his. A warmth began to gather against my bare arms, and out of the corner of my eye, past the red dust that had gathered around our two souls, there was a faint blue light. The same light that had brought me into this memory.

"No," I gasped. I could still feel the warmth of his lips on mine, the sweet candy taste of him, but my heart dropped into the pit of my stomach as my future king began to fade away. "Don't leave me yet!"

"Our time is up, someone is coming . . ." His speech was flickering, but before he was completely gone, he whispered something in elvish and placed his hand over my heart. Then in words I *could* understand, he said quickly, "The beating of my heart, so you know I am with you even when I am not. Do not fear. Fight."

And then the memory evaporated.

When I reopened my eyes, I was in my bed inside my room at the residence of 17 Serendipity Lane. There was a second heartbeat next to my own, and as I rose, I saw that I wasn't alone.

❦ 4 ❦

Cee-Cee's eyes fluttered open. She came to slowly, rising with a confused look on her face. Her hair looked pinker if that was possible.

"What happened? When did we get here?" she asked.

"I don't know." I rolled off the side of my bed. "Toby must have brought us here."

"Toby?"

"Yeah, it's, uh, a long story."

I woke up my wand and flicked it in Jeremy's direction, rolling him over like a log until he woke.

"What the hell?" he grumbled, grappling to his feet before backing against a wall and knocking his head on the low ceiling in the corner. Rubbing its side, he said, "Just because you are mastering your magic quicker than you should doesn't mean you have to use it on us all the time—wait, where are we?" His eyes scanned his new whereabouts. "Oh, rad. How'd we get here?"

Before I could try to explain anything, a hologram of an arrow flew through my closed window and dug itself into the wall. All three of us jumped in place, before focusing on the flag that hung down from it.

"Violators of the lockdown," Cee-Cee read, her expression forming into a scowl. "One Anastacia Montgomery, descendant of Hecate, and one Jeremiah Love, human in disguise. Fines or punishments will be handed out in Market Circle when the sun has risen for her second cup of tea." Her eyes slowly rolled over towards mine, passing over Jeremy who had brought his hands up to cover his pointy ears. "What does any of that mean? And who the hell is Hecate?"

My legs suddenly felt like Jell-O. I crouched down into a ball—my wings folding around my body as if I could make all this go away. We'd been here for about five seconds, and already Garlandia was turning on us. "I have no idea, but it can't be anything good."

Cee-Cee grabbed for the hologram flag as though she could pull it down, but as soon as she touched it, it disappeared. "Violators? And a whole lot of other nonsense— but *violators*?"

Just then a sharp little knock coming from downstairs intervened. All three of us looked to one another, but it was I who jumped up first. There were too many thoughts running through my head for me to be afraid of what or who it could be, but as I allowed my wings to float me down the stairs to the front door, I saw there was no reason for worry. I could already see through one of the tiny windows embedded in the door that it was only a faery of the smallest variety.

"Hello?" said a nasal, male Ardeen once I opened the door; he was wearing the tiniest and fluffiest, bright blue suit I'd ever seen. Reading off a very small piece of parchment, he stated, "Miss Makayla Wood, also known as Lala Abberwockey of the Erwain descent?" When I didn't say anything, he ripped off his glasses and levitated closer to my face. "Is that you?"

I flinched my head backwards. "Yes."

"Fine," he said, before pulling out his wand and flying inside the house without an invitation.

"Um, okay. Come on in, why don't you." I shut the door and followed him towards the kitchen.

Jeremy and Cee-Cee were hanging over the banister, shifting their gaze from me to where the tiny faery had just gone off to. Cee-Cee mouthed the words, "What is that?"

"Are you coming?" squeaked the faery, reappearing in the space before the kitchen. He seemed impatient, placing a hand on his hip as he floated midair.

"Sure?" I said questionably, waving down my friends to join me.

All three of us came to a halt once we stepped into the kitchen, for in the same amount of time it had taken us to get from the stairs to where our guest was, he had already managed to make piles of what looked to me to be full-sized legal documents.

"What is all this?" I asked, stepping up to the yellow kitchen table and picking up what appeared to be some sort of handwritten deed.

"Don't!" the Ardeen faery squeaked, flying over and swatting the paper out of my hands, allowing it to drop back down into the pile. "Don't touch anything!" He closed his eyes briefly and wiped his hands down the front of his frilly suit. "I finally have it all organized. All I need from you is a signature and the house is yours. Now then, let me see here . . ." He flew away for a moment, shuffling through his piles manically until he seemed to find what he was looking for.

"The house is *mine*?" I questioned. "But wouldn't that mean that the owners aren't coming back?"

"Uh, duh," said the faery, flying over to where I was standing, the piece of paper in his hands four times his size.

I fell into the chair nearest me, and Jeremy's hand found my shoulder.

Preparing for an answer I didn't want to hear, I asked, "They aren't coming back because they don't want to? Or because they are dead?"

The faery dropped the paper in my lap and landed on my arm. "Dead. Now sign."

My chest instantly constricted and every color in the kitchen dulled.

"Oh shit," Cee-Cee muttered, just as Jeremy sank down so that he was level with me.

"No—no, they—they left," I said, fighting my shallow breaths. "They are safe. They—"

"They?" the faery said, crossing his arms over his chest. "Who are *they*? The house you are coming into belonged to one."

I dropped my gaze down to meet the faery's. "To one? Whose house am I inheriting exactly?"

"The residence of Miss Helene Voss, of course."

My shoulders instantly relaxed, though I still felt as though I had ingested a handful of rocks. "Oh, I see."

The faery fidgeted with his sleeves before pointing down to the place where he needed me to sign. "Yes, I have been waiting for you to arrive for weeks. Now then, if you would please leave your mark on the line then I can be on my merry way. I have forty-nine other appointments today. Everyone is trying to get their affairs in order."

I picked up the piece of paper and began to read through it. None of it made any sense. "I don't know how comfortable I am signing this without having a guardian present."

The faery scoffed. "A guardian? *Please*. This is a generation house, just sign the bloody thing."

"What's a generation house?" Cee-Cee asked. Her and

Jeremy had backed away and were snooping through the piles of paperwork.

The faery flew over and smacked Jeremy's hand away from a piece of paper he was about to pick up. "Exactly what it sounds like—a house passed down through the generations." "And who was the original owner?" I asked, still skimming the blotchy handwriting.

"It says right there," the faery said, growing increasingly impatient and pointing to a name I didn't completely recognize.

"Allender Voss. Who's that?"

"For the love of Terry McGaphagin, may his sweet harmonies rest in peace." The faery sighed while Cee-Cee, Jeremy, and I, all gave one another sordid looks. "If this is what the next generation is proving to bring us, then we might as well just fall flat on our backs and die."

He ignored my scorned reaction as he tapped the names on the page with the tip of his wand. "Allender Voss left the house to one, Maude Voss, but then due to disagreement signed the rights over to his second daughter, Helene Voss, who then died at which point his granddaughter, Makayla Wood, also known as Lala Abberwockey, became the sole heir of the cottage. The residence of 13 Ambiguous Fox." He then reached down and grabbed my wrist, shaking it. "Now pull out your wand, would you, and sign the damned thing!"

I scooted my chair away from the table before standing up. "My grandfather," I whispered, cupping my hands over my face as I backed against the kitchen sink.

Jeremy and Cee-Cee gathered around me, making sure I didn't collapse. Spacing my fingers out over my eyes, I looked from one to the other. "Do you remember what I told you about him—about what Helene told me before she was turned to stone?"

The two of them nodded.

"This could be good," Jeremy said. "Maybe there's something in that house that will help us figure out how to find him."

I nodded. "Right. Okay . . ." I pulled out my wand and looked at the agitated faery. "How do I sign this thing?"

He fluttered over to the deed and pointed a tiny finger at the line. "You only have to place the end of your wand against the contract and say your name and that you accept."

"That's all?" I asked.

"Yes."

"Okay, fine," I replied, laying the pointy end of my glowing wand just above the line. But before I said anything out loud, I took a brief moment and looked at the little faery. Anything that activated my wand revealed Titania's mark, and Toby had warned me to keep it under wraps until the time was right—whenever *that* was. "I need you to turn around before I do this."

"Absolutely not," he huffed. "The biggest part of my job is witnessing the signature." I paused, weighing out my options.

"What about Jeremy and Cee-Cee?" I asked. "They could be the witnesses."

"I'm your family's keeper, I am the only one who can be a true witness."

I cocked my right brow towards the ceiling. That's what Toby had called Gwen. "What's a keeper, exactly?"

I thought for a moment that he was going to combust, that pieces of his ridiculous suit were going to go everywhere. It was obvious he just wanted to move on to his next appointment. "I handle all the details of your family tree. All your belongings and such—"

"So, you're like a lawyer?" I asked.

"I don't know what that is."

"You are," I answered for him. "And I assume then, that

you don't just handle our property, but our secrets." Gwen had been doing nothing but managing secrets.

"That is part of my job, yes," he said, his expression teetering on hesitant.

A partial smile escaped my parted lips. "Okay then, I will sign in front of you."

And that's when the faery's entire demeanor changed, as though he knew his day had been scrapped. He must've had an inkling of what was about to happen, but it seemed he'd been in denial up until this point. As I touched my wand to the paper, he drifted down to the table and took a seat, his legs dangling over the side and his shoulders drooping.

"Go on, then," he muttered unhappily.

"I, Makayla Wood, accept," I said. But nothing happened.

The faery took a deep breath. "You have to say your full name."

"Oh—but I gave that up," I said, frowning.

He shook his head. "That wasn't up to you. Your full name is Makayla Wood, also known as—"

I shook my free hand at him. "Okay, okay, I get it." I focused my gaze back down to the legal document. "I, Makayla Wood, also known as Lala Abberwockey of the Erwain descent, accept."

Immediately the end of my wand glowed brighter, and the star and diamond showed themselves. On the paper, a crown appeared as my signature.

"Cool," Cee-Cee and Jeremy said together.

The little faery, my family's keeper, sighed as soon as it was done, tapping the air in front of him with his wand. Immediately a male faery appeared like a ghost, wearing striped pajamas.

"Pack up the kids, Claude. Code lilac."

The image of the Ardeen placed a hand to his chest. "NO! We've only just redone the kitchen!"

"We don't have a choice," said my keeper, his eyes now thin little slits as they traveled up to mine. "My secrets are now worth more than our Skyway home. We must go to Raton." He waved his wand over the image of who I assumed was his husband, and the faery in striped pajamas was erased. "Happy?" he asked, fluttering up over the table and gathering all the paperwork into one very tall pile, before waving his wand over it and making it disappear.

"Happy?" I protested. "You made me do it."

"You made me do it," he repeated in an unpleasant manner. "I should've listened to my mother and become a fashion designer, but no, I had to follow in my father's footsteps—stupid dying request."

"Wait," Jeremy said. "You're leaving because of what you now know about Makayla?"

Hovering before the three of us, looking almost angry, he said, "It is my job to keep secrets. If I stay here, they will do all they can to rip them from me. I have to go now, before it's too late." Looking down at my wand, he said, "I assume you are wise enough to know not to use that in public—not yet."

I nodded my head.

"Fine. I must go."

"Wait! What about the keys to the house?" I asked.

"Keys?"

"Yes, won't I need them in order to take possession?"

"The house is yours. It won't let anyone in but you, and anyone who you allow to enter."

Jeremy, Cee-Cee, and I all shared a look. "So, once we are inside, not even the king could get us out?"

The faery shook his head. "But that doesn't mean you would be safe forever. What King Loral wants, he gets. If I were you, I would figure out what you are doing about that" – he pointed down to my wand— "and get on with it." Rolling his eyes, he unfurled his arm before bowing to me. "I suppose this is in order." Then there was a loud bang, and he was gone, blue dust falling from where he'd been just a second ago.

"Oh, he just bowed to you," Jeremy said.

Ignoring him, I muttered, "How do they do that?" while reaching for the fading dust. Besides morphing, POPPING seemed like something I truly needed to master.

"Well shit, yo," Cee-Cee said, falling back into a chair. "What do we do now?"

"One thing is for sure," Jeremy said, rubbing the points of his ears. "We do *not* go to Market Place or whatever that ghost sign said."

"I don't think we have a choice." I leaned over the kitchen table. "If we don't, they will just come get us. That's kind of how it works here. That is, unless . . ."

"Unless what?" Jeremy asked, inching closer to me.

"Unless I can get you guys back. I don't know why Toby would've brought you here, especially if he knew there was any chance of you getting into trouble."

"Are you kidding—we ain't goin' nowhere," Cee-Cee said. "We're in this with you now. We aren't just going to let you stay here alone."

"Yeah," Jeremy said half-heartedly. It was clear from his unsteadiness that he would have no qualms about returning to his own world.

I gave them both sympathetic looks. "I appreciate that, you guys, but this is some crazy shit we're in. I barely know this world, and the two of you most definitely don't know anything about it."

"We aren't going home—even if you can figure out a way to get us there," Cee-Cee said defiantly. "I knew it, the day we first saw you. We were supposed to meet. That means something, Makayla."

I studied her. She hadn't ever said anything relatively close to that before. "Fine, but we need to find out what this violator business entails. Don't let the talking animals and flowers fool you, this place is dangerous."

"Who we gonna have help us?" Cee-Cee got up and peered out the window. "You got any faery friends hanging around out there?"

I bit the end of my finger, trying to figure out where to start. Suddenly my wings raised up behind my shoulders. "Cajun Cathy's."

"What?" Cee-Cee asked.

"That's where we're going to go. That's where everyone hangs out here, and if anyone can help us figure out what's going on, they'll be there."

"All right, then. What are we waiting for?" Cee-Cee said.

"Yeah," Jeremy seconded, looking wildly unenthusiastic. "Let's uh, march on out there. I can't wait to have my legs and arms pulled off."

"Don't be silly, Jeremy," I said sarcastically. "They don't pull people apart here, they just turn them into statues, or in the case of the fey—they expel our dust."

"Oh . . . good. Well, I do hope there's a place to buy a new pair of pants nearby," he said, shooting Cee-Cee a nasty look.

There was no denying it as we walked along the cobblestone path towards the smell of jambalaya, a foul energy had burrowed itself into the forest. It was far quieter than I remembered it being, and the sound of wooden flutes being played was nowhere to be found. Every once in a while, we spied a gnome or a flower scurrying about, but as far as faeries or Wood elves, there were none in sight.

"This feels wrong," Cee-Cee said, peering through the distant trees.

"I don't like it," Jeremy seconded.

I knew, if anything, that I had to get Jeremy home. I just had a really bad feeling that something terrible was about to happen.

"It's okay," I lied, my wand down by my side, and my wings raised like the hairs on the back of a hunted animal. "Toby wouldn't have brought us here if he didn't think it was safe." Another lie. Of course it wasn't safe. What the hell was he thinking?

"Maybe we should just go straight to your aunt's house—no one can get to us in there," Jeremy said.

"Eventually," I answered, "but I need answers first. I refuse to wait until someone gets turned to stone right in front of my eyes again."

Just then an Erwain faery snuck out from behind a tree, displaying a purple dress. She was a squatty thing with scraggly green hair and saggy pink wings. It was the faery who owned the dress shop at the farmer's market, where I'd first met Toby.

"Evening dress for you, my dear." She stayed in the shadows while pushing the dress into my face. "Such a pretty color for a pretty young face—wait—*young* face! Miss Makayla Wood, is that you?"

"Esmerelda?" I questioned.

"Why, yes. You know my name?"

"Of course. I have a good memory." It was a trait I was looking forward to using in law school, but that was no longer in the cards. "What are you doing? Are you—" I looked around at the seemingly desolate forest. "Are you selling your dresses here instead of the market?" That seemed terribly out of character for this faery. She had a reputation for holding her retail products over all the rest of them, and her prices were evidence of that very truth.

Refolding the dress in her arms, Esmerelda grew quite fidgety. "It's not that I want to do this! Peddle around my exquisite fabric like some kind of common cotton weaver, but I—I have no choice. They took away our market, and as you know I use only the highest quality threads to make my dresses." She nodded as she spoke. "I cannot just let these masterpieces fall apart on me, now can I?"

"Of course not," I sympathized. "But what do you mean they took away the market?"

"Exactly that," she chirped. "Two weeks ago, now."

"Why would they do that?"

"King Loral said they needed the space. For the

questioning and such. Too many violators, and he doesn't like to crowd the castle."

Cee-Cee poked my side. "Market Circle must be where the farmer's market used to be."

Nudging his head in between Cee-Cee and me, Jeremy asked with a quivery voice, "What is it, exactly, that they do to the violators?"

Esmerelda shrunk down even more than I thought was possible, hugging the purple dress to her chest. "It's terrible," she whispered. "No one gets away. They pretend like it's a trial but it's not. Most every faery I've seen go in gets taken to the castle—to the dungeons I presume, and who knows what they are doing to the elves."

Jeremy gulped.

"Why are they being brought in?" I asked.

Esmerelda shook her head, lowering it as she whispered yet again, "A slip of the tongue, a foot out of line—who knows. Best to just keep your wings and head down. And don't forget, they catch you flying anywhere, and you might as well blow your dust in their faces, cause they're going to get it out of you just for being able to spread your wings."

"Are you saying we aren't allowed to fly?" I asked.

She lifted her eyes to the clouds. "Do you see anyone up there, young Erwain? If you flutter above the trees, then you are giving Loral's army permission to shoot you down."

I followed her gaze, and sure enough, there wasn't a single witch or faery to be found.

"This sounds like a witch hunt," Cee-Cee said under her breath.

"Oh no, dear, the witches are the only ones who seem to be safe. Still keeping to themselves, of course, just in case—but at this time it's the faeries and elves King Loral is weeding out."

"Isn't anyone doing anything?" I asked, as quietly as I

could muster. I knew it wasn't safe to be talking about such things openly, but my blood was beginning to boil, and I was itching to fly only because I knew I couldn't.

"Don't you think we would if we could? No one wants to face those dungeons, Miss Wood. The smart ones POPPED from the kingdom before the king placed the traveling ban in effect."

"I don't know how to do that."

"It doesn't matter. You wouldn't be able to POP from the kingdom anymore anyway—there are enchantments in place that won't let anyone leave. We are living in a cage, so to speak." Esmerelda took a deep breath then held up the dress once more. "Anyway, don't suppose you want a dress. I'll gift it to you, seeing as you are *the* Makayla Wood—been a lot of chatter about you ever since you left weeks ago." She leaned super close to my ear. "Lots of chatter."

I narrowed my eyes down at her. "I didn't think you ever gave anything away for free."

"I don't. But like I said, you are no longer simply a lost Erwain. There's something like royalty hanging around your shoulders and everyone knows that. Here." She hung the dress over my arm. "It's just good marketing. Faeries see you wearing it, they'll want one for themselves. Just remember me when this is all over. If the rumors are true, you may need a whole new wardrobe."

"All right," I said, accepting the dress. "Thank you."

"You're welcome," she said, and bowed ever so slightly to me before backing away into the forest.

When I faced Jeremy and Cee-Cee, both their eyebrows were raised.

"That's the second one to bow to you," Jeremy said.

"So what," I retorted, leading the way once more towards Cajun Cathy's. I couldn't tell them what Toby had told me—that there was an entire rebel army who had sworn in under my name, and that it appeared that some of the citizens of Garlandia were wise to that fact. I couldn't say it out loud— not yet, not here.

"We aren't the only ones who know what's goin' on here, Makayla," Cee-Cee said as if reading my mind, her gaze falling to the wand in my hands. "I think they have a feeling, or some kind of heavy intuition that you are—"

I slapped my hand over her mouth, causing her eyes to bug out. "I don't think it's wise to speak too freely out here, right now." Even though it was probably just me being paranoid, I could've sworn I'd been seeing flashes of blue all around us. Last time I saw that Herbert was turned to stone. My hand fell from Cee-Cee's face and her chest rose. "Let's just get to the restaurant."

But we didn't make it there, not before finding a few more brave merchants from the farmer's market who had set up their shops along the cobblestone path. One of them being the wood elf's booth Jeremy had bought his leather shoes from, and another being a booth with three walls, stacked with shelves of crystal balls. I remembered the witch manning it from that day at the market . . . something about the way she'd looked at us as we'd walked by had bothered me. As we attempted to pass her tent, she shouted out to us.

"Oi! You three! Specifically *you*, sister!" Her eyes were pointed at Cee-Cee like blackened arrows.

Cee-Cee paused and stared back at the beautiful witch. A young-looking blonde, wearing a white dress with a black shawl covering her bare shoulders. Around her hips hung a leather belt, and dangling from it were three small glass bottles.

"Me?" Cee-Cee questioned, a hand on her chest.

The witch's smooth, pink lips, widened. "Yes, you. Do you see any other sisters here besides the two of us?"

"Sisters?" Cee-Cee looked at me questionably. "What's that girl talking about?"

I shook my head. "I have no idea."

During my time in Garlandia, I had only been in contact with one witch: Cathy. And she had proved strange, yet curious. At least she'd given me a food weapon when everyone else had expected me to eat with my hands.

"Come, Anastacia. I've been waiting for you to return since I recognized your face weeks ago. I have something for you."

Cee-Cee tucked her chin and turned her head sideways. "How'd you know my name?"

"Come," the witch said, waving her forward. "Let me see your palm, sister."

Cee-Cee looked at me as if I was going to tell her whether she should or shouldn't.

Weary as I was about this sorceress, it was peculiar, the way she was speaking to Cee-Cee, and I wanted to know what her game was. "Maybe she knows something," I said, shrugging my shoulders while simultaneously retrieving my skepticism and wearing it proudly.

The three of us inched towards the booth, Cee-Cee apprehensively placing her hand into the witch's. A crystal ball near where she stood began to change color. Green . . . just as it had at the market that day.

"Ah, just as I thought," said the witch, tracing a line down the center of Cee-Cee's palm. "A descendant of Hecate. The dark one."

"What the hell you mean, the *dark* one?" Cee-Cee said, her mouth open, obviously assuming that the witch was speaking about the color of her skin.

The witch raised her eyes to meet Cee-Cee's. "Your mother's blood . . . the power was derived from her . . . Anastacia, do you not know what you are?"

"Other than a damn beautiful girl from the burbs, does it look like it?" she said defensively.

The witch stepped away from Cee-Cee's palm. She traced the heads of all the crystal balls until the tips of her fingers landed on the one that had been changing color. It was now filled with smoke the likes you'd intend to find floating over a dark swamp.

"Your mother left you years ago."

Cee-Cee frowned. "She died."

"No, she didn't." The witch lifted the ball and set it into Cee-Cee's hands. "She left, and from the looks of it, she wrapped a spell around you first."

Cee-Cee squinted at the witch before looking down into the ball, but as she did, her expression softened. Her eyes nearly immediately started to water as she watched what I could only assume to be a scene unfolding, though neither Jeremy nor I could see the nightmare or vision that so obviously was about to leave our friend haunted. When it was over, she looked back up at the witch, her jaw had unhinged.

The way this crystal ball dealer looked at our friend made my stomach sour. It was like Cee-Cee made her hungry, but for what I couldn't be sure.

"What is it, Cee-Cee?" I asked, watching as her expression satiated into some kind of sad confusion. Jeremy Love wrapped his hands around my arm in what I could only construe as anticipation.

"This isn't—it's not possible," she whispered, shaking the ball with both hands. "I saw her in the hospital. I was at her funeral."

"Closed casket?" asked the witch, a grin surfacing that made my head pound.

"Cremated."

"I see." She reached forward and retrieved the ball.

"Wait—I wasn't done with that!"

"I'm afraid I can only give you a sneak peek for free." She laid the ball back down on its stand.

"I'll buy it from you," Cee-Cee said without hesitating, pulling at her empty pockets before redirecting her gaze to search mine and Jeremy's. "Did you guys bring any money with you?"

"I don't take money," the witch said before either one of us could shake our heads.

"Then how am I supposed to pay," Cee-Cee asked. "I need that ball. If what I saw inside of it was true, then—"

"You will become my student," the witch said matter-of-factly, grabbing a box from under a table and wrapping up the ball. As she spoke, she placed it in the box along with a business card. "You will start tomorrow."

"Wait a second, I don't even know you. How—How do I know you didn't just *make* me see something you wanted me to see?"

"Ex*cuse* me," I said, taking a step closer. "But how do we know that our friend can trust you?"

A dimple formed on either side of the witch's lips. "Makayla Wood. Oh, how I have heard your tale."

A firm line appeared between my brows.

"I'll tell you what," said the witch, "the two of you can come with her if it makes you feel better. But the truth of the matter is, your friend has much to learn, and I can help her."

"Can you help us not get turned to stone, too?" Jeremy muttered under his breath.

The witch turned her attention onto him. "What do you mean, elf?"

I piped up. "We've been accused, or I should say these two have been accused of being violators. But if being here is their crime, they had no choice in the matter. We didn't ask to come here from our world—someone brought us in."

The witch kept her eyes on mine for a second, then

allowed them to travel over to Cee-Cee and Jeremy. Finally, she said, "I can free Anastacia, they are not after witches—but as for you, elf—"

"He's not really an elf. I made his ears that way," I admitted.

"And I'm not a witch, yo. I mean, I would know if I were."

"Anastacia, your blood runs thick with dormant spells. Your mother kept this from you, she crossed you." She handed the boxed crystal ball to Cee-Cee and placed a hand over her wrist. "Tell me it isn't true, that with your feet on Garlandian soil, you've never felt more at home."

Cee-Cee said nothing, but I could tell the witch's words were resonating deep within.

"Your soul found mine so that I could release what's inside of you."

Cee-Cee stared down at the box now in her possession. I could almost see the wheels turning in her head—they were most likely turning in the same direction as mine. Finally, she looked back up at the witch, and holding out the box, said, "I can't do this, not unless you can help the both of us." She nodded towards Jeremy. "He's like my brother. He's family."

The witch bit her lip and studied Jeremy as though she was assessing his worth. "Fine, but I will have to pay, which means you will be in my debt," she said to Cee-Cee.

Cee-Cee pulled the box back towards her stomach. "Whatever you want."

"I want you."

Icy fingers ran down my spine. It was all I could do to just stand back and watch, but I somehow knew this person might be Jeremy's only hope.

Cee-Cee bobbed her head up and down. "I will be your student, or whatever—just help us."

"All right, then." She traced her finger around Jeremy's jawline, causing him to clench up. "You will have to pretend you really are an elf. They hate humans more." Jeremy gulped as she raised a hand and signaled to the elf who was running the leather goods hut. "Oi! Heime! May I have a word?"

Jeremy, who had already been fidgety, grew even more uncomfortable as a familiar wood elf meandered over to where the four of us stood.

"Dora," said the elf, addressing the witch.

"As of yesterday's raid, you need an associate, isn't that correct?"

"Yes," he answered dryly.

"Good. Meet Jerry."

"It's Jeremy," Jeremy said, looking anywhere but at the elf.

"Call him what you want, but he needs a new name and a new passport. His old identity needs to be erased. Can you do this?"

"Erase my identity?" Jeremy paled as the witch nodded.

"It will cost you," said the elf, ignoring Jeremy's reaction. "Prices have gone up since the regime has cracked down."

"But can you do it? If not, this boy is going to die today."

Jeremy's mouth unhinged and he froze, as if someone had stuck their entire arm down his throat. I lunged for him and grabbed his hands into mine, attempting to calm him.

The elf's gaze shifted to meet Jeremy's, before slowly falling to meet his feet. "Are those shoes from my booth?"

Jeremy looked down at what he was wearing and then raised his gaze back up to the elf's, nodding slowly.

"I like those shoes. Nobody ever buys them." He paused. "Fine. I will help him."

"Good." The witch came around and took a hold of Jeremy, handing him over to the elf like he was a purse that had been recently purchased. "We can handle the details later; you know I'm good for it."

"Yes," the elf said, holding Jeremy by the arm.

"Wait—am I just supposed to go with him? Like right

now?" Jeremy asked, his eyes pleading with me to do something. "What about the hearing?"

"The human boy they were after will no longer exist in a moment. The trace will lift from your shoulders," said the witch.

"His identity will be completely scratched?" I asked. "Like, in this world *and* the one he's from?"

"If you want your friend to live, then yes," Dora replied.

"Is this the only way?" I furrowed my brows, feeling very angry with Toby all the sudden for causing all this mayhem.

"Do we have a problem here?" asked the elf.

Jeremy and Cee-Cee looked at one another fleetingly before she grabbed his shoulder. "Go. It's safer."

"What if I don't see you again?"

"If you don't do this, I may not see you after the sun has its second cup of tea anyway," Cee-Cee replied.

Water began to accrue around his eyes.

"I'm so sorry," I whispered, squeezing his arm.

"It's not your fault," he muttered, turning towards the wood elf, who then locked his gaze onto Jeremy and gave him an 'are you ready,' look.

Jeremy's chest rose and he nodded, and then the elf named Heime pulled out his wand and flicked it at our friend.

Cee-Cee and I jumped, taken by surprise at the hastiness of it all. However, it appeared that nothing had happened, except that Jeremy's features may have sharpened a little and his skin became a bit more weathered.

"What was that?" I asked.

"Just a realignment of his energy," Heime explained. "Every soul has its own imprint, and it is from this that King Loral tracks those without wings. Your friend's energy has now been rearranged, that is all."

Whispering, while my gaze jumped around like a grasshopper, searching for flashes of blue between the trees, I asked hastily, "And you just did that—*here*? Like, out in the open?"

"Best place to hide is in the front line," Dora said from where she was writing something in what looked like a log of purchases.

Jeremy's mouth was unhinged as he stared blankly at Cee-Cee and me. "I don't feel any different." He paused, raising his nose into the air. "Except I can, like, *see* the wind . . ."

Heime gestured towards Dora. "I'm holding his wand as collateral until I receive payment."

"You'll get it," she snipped.

"W—Wand?" Jeremy stammered.

"Yes," Heime replied. "Every elf comes upon their magic tool early in their making. We aren't like faeries in that it comes from our soul—it will appear to you shortly."

"We?" If Jeremy's eyes had grown any wider, they would have fallen out.

"Did you just turn him into an actual—" Cee-Cee started but was immediately cut off by Dora.

"I think we're done here, Heime. Thank you for introducing your new apprentice to us, but that's enough chatter." As she spoke, she glanced at me and then out into the trees. I looked out, seeing nothing; still, I had to assume she was erring on the side of caution. We'd been pressing our luck for long enough. "I must get back to work, and I am assuming these two have somewhere to be very shortly." She peered up through the leaves and pine needles, assessing the placement of the sun before tearing apart a piece of parchment from her log. She jotted something onto it and then passed the note to Cee-Cee. "You'll be needing to give this to the guard as soon as you pass into the valley."

Cee-Cee accepted the piece of paper and looked down at it, scrunching up her nose. "What does it say?"

I looked down at the note, but it didn't appear to be written in any language I knew of.

"Come, Bally," Heime said to Jeremy. "It's time to learn how to stretch leather."

"Bally?" he whispered, reluctantly following the elf, but not before waving good-bye to us. "Fix this," were his last words to me.

I simply nodded my head. I hadn't made a list for a long time, but it wasn't because I'd given up on who I used to be. That anal-retentive git still lived inside me, it's just that I'd grown up quite quickly in the span of a few weeks, and I knew that not everything could possibly be perfect. The simple truth of the matter was, if I had a list of things to do now, I would run out of paper. But 'fixing this' was definitely on that very long metaphorical list of things to do.

"I will be expecting you tomorrow," Dora said, her cool, yet cutting voice interrupting my thoughts.

"How will I know where to find you?" Cee-Cee asked, both doubt and fear saturating her voice.

"My address is written on the card inside the box." Her eyes drifted to mine for a mere second. "Feel free to bring your faery if you so desire."

"I'll be there," I said through a very tight jaw. The longer I was in her presence, the more I detested her. I didn't know if that was quite fair, but the feeling in my gut—the one that was screaming to press on with this affair with caution—was growing stronger.

We took our leave shortly after that, feeling awfully strange deserting our friend.

"He *will* be okay, right?" Cee-Cee asked, as though I could truly give her an answer.

"My intuition tells me that Heime is trustworthy, and if I've learned anything since my wings have appeared, it's to trust what I feel."

Cee-Cee wiped her eye and I knew she was trying to hide the fact that she was silently crying. "What does your intuition tell you about Dora? About the things she said to me."

My gaze bounced from a stone statue of a squirrel wearing glasses to a female gnome, her mouth open in what could only be described as protest. In her outstretched palms, now fused to her body, was what appeared to be a rock. She must've been trying to barter for her life.

"Makayla?" Cee-Cee asked when I didn't answer.

"I think," I replied, setting my gaze back on the path that would lead us not to Cajun Cathy's but to the place where we had once enjoyed a farmer's market. "I think we would be wise to tread carefully around Dora."

"What makes you say that? Do you think she's lying— about—about me being a witch?"

I looked at my friend. The pink hair I'd given her softened her appearance. "I think, Cee-Cee, everyone is born with magic on some level. I am a prime example of what we can hide from ourselves."

"What if I'm not just a witch . . . but a *bad* witch?"

"Cee-Cee, what did you *see* in that thing?" I gestured to the box in her arms. But she didn't answer, instead she only gave me a chilling stare before shaking her head. "Fine, you don't have to tell me. I'll tell you this, though, as with anything there is both light and dark in all magic. It is up to the one who feels its power to weave its cords in one direction or the other." I knew this better than anyone. I'd spun magic directly from my soul, and although I hadn't done it on purpose, the effect of what I'd done was more than just a permanent purple streak in my hair.

Maude had said to be careful, that spinning from one's soul had the ability to change someone. I hadn't given it much thought then, but recently, now that I'd been practicing magic regularly, I understood. I'd felt the temptation—it was there—

to spin magic straight from my soul. The darkness existed directly next to the light; it existed as a whisper, and it spoke into my ears every time I cast. But that was why we used wands instead of ourselves—because we weren't meant to have raw electricity that near to our hearts.

It wasn't until we crossed underneath Edmond and Bernice, the pair of unhappily married trees who stood between the forest and the market, that Cee-Cee chose to speak again. "What I said earlier, I meant it. The first time I saw you, I knew I needed to know you. Do you think it's because I knew you could bring me here?"

"I'd like to think it was because you saw someone who desperately needed a friend or two."

She bit down over her lip and nodded. She didn't say another word, but she didn't have to. She'd already made up her mind that everything Dora had told her was true. And if there was a hope that her mother was still alive, then she was going to do anything it took to find her.

❦ 6 ❦

The marketplace looked as though the sky had fallen upon it. Pale blue fabric moved like waves of the sea as the Garlandian knights paced over the grounds. The knight who was stalking up to Cee-Cee and I was on horseback, a large sword hanging from his side.

"Who goes there, you who crosses into the king's court?" the elf demanded.

"My friend was summoned," I stated, my wings lifting behind my back. The elf followed the edges of them with his eyes, then gave me a warning stare. Ever so slowly, I allowed them to sink back down.

The elf pulled out a black wand and pointed it at Cee-Cee. "Name."

"Anastacia Montgomery," she stated, a drop of sweat slowly dripping from her right temple.

"Violation?"

"It—It was be—because of—um . . . Wait—here!" With a shaky hand, she handed him the note Dora had given her.

The elf reached down and snagged the paper from her grip then brought it up to his eyes for inspection. He appeared to reread it several times before shouting to someone in the crowd. "Sir, may I have you for a moment?"

The crowd of knights encircling whoever it was this elf called 'sir' parted and I held my breath, hoping to the stars and back that it would be Toby. But I was sorely wrong.

As soon as the charcoal dark eyes of the elf I most despised in the world spotted me, my insides crowded together as a ripple of nausea ran through me. "Rally," I cursed his name under my breath.

Upon spotting us, he froze, a sickening expression transforming onto his wicked face. As he began to move away from his goonie followers, I took note that he was not alone. Clinging to his side and staring at him with starry eyes, was a female elf with an unfortunate acne problem and a crooked nose. The fabric of her dress matched the ballgown Toby had given me not so long ago, denoting her status.

"My, my, my," Rally said, once he'd come upon us. "If it's not Lala Abberwockey in the flesh and dust. How did I guess I'd be seeing you sooner than later? What did you do to find yourself here?"

"We aren't here for me," I spat out. "My friend was brought here with me unwillingly, and now she is being called out for illegal immigration."

"She brought this with her," the knight said to Rally, handing him the note before being dismissed.

Rally read over the words. When he was finished, he looked Cee-Cee up and down. "You are a friend of Dora?"

"I just met her." Cee-Cee's voice was tame, but I could more than sense her distaste for Rally—it was pungent.

Rally stepped away from the homely elf and so close to Cee-Cee that they were practically neck and neck. Cee-Cee clenched up and her nostrils flared as Rally inspected her eyes. Her lips twitched, but she was smart enough to restrain herself from speaking out of turn.

Finally Rally took a step back. "I can't believe it."

The female elf, still off to the side, kneaded her hands together, as she said, "Can't believe what, Rally bear?"

Speaking directly to Cee-Cee, he said, "The tracker said what you were, but it didn't seem possible. Hecate's blood is rare—there hasn't been a direct descendant for years." Nearing her once more, he reached for a strand of her pink hair, ignoring the female elf's unhappy stare, as he placed his lips a little too close to her ear. "You are as beautiful as Hecate herself. Where have you been hiding?"

Cee-Cee's answer was short. "I wasn't hiding. I've been living with my dad."

A curious smile manifested over Rally's face. "With your dad." He chuckled and then took a step back. "I apologize for the mix up, Miss Anastacia. Give Dora my regards."

Even though he was being friendly, a rare trait for him, I didn't care a lick for the way he was looking at my friend, nor did the female elf who was accompanying him apparently.

Stumbling forward, the female elf jutted her hand out, I guessed for me to slap. "I'm Princess Louisa. You must be the lost Erwain, tales of your reappearance made it all the way to my kingdom."

I hesitated only a second, watching as Rally gave me a look of warning as he stepped back in line with Louisa; but all that made me want to do was become fast friends with the homely elf. I slapped her hand and accepted the one she reciprocated across my face.

"So nice to meet you, princess. And I hope you don't mind me saying so, but the two of you look most excellent together."

Louisa cooed and squeezed Rally closer to her.

"Aargh!" He shifted rudely away from her embrace. "Louisa, what happened to those mints I gave you?"

The princess's face turned bright red, and she looked

morbidly embarrassed as she pulled out a small container and stuck a little white tablet into her mouth. "Sorry," she said, then looking up at me, explained, "just a bit of a halitosis condition."

Rally crumpled up the bit of paper into his fist. "You two should move along. Get back to your end of the woods, so to speak."

"Gladly," I snipped. "Come on, Cee-Cee, let's get out of here."

"Wait a second." Rally laid a finger over his lips. "Wasn't there someone else that was supposed to be here . . ."

Cee-Cee and I glanced at each other in nervous anticipation.

Returning my gaze to Rally, I rolled back my shoulders and made sure to steady my voice. "I'm sorry—what?" I could've sworn I caught Princess Louisa giving me a funny look out of the corner of my eye.

"Didn't I see you here with a human boy once upon a time?" Rally insisted.

"I don't know what you're talking about," I lied.

Princess Louisa shifted her feet, and as she did the sun reflected differently from the sword hanging from her side. It blinded me and I looked away.

"I think you're overthinking things, Rally bear," Louisa cooed into his ear. "If they were hiding anyone, the truth would be spilt all over their hands." She ran her fingers through his hair, and he growled. "No one can hide anything from you—you're too smart."

"Stop that!" he exclaimed, pushing her from his side. "You know how I feel about public displays of affection." Readjusting himself, he waved a hand flippantly in our direction. "Go on—get from this place."

"Fine," I said, an indecent smile forming along the lines of my lips. I should have simply taken the rare gift of Rally's dismissal and run, but I couldn't help myself. "If you don't mind me saying, you two are just perfect for one another." I winked at Rally. "Whoever got the two of you together, really pulled one over on you."

Louisa beamed. "Thank you, Miss Makayla."

Rally looked like he wanted to tear my heart out. We both knew it was Toby who had somehow managed to set them up —a way of keeping Rally preoccupied and out of his hair. Poor Princess Louisa wasn't really on top of the list of wanted elf mates, but she was notorious for being a daddy's girl and getting what she wanted. After hearing of Rally's love for her, a letter Toby wrote in Rally's penmanship, she absolutely *had* to have him. Now he couldn't leave her, not without feeling the wrath of a king with a daughter scorned.

Just as Cee-Cee and I turned to leave, Rally shouted angrily at my back, "Too bad—what they're saying!"

I glanced back at him.

"That Sir Toby was taken by the Easternly Witches upon his travels back into the kingdom from Anemone."

I froze. My heart began thumping just at the mention of Toby's name, so loud in fact that I felt as though everyone was able to hear it. Unable to move right away, I pushed past the rapid beating to feel for the extra rhythm Toby had given me for reassurance. But suddenly it was all too quiet in my chest. Cramming my eyes shut, I strained my internal ears to hear for it. Finally, I came across a very soft beat next to my own, but it was no doubt quieter than it had been when I first woke.

Facing him once more, I stood taller. "That's unfortunate."

"If the rumors are true then his fate is surely at an end, for they are but time weavers who come from the ground. No one escapes them. They are, in essence, death."

My tongue felt swollen, my mouth dry. I couldn't tell whether what he was saying was true, or if Toby's heartbeat was only quieted by the heaviness of mine. But just then, a chilly wind soared past my cheeks, stealing away my indecisions, and landing directly in front of Cee-Cee.

The wind circled her as though it were alive. Her hair was in its folds, and in her hands the box she was holding opened. She stared down into her newfound crystal ball. When she looked back up, her gaze fixed onto Rally's, and her brown eyes were glowing an emerald green.

"He is lying," she said, her voice thicker and deeper than usual. "The elf does not know where the blood of his superior flows."

Rally's eyes narrowed. The way he was looking at Cee-Cee —it was like he was seeing the face of someone who he'd watched die in his arms. Like he couldn't believe he was seeing what he was seeing.

The whirlwind stayed with Cee-Cee for but a second longer, before flying away; at which point her eyes dulled to brown, and the box in her hands folded itself back up.

When she realized everyone was staring at her, she stated a very quiet, "What?"

"Hecate . . ." Rally whispered, before taking Louisa's hand and pulling her along back into the throng of the pale blue army. "She cannot protect you forever, faery," he said in my direction, "and she won't. Not if Dora has gotten involved." But whatever had happened, it had obviously shaken him, for he couldn't seem to get away fast enough.

7

"That was so totally wicked!" Cee-Cee exclaimed as we ran back through the forest.

My wings levitated over the forest floor, but never past the tops of the trees. We'd gotten out of that place once and I didn't want to chance that we could do it again. Although, I was pretty sure that no matter what happened, Cee-Cee would remain safe.

"If I dare to say it," I said, my chest heaving, after we'd collapsed into a tree who proceeded to shout at us for doing so, "it almost appeared as though Rally liked you. Like, *like liked* you."

Cee-Cee shivered as a disgusted sound rose from the back of her throat. "Gross. He touched my hair." She pulled out a strand and looked at it like she wanted to cut it off. Her eyes refocused and suddenly she was more alert. "Hey, look where we are." She pointed her arm up at a sign.

I looked up. "Ambiguous and Fox."

Crawling up to stand, she pointed at a stone-wall cottage buried behind the trees. "Is that it? Your aunt's house?"

"It must be," I replied, my wings pulling me up to my feet, proceeding to walk towards the forest residence.

It didn't look like somewhere my Aunt Helene would have lived. Granted I didn't have much time to think about her dwellings while she was alive. I was too busy believing she was out to help me, when in reality she was trying to get me to find my faery dust so that my wings would free themselves and she could take them from me while my guard was down. Too bad for her she'd underestimated me. In any case, if I had given it much thought, I wouldn't have pictured this snug little bungalow as the place where she resided. Helene, with her fishnet tights and dark aura—well, it would have seemed more fitting that she lived in a darkly lit dungeon of some sort.

"Never judge a book by its cover," I muttered.

"What?" Cee-Cee asked as we stepped up to the wooden door.

"Oh, nothing—just thinking out loud." Pulling out my wand, I held it stiffly by my side. The front stoop was engraved with the number 13. 13 Ambiguous Fox. Charming address.

"What do we do now?" Cee-Cee asked.

Placing my free hand over the doorknob, I gave it a twist and pushed the door easily open. Stepping carefully over the threshold, I turned and shrugged my shoulders at her. "Just go in, I guess."

After the two of us were inside, a sharp wind pulled the door shut, causing both our shoulders to shoot up towards the ceiling.

"Dang, this place be spooky," Cee-Cee said, carefully putting down the box in her arms and rubbing her bare shoulders with her hands.

Draping the purple dress Esmerelda had given me over a chair, I added, "More like absurd. This doesn't feel like Helene." After another minute of scoping it out, I added, "It's as though it hasn't been lived in at all."

The white walls were bare, the fireplace appeared as though it had never felt heat, and there were three simple pieces of furniture in the room guarding a coffee table that had but a single copy of *Wicked Style* on top—a fashion magazine for the modern magical folk.

But as we were about to find out, there wasn't a lot of time for dissecting the home for clues to prove my aunt had ever lived there, for a second later a loud POP ensued somewhere inside the house causing Cee-Cee and I to jump immediately into one another's arms.

"I thought no one could get in here unless you let them in," she whispered.

"That's what my keeper said," I replied, clutching her to my side as the two of us clung to the nearest wall and waited for whatever else was in the house with us to show itself. But not even a second later, all my apprehensions melted away.

"You can let them in," said a smooth female voice, "or they can come in as long as they are needed; but don't worry, anyone who is a potential threat will never be able to come inside."

"Contessa!" As soon as I recognized the Erwain, I ran from Cee-Cee's arms straight into hers.

She hugged me tight, her bright orange wings folding around the two of us. "We've been waiting weeks for you to return," she whispered into my shoulder. I knew just from her touch that the whimsical faery I'd last met was gone—replaced by an encumbered soul.

I shifted my gaze so that I could look into her eyes. I didn't remember them being golden. "I thought you'd be gone, too," I said.

"We volunteered to stay, to wait until Sir Toby sent word that you would be coming back."

My eyes hardened. "You've been in contact with my—with Toby?"

"Yes. And before you ask, Tanker and Maude have already gone; their location is confidential. They couldn't tell us in case the guards came for questioning." She looked away for a brief moment. "They already have once."

"But they *are* safe right?"

Contessa nodded her head. "Yes." Laying a hand over my cheek, she repeated herself, "Yes, they are. And now we need to figure out a way to get you to them."

"No," I said obstinately. Contessa frowned. "I can't. Not until I find Toby."

Contessa pulled her hand away, growing even more serious if that was possible. "Makayla, our contact with Sir Toby has been stifled. We can't just sit around and wait on the off chance that—"

"Wait, you're in contact with him? Right now?"

Contessa dipped her chin and looked down at her hands. "We *have* been in contact with him. Like I said, our communication has been disrupted." Returning her gaze to mine, she continued. "I'm sorry, Makayla. I know this is troubling information, but we can't wait for him to return to us. We are on strict orders to get ourselves and you to your parents as soon as we can."

"Why wouldn't he have told me he was in contact with you?" I muttered. Then, sorting through my thoughts, I looked back at the faery. "How can you get me to my parents if you don't know where they are?"

Her shoulders slumped. "That's a good question. But I think the answer is in here." She scanned the walls. "Generation houses are known for keeping secrets. If not, the butterflies should be arriving soon." Suddenly Contessa's eyes froze from where they'd been wandering, pausing over Cee-Cee's boxed crystal ball. Cee-Cee, who had been standing quietly next to it while the two of us reconnected, took a step closer to it as though she was protecting it. Contessa's gaze met hers.

"Who's this?" Contessa asked, the corners of her lips turning down.

"Oh, I'm so sorry. This is my friend Cee-Cee," I answered. "I didn't mean for her to get dragged into this, but when we woke up this morning, she was here with me. What did you mean about the butterflies arriving soon?"

"I see." Contessa didn't seem to hear my last question. Instead of answering, she moved towards the box, and past the apprehensive look coloring Cee-Cee's face. As soon as she reached it, Contessa flipped open the lid and simply stood over the ball, looking down at it as though she'd come across a severed hand. A bit of orange and black dust began to emanate from her shoulders. "Where did you get this?" she whispered.

Cee-Cee shot me a nervous look before answering her. "A witch in the forest. The ball seemed to know me, so the witch had me take it."

"Dora." The way Contessa said the name revealed the way she felt about this particular character. This was not a friend. "And what else did she say to you?"

"Th—That I'm a descendant of Hecate. That my mother was a witch. That I'm a witch."

Contessa looked up at Cee-Cee. A bit of her dust danced away from her and over to where I was standing, gripping my wrist as though it were a hand trying to pull me away. Every inch of my skin prickled.

"Contessa?" I questioned. "Are you all right?"

The faery held very still for a moment, before backing away. "No . . . No, I'm not." There was something different about her, but I couldn't put my finger on it. "But neither Owen nor I have been taken yet, so that's something. As for you needing to wait for Toby, we can't make you do anything, but neither Owen nor myself can afford to wait much longer. There are rumors that black magic has infiltrated the castle walls." As she said the words, she gave Cee-Cee a strange look. "That the guards aren't just expelling dust from the fey, but that they have found a way to keep it from reproducing once it has been detached."

"You mean permanently destroying our dust—our magic?" I asked.

"Yes."

"That's horrific!" I exclaimed. "What happens to the fey who have been victimized in this way?"

"No dust equals no magic, equals part of their soul being taken away."

"They can't do that," I muttered.

"No, they shouldn't be able to do that. But the seeds of darkness grow more steadily in the absence of light. It is an unnatural thing that is headed our way."

I suddenly felt like I needed to sit. Collapsing into the nearest chair, I said, "Tell me, who is left here—in the forest?"

Contessa's eyes hardened; she was still surveying Cee-Cee, who was clasping and unclasping her hands in a way unlike her usual character. "A handful, that is all. And those of us on the council. For whatever reason, King Loral is keeping us on the sidelines. Probably with the assumption that the longer he waits to question us, the more answers we will have for him." There was a small silence as all this information fell around our shoulders. "I must get back to Owen before he gets worried," Contessa finally said, reaching for my arm. "The two of you should not leave this house. And as for you" –she gave Cee-Cee a piercing look— "the last thing you should be doing is meddling in any sort of business with Dora. She is not your friend, girl."

Cee-Cee opened her mouth as though she was going to argue, but quickly shut it, taking a step back.

Returning her attention to me, Contessa said, "If you are

smart you will start pillaging through this house. There must be answers somewhere in here, and even if Toby does return in time, you'll need a place to hide. We all will for that matter. Your safety is not yours alone, Makayla. You have the power to change everything. Be wise in your decisions and listen . . . listen for the butterflies." And then once more there was a very loud POP along with an orange dusting where Contessa had been but a moment ago.

I looked over to where Cee-Cee was standing. She looked as if she'd just been given news that the authorities were coming to take her under arrest.

"What now?" I whispered. "What do we do *now*?"

Cee-Cee grabbed the box containing her crystal ball and fell to the couch. Carefully pulling the orb from the container, she centered it over its stand and placed it on the coffee table. I scratched the area above my brow. "Everything Contessa said were things I didn't expect, nor want to hear."

"Are you seriously, like, surprised?" Cee-Cee said, placing her hands on either side of the ball. "That king is vile. I'm just curious why your friend looked at me like I was a threat to you."

I stared at the ball. "Probably because you got messed up with the wrong crowd. I felt it when we were there with her—something isn't right with Dora."

"Yeah well," Cee-Cee said flippantly, "she seems to think my mother's still alive, and so do this ball. So excuse me for wanting to dig a little deeper."

"So that *is* what you saw in there?" Cee-Cee looked up at me. "That your mother is still alive?"

She didn't answer, instead she returned her gaze to the crystal.

I took a deep breath and let it out slowly. It seemed rather obvious that Dora was either baiting Cee-Cee with false hope or had some kind of foul intention. But I didn't have the energy it was going to take to persuade Cee-Cee to see that, not when I was already worried to death that something had happened to Toby.

Biting my fingernail, I pondered out loud, "Why wouldn't Toby tell me that he was in contact with Contessa?"

"Got me," Cee-Cee answered, peering into her ball like she was adjusting a microscope.

"All I have are more questions now." My heart was beating so fast there was no way to distinguish whether or not Toby's was still mixed in with mine. Pinching the fabric of the blue couch between my finger and thumb, trying to keep my mind at bay, I stated, "I wonder what she meant about listening for the butterflies."

And that's when Cee-Cee looked up, her back suddenly erect. "I don't know, but that might be a good place to start."

I followed the direction she was pointing, towards the window. I gasped as I stood up, my wings rising steadily behind my back. For there, levitating on the other side of the windowpane, was a giant purple butterfly.

8

Rally walked into the throne room with a stifled gait. He peered around the vast space until his eyes met the frosty hair tied into a knot at the nape of the king's neck.

"Sir." Was all he said.

Sebastian Loral was the closest thing he'd ever had to a father, and even though the king of Garlandia had never been one for affection, it was no secret amongst the guard who his favorite was. Yes, Toby was next in line, but everyone knew who Loral had been grooming. Ever since the day Rally had been dropped off to the castle, a mere babe.

The king didn't turn from the window he'd clung to. "What is it, Rally?"

"Makayla Wood has returned to Garlandia."

"I've heard."

"She's not alone."

King Loral hadn't moved except to breathe from the moment Rally entered. Still, the elf seemed to freeze. Keeping his gaze to the sheet of glass separating him from the going's on outside the castle, he moved his head so slowly in Rally's direction that one might have heard a creak.

"It is not possible for anyone to get in or out of the kingdom. Makayla was the one and only exception."

Rally's chest rose and his lips sealed shut only briefly before he stated back to his lord, "The girl who has come with her is a descendant of Hecate."

This time, Sebastian allowed his eyes to burn into the figment of the son he never had. "That's . . ."

"Nearly impossible. I know, sir. But the tracker doesn't lie and I—I could smell it on her." His gait shifted and his shoulders lowered. "The girl posing as Makayla Wood's friend is one of the last bloodlines belonging to the Crone."

He spit out his next words as if they were toothpicks. "Posing as her friend?"

Rally began to dance backwards with his proposition. "Perhaps posing is the wrong word."

The king finally pushed away from the window, creeping towards Rally like a mountain lion stalking its prey. One foot moved in front of the other in a slow-paced march, the boots around his feet making no sound against the marble floor. "Speak plainly. Who is this girl and why is she here?"

Rally didn't fear this elf who he'd seen burn men to the ground by merely staring at them. In fact, he'd grown to look up to his superior; then again, affection wasn't allowed, and he'd needed something to fill that void. Also, his mother had instructed him to keep himself tucked into the folds of the elf's robes. Trepidation, he had not, but his wits told him to respect the magic stirring within King Loral's blood—even if it was an unnatural thing.

"I—I believe the girl may not know who she is. Dora has claimed her, perhaps the witch brought her here." Rally struck out his arm and pointed out towards Market Circle. "She had a note from the witch. It saved her from the dungeon."

Loral's cheeks darkened, becoming the color of clay. "I am the end all. Not the witch from the end of the woods."

"I am aware of that, sir. But I know you and Dora have a connection, and—"

"NO MORE OF THIS!" he bellowed, causing the curtains to shake around each and every window lining the throne room. Everything stirred, minus that of the water that sat before the throne. Lowering his voice, stepping up to the closest thing to a son he'd ever had, Sebastian said, "What are the chances of her truly being unaware of her power?"

Rally's Adam's Apple dipped down then back up as if it were a lever. "I'd say nearly one hundred percent. Hecate herself breathed through the girl and she didn't so much as blink an eye after."

The king's left fist clenched together, and he lifted his chin. "You say Dora has already connected with this girl?"

Rally nodded.

Loral's head turned towards the throne, and he said so softly that Rally had to strain to hear his speech. "She said this day would come. That when it did, we must tread lightly, for more than two winds would find one another. However, it will not be a funnel cloud coming to destroy what we've built, but a tsunami." Lowering his gaze, refusing to meet Rally's, he added, "The question is, will this aid in our fight against that insect Titania, or will this complicate things further?"

Rally's mouth unhinged as he prepared to find the words to answer his lord (even though he hadn't the faintest idea what to say). He'd been groomed but only handed enough information to keep his head out of the clouds and into the magic handed to him. Either way, Loral beat him to the punch.

"Go now, Rally. Summon the Huntress of Lorelei Wood. Tell her what you told me."

A heaviness set in over Rally's chest and the corners of his vision dimmed. "You want me to—but I haven't reached out in so long . . . What if she doesn't answer?"

This time the king shot his glare to fit perfectly into his student's eyes, causing a chill to run down Rally's spine. "I've forgotten. Are you the one who gives the orders around here, or am I?"

Rally immediately rolled his shoulders forward and bent to one knee. "I apologize, sir. I was caught off guard."

The king scoffed. "Get up." Rally obeyed, quickly reforming his posture, and standing at attention. Loral sauntered over and stopped just short of walking past him, so that his lips were but inches from the half elf's ear. "Never bow to me, son. You're not a faery."

Rally nodded too quickly. "Yes sir."

A moment later, the king was gone.

୶୬ଛ

Rally's quarters were just across the hall from Toby's. The two boys had been raised together. Brothers, or maybe cousins more like. That was how they'd viewed themselves. That was until Toby started coming apart at the seams shortly after that *faery* stepped foot into the Garlandian forest.

Why had he gone and ruined it all? He was the only elf in King Loral's company that Rally felt comfortable around, though no one would ever know that. Rally was very good at keeping himself steady and in line. He also knew verbatim the law as according to his ruler; and his mother had infused him with the inability to question authority.

He closed the thick wooden door to his room and ensured it was sealed properly. No one was in this part of the castle this time of day. There were far too many violators, and the knights were occupied with the handling of fugitive elves, fey, and the very occasional witch. Still, what he'd been ordered to do might be construed as . . . confusing. Questionable. Even if it was an order from the highest commander, he didn't want to have to explain himself to anybody.

Turning around to face his quarters, he tapped the four corners of the room. Within seconds a marble chalice the color of tourmaline, a collection of herbs and retracted stardust, lake water from the ninth underworld, and the ash from his mother's homeland began to circulate from where they'd been hidden. He remained planted as they danced together over his head before setting down and coming together in a perfectly deranged recipe designed to wake an ancient voice from her resting place.

As soon as the water found the chalice and the ingredients fell into their place in the water, Rally came to his knees. His wand tight in his hand, he took but one deep breath before closing and reopening his eyes. With his chest stilled, and with the ice King Loral had deposited in his chest and spine just moments ago still solidly in place, he stiffly brought the tip of his wand to the edge of the chalice and tapped it six times. He might as well have been summoning a demon.

"Savannah, Huntress of Lorelei Wood, can you hear me?"

Nothing happened for nearly three minutes. Rally began to hesitate. It had been some time since he'd last attempted to find the unbeating heart of the witch who had been crucified for trying to reign in all that was lost when the cult of the bad village was laid to rest. But just as his self-doubt began to rain down over his shoulders, the dim lights in his quarters began to flutter until all that surrounded him was darkness.

Mildew filled his nostrils, ice pricked at his flesh, and the dankness of a cave buried several football fields underground pounded against his skull. This was where they'd sent her . . . the people of Lorelei. It was a punishment. A death sentence. The thing is, not everything or everyone can be killed; at least not instantly. What he'd seen just that day was proof enough of that.

A scuffle in the corner grabbed his attention and he lifted the wand he still clung to. The darkness filled with the stardust his magical tool had inhaled, and though it was a sort of black glitter that erupted, it was enough to make out the outline of the squid-like creature that scampered out into the sparkle and fade.

He'd asked his superior only once—when he was eight—why Savannah looked this way now; he'd been too young to understand that some things are best left alone rather than brought to light. King Loral had only told him not to see her as she'd once been, for she no longer existed the way she had when her identity was defined by the witch's wand she'd been granted while living in the flesh. Her physical self was no longer a thing, and so she'd become a twisted recreation of what her spirit could afford to portray.

Rally never asked any more questions and Loral never offered any more council on the subject.

As he continued to hold out his wand, the creature spoke directly into his mind, using a raspy voice that made one suffer at their own breath. "Rally. . ."

"Yes," he answered stiffly.

"It's been so long . . . I'd thought you'd never return."

He closed his eyes and tried not to breathe. It was not just the decay of body in this place that made it foul, but that of spirit as well. Savannah hadn't just been sent to die in this underworld but had been sentenced to a slow rot. It was a punishment Rally wouldn't wish upon his worst enemy—even that of a certain red-headed faery.

"I've come because there's been a development as of late." The squid-like thing scampered around his feet, and he tried not to upend his lunch. Bringing his free hand to his mouth, he made a fist and held it before his nose and lips as if it might buffer the stench of decay. "The Hecate line . . . specifically the witch you'd been trying to track before you were captured. I believe she's returned."

The creature slithered into a spot directly in front of where Rally was planted and very slowly began to pull from stardust and whatever else Rally had sucked into the end of his wand. It wasn't enough to reform herself permanently, but it did allow her to show herself as he had once known her. It was enough to fill his heart with the sentiment she would need him to cling to as he moved forward with her bidding.

As soon as the image of the woman he'd known became whole again, Rally felt his heart pump pure blood for the first time in a long time. She walked over and placed a cold hand against his warm cheek. "Summon the Robes of Lorelei. It has been some time, but I must believe they are still out there. Only they will know what comes next. Explain to them that I can no longer serve the Crone, but in you they may find what has been lost. After all, you have my blood."

Rally took one final deep breath, sorting through the decomposing air particles that filled this cave—striving to find the scent of the woman who had once held his hand and led him from one world into another.

"Yes mother," he replied.

And then light disturbed dark. There was a shriek as the woman touching his face shrunk back into a cretin and he was pulled from her grave back into his room, where he was at once awakened to find he wasn't alone.

"What in the world are you doing, Rally bear?"

Rally swayed from where he was hunkered over the chalice on the floor of his bedroom. "I was just—" She was staring him down, only about a foot from where he was crouched. He dug down deep for his knightly persona. Coming to standing, he acted as though there was nothing more on the ground than a cluster of plastic army men. "How did you get in here? I secured the door."

Louisa cocked her hip to one side and her head to the other. "I am yours completely; I should never be locked out from your heart." As she said this, she pressed a palm to his chest. It was all he could do to keep from retching all over the illegal spell ingredients.

Instead of displaying his truth, he tucked it in and used his remaining strength to soften the corners of his mouth. "Yes love, you are so right. I would never lock you out intentionally." As he cursed his lost cousin, his once brother in this castle for setting him up with this filthy excuse for a royal elf, he took her hand in his and began to move the two of them towards his door, which had been left wide open. As soon as her back was turned to the magic he'd been practicing, he waved his wand behind his back and dispensed the items back to where they resided in hiding. "Come now. I have some correspondence to tend to and I believe I've a surprise for you down in the dining hall."

"Oh?" she questioned. She tried to turn and look back at the spot where the ingredients had been only a moment ago, but Rally urged her quickly out the door.

"I know you've been complaining that I have been absent more than present, so I found you someone to love while I am at work."

Once they were in the hallway, she shot him a conniving stare. "Rally bear, what have you gone and done?"

"Just you wait, my love," he said, trying not to choke on the false affection.

Hopefully the distraction would perform as he needed it to. This princess was already an unwelcome stain in his everyday life, but now more than ever he would need her big nose and buck teeth out of his way.

His life was no more his own than Makayla Wood's. The

difference was he hadn't come to this place to scoop up the evil and throw it into the fire. He'd been born into strategy, and though he'd never been given a voice of his own, he knew what his next steps needed to be.

Lorelei . . . the world where the merpeople ruled even the dry land. This is where it all began, where his mother had seeded him into her womb using an elf who she thought could get her closer to their leader. She'd been wrong, and she would now suffer until there was nothing left of her but the stench of rotting air.

She'd put the future of their bloodline in his hands. The Robes of Lorelei, they were few, but they were there . . . and it was now up to him to find them. Their priestess had returned.

❧ 9 ❧

I was hesitant at first, taking fixed steps towards where the butterfly was lingering just outside the living room window—Cee-Cee mere inches behind me. When I was close enough that all that stood between us was the thin sheet of glass, I carefully pulled open the window and let out a shallow breath.

The butterfly didn't move, keeping to its spot directly across from my nose. It appeared to be staring at me.

"Are you an intellectual?" I asked.

But there was no reaction.

"*To find us, you only need to whisper into the heart the name that still breaks mine apart.*"

My head jerked back, and I almost fell backwards. "What the—" Had that raspy, child-like voice just come from that butterfly?

"It's, like, staring at you," Cee-Cee said.

I steadied myself, staring back at the insect. "Did you not hear that?"

"What?" Cee-Cee questioned.

"That voice—that creepy voice."

"*Raton.*"

"There it is again!" I exclaimed, pointing at the butterfly, but it flew away before I could reach forward and capture it.

"Makayla," Cee-Cee said, a worried look appearing on her face. "I didn't hear anything. You better not be losing your shit. I don't think I can hack this place without you."

"It got away!" I practically jumped out the window, searching for the butterfly, but it was totally gone. Once I was back on my feet, I pulled the window shut again and slumped down onto the nearest couch, my gaze moving back and forth as I tried to assess the situation. "I heard it. Like a riddle." I closed my eyes and repeated the line, embedding it into my brain. "To find us, you only need to whisper into the heart the name that still breaks mine apart." I bit my lip, thinking over the words. "And then it said one word: Raton. Where have I heard that before?"

"Raton?" Cee-Cee repeated the word. "Sounds like a place."

"Raton . . . Raton—wait! That's what that little faery said this morning!" My mind was quickly putting the bits of information together. "My keeper! While he was fuming about having to pack up and leave, he said they would need to get to Raton."

"So, it's a safe land," Cee-Cee mused.

"It must be." I racked my brain. "But what in the world could the rest of that mean? Whisper into the heart? My god, that could be anything!"

"This place is so frustrating," Cee-Cee said, staring out the window into the forest. "I wonder who sent that butterfly here. Do you think it was your faery parents?"

"I don't know, it could've been. They left no clues back at their house as to where they were going."

"Well we didn't really have a chance to look for any," Cee-Cee pointed out.

"True. Maybe we should go back to 17 Serendipity Lane for a bit. Nose our way through the house. There could be something there that could help us."

"Sure," Cee-Cee agreed.

But just as we were getting ready to leave, a loud trumpet sounded from somewhere in the forest, and when we opened the front door, we saw what at first glance was a parade of knights; but upon a more discerning study, turned out to be a death march. For at the lead was a knight pointing a sword down at a small creature whose hands were bound behind his back. I recognized him immediately, and so did Cee-Cee. It was Mort.

"What could that little crap bag have done?" Cee-Cee asked as we watched the little gnome being taken away from his forest home.

"Nothing," I answered in a whisper. "He's just a little mailbox gnome."

I closed the door and pulled Cee-Cee away from it. "Perhaps we wait to leave just yet." Contessa *had* mentioned there could be clues hidden *here*. "Let's stay put for now and search through this house instead."

She nodded her head very quickly. "Yes, let's."

ॐ

We decided to wait to leave again until the next morning. We had planned to escape back to my birth parents' cottage around evening, but dark fell early and there were two more 'violators' marched past the living room window that day. A female Wood elf with a dangerous mouth on her and what appeared to be a male witch. Apparently, witches weren't entirely safe after all.

Speaking of the magical breed of wingless beings, we'd seen a couple faces peering at us from the woods. One man and one woman, both adorned in the typical witch's garb. Every inch of their skin was covered, and these two in particular wore tattered clothing, as though they'd refused to update their wardrobes after being alive for several hundred years. I hadn't been in Garlandia long enough to know the difference between a good witch and a bad witch (for Dora, with her blonde hair and round cheeks, would at first glance put her opponent at ease). For all I knew, that was her game. As for our new 'friends,' we'd caught them lurking around 13 Ambiguous Fox at least twice during the day. What they wanted from us—we didn't know. And we didn't want to find out. We had too much on our plates, so we had no choice but to ignore their existence.

Since we'd decided to stay put, we went ahead and began rummaging through my new house, searching for clues. But the more we dug, the more it seemed fairly evident that it had either been cleared of all Helene's possessions, or that my aunt had spent hardly any time here while she'd been alive. Save for the small closet in the master bedroom, crammed with dresses and shoes, there was no evidence of her at all. If this was all that was left of Helene, then it pointed to one conclusion: my aunt was obsessed with only two things—killing me and fashion.

Other than the closet, all we'd managed to find were two bedrooms, one bathroom, a kitchen (with a family of intellectual mice living in a cabinet that they had designed into a three-level home) and of course the living room, which we had first entered.

It was a small, quaint living quarters and there was nothing, not even a slip of paper nor a rogue hair swept away into the corner, to lend its hand in the direction that I was hoping for. Namely, Raton. Then again, I couldn't very well expect things like that to just walk out and shake my hand. Or slap it, more like.

Having made the decision to spend the night, Cee-Cee and I laid side by side in the bigger of the two bedrooms. Neither one of us slept very well, between the questions fluttering around our heads, to our fears of what might happen the next day, and of course how Jeremy Love must've been feeling all alone in a strange land.

"He's seriously been turned into an elf, hasn't he?" Cee-Cee said after three hours of pretending to be asleep. It was the first time either of us had brought him up since we'd been forced to part ways.

"Probably," I murmured. "But I daresay that there are worse things. He did love that Wood elf's shop. That's something, right?"

"I guess so." But I could feel the heaviness in my friend's gut, and it made my guilt bubble further up to the surface.

After a few more silent moments I said what I'd been thinking for weeks. "I'm sorry you guys met me."

Cee-Cee rolled over immediately, propping her head up with her elbow. "Don't say that, girl. Don't you ever say that again."

"It's true." I kept my gaze attuned to the ceiling. "You guys would be getting ready to go into your last year of high school if you hadn't met me. And god knows what your parents are thinking right now."

Cee-Cee was quiet, contemplative. Playing with my wing like it was a strand of hair, she said, "It's gonna be okay. My dad will get over it once he has me back safe and sound, and Jeremy's parents, well—let's just say, they not gonna go looking for him if he disappears. Besides, I'm sure there's a faery spell or something that we can concoct to make them forget all about everything when our parents do figure out we're gone."

My forehead wrinkled. "What do you mean—about Jeremy's parents?"

Cee-Cee took a deep breath. "They just, you know, they aren't that nice."

"Aren't that nice?" I made a face.

Cee-Cee stared at me for a moment, eventually letting go of my wing. "It's like this, okay. Jeremy and his family were all real close when he was young, but then one day he came out, cause he thought his family would accept him; but as soon as he did, they all just sort of crept away. His mom, his dad, and his big brother. They just stopped paying attention to him."

My jaw dropped. "Wait, what? His family doesn't support him being bi? That sort of ignorance still exists?"

Cee-Cee shot me a look that poured white girl privilege all over me like sticky syrup and I quickly decided that maybe I should think sometimes before I talk. I may have had a target on my back my whole life, but I had four parents who loved me to the moon and back, and let's face it—until I stepped foot into Garlandia, I'd known only privilege.

She laid back down, facing the ceiling. "That's when I met him. It was just around the time my mom died, or when we thought she died . . . The two of us kinda just became instant best friends."

"Wow," I said. "I can't believe that. Jeremy is so sweet. I can't imagine anyone treating him unwell."

"Yeah, well, Garlandia ain't the only place with problems, ya know."

I placed my hands under my head. "No, it isn't. So, what do you think about your mom and all that? You *do* realize that Dora could've planted whatever you saw into that ball."

"Believe me, I thought about that. But here's the thing." She folded her hands over her stomach. "I'm not so sure I ever believed she was dead."

"How can you say that? Until today you would have had no reason to believe otherwise."

"I don't know," she muttered. "It's kind of like when you

get hungry, but you don't have time to eat. For a little while, the feeling in your gut, it's like your stomach is eating itself cause you're so famished—but then, after a while that hunger just goes away. You still need to eat, but you somehow forget that you need to." She paused before going on. "I just remember being at her funeral, sitting in that first row, in that gray folding chair, staring at my mom's urn. Somewhere deep inside, a part of me was mad—and I mean *hopping* mad—cause I felt deserted. Like I knew she'd just gone and pretended that she died."

"How come you never said anything then?" I asked suspiciously.

"Cause I forgot about it. Like the hunger, you know. And it wasn't until that ball was set under my eyes and I saw my mother's face, that I remembered that burning feeling inside—like ropes on fire knotted up in my belly."

"If she *is* alive—then what?"

"I'm not sure."

"Would you be mad at her? I mean, she had to have left for a reason, right?"

Cee-Cee was quiet for a long time, but when she finally answered, her voice sounded different, so unlike her own that I felt the hairs raise on the back of my neck. "I would make her wish she'd died the first time."

I immediately began to question Cee-Cee's violent response, but upon second thought, I chose not to say anything at all. Something had been dug up and there were too many roots to gather.

"All right, then. Good night," I said, turning on my side, facing the opposite direction.

"Good night, Makayla."

As the rhythm of her breath slowed, I continued to stare at the wall. For the first time since I'd known Cee-Cee I felt uneasy.

10

The next morning, we rose early. Partly because our sleep had been restless, but mostly because we wanted to get to Tanker and Maude's house before the forest marches began. I changed into the purple dress Esmerelda had given me, and Cee-Cee found a dark blue velvet dress with pointy lace up black boots in Helene's closet. If she was in fact a witch, she definitely looked the part.

We'd just exited the ambiguous residence when one of the stalker witches from the previous day snuck up beside us and grabbed Cee-Cee by the wrist. I'd barely gotten my wand out before the woman stuck her nose in my friend's face.

"It's in there with you, isn't it?"

Cee-Cee was struck with either fear or a loss of words—perhaps both. Before she could answer or question the filthy witch, I put my wand to our assailant's head like it was a pistol.

"I don't know your game, but you best back off."

The witch didn't pay me even a morsel of attention. Instead, she looked deeper into Cee-Cee's wide eyes. "She'll pull it out of you. I don't know what she's up to, but I know she will." The witch shook her head, completely ignoring my act of defensive magic. "If you can hear me, our lost child—don't let her." A tear ran down the woman's dirty face, bringing the true color of her pale flesh to the surface. "We almost didn't survive the last time. Please . . . do not bring her back."

Cee-Cee's chest had lifted to the sky, and I hadn't seen her blink for at least a minute. I was just about to use my big girl voice and threaten the witch (pretend as though I knew how to hand out curses) when she pulled away. I kept my wand pointed at her head as the male witch, who we'd seen along with her the day before, came out of the brush and took her arm in his. Before he was able to pull her too far from where we stood, she pointed a jagged finger at Cee-Cee's heart.

"The Robes have been summoned and are fluttering in the wind. Malina, if you can hear me, you must let go. *She* cannot exist without you, and their cause is nothing without her."

The man pulled the shaking woman into his arms and together they ran off into the woods, muttering something about a final escape.

I didn't lower my wand, not until their footsteps were but a distant memory, and even then it was hard to let the tool fade back into my soul.

"What . . . just . . . happened?" I asked.

Cee-Cee's dark skin had paled to the color of sand. "Her soul was so tired."

I loosed a heavy breath as I stared questionably at my friend. "What?"

"I could, like, *feel* it. Like she'd spent her whole life fighting just to come up against . . . a bad village."

My eyes widened. "Why do you say that?"

Other than a brief mention of the key, I hadn't whispered a word of what Toby had told me in my father's memory—there hadn't been time. Not a single thing about the organization called the Bahidicaras had escaped my lips. How could she know that?

"It was written in her soul." Cee-Cee said, very slowly letting her guard back down. Little by little, she faced me. "What do you think she meant by all that? Who is Malina?"

I shook my head. "I don't know." And that was the truth. Just when I thought things were starting to come together—that this puzzle was getting put together—the picture kept getting bigger and more pieces were thrown in my lap. "I'll tell you one thing though; I don't think their home is decorated in light blue and I doubt she goes to bed singing Loral's praises. I think she was trying to warn you . . . or us."

Finally, after what felt like a lifetime of standing there, surrounded by a mystifying fog, Cee-Cee shook her head and started marching towards the path that would lead us to our next destination. "I feel haunted AF all the sudden. Let's get outta here."

"Yeah," I said, following suit. "Now you know how I feel."

Except I'd been carrying the ghost of a faery queen all my life, and from the look on that witch's face, I couldn't very well entertain that the ghost Cee-Cee might be carrying had come back to throw streamers and balloons down for the justice that was to prevail. If anything, what was brewing inside my friend, and whatever Dora found so enticing, reeked of groundwater.

We made it back to 17 Serendipity Lane without seeing anything disturbing—other than the lack of souls out of their homes—but as we would soon come to find out, that was just chance. For the king's army was out at all hours, yanking fugitive Garlandians from where they were attempting to hide after failing to show up for their reckoning. So far, we hadn't seen anyone returned; and like much of the land, when we entered back into Tanker and Maude's home, it was far too silent.

"I hope they took Kevin and the birds with them," I said, as Cee-Cee set down her crystal ball on the kitchen table. They were the first words either of us had muttered after our disturbing, witchy encounter.

"It is a little lonely here without them, isn't it?"

"Yeah," I said, my eyes peering over the counters for clues as to whether anything had been moved since we'd been gone. But it didn't appear so. If anything, it felt as though the inside of the cottage had been put on pause.

"You think they got anything to eat in here?" Cee-Cee eyed the fridge with a lone hand over her stomach.

"If they don't, I know there's a garden full of veggies outside." I scanned the contents of a few cabinets, along with the fridge. There wasn't a lot to choose from but there was a start, and if there was one thing I was good at, it was being resourceful.

I headed out to the gardens with a basket, pulling out carrots and squash—being careful not to disturb the pink-petaled flower near the door. It was not keen on being plucked, and it reminded me of this with a distasteful glare as I perused its blue potted residence.

When I returned to the kitchen, Cee-Cee was staring up at the light, not blinking.

"What are you doing?" I asked hesitantly.

"Seeing if I can turn it off. You know, like with my witch powers."

I tried to stifle a laugh. "Cee-Cee, it doesn't work like that. Magic doesn't just come when you ask it to." I set down the basket. "It's like your heartbeat. It's not something that can be forced. It's a part of you, yet it is its own entity at the same time. It has to get comfortable with you before you can get comfortable with it."

She was quiet for a moment before dropping her gaze down to meet mine. "Look at you Kayla, you sound like a royal-ass faery all the sudden."

I smiled, grouping together vegetables and the other ingredients I'd found according to taste pairing. It wasn't the worst compliment I'd ever been given.

A little while later we were digging into toast, smothered in eggs over easy, tomatoes, zucchini, and cheese. We each ate twice as much as we should have, but we were starving. The only thing we'd found to eat at Helene's were some stale seaweed crackers and a pitcher full of some questionable juice, with what looked like eyeballs floating inside it.

When we were done Cee-Cee went directly back to her ball, an obsessive habit she was claiming quickly, and I began cleaning up our mess and putting away the leftovers. I was running a damp cloth over all our crumbs when I heard Cee-Cee curse behind me.

I flipped around so fast that my sparkly red hair whipped my cheeks, and when I saw what she was referring to my heart turned ice cold.

"Is that—" I started, with my eyes centered over the crystal.

"Toby," she finished for me.

His features filled her ball, and he was shouting at what appeared to be ghostly hands shrouded in a dark fabric as they tried to reach for him.

"What's happening to him?" I shouted, lunging for the table, my face inching closer to the ball. "What's he saying?"

"I don't know," Cee-Cee said very quietly, her hands reaching up to cup the crystal on either side. "This thing is like vibrating—feel it."

I reached for the ball, but before my hands could actually touch it, a spark of green electricity shot out and struck me so hard that I fell back against the floor. When I scrambled back up to my feet to look for Toby again, Cee-Cee was grabbing frantically for my arms to help me up and my future king was no longer there. And neither was his heart's beat that I'd been feeling in my chest.

"Where did he go?" I asked, my hand over my sternum, feeling for the ghost of him.

"Who cares where he went! Why did that just happen?" Cee-Cee exclaimed, but when she saw the sheath of panic spreading over me, she reevaluated her speech. "I mean, shit yo." She took a step back and placed her hands on her hips, attempting to steady her breath. "That was crazy. But um, I'm sure it was nothing."

For the first time since we'd known one another, I bared my teeth to her. "*You're sure it was nothing*! Are you stupid or just dumb?"

I didn't wait for a reaction. Sure, my hasty verbiage had been rude, but until now I'd been keeping my cool about the internal struggle that I was dealing with every second of the day—*because my king was missing*. Toby was missing and I hadn't had a single moment to myself to give mind to the fear of losing the love I'd just found. No, there had been no time for that because this future queen was already buried by the burdens of others.

I swept myself away and marched out from the kitchen and up to my room, quickly searching for a bag and rummaging through my things until I found what I was looking for: the few runes I'd received as payment from the gnomes last I was here, and the secret stone Toby had given to me just before we kissed for the first time. I then stormed out into the hallway and paused in front of one of the framed family portraits. The last time I'd been here I'd been mesmerized by the old snapshot of the large, gruff looking

THE POOL OF AESLIN

man, who didn't look like a faery at all—except for the enormous wings sprouting from his back. He looked instead like he belonged next to a Harley Davidson in front of a bar filled with stale cigarette smoke and faded pool tables.

But I hadn't paused in front of it this time because of all that. Sure, it still seemed strange that I had a faery grandfather at all, regardless of what he looked like. It was what was levitating next to his head that caused me to pull the frame from the wall and smash the glass, grunting as I did so, before pulling out the photo and holding it closer to my eyes.

"That's it," I rationalized.

When I rounded the stairs and headed back for the kitchen Cee-Cee peered out from around the corner, an apologetic and confused look on her face. "Hey, so listen, I'm sure he's fine. It's gotta be a trick. You've got enemies like a pound puppy got fleas—anyone could've infiltrated this thing." She gestured to the crystal ball. "It was just something to scare you, you know."

Thick, hot breaths were exiting and entering my nostrils as I pulled the photo up to my chest so that it was facing her. "That message back at Helene's"—I still couldn't call it my house— "I know who it was from."

Cee-Cee's expression transformed from surrender into awestruck as her gaze centered in on the picture. "Is that the—"

"The butterfly that came to our window yesterday —yeah."

"How old is that picture?"

I shrugged my shoulders. "I have no idea."

"Butterflies don't live that long."

"Not in the world we're used to, but who knows about here. What I do know for sure now is where that message came from." I looked over Cee-Cee's shoulders. "Raton . . ." I lowered my voice, placing a free hand over my half empty chest. "Not just any ordinary safe land, but the rebel camp." I thought back to the riddle the purple butterfly had left with me and stared down at the stiff expression on my grandfather's face. I was supposed to whisper into the heart the name that still broke his apart.

"My grandmother."

"What?" Cee-Cee questioned, still treading carefully.

"Look at him. There is only one thing that could break this man's heart. A woman. We have to find out her name, and then we have to find out what heart he speaks of."

Cee-Cee nodded, before saying hesitantly. "Just, uh, after we go see Dora, okay."

My eyes were piercing, but I couldn't argue with her. For one, it wasn't as though Cee-Cee had much of a choice, she'd made a deal with the witch. And secondly, I had to know if what we'd seen in that ball had been real—I had to know if Toby was okay. And it seemed to me that if there was anybody in the know in this forest, it was Dora.

11

With a bag over my shoulder filled with stones, my spell book, the picture of my grandfather, and Cee-Cee cradling her crystal ball in her arms like it was a baby kitten—the two of us braved the forest. Dora's address was foreign to me, if one could call it an address that is. All the card that she had given to Cee-Cee said was, "For Those Who See When Others Go Blind—Lantern's Edge." To find the place, I'd done a hasty spell with a quick flick of my wand to take us to our destination.

The tracking spell I'd conjured, thanks again to Maude's book of spells, was leading us deep into the woods via the hologram of a yellow butterfly. We'd surpassed the tree named Frederick where Helene would remain inside as a statue forever and were further into the woods than I'd ever been. This was not a good sign, because if there was one thing I'd been warned of, it was that the further one got into the forest, the darker it became, and I don't mean for lack of sunlight.

Eventually, after what felt like hours, the earth turned to rocks and the air chilled so quickly that I could've sworn my breath was crystallizing in my lungs. The creek we'd been following thinned then grew wide again, so wide in fact that it seemed the entirety of the forest floor was under a thin ribbon of water. Eventually our yellow butterfly slowed and flew towards a patch of trees about fifty feet in front of us, and when it stopped, it vanished.

"What the—" I started.

"This has gotta be it," Cee-Cee said, her teeth chattering from the unfriendly chill. "Lantern's Edge."

"Where's the cottage?" I asked, squinting at the spot the butterfly had disappeared into.

"I don't know. Probably wherever that butterfly went."

I peered around the trees, and then up to the faint bit of light I could see trying to find its way through the thick branches above. If it weren't for that speck of sun, I wouldn't have been able to tell if it were night or day.

"Sooooo, I guess we follow it," she said, before following the lead of the vanished charm.

I lunged forwards and snagged Cee-Cee's shoulder so fast she almost dropped her ball. "Wait!"

She glared back at me, and I felt like I was standing on the edge of a mountain cliff, holding onto a friend who was trying to jump. "Makayla, let go of me."

My fingers gently released from the crushed blue velvet that covered her shoulder and I took a step backward, assessing what to say or do next. "Look, I just have a really bad feeling about this."

The expression on her face softened. "Do you want to know where Toby is or not? Because for whatever reason, that witch knows things that we don't. She can tell me where my mother is, and she can probably tell us if Toby is in any serious danger."

That had been exactly what I'd been thinking *before* we got to this creepy part of the forest. Now I wasn't so sure. There was definitely a voice screaming inside my head to turn around, and fast. That Toby was fine, and that this was all some sort of trick to line things up by the hands of an old crone. But my anxious heart, the part of me that always acted on impulse, couldn't deny the slim possibility that my intuition was off. That Toby was seriously in danger, and this witch could help.

"Fine." I puffed out my cheeks as I deflated. "But for the record, I think this is all a mistake."

Cee-Cee took my hand in hers, pulling me gently along.

"I guess in some regards I *am* like any other teenager," I muttered.

"Whatchu talking about?" she asked, clutching the ball tighter to her chest.

"My friend asks me to jump with her off a bridge, and I do it."

She ignored my last comment, and the two of us continued to march over sticks that crunched under our shoes and fallen pine needles that offered a cushioned floor for our feet to walk upon. When we arrived at the spot where the butterfly had vanished, the air around us shifted and a blur of light spun around our heads until it disappeared to nothing. It grew dark, and then we were standing exactly where we had been just a moment ago, except now there was a brown stone cottage directly in front of us, a wooden sign that signified we were at our destination—the title of Lantern's Edge burned into it—and the air was filled with the scent of what I could only describe as enchantments. Because magic *did* have a smell —I'd learned that. As if every spell that had ever been woven had its own personality. Like when I changed the color of something, it smelled like cloves; and when I'd done the spell to talk to Toby, I smelled the two of us: cinnamon and ginger. Here it smelled like charcoal . . . like how a fire drenched by rain might smell.

Still clutched together, Cee-Cee and I addressed our

surroundings, realizing that we'd crossed into some sort of charm. For everything past the sign that read Lantern's Edge was blurry and shiny. Almost like the charms Toby had activated around us during those first few times we'd been alone in the forest; except this was much thicker, and if I had to guess much more impenetrable. My heart began to race just thinking about the possibilities, that this witch could most likely keep us here for ages and nobody would know.

A second later Dora appeared in the doorway, her hands loosely by her sides and a frightening smirk drawn on her face.

"Welcome Anastacia," came the smooth voice of the witch.

She was wearing the same thing as the day before, and as she motioned for the two of us to come in, the glass vials dangling from the leather belt around her waist danced back and forth. As I walked past her into the cottage, I tried to see what was inside them, but they appeared empty.

"Welcome," she repeated, once we were inside. "Nice to see you again, Makayla."

I cringed automatically when she said my name, stepping back uncomfortably over the dusty wooden floorboards. It was exactly how I imagined a witch's home to be. Dimly lit, shelves full of spell ingredients—random herbs and oils— books lining the walls and stacked on tables. It was cluttered, but one could assume it was organized to her standards.

"So," she continued when neither of us had said a thing— Cee-Cee looked too frightened to find words. "You are here, Anastacia, because you need to learn about your roots." She turned her head towards me and clicked her tongue. "And you are here because it is wise to keep your enemies close."

Her gaze remained locked over my mine for a moment before she laughed softly to herself.

"What do you mean by that?" I questioned, praying to

Gaia that I was exhibiting anything other than anxiety. "Are you suggesting that I'm your enemy?"

"No, Makayla. I never said *you* were *my* enemy. Now then —" She retrained her gaze to settle on Cee-Cee, who was still clutching her crystal ball. "I think it may be time that you set that down. Come, you two will have a seat. 'Tis teatime."

I remained frozen in my spot as Cee-Cee slowly followed Dora's lead, setting down her ball and having a seat at the round wooden table. Once she was sitting, she turned and stared at me, willing me to do the same—but it was like I couldn't move my feet.

"Dora," I said. The witch turned from where she was pouring hot water into three cups. "Did you send that vision to us this morning? The one in the crystal ball?"

"What vision?" she asked innocently.

"We saw somebody very close to me, and he was—he looked like he was in serious trouble."

"*You* saw this?" she questioned.

I nodded my head.

"Interesting," she cooed, snapping her fingers over the three mugs, causing them to disappear then reappear over the wooden table.

"Why is that interesting?"

"Because only Anastacia should be able to see into the ball. 'Tis hers, not yours. Unless her soul wanted you to see it, which is entirely possible."

My gaze shifted from Dora's to Cee-Cee's, who was shaking her head quickly. "I wouldn't even know how to do that."

"Anastacia," Dora said, coming up to her side and placing her hand over her shoulder, "there are many things I am sure you have done over the years that you didn't even know you did." She sat down next to Cee-Cee and patted the third empty seat, peering in my direction. "Now, let's have a little chat and see what our leaves tell us, shall we?"

I hesitated, contemplating whether to do as I so wanted and fly out that front door as quickly as my wings would take me, or stay here for Cee-Cee. In the end, I'd already sent one friend off into the hands of a stranger. I couldn't do that again.

"That's better," Dora said after I was seated, my bag thumping loudly next to me on the floor. Cupping her hand around her own porcelain mug, she brought the tea up to her nostrils and inhaled its scent deeply. "Ah, lavender and coriander, my favorite. Go on then," she said, looking back up at the two of us. "We can't read your leaves unless you drink."

I stared suspiciously down at what was before me. Last time I'd taken a foreign drink from somebody in Garlandia I'd woken up chained to the wall of a tree's basement.

"Aw, come on, 'tis only tea," Dora teased, as though she'd read my mind. She took a sip of her own and nodded reassuringly in my direction.

Hesitantly, Cee-Cee and I lifted our steaming mugs up to our lips and ever so slowly, sipped. Immediately, my taste buds were overcome with the flowery scent of lavender. It wasn't terrible, but I was definitely more of a coffee or more recently, a licorice root extract drinker.

"Ooooo, that's really good," Cee-Cee said, slurping down some more before resting it on the table.

"I knew you would like it, Anastacia. Coriander is one of Hecate's favorite herbs."

"Who is this Hecate character anyway?" I blurted out.

At some point, between the time we'd met Dora the day before, and now, I'd remembered something about this so-called Hecate. "You referred to her as a witch, as the dark one, but I seem to remember from mythology that she was a goddess."

"Of course. Makayla Wood, the scholar," Dora said, her intention anything but complementary. "Books don't always tell you everything you need to know, nor do they always tell you the truth. Hecate was first a witch, you see, but she rose to the status of a goddess."

"How is that possible?" Cee-Cee interjected between sips of her tea.

"I do not claim to know the specifics," Dora answered. "'Tis as much a mystery to our kind as it would be to an ordinary being. *But* there is speculation that she used dark magic to get there, and that is why so many witches born from her bloodline turn towards that path."

Cee-Cee's eyes grew like two oversized figs. "Towards dark magic?"

"Yes," Dora nodded her head. Seeing the panic in her protege, she quickly laid a hand over Cee-Cee's. "Do not worry, Anastacia, magic is a language. All witches, just as all faeries and elves and anyone who knows how to speak to the wind and fire, they must learn every word—it doesn't mean you say certain things out loud. But to be ignorant of what something means is simply dangerous."

By now I was frowning, hard. "From what I have seen of dark magic, it is all consuming." Helene's image, the last look she gave me before being turned to stone, was forever embedded in my mind. Helene had allowed heartache to turn her soul, and in the process had become consumed by burning magic via the dark elements.

"Everyone has choices to make in every world. 'Tis part of life. Drink." Dora pointed to my still full cup.

I reluctantly sipped on the concoction as Cee-Cee eagerly finished hers and scooted it towards Dora for inspection. "What does it say?"

Dora, her shoulders hunched together, leaned in over the

leaves. "Ah, you see this wavy line, it denotes a journey in your future . . . and it is ever so rocky." I could have sworn I saw her smile, if not a bit wickedly. "I see mountains . . . and a sharp, unharmonious wind."

Cee-Cee's color paled. "She spoke of that."

Dora leaned in closer. "Who spoke of what?"

Cee-Cee's eyes grazed mine as I shook my head carefully in her direction. "Um, nothing," she said, nervously tucking a pink stray hair behind her ear. I didn't think it wise for her to say anything that could lead the witch into speculation, and I was growing more and more wary about this entire ordeal the longer we sat there. Cee-Cee continued, "Just, in the ball yesterday I thought I heard a voice whispering to me something about mountains, but it wasn't very clear. I could have been wrong; it was pretty fuzzy."

I noticed that Dora took a specific interest in this information, but she said nothing. "The ball spoke to you because there is something in your life you must know about. That ball has been waiting for you for a long time, Anastacia. A long time."

Cee-Cee was silent for a brief moment before the animated girl I knew finally showed herself. Pushing her teacup aside and jutting out her chin, she demanded, "All right, listen—you know where my mom is, or what? A lotta weird shit be happening ever since I met Makayla, but now this is personal. So, is she alive?"

I stopped sliding my full teacup back and forth between my hands and watched for what was about to happen next.

"Well then, I was wondering when you would come out with it." A thin smile remained on Dora's face as she sipped the rest of her tea and stared down into her leaves. She paused over the teacup for long enough to cock an eyebrow skyward, and then turned her attention back on me. "I have answers, Anastacia, just as I think your friend has answers."

I gave her a suspicious look before realizing she meant she wanted to see my leaves—that she more than *desired* to see what was in my future. My dust began radiating around my cheeks and I allowed her to see green and orange fester into an unhappy brown. Then, standing, holding my teacup stiffly in my hand, I stared down at her. "You want to mess with her" —I pointed to Cee-Cee— "that's up to you and her. But me, I'm off the table." Meeting Cee-Cee's eyes, I said before pouring the contents of my tea onto the floor and stomping over the leaves, "I'll be outside, waiting for you to be done with this hack."

"Makayla," the witch sang out in a sweet voice soured with bitter lemon.

I turned only my cheek back towards her.

"Don't you wish to know whether Tobias is in trouble?"

I flipped all the way around and stared down at her with piercing eyes. When I didn't say anything, she continued to curl her lips up, almost mockingly.

Patting my seat, she continued, "I can help you locate him. Settle that rapidly beating heart of yours. It's beating so fast, it's as though there are two in there."

I opened my mouth to retort, but quickly stopped myself. The ignorant witch had just given me a free pass and she didn't even know it. As soon as she'd said it, I'd felt it . . . I'd felt *him*. Though the beats were quieter, he was still there. Toby was alive.

I gritted my teeth so as to hide my smile. It couldn't be clearer to me that this seedy witch was after something, and I was beginning to think it had nothing to do with Cee-Cee. Either way, I was sure the way she was getting her information —*strict confidential information*—wasn't by using authorized magic.

"It is by the beating of my heart that I know I don't need your help."

She stayed perfectly still and calm. "You didn't seem to be so sure of this when you first walked in here today."

I sneered at her. "That's because I let unease enter my heart—doubt. Those emotions are so strong they can interfere with magic. They made his heartbeat fade. I let Garlandia's devastation infect me for just a second too long, but I've just been reminded that I'm immune from this sickness. Now let me warn you, *witch*, that whatever dark magic you spun to make me frightened that Toby was in trouble, whatever you are doing to Cee-Cee to make her think her mother is alive—it's not working on me anymore, and it is my mission to put an end to all this disease in *my land*."

Amusement heavy in her person, Dora replied, "Spoken like a true queen, Makayla Wood."

I bared my teeth.

"But I will have you know that Anastacia's mother *is* alive, very much so, and your future king—his days are numbered."

"Bitch," I said, my eyes narrowed on her. Then, returning my gaze to Cee-Cee, who had cowered down into a frightened shell of herself all over again, I reiterated what I'd first said, "I'll meet you outside—past the sign and all that other witchy garbage." Then I marched out before either one of them could stop me, not coming to a halt until I'd come out of the enchantment and was staring through the endless trees separated by nothing more than darkness.

I allowed my knees to unbuckle, sitting cross-legged on top of the forest floor and dropping my head into my hands. I wasn't abandoning Cee-Cee, I told myself. I hadn't abandoned Jeremy either. All this was just an unfortunate series of mistakes. They were good friends . . . great friends, and now because of me Jeremy was an elf, and Cee-Cee—I didn't even know what to think about what was arising from her soul.

I lifted my head from my hands and screamed, attracting a flower who had been striding around on its roots. It paused directly in front of me. Its fangs were the size of its purple petals. Shooing it away with my hands, I screeched at it, "Go away!"

As it stood there, it began to smirk at me. "Tasty little Erwain, all alone in the forest."

Completely unthreatened by this carnivorous daffodil, I stammered out through a tight jaw, "Get out of here, would you. I'm having enough of a bad day without talking flowers looking at me like I'm dinner."

The flower continued to pedal around me. "Fey don't often find themselves this far into the woods. They don't like the chill."

"I'm literally, like, fifty times your size, so why don't you back off." I shooed it off again and rubbed at my temples. But it wasn't leaving, and when I looked over again it had grown a size bigger, its fangs dripping in saliva. I sat up a little taller.

"Fey are a delicacy, hard to catch—what with your wings and all. But you can't fly right now, can you?" It inched forward and grew a little more in size. "The king has seen to that."

Okay, now I could feel that my own heartbeat was beginning to race next to the steady one Toby had installed next to it. I wondered if he had echoed my heartbeat as well— if he knew when I was in trouble. Then again, there was sort of a red X over my head. Being me right now was simply dangerous.

"Look," I said, keeping my voice level as I stood. The flower followed me as I backed away, licking its fangs. "I'm just waiting for my friend and then we'll be out of here."

"Too late, I'm afraid I can't let such a luxury as this out of my sight."

It grew once more, the top of its highest petal now up to my knee. Not wasting anymore time, I reached inside my bag for my book of spells. I tripped over a fallen branch but caught myself, keeping my breathing steady as I backed myself into a tree. The flower doubled in size as I flipped through pages of the book, searching for the code that could get me out of this predicament. I'd begun working on defense spells back in the human world, but they were quite complicated and required exact wording.

With my wand pointed at the faery-hungry flower, getting so close I could feel its sickening sour breath on my skin, I muttered the start of the spell I'd been working on back in the human world. But I only got two words out before the petal mongrel interrupted me.

"It lacks confidence, it does," seethed the flower. "I can feel it in your heart." It licked the air in front of me. "Your trepidation."

My eyes dropped to the carnivorous plant. "I do not fear."

"Then why does it shake?"

I stared down at my wand; it was shaking like a leaf. Pressing my lips together, I steadied the wand, pulling from the energy swarming around it. "I'm stronger than you think I am," I said to the flower before lighting the end of my wand with the words on the page.

"Et essex malus, mi a forbid—" Dust was free flowing from all parts of me, infiltrating my wand. But before I could summon the spell in its entirety, the flower shrieked, breaking my concentration.

"What is that!" It was staring at my outstretched wand, beginning to shrink back down to its original size, and this time it was the one backing away. It pointed a shaking leaf at me as it turned and began to run. "It's the mark—she's back. The rumors are true! She's back!"

My heart continued to race as I watched my predator

disappear, before staring down and finding that my activated wand was shining brighter than ever, the star and diamond clear as day.

"Shit!" I exclaimed, jumping away from the tree and shaking away my wand. I'd been concentrating so hard on not getting eaten that I had forgotten all about the implications of using my magical tool. For once, I was glad I was tucked this far back into the forest. If I'd let my wand shine that bright back where the sun danced freely, the wrong sort may have easily spied it.

Eventually I made my way back to the sign and took a seat, scouring my surroundings and trying not to bust out a rib with my labored breathing. "It would be helpful," I said to Titania as though her ghost could actually hear me, "if you were more than just a bloody diamond encased star."

Sure, it was pretty cool that she'd seen such a fire in my soul that she decided I could be the one to finish her charge, but it wasn't like I was infused with anything other than her fury. I wasn't any more powerful than any other faery; I was just a regular Erwain. If anything, I was weaker because I'd been acting as a human for the past seventeen freaking years.

I turned my head back to stare at the invisible witch's house and sighed. I was headstrong, that was all I had going for me. Willful. It had gotten me far in the human world. All I could do now was retain the person I'd grown into, wings or no; because right now I had more than swords pointed at my head, more than ivory wands waiting to turn me to stone. I had a witch from the darkest end of the forest trying to see into my head, and a friend who quite possibly had been bred from a sorceress so dark she rose over her peers with a crown of daggers.

Yet, I was the one they were all looking to . . . to clear away the infection. To kill the king.

Maybe even more than that.

Cramming my eyes shut, I whispered to myself a chant that I'd repeated for much of my youth. Five words that raised me light years above the rest of my peers.

"I will not back down."

It wasn't much. But these words were all I had.

❧ 12 ❧

Cee-Cee reappeared by my side sooner than later, which at first made me think that Dora was freeing her of their malevolent contract, but that was just me making assumptions.

"Why are you so pale?" she asked after walking up to me.

"Never mind that." My chest was still heaving from my near-death experience with the fey hungry flower. "Where's your ball?"

"I left it there." She started back the way we came, and I didn't hesitate for a second to follow. "Dora said that it'd be best to learn how to interpret its messages as I progress. Apparently, the reason I saw anything at all when I did was because it had pent up energy waiting for me—but since I'm crossed, or whatever, I'm not going to see anything until we undo what my mom did to me to keep me in the dark."

A puzzled look washed over my face as I started walking faster, trying to get us out from this part of the forest as quickly as possible. "What's that mean, that your mother crossed you?"

"Dora said it was a spell—kinda like a hex. But it was never meant to harm me."

"Why would your mother do that to you unless she was protecting you from something?"

Cee-Cee shrugged her shoulders. "Maybe she wasn't protecting me, maybe she was protecting herself."

I took a pause from constantly peering over my shoulders for hungry flowers, and or knights out for faery dust, and searched the energy around Cee-Cee. "Protecting *herself*? From what—you?"

"Dora said she had to have Hecate blood, too, in order to hand it down to me. Dora said the power locked inside me is fierce. She said one possibility is that my mom went dark, and that she could have seen that I had the power to stop her from whatever she was up to. If that all was true, then she would've desired to end that possibility before it had a chance to grow into something, thus the hex."

I more than frowned. "That sounds like a load of crap."

Cee-Cee stopped walking and turned towards me. "What's wrong, Makayla? You mad you ain't the only one with magic anymore?"

What? "Cee-Cee?" I questioned, aghast that she would even come to that conclusion."

Whatever." She started walking again. "Dora said you wouldn't understand. Witches and faeries are just too different."

"How? Just last month we were both human."

"No, we weren't."

"As far as we knew we were. I was a girl who needed friends, and you and Jeremy saw that."

She kept her gaze forward, but I could tell by the way she was squinting her eyes that she was crossed in more than one way.

"She's trying to turn you against me, Cee-Cee."

"She knows things, Kayla."

"I don't doubt that she does, but—"

"And she saved Jeremy, and that wasn't for free. Regardless of what you say, I gotta be going back there tomorrow, and the day after that."

"Seriously? Don't make it sound like it's a chore; even if Jeremy was safe at home, you'd still be going back there."

She remained silent for a little while longer, the only sound being that of Helene's boot heels clacking away as we hit the cobblestone. It wasn't until the air warmed, and the trees were grouped further apart, allowing the sun to color our faces that she seemed to relax.

"I'll be careful," she said very quietly, once we saw the sign for Serendipity Lane.

I tried to accept that, but all I could think about was what I might be able to trade to Dora for Cee-Cee's freedom, so that she had a choice as to whether she returned or not. "Let's grab some food from Tanker and Maude's and then go back to Helene's. I want to check her house for clues again."

"Sure," Cee-Cee said, but there was a guarded quality to her tone.

Later, with twilight upon us, I was hunched over my spell book searching for anything that could point me in the direction of a crossing spell, when I heard a yelp coming from the master bedroom. Dropping the leather-bound book, I practically flew through the tiny cottage. When I arrived, Cee-Cee was crouched down inside the tiny closet, piles of shoes and various dresses and robes spread out all around her.

"What's going on?" I asked, bending down to try and see what she was up to. As usual, as soon as I got too near the ground my wings got in my way like a bunchy graduation robe.

"There's something back here." Her voice was muffled by all the fabric.

"You mean other than ten thousand pairs of knee-high boots?"

"Listen." She knocked on the closet wall. It sounded hollow. "I mean, it could just be how it's built—but if it's not, then" —she pulled her face out and looked at me— "there could be something in there that could help us."

I hesitated only for a second. "Get out of the way, let me in there."

She scooted out of the closet, and I slid in, pulling out my wand and illuminating the space with my brightly lit star. I knocked on the wall, hearing the vacancy on the other side. "I'm right, aren't I?" Cee-Cee said. "There's something behind that wall."

I pulled out from the closet, allowing the magic in my wand to drain as I laid my hands over my knees. "Yeah, but the wall is seamless. There are endless spells that Helene could have used to hide something in the house. Obviously if it's something that can lead us to my grandfather, it would be properly locked up."

Cee-Cee cupped her hand around her chin, thinking. "What if she didn't concoct the spell? This is a generation house, so maybe it's in the family. You know what I'm sayin'?"

I jumped up. "I think so."

"Where you goin'?" Her voice trailed behind me as I ran back to the spell book and quickly started flipping through it.

"This thing has spells in it from the very beginning of Maude's life—spells that her and Helene worked through together. There might be something in here that could lend us a hand."

"That's an idea," Cee-Cee mused, munching on a carrot as she flopped down onto the couch next to me.

"Don't eat all those," I said distractedly as I continued to skim the diary entries above each spell. "I need the ingredients to make iced mud cream for the gnomes." In between everything else, I still had to find a way to get my hands on more runes so that Toby and I could figure out his mother's clue.

Cee-Cee scrunched up her face in confusion, but I didn't have time to explain. "Never mind why."

"You're so weird sometimes."

"Whatever. Wait, here's something." I dropped down from the couch onto the floor, spreading the book wide open over the coffee table. "It's called 'Daddy's Secret Room.' It says here that Maude and Helene were shown a very special secret place that if they ever needed to find something or someone, they could find it in Daddy's special space." I looked up at Cee-Cee and we shared an excited look. "All we do is draw a keyhole with the end of a wand over the space where what we're looking for can be found. Then we place the wand through the keyhole and turn. If the magic isn't right, it won't work."

"What's that even mean?" Cee-Cee asked, frowning. "How you supposed to know if your magic's right or not?"

I shrugged my shoulders, already lifting my wings and floating back to the room. "Maybe it knows whether I'm family or not by my wand," I said over my shoulder. Diving back into the closet, pointing my wand at the wall, I added, "My wand *is* made from my soul, after all."

Cee-Cee fell to her knees behind me and began pushing her way in. "Wait for me, I want to see, too."

Once she was inside, I pulled from the energy around us until my wand was filled with the force it needed to work the spell. Keeping my hand steady, I traced the outline of a keyhole onto the wall, and when I was finished, stuck my wand through it.

"Oh my god!" Cee-Cee clapped her hands together. "It went through, that's so cool!"

I tried to contain myself, but she was right—it was damn cool.

"What are you waiting for? Turn it already!"

"Right," I said, then gave it a turn. As soon as I did, a doorknob appeared to the left of the wall and Cee-Cee and I started giggling like two little girls. "I think we just found Narnia," I said.

"Open the door!" Cee-Cee exclaimed.

The two of us scooted forward, unable to stand because of the cramped space. I gripped the handle and opened the door. At first there didn't appear to be anything, so I lit the end of my wand once more and shoved it in the small opening. It didn't take long, though, to see what was hiding on the other side. It didn't look like much, at least not in the dark space, but once we pulled it out and spread it onto the floor and under the well-lit bedroom, we saw what a huge discovery we had made.

"It's a map," Cee-Cee said, her eyes moving rapidly over the large drawing.

"Yeah." My finger was lying over my bottom lip as I tried to sort out what I was looking at. "A map of Garlandia."

Falling backwards on her heels, Cee-Cee sighed. "How's this supposed to help? We're looking for Raton."

I continued to study what laid before us. From the castle to the trees, to the many assorted cottages . . . everything down to the last pebble was on this map. But there had to be something in there that pointed to where we needed to go. Why else would it be locked away?

"I don't know," I said to her, "but there's answers here, I can feel them."

❧ 13 ❧

The next morning, I barely noticed Cee-Cee preparing to leave because I was still completely engulfed by the map. It wasn't until she said, "I'm going to Dora's—be back later," that my head snapped back to attention, and I flew over to the door, slamming it shut.

"Don't go," I pleaded.

"Dude, I have to. Look, if you're freaking out just come with me. You don't have to come inside."

I pictured a herd of hungry carnivorous daisies closing in on me and shuddered. "No way."

"Well, I gotta go. Or did you forget the part where I agreed to do this cause of our friend, Jeremy."

I let out an exasperated breath. "Fine. But I don't want you walking through that forest by yourself." The peculiar witches who'd accosted us the other day hadn't shown their faces since, but the fact that they'd appeared at all had me uneasy. Plus, who knew what else was getting ready to pounce.

"What do you suggest we do then?" she asked, jutting out her chin and placing a hand on her hip. She was wearing another one of Helene's outfits. A bright green dress with a slit up the side, and a pair of purple boots that did not look comfortable in the least.

"Cathy's!" I blurted out.

"Huh?"

"We never got there the other day, but it's on the way. I bet we can persuade someone to escort you to her creepy cottage, either that or pay them to."

She gave me another discerning look. "And what do you plan on paying them with?"

I glanced over at my bag lying over the couch cushion. I needed every last rune that I had—at least until I knew whether the ones I had were valuable to me or not. "We'll worry about that when we get there," I said, grabbing the map and folding it up before throwing it in my bag. "C'mon, let's go."

⚬⚮⚬

The jambalaya shack looked run down when we arrived—or more so than it usually did. The smells coming from inside, though, were very much alive.

There were but three souls inside its walls, and to my happy surprise I recognized all of them. If my memory served me right, which it always did, their names were Puck, Adlar, and Teagan.

"Uh, that's a bear," Cee-Cee said, gripping my arm as she stared at the large brown bear sitting by himself and eating a healthy helping of Garlandia's favorite dish.

"It's fine, he's on the council. I wonder why they're not sitting together," I murmured, ignoring the strange look on Cee-Cee's face as her eyes bounced from Puck the bear, to Adlar the Wood elf, and Teagan the gnome.

"Hello there, dears." Cathy the kitchen witch panted as she scrambled her way through the empty chairs and tables to get to us. The way she moved, it was like she was programmed. Set on a repeat circuit of cooking and serving. "Two for lunch, then?"

"Yes please," I said.

"Do we have time?" Cee-Cee asked, raising her eyebrows.

"Don't worry, we'll get you to Dora. I'm sure she can tell whether you're coming before you even wake up in the morning." I rolled my eyes, allowing them to land on Adlar's. His pointy ears seemed to have perked up at the mention of Dora.

"Right over here," Cathy said, as she directed us to a four top in the middle of the room. "Be right back with your food."

"Thank you, Cathy." Mimicking a bobble head doll, she strolled away. "I don't think she remembers me," I said after she'd gone.

"Pssst."

Cee-Cee and I turned our heads in the direction of the small gnome sitting on a highchair at the table semi-across from us. Puck and Adlar were facing us too.

"Hey." I waved to them.

The gnome placed a finger over his mouth. "Don't be sayin' nothin' you shouldn't out loud, ya hear me?"

"What do you mean?" I whispered back.

Adlar pointed towards the kitchen. "Something's not right. Too many 'violators' being taken shortly after dining here."

"Then what are you all doing here?" I questioned.

"Spying back," grunted Puck, shoveling more food into his big bear mouth. Cee-Cee tucked her chin to the side and made a disgusted face.

"Isn't it kind of curious, though?" I asked. "Three council members *not* sitting together."

"Ain't no more council," Teagan shouted as quietly as he could. "At least as far as the king is concerned."

I furrowed my brow.

"Oh, come on, Makayla Wood," said the bear, "don't act so surprised."

Adlar sat back in his chair and crossed his arms over his chest. "What's this I hear about you speaking with Dora?"

"You know her?" I asked.

"Everyone knows Dora. Why are you two concerned with her?" His eyes darted from me to Cee-Cee.

"We have unfinished business," Cee-Cee said when I took too long. "She helped us with something, and I traded my time."

Adlar wrinkled his forehead before shaking his head. His skin was the same color as Toby's, his hair almost as white. "You traded more than that."

"What's that supposed to mean?" I asked.

"Let's just say that those who barter with Dora have a habit of never fulfilling their debt."

"Is that so," I said under my breath, redirecting my gaze back to Cee-Cee. I didn't have to say anything out loud for her to hear my next words—*I told you so*.

"What r the two a ya doin' in here, anyway?" Teagan asked. "Shouldn't ya know better than to leave yer house. Ya git to where yer goin' n ya stay put."

"I have things to tend to," I stated.

All three of them engaged in a shared look, but immediately went back to minding their own business once Cathy rushed out of the kitchen with two steaming hot plates.

"Here ya are, dears," Cathy said, sliding the plates under our noses and handing Cee-Cee a fork but ignoring me.

"Oh! Could I have one of those too?" I asked, trying to catch her before she ran off again.

"No dear, those are only for witches and elves."

"But don't you remember? I don't like to eat with my

hands, and I forgot to bring back the one you gave me last time I was here."

She placed her hands on her hips and leaned back, giving me an inquisitive look.

"We sat together and shared a meal. You told me you used to work for the king . . ." Her cloudy eye seemed to center in on me in a curious way, and I found myself trying to look anywhere but directly at it. Call me crazy, but I could've sworn I saw a face staring back at me from inside that eye. "You know what" —I waved a hand in the air— "I messed up. That never happened." I scooped up a handful of goop and licked it off my hand, stopping to pose with a thumb's up as if it were for a cereal commercial. "Delicious, thank you."

She stared down at me for another second, before shaking her head and shuffling back to the kitchen. When I looked up, Adlar was mouthing the words, "Be careful."

We ate the rest of our meal in silence. When we were done the five of us met outside.

"Come on, behind these trees," Teagan said, scampering towards the hideout.

"It's her," I said, breathing far too quickly. "That eye of hers . . . something isn't right with it."

"Mind control," Adlar said. True to his race, he stood tall and kept his facial expressions stiff. "I think King Loral has got that poor witch under some sort of spell."

"But she ain't all there, is she now?" Teagan tried to reason. "Poor ol' bat hasn't made a lick a sense since she came to us in the forest."

"I tried to bring this up with you all last time—there is something not right about her. I seriously think that whether it's her fault, she is linked to that castle." I pointed in the direction of King Loral's home base.

"Unfortunately, it's too late to do anything about this," said the bear. "I think, perhaps, we have other matters to discuss at this time. Like why this friend of Makayla Wood is getting involved with Dora."

"She knows something about my missing mom," Cee-Cee volunteered. "And she knows things about me as well."

Adlar remained quite still as he stared at Cee-Cee with his cold, dark eyes. "Of course she does, it is how she lures in her victims."

"I am not a victim!" Cee-Cee shouted, causing the rest of us to shush her. Lowering her voice, she repeated, "I am no victim."

"No one ever starts out that way," said Puck. Then resting his gaze over my shoulders, continued, "We have no quarrel with you going to see the witch, friend of Makayla Wood, but as for Makayla herself" —he bowed his head towards me—"I apologize, but we cannot let you travel in Dora's direction. It is too dangerous."

"Believe me, I don't have any plans to travel there ever again," I chirped back. "However, I don't want Cee-Cee going on her own. It's actually the reason we came here today, to see if I could pay someone to be by her side."

"There is no need for payment," Adlar said. "But I am afraid no one knows where the witch resides. She is quite secretive."

"We know where she lives," I said, flicking my wand just as I had the day before. A second later the same little yellow butterfly popped out the end of it.

Adlar's eyes grew for a moment, then shrunk back down as he gave me a very studious look. "This takes you to her?"

"Yes," I answered plainly. Then, looking around our small circle, observing the questionable stares coming from everyone but Cee-Cee, I asked, "What? It's a spell I found in Maude's Book of Shadows. It's just a simple tracking spell. I'm guessing you've all used something similar before."

"It is not that, Makayla Wood," said Puck.

"Well she's—no one's we's known has ever been able to find her lodging," Teagan added. "Not a single soul."

"Oh," I muttered. "Well, we were invited . . . I guess that's why my spell worked."

It was quiet for another moment, everyone looking from creature to faery, faery to elf. Finally, Adlar broke the silence. "We do not have time for the workings of questionable magic. Puck, you will take Makayla's friend to Dora and bring her back when her session is over." He signaled to the leather pouch hanging around the bear's neck. "See if there is any way we may barter for the girl's freedom."

Puck nodded his head and then gestured for Cee-Cee to follow him. "The chances are not good, but I will speak with her. Come, friend of Makayla."

"Go," I said, trying to ignore the apprehension filling in like shadows around Cee-Cee's eyes. I gave her a quick squeeze and then pushed her towards the bear. "Don't worry, we can trust them, they are friends."

Cee-Cee nodded her head with uncertainty, but followed Puck, nonetheless, leaving our small circle with just Teagan, Adlar, and myself. As soon as it was just the three of us, Adlar took two steps in my direction. "Did you find it yet?"

"What?" I asked.

"The key."

❧ 14 ❧

Teagan, Adlar, and I found ourselves sitting around Maude and Tanker's kitchen table. Adlar and I across from one another and Teagan between us, sitting on a stack of books so he could see over the table. Adlar had waited to explain himself until we had gotten safely indoors where he could be sure our conversations were private.

"You're Toby's cousin?" I asked, after learning of the connection. "How?"

"My mother was his father's sister."

"Then that means that he is part Wood elf as well?"

"He is an elf," Adlar stated. "The difference between Aeronian and Wood elves is in name only. Status quo. Our blood runs the same way, our magical origins from either Danka or Lanake, the firsts of our kind."

The tips of my fingers dug into the sides of my head as I soaked in all this new information. "So, you two have been working together from the beginning?"

"Yes. My aunt, his mother, sent us on a mission to collect all the remaining sons of Lanake, to use them and their strength against King Loral when the time called for action.

Over the years we've grown our numbers large, and there are many swords that have been sworn in under your name, Makayla Wood—but unless we have that key, we cannot hope for much. The king will remain indestructible."

I had to focus on one thing at a time, otherwise my mind would spin out of control. "Just—how did you know about the key? I mean, how did Toby get word to you?"

"We have our ways," Adlar replied. When he could see that I wasn't satisfied with only that answer, he lowered his shoulders and pulled a thick silver ring from his middle finger, tossing it across the table.

I picked it up and studied it. It didn't look all that interesting. Lots of elves wore jewelry. Toby wore one just like this—

"Oh," I said, putting it together.

Adlar held out his hand, impatient to get his ring back and slipped it back on his finger. "It only works when it's on. The ring grows hot when there is a message, and the message is found engraved inside. It is in the language only those who have known the hills are aware of."

I placed a hand against my chest, feeling the two heartbeats inside. Unaware it was happening, a hot tear rolled down my cheek. "Have you talked to him recently? Is he okay?"

"Of course. He is laying low. The king sent for a set of crones to take him down on his way back from Anemone, but Toby is far too smart to be taken by witches. Regardless, his uncle must not know that he is okay. As of this moment, he thinks that without Toby you are virtually defenseless. If he realizes that the other half of you is still out there, he may pounce earlier."

I wiped my eyes, nodding, then looked around the kitchen. "How are we to be sure we are safe talking about this here?"

Teagan, who had been staying relatively quiet, spoke up.

"He's got all's his goonies up at that market, ya know—takin' lives of the innocent. Minus Cathy's, he ain't got ears in the forest anymore—only the taboo curses around a certain name that we all know, belonging to a certain faery." He stared at me funny as he said the last part. "You've got to excuse me, Miss Makayla, as it just doesn't seem real. Not that I don't believe it —I do—it's just been a long time comin'."

I smiled at him as I wiped my nose with the sleeve of my purple dress. Focusing on the little gnome, I said, "You can talk about how it doesn't seem real but imagine how I feel."

Adlar cleared his throat. Interrupting our little moment, he pointed to my bag lying on the table. "I can feel them in there, the runes. Have you figured out if any of them are the ones we are seeking?"

I pulled at the bag and turned it upside down. My spell book, three runes, the secret stone Toby made me, the map, and the picture of my grandfather all fell out. Immediately Adlar was drawn to the secret stone.

"That one doesn't count," I said, lunging across the table and stealing it away from his hands. "Toby made this for me."

Adlar gave me a strange look but didn't linger. "I thought it felt new."

I laid it in front of me. "I don't know how to open it."

"It doesn't matter. That one's not ready."

"How can you tell?" I asked, frowning.

"They change color when it's time. That's its way of giving he who holds it permission. Then you simply ask to know its secret and it tells you; afterwards it is engraved with the symbol of what it unlocks." He sorted through the small pile of runes, assessing their marks.

"Do you recognize any of those symbols?" I asked.

"Well, that one's Quartz River," Teagan said, pointing a stubby finger at the one closest to him.

"Yes, it is," Adlar seconded, picking it up.

I flexed my brow. "A river? We are looking for something to unlock a pool. Though, I suppose the pool could be referring to any body of water. Have either of you heard of the Pool of Aeslin?"

They shook their heads. "We've been trying to figure it out ever since Toby sent me the message. There is no history of that name anywhere." He set the stone aside. "We will try this though, there is no harm in it." Then he sorted through the other two, pulling them up and tracing the symbols etched on top. "These are useless," he said, after inspection, pushing them back towards me.

"What do they say?"

Pointing at each one, he translated. "This one says Jake, and this one says Oliver. They've both been made too recently to match what we are seeking. I am guessing that if you give the stone to the owner, he will give you something in trade."

"Great." I threw my hands in the air. "So, we have a lot of nothing."

"No's we don't—we's got the river stone," Teagan said.

"True." I raised a single shoulder. "I guess we should go try it." I pulled out my map and unfolded it, searching for Quartz River.

"What is that?" Adlar asked, peering down at the map.

"This? Oh, I found it in Helene's—I mean, my house—last night. I think it's a clue to something, but I don't know enough about Garlandia to know how to use it."

"That's old magic, that is!" Teagan exclaimed, standing up on his stack of books and staring down at the map.

"What do you mean?" I asked, looking up at the two of them.

"It's a shield," Adlar replied. "That's faux. The real map lies underneath it."

I couldn't be more confused if I tried. "You are going to have to explain."

Adlar remained still, then rubbed his hands together; they were so rough and brown that I half expected sawdust to pile up underneath them. Then, slowly pulling his hands apart, a very soft light shone through the space. Holding his hands steady as though he didn't want to disturb the energy in between them, he stood and hovered over the map, continuing to pull his hands apart—the light stretched as though it were a fragile elastic band as his palms faced the illustrations below— and then the light shown over it. He held it steady, and when the moment seemed right, he lifted his palms. As he did this, he lifted away a map from the map.

My jaw dropped as he set the top copy next to the newly revealed bottom one.

"I can't believe that just happened. I've been studying that thing all night!"

"The top copy is simply a map of Garlandia," Adlar said, inspecting it. "This one" —he pointed to the real map, which from all intents and purposes appeared identical to the other one— "will lead you to where you are supposed to go."

"Amazing," Teagan said, apparently still in awe. "They used to use these fer treasures—you think ther's gold in ther?"

"Step off, you greedy little gnome," Adlar said quite seriously, still perusing the new map. "I have a feeling this is something more important than that." He laid his gaze to rest over mine. "You found this in *your* house?"

"Yes. It was behind a wall. I had to use a spell to get to it."

Adlar pulled away, taking his seat once more. "It is said that before Danka was eliminated, those who were courageous enough to run away found tunnels within the land."

"Danka. Who is this Danka?" I asked.

Adlar inhaled a deep breath through his nose. "There once were two brothers. One was good, one was bad. He was not the good one. It is said he was the first one to summon darkness. During his reign, slavery and executions were so prominent in his land, that those living under his brother, Lanake's rule, began to try and hide souls from Danka's kingdom. Tunnels were hidden throughout every land. Underground pathways that led to safe places—each one an undiscovered paradise protected by magic."

"You are insinuating that *this* map could lead me to one of those tunnels?" I eyed the picture of my grandfather as Adlar nodded his head. Then, more to myself than anyone else, I said, "It will lead me to Raton."

I held the photo of Allender Voss in my hands. It was almost as though he was staring back at me, willing me to put it all together. The butterfly had delivered his message: *To find us, you only need to whisper into the heart the name that still breaks mine apart.*

Excited, I stabbed the real map with my finger and shouted, "There's a password! This will lead to somewhere, something with a heart—and from there all I have to do is whisper a name!" I stared up at the two of them questionably. "Does either one of you know anything about my grandparents? Specifically, my grandmother."

Immediately the two of them gave one another grave looks. Teagan looked away, but Adlar was brave enough to look me in the eyes. "Your grandfather left after your grandmother died. Her name was Cecilia, and she was King Loral's first victim. To this day her statue sits outside the castle walls."

✣ 15 ✣

It was all beginning to make sense. Everything I'd read in my mother's spell book, and all the family woes that seemed to sit in the dark corners of this house. The things my birth mother never wanted to discuss, because it hurt too much to do so.

"What did she do? My grandmother?" I asked, after finding out the terrible truth.

Adlar's hands were clasped over the kitchen table like a clam shell, and as he began to reply, he let them open. "She was a faery, and it was right after Sir Toby's uncle was crowned king. I assume he was asserting his power, showing the kingdom what *his* Garlandia was going to look like. Shortly after that, your grandfather disappeared and rumors began to spread that he was forming a rebel army against King Loral, against elves in general."

"Is that part true?" Because if it was, I didn't want to believe it. That kind of thinking was no different than how things were now.

"I think it was . . . in the beginning, but from what I've heard Allender has finally let that go. He is after only one elf now and has spent the better part of 200 years plotting against how to undo the king who took his wife."

The wheels were turning quickly in my head, and I couldn't sit there any longer. Folding up both maps, I threw them into my bag, along with everything else and picked up the one rune we had a chance of using against our ruler.

"What r you doin' then?" Teagan questioned. "We's need to look at that map."

"I know, but I can't concentrate knowing that this might be the key." I held the stone tightly in my grip. "We have to go try this before we do anything else."

Adlar stood. "I agree with Makayla. The Quartz River is a fair jaunt without horses or being able to fly. We should go now. If this isn't what we are looking for then we are going to have to figure out another way to get our hands on more runes." The last part was directed at the gnome.

Teagan looked away. Neither Adlar nor I said anything, but it was common knowledge that in Garlandia gnomes hoarded runes like crazy. We wouldn't bother poor Teagan until the time came, but unless we had the key we were searching for in our possession, we were going to find ourselves against a wall; and the only way to knock through that wall was to search his and every other gnome's home that we knew of.

There were several rivers flowing around Garlandia. The Quartz River, thankfully, ran inside its walls, otherwise we wouldn't have been able to access it because of the travel restriction.

It ran along the mountainside, west of where Tanker and Maude lived. We'd been hiking uphill for what had to have been three hours when I pulled out the shield map and stared at its location. In truth, both maps looked identical, and that was the problem. I had to find the one discrepancy and follow that lead.

"We's almost there, ain't we?" Teagan said, looking down at me from where he sat on Adlar's shoulders.

"Yeah." I traced the jagged line that ran through the hills. "Should be just past these boulders."

"Those aren't boulders," Adlar replied, peering at the map.

"What are they then?"

"You'll see. Let's just keep moving."

I folded up the shield and followed their lead, sneaking peeks over my shoulder as we moved along. "It's eerily quiet out here. Is it always like this?" There wasn't even the sound of birds chirping. One didn't realize how normal that was until it was gone.

"No." Adlar said, the word heavy on his tongue. "This is where the young fey used to play . . . back when there was young fey."

"Ardeen and Sheridan faeries can still have children," I argued.

"Yes, but do you see them often?"

"No," I answered.

"They's too scared to lets them out of their homes," Teagan interjected. "Damn shame. Elves build and create, that's what they do. Gnomes dig up treasure, that's what we do. And faeries keep light in our hearts . . . that's what ya's supposed ta do. We's never see fey playin' anymore. Now they's clipped your wings on top of it all. Damn shame," he repeated, shaking his little head.

Adlar placed a rough hand over my shoulder as we took our last few steps up the mountain. "We will change it, Makayla Wood."

I forced a smile. "We will. Hey" —I paused— "isn't that a river I hear?"

"It is," Adlar said, "and there they are." He pointed to two very large crystals, bigger than I ever knew they could be. One was pale pink and one white.

"Quartz," I said.

"Yep. Fey do love those shiny rocks, then," Teagan said.

As I stared at them, almost hypnotized by the energy coming from them, my wings lifted and extended behind me, raising me from the mountain over the rocks to where the river ran.

"Be careful, Miss Makayla!" Teagan shouted, cupping his hands around his mouth. "Don't be goin' above the trees, then."

"I won't!" I yelled back down, fluttering over the river. It was so clear, and from this height I could see the crystals lining the bottom of it like a shimmering pathway.

Very slowly, I lowered myself so that I was levitating just over the river flow, my feet so close I could feel the water's breath over my ankles. I waited for Teagan and Adlar to pop their heads over the side, and then nodded to them before letting go of the stone I was still gripping tightly in my hand.

It fell with a loud splash and sank to the bottom. I held my breath, unsure of what was about to happen. I didn't have the faintest idea how these things worked. Would a message come through the water? Would something appear unto me? But as I floated over those waters—my chest filled—the stone I'd dropped into the Quartz River turned into something small and red.

I scrunched up my nose and allowed my wings to soften, my feet diving into the shallow river, soaking the black flats encasing my feet.

"What is it?" Adlar asked, taking a step closer.

I bent down, uncaring of the fact that I was getting my beautiful new dress all wet, before pulling away the object.

"It's a shoe," I said unhappily.

As I stared down at it, trying to decipher if it perhaps had more meaning than it was letting on, a bit of grass that had grown wild near the edge of the river shook, and from it exploded a very old gnome. Scampering away from his hideout, he jumped into the river and paddled over to where I was crouched down, giving a bit of a jump and stealing the shoe from my rightful hands.

"That be mine," he grunted, paddling back to land before running off. "Damn stupid Hank! Bribing that elf to hide my shoe. Over a hundred years later! Oh, I'll get 'im, yet." He scampered back up onto land and put on the shoe. Sure enough, it matched the very weathered one he wore on the other foot. And then he ran off into the woods.

I sighed before looking back at my companions. "Well, that didn't work."

Adlar pulled Teagan from his shoulders and set him on the ground. "We need more runes."

"Where do we find them?" I asked. "Toby was right. There could be endless keys out there, and this place is huge—how are we to find the right one?"

Teagan had taken a seat next to the river, placing his toes into the water. He had his head down and his hands roped together, twiddling his thumbs.

I stared at him, as did Adlar. "Oh Teagan," I sang sweetly. He looked away. "I think we both know where we could find some more."

He made an irritated noise, cranking his head further over his shoulder.

"Teagan," Adlar warned.

The gnome looked up, aggravated. "No. I knows what yer thinkin', and the answer is no."

"Come on, Teagan," I said. "We know you have some. Just let us look through them and see if anything matches what we're looking for."

He continued to fidget, growing increasingly uncomfortable. "I's been workin' on that collection my whole life."

"We aren't going to take it from you," I insisted. "Please Teagan, what if you have it."

The gnome grunted, swinging his head from left to right, then finally pointed a stubby thumb up at my face. "Fine. But just the two of ya get ter look, and not without me lookin' over ya."

"Of course," I said.

"And I don't want ya tellin' anyone that I letcha, otherwise they all be wantin' a peek."

"We promise," I said, looking up at Adlar.

The elf nodded his head. "We should go. Our time's running out and we've already wasted almost a whole day." As we began to trek back down the mountainside, he pulled the ring from his finger and whispered something into it, before placing it back on.

16

Ever since I'd learned how to crawl, at four-months-old,
I'd been one hell of a multitasker. But between
keeping tabs on Cee-Cee, looking for a single rune in
a country stacked full of them, worrying that the second
heartbeat next to my own could go away any second, and
keeping a constant watch over my shoulder for hungry flowers
or castle elves ready to expel my dust, I was finding that my
workspace was getting cluttered. I needed to use every
moment to my advantage, and I needed to find out more
about my grandfather.

"He was all work n' no play," Teagan said, after I'd begun
asking about him.

"Cecilia was the one thing in this world that grounded
him," Adlar added.

I levitated just over the ground so I could read the maps as
we traveled back the way we'd come. "Do you think that's how
we get in?" I asked, "Through my grandmother's statue?" My
eyes perused the area around the illustration of the castle. If
only the statues had been marked on here as well, then I would
know how to find Cecilia.

"Not a possibility," Adlar stated. "Those maps are too old; the passage has probably been marked there for thousands of years. And even if it could be the statue, the king's spell over his victims protects against any meddling with his magic."

"Right," I muttered. I thought back to when I'd tried to move Herbert after he'd been turned to stone, and how Tanker had immediately stopped me. He'd said the king would know.

"What happens if you touch them?"

"No one knows," Teagan said, perched back up on Adlar's shoulders. "Don't get the chance to ask 'em, if ya knows what I mean."

I pictured King Loral and felt my lip curl up as though I'd just walked past a garbage can full of rotting meat. Though as far as I was still concerned, he was faceless—he hadn't yet had the nerve to meet me in person.

"What could turn someone so foul?" I asked. "Was King Loral always like this? Before he was handed the crown, I mean?"

"There's not an easy answer for that," Adlar reasoned. "Before he was king, he was quiet, kept to himself. Stood in formation with the rest of the knights while Anthony led the front. It wasn't until the death of his brother that anyone really noticed him at all."

"At least that fits together," I said.

"What's you mean?" Teagan questioned.

"Back before I knew what I was or that this place existed, I was on the path to becoming someone who represents a fight. A huge part of my job would have been strategy. In order for me to take down my client's opponent I would have had to lay low and keep my strongest punches for the end."

"I don't knows that I'm followin' ya all that well, Miss Makayla."

I stared from Teagan down to Adlar.

"Loral was playing dead, waiting for the perfect moment to come back to life." I paused. "Kind of like he's doing right now . . . with me."

Neither Teagan nor Adlar replied to my comment right away, but I knew that they now understood what I'd been trying to say.

Finally, Adlar spoke, reassuring me with his calm and steady voice, "It is a good thing that you have a strong council, then. To help you fight."

I turned to him, his expression as weathered and stony as usual.

"It *is* a good thing. And if all goes well, the king will never see us coming."

The rest of the hike down the mountain was fairly quiet. We didn't see a single soul out of place. As for the maps, I'd had no luck finding the discrepancy between the two pieces of parchment. The day had been anything but progressive, which was why when I saw Jeremy Love dropping a pair of shoes into a young Wood elf's arms and taking a stack of wood in exchange, I felt relieved.

I hung back, still hovering just about an inch or so over the ground, waiting for his customer to go, before fluttering over towards him so quickly I practically fell on top of him.

"Oi!" he shouted, sounding very Garlandian. "Makayla!" He beamed when he realized it was me who had barged into him. He threw his arms around my waist and pulled me in, whispering into my ear, "Dude, I'm like a real elf now."

"I know." I pulled away and stroked his ears. "I'm sorry."

"Sorry? Why?" His eyes were positively glowing. "I've never felt so right in all my life! Not to mention I'm getting a free internship in fashion design."

A bit of moisture accrued around the edges of my eyes. Stroking his cheek, I chuckled softly. "Well, you do look really good—"

"Oi! What are you doing?"

The two of us turned and stared into the tent at the Wood elf named Heime.

"Are you two *trying* to call on the guard?"

Jeremy and I looked to one another for some sort of answer then back to his mentor. But another elf's voice shook us apart as Adlar came running up behind us, pulling Teagan from his shoulders and dropping him to the ground.

"It's against the law for fey and elves to embrace," he reminded us, his gaze perusing the woods to our left and right.

"Oh shit, I wasn't thinking," I said, standing more erect, my guard up all the sudden.

"It's fine," Adlar said, his jaw quite stiff, "we are alone." Then looking up to Jeremy, he held out his hand. "I don't believe I've met you. They call me Adlar."

Immediately Jeremy's eyes softened, and his hand trembled a little as he reached out to shake it. I stopped him before he made the mistake, placing my own hand over his and mouthing the word 'slap.'

"Oh, right," he said, slapping Adlar's hand, before he turned his blushing cheek so that it could receive a slap in return. "*Very* nice to meet you. I'm Bally."

"Yes, I heard Heime had a new apprentice. Good to put a face with the name." Adlar turned towards the tent. "Oi Heime. I am looking for a new vest. Might you have something to look at?"

As soon as his back was turned Jeremy turned his cheek to me. "He looks just like Toby."

I snickered. "That's because they're cousins."

His eyes lit up. "What? How?" It wasn't really a secret that Jeremy had a crush on my future king.

"I'll tell you later." I gestured to the next merchant over. "Is that Dora's tent?"

"Yeah. Those two have been over there all day," he retorted, speaking of the witch and Cee-Cee. Suddenly he grew quite serious. "And Makayla, I've heard things about her. Bad things."

"Like what?"

He looked over his shoulders, noting that Heime and Adlar were invested in a conversation pertaining to an assortment of leather vests. "That Dora only takes interest in that which will make her grow stronger."

I inhaled a long breath through my nose. "That sounds about right." Then, seeing the worry in his eyes, I quickly retorted, "But I think you and I both know that Cee-Cee is too defiant to let herself get *taken in* by anyone."

"Back where we came from, maybe—but Makayla, this place is different."

I hesitated, because I wanted to argue, but the truth was that there wasn't anything to argue against. He was right.

"Look, I have to get going, but don't worry about her. Just manage to keep yourself alive and do what Heime says."

He stared at me for a moment before nodding his head.

"I'll talk to you soon," I promised, and he lifted an orange, leather-stained hand, waving good-bye as I turned towards Dora's tent.

Cee-Cee was dusting off the crystal balls with a white cloth when I appeared before her. As soon as she saw my face she started beaming. "Hey girl! I've been waiting for you. Puck said you'd come get me when you were done with whatever you been doing all day." She leaned in over the balls, and asked quietly, "Any progress?"

I shook my head. "Where's Dora?"

Before Cee-Cee could answer, the blonde witch appeared around the corner, her pink lips settling into a close-mouthed grin that made my stomach churn. "Hello, Makayla."

"Dora," I said, my teeth clenched so tightly I thought they might shatter.

She clasped her hands together in front of her stomach. "Anastacia, you may leave for the day."

Cee-Cee's eyes twinkled. "Cool. I'm starving." She looked at me. "You hungry?"

"Sure. But before we go, could I speak with you for a moment, Dora?"

The witch remained still, absorbing my mere presence for a full minute before responding. "Of course. Let me just get Anastacia squared away first."

She lifted her skirt and stepped back into her tent. Pulling out a small brown sac, she turned and handed it to Cee-Cee. "You know what to do."

Cee-Cee dropped the cloth, still in her hands, and accepted the sac. "Yes, ma'am. Shall I leave my ball?"

"That is up to you. Will you be back?"

My ears perked up at the question. Was she letting Cee-Cee go?

Cee-Cee seemed unsure. "I'll let you know tomorrow."

The witch smiled. "Good. Now Makayla, what is it you wanted?" She laid a hand on Cee-Cee's back, almost as though she was marking her as her own.

"Could I speak with you privately?" I asked, shooting an apologetic look in Cee-Cee's direction. But my friend didn't even seem to care. Instead she simply gestured towards Jeremy's tent and volunteered to leave us.

Dora grabbed her by the forearm before she got too far. "Anastacia, would you take this to Bally. I owe Heime a fair bit of stardust."

Cee-Cee accepted the small pouch, the bottom of it glowing through the fabric, before stepping away from the tent and allowing Dora and I to speak.

"What is it you desire, Miss Wood?"

"Nothing. Not from you," I said unhappily. "I only

wanted to inquire as to how long it is you plan on keeping Cee-Cee."

"She is free right now."

I cocked a brow.

Dora clasped her hands together once more. "I have given her what she needs to undo the magic her mother spun around her shoulders. Once she remembers all that has been forgotten, it will be for her to choose whether she wants to remain my student."

I bit down over my lip, scrutinizing every inch of the witch's body. When I was done, I stared her down. "Is it really, though?"

With a sickening smile slithering onto her face, she replied, "I don't mess with free will, Makayla Wood. That is something you may have to accept."

"And what do you mean by that?" I scowled.

"Just that your friend's choices are all her own."

I placed my hand on the table before me, careful not to touch any of the glass orbs. "I don't like you, Dora of Lantern's Edge."

With her eyes still centered perfectly over mine, she said, "I don't seek acceptance."

"Then what *are* you after?"

But she didn't answer. Instead she unclasped her hands and took a seat in the chair behind her, the vials hanging around her waist dancing as they always did when she moved. Try as I might, I did everything in my power to see *what I knew* lay beneath the surface she'd provided—but her shield was too strong.

"Fine," I replied. "I'm sure we will be having words later."

"That is something we can agree on."

I gave her one final cold stare before stomping away, meeting up with Cee-Cee who was walking back to me with Adlar.

"Teagan's run off," the elf said. "I'm assuming he's having anxiety about sharing his stash with us. Probably the fewer to touch his things the better. I suggest the two of you get back indoors and I will go see to the gnome."

"Sure," I said. "Would you come to Helene's, I mean, my cottage when you are done?"

"If it is safe," was all he said, before he scanned the forest, and turned from us—fading away into the trees.

17

The Easternly Witches had finally gone. The wind was now its own, yet it was still howling and most likely would until the end of days.

Toby knew this route was haunted, that those who traveled along the roots of these trees crawling over the mountain's edge—like fingers pulling at the path—that hardly anyone without wings made it out alive. Good thing then, that his uncle wasn't wise to the fact that he did have a set in his possession.

"Is it safe to leave yet, Sir Toby?"

He stuck his head out of their shelter and stared into the purple sky.

"The sisters have given up, but I have yet to receive the message I seek from my cousin. We must remain where we are until the moment is right, otherwise my uncle will grow wise."

Petal pushed her nose out from the cave where they were taking shelter and stared down into the valley below. They were supposed to be between Anemone and Garlandia, but the faulty route King Loral had instructed their guard to take them on had led them through Breya's Pass.

Toby had heard of this trail, of its taboo; he'd been warned against it many times back when his parents were still living. According to the myths, when Danka first took a wife, it was from the arms of his own brother. She was named for her soul, Breya—meaning purity. Lanake and her had been matched together to double their light. But Danka was vengeful of his brother, and as was his pattern, he found a way to take this extra light from him, stealing Breya into his dark fold and eventually suffocating her with his iniquitous soul until she was nothing more than an empty vessel.

Her weakness proved useless to him, and so he strapped her, his first queen, to a horse and sent her into the winds. The Easternly Witches, spirits of the undead who crept amongst the charcoal-like mountains—between the lands where it was rumored that the moon never shone—it was into their hands Breya fell. They fed upon what was left of her light, sucking her dry, and when there was nothing more to feed from, they threw her body into the folds of the mountain.

The pass where she'd been left to die was said to be cursed. Toby had heard many different stories pertaining to why it was no traveler would dare walk its path; but the most common of them all was that Breya's soul, unable to weep for her lack of existence, drained the light of every passer's by—trying to regain the essence of her once pure heart.

Days they'd been there, hidden inside a cave along the pass, and so far they had yet to meet their end.

"Is there any way to know, Sir Toby, if King Loral believes us to be dead?"

Toby raised his hand into the wind, a wisp of what looked like yellow light curling around his finger. "I'm afraid not, but we must assume he believes he has only one opponent to face off now."

"And how do you think she will fare? This is, after all, her journey."

The yellow light evaporated, and he dropped his hand down by his side. "It is all but perception." The silver vial hanging from his neck shimmered in the bit of light they were afforded from their vantage point. "She said it herself, that she is not the same girl she used to be."

"Is she a warrior, though?"

Toby lifted his hand, petting Petal's cheek. She let down her guard for just long enough to sigh.

"She never would have made it this far if she wasn't."

"And as for you, Sir Toby? You've managed to build armies in her name in all the surrounding lands—you've found every last son and daughter of Lanake that you were afforded. When the time comes, do you think you can—"

The whisper of a scream interrupted their conversation, and a chill icier than a first winter's freeze infiltrated their chests. A shadow crept onto the edge of the mountain where they stood, and as they cautiously began to move backwards into the cave, a form began to manifest before their eyes.

"Is it the witches?" Petal gasped. "I thought you said they'd gone."

"This isn't the sisters," Toby said calmly, with perhaps a guarded quiver suffering near his tongue. He clasped the vial his mother had left for him tightly into his hand, the other on Petal as though he was preparing to jump onto her back, as they backed further into the cave.

The form continued to unfold, and within seconds a shrouded young woman appeared before them. Her hair hung in chopped layers, as though it had been pulled out in clumps; there were many scratches on her face, and she wore a dress that may have at one time been white with gold lining. But as it was, it was the color of muddy earth and tattered to shreds. She lifted her chin, and two dull green eyes looked up into Toby's.

"Did I hear his name? Did you speak of Lanake?"

Toby stayed very still. "Breya." Petal whinnied a warning, picking up her front hooves and stomping them down. "Wait, Petal," Toby said, trying to calm her down. "Let us see what she wants."

"What I want? It is no longer about that." Her eyes slowly rolled to the sides, and she swung a careless arm out towards the west. "The last soul I came upon was also hiding from malevolence."

Toby puffed up his chest. "How do you know that is what we are doing?"

She turned to face him again. "No one stays here otherwise."

"What happened to this soul you speak of?"

She tilted her head to the side and waited a straining moment before answering. "She left footprints in the ashes of dragons' breath."

Petal cursed, and Toby put out a hand to keep her from stomping forward out of the cave.

"You let her leave?"

Breya's sheer expression appeared offended. "I am not the enemy. It was I who shared with her the secret dwelling for scorned souls."

"I apologize. Would you then share this information with us?"

A crooked smile formed on her face. "You aren't traveling away from devastation. You are moving towards it. Willingly. And you know."

"I know what?"

"That the same wickedness that tore your country apart so very, *very* long ago—that it has returned."

"I was warned of this, yes."

Breya lowered her head to her shoulder, her voice feathered when next she spoke. "It is said that the Crone lives not in a body any longer, not one of her own anyway. The wicked was cursed by the wicked . . . Who to trust, young heir? Who to trust?"

"I do not like where this is going. Brace yourself, Sir Toby," Petal whispered hastily behind him.

"Stand down," he whispered back at her, his gaze locked firmly on Breya's ghost. "We aren't going anywhere."

"No," said the ghost. "You aren't."

As he watched her move towards him, Toby felt his chest constrict.

❧ 18 ❧

I didn't want to get out of bed. Call it intuition, fatigue—burnout. Whichever, whatever it was, the dull throbbing in the back of my head and the frighteningly quiet second heartbeat that was supposed to be inside my chest didn't help matters. Nor did the silence inside the residence of 13 Ambiguous Fox. Cee-Cee hadn't slept beside me, and she wasn't in sight. The question was, where was she, and what had happened after her uncrossing?

The night before had been . . . jumbled. Both Cee-Cee and I had been given assignments and one dark twisted mystery didn't have anything to do with the other. At least that was what I'd assumed. I'd spent most of the evening with my neck craned over the two maps, my fingers tracing each segment of each parchment, searching for the difference in the two. I was silently begging for a piece of the puzzle that might as well have been eaten by the dog. Meanwhile, Cee-Cee had been given some oils and herbs that she was to bathe in as part of the uncrossing spell Dora had set her up with, and she was on a mission to undo the ties her mother had spun around her from head to toe. I was literally too preoccupied to put any energy into asking her to take a moment to think before doing something that could potentially change her life.

"Do we have matches?" she'd asked, rummaging through the cabinets in the kitchen. "I'm supposed to light these three candles and walk through them into the tub."

"I don't know," I'd answered distractedly. "I've got other things on my mind, Cee-Cee." It had grown dark outside, and I still hadn't heard back from Adlar about whether we were getting any closer to finding the key to the Pool of Aeslin. Also, I wasn't exactly keen on Cee-Cee actually following through with this spell; but as she'd reminded me earlier that day, Dora had told her she was free to come and go as she liked after she undid these bindings.

Free. We would see about that.

The family of intellectual mice had fashioned a lock to keep us from intruding in their home, and I could hear Cee-Cee in the kitchen, banging on the cabinet as though it were a door.

"'Scuse me?" A squeaky voice shouted out as though extremely aggravated. "We are having a family dinner."

"Sorry," Cee-Cee answered, an edge to her tone. "Just wondering if you could point me in the direction of some matches."

The mouse huffed in annoyance. "Mistress didn't have matches. Used her wand."

"Oh . . . right. Sorry, you can get back to your—" and then I heard the cabinet slam shut and a lock turn.

A moment later Cee-Cee was standing over me. "Hey, could you do me a favor?"

I'd looked up at her, rolled my eyes, then tapped my wand at the candles in her hands, lighting them with ease before shaking my wand away and returning to my work.

"Wow, you're getting really good at that. You didn't even have to say it out loud this time."

"Yeah. I'm good at things," I muttered. "That's kinda my thing."

"Right. Okay, well, I'm going to go do this." She continued to stand there, and I knew she wanted me to be more curious about her spell, but I just didn't have the time to pretend to be excited for her. "I'd ask you to come help, but I'm supposed to do it on my own."

I waved a hand in the air, concentrating too hard on my task to pay much attention. "Yeah, okay."

I continued to peruse the maps, all the while trying to shut out the sound of water running, followed by a series of chanting, and then a tortured silence. Eventually I couldn't take it anymore. Shoving away from the maps, I stood and traveled over to the bathroom to check on her.

Whether it was intentional or not, Cee-Cee had left the bathroom door unlatched. There was no more chanting of unrecorded language coming from where she was supposedly immersed in water by the time I snuck up on her. With the tip of my wand, I cracked open the door just enough to peek inside.

The three candles I'd lit were set up just before the tub in a triangle, their flames unnaturally high. The air smelled of lavender, along with some other plants I couldn't name. My jaw fell when I saw what was lifting from the water Cee-Cee bathed in. Steam mixed with a darker smoky fog, lifting very thin strands of blue and white light; and as they lifted, they came untied. There were too many knots to count.

I didn't stand there long before backing away, my head was fuzzy and my neck sore from craning over the maps. I needed to crack the riddle and find the passageway into the safe land, and I needed to find this key before I could even think of facing King Loral. But after what I'd just witnessed, I knew I wasn't going to be able to concentrate for the rest of the night.

I laid down in mine and Cee-Cee's bed and aimed my

wand towards the ceiling, stating quietly under my breath, "Sagious poppious, verilous malus." As soon as the words were out of my mouth, red, blue, and yellow light shot out from my wand and fell down over me like a sheath of distilled uninterrupted sleep. The spell would ensure I woke up well-rested, and not only that, but no one would be able to get within five feet of me until I woke. Cee-Cee wouldn't be able to sleep next to me, but I had a feeling that wasn't going to matter, and my assumptions were right.

Even with the spell, I woke with a throbbing front lobe; and as I sat up on my elbows and blinked my eyes, I found the sunlight coming through the window to be piercing. Unsure about what to expect once I left the room, I hesitantly got out of bed, stretched my wings out behind my back, and cautiously fluttered through the quiet house. I peered first into the second bedroom, finding it empty. From there, I entered the main living area . . . where I located Cee-Cee. The second I set my gaze on her, the breath in my lungs sank.

She looked the same and her hair was still pink . . . but I knew the moment I entered that room that something wicked had happened the night before. She was levitating cross-legged over the coffee table in the living room. Her eyes were closed, and she was whispering quick and short verses over and over again. The language was completely foreign to me. It reminded me of the sort of insect-like verbiage you'd hear from a demon in a movie about possession.

I crept around her, circling her energy as though I was facing a sleepwalker. I knew it would be unwise to alert her of my presence too quickly. But I didn't have to wait long, for after making one lap around her floating body, she opened her eyes and stared directly down at me.

I yelped a little at first—her eyes were fully dilated. Just as quickly as her eyes popped open, they returned to normal, and she set herself gracefully back down onto the ground.

My voice shook as I offered a "Good morning." It was all I could think to say. When she said nothing in return, I added, "So, it worked then."

Though the energy from her soul seemed seedy, it was more relaxed than I'd ever known it to be. I suppose it really did feel as though it had been freed of something . . . mostly. There was something about her I couldn't yet put my finger on. Something she didn't want me to see.

"I feel amazing, Makayla." Her voice was clear and crisp, but it was nothing like Cee-Cee's.

I stepped in closer to her and took her hand in mine, studying her. Everything about her seemed older now, as though her soul had matured overnight . . . or over the course of a spell.

"Do you—do you remember anything? From before your mother bound your magic, I mean?"

"I remember everything."

My head slowly fell to my shoulder.

"I see. Why did your mother do this to you?"

She stared down at my hand wrapped over her own, as if she wasn't quite sure why I was touching her. I felt a stabbing sensation in my ribs and carefully took back my hand.

"She did it when I was three years old. Long before she left." She straightened out her neck.

She hadn't answered my main question.

"And your magic?" I asked, trying to keep my voice steady.

She lifted her hand. Snapping her first finger and thumb together she made a flame and held it over her palm. "What do you think?"

I carefully fell onto the couch, my gaze surrendering to where the maps were spread out over the table. It wasn't that I cared that my new best friend was a witch; it wasn't even that she had Hecate blood running through her veins. I didn't know enough about witches or their origins to form an opinion about any of that. No, it was something else. I chanced another look into her eyes. Immediately my heartbeats tripled.

"I think you don't need me anymore," I whispered. In the silence that followed, I felt her preying over me. Dissecting pieces of me. "I mean, of course, we still need each other—"

"I know what you mean," she said, coming to her knees. "Here, let me help you with this." She was inching closer to the maps. "It works a lot better if you raise it up." She placed her palms face down over the true map. "You must make it 3D."

"Wait—what?"

I sat forward in my seat as the illustrations on the map came to life. All the trees, the castle, the cottages . . . and then the same on the shield map. Once they were raised, Cee-Cee stood up and pointed down into the forest, to a spot not terribly far from 17 Serendipity Lane. There was nothing but a blank space on the shield, but on the actual map there was a fairly large tree. She snapped her fingers over the tree, causing two tiny blue birds and a yellow bird to fly out of the map, eventually fading into nothing.

For a second, I let my newfound worries evaporate as if they were nothing more than someone else's worrisome faery dust that had gotten too close to my spirit. "Holy shit, you figured it out!"

"Of course I did," she said, sounding bored as she flopped onto the couch, crossing one leg over the other.

And just like that, the dread was back in my stomach. The way this version of Cee-Cee moved—the way she peered around the room as if she could see into pockets of space that no one else could—it wasn't my friend. Even her dialect had changed.

I hovered over the found tree for a moment, memorizing the crossroads that it grew next to, before looking back up at her. She was studying her cuticles as though nothing was unusual. Before I spoke again, I took a step backwards, choosing my next words carefully.

"Do you feel any different?"

She scoffed. "What do you think? Of course I do."

"How so?"

"A little angrier for one."

"You're angry?"

"Yes." Returning her gaze to mine, she said, "You wouldn't understand. When you hid your wings from yourself, that was you crossing *yourself*. Even though you don't remember doing it, you had only yourself to thank for that. But me—Gloria did this to me."

"Who's Gloria?"

"The witch who birthed me."

I stepped around the coffee table, continuing to study her. Those eyes, they didn't belong to Cee-Cee. I wasn't overreacting. I had no idea who I was sharing my space with anymore.

"I'm sure your mother had a good reason," I said tentatively. Her head ticked when I said the word mother. My skin began to crawl.

"No." She shook her head. "I remember the very instant she folded the invisible ties around my body . . . there was panic in that woman's heart. She crossed more than me, she crossed the line. She used illegal magic. She tied me up and let in a ghost to see out of my eyes." She'd whispered that last part, but it was still loud enough that it caused me to flinch. Seeing the alarm go off in my eyes, she sat up a little in her seat. "At least that's what it felt like."

"It felt like she planted another soul into your body?"

As though my thoughts had been broadcast over my forehead—that I was on to her—the imposter looked to the ceiling, surveying it as though she could see invisible creatures crawling upside down on its surface, and she asked, "Are you afraid of me, Makayla?"

The blood running in my veins went cold, and my dust froze. "What?"

My wings were curled at the ends—those eyes of hers were focused on me like a predator.

"I can hear your blood flowing. Your heartbeats . . . both of them. His is slowing, right now, as I speak to you. Do you think he'll make it back, your king?"

I shivered from the inside out. "Who *are* you?"

"The second heartbeat he placed next to your own beats slower because you worry he's gone. Makayla Wood fears." She pulled at a strand of hair, curling it between her fingers and then drawing it under her eyes. "You're judging me, Makayla. I can feel you doing it. The funny thing is, we are similar in so many ways. In fact, you've spun magic from your soul, strong magic. You took years from your life, and it will forever show."

I ran my hand over my head, over the purple streak. "I did what I had to do."

"They say it feels good to cast directly from your soul. Almost as good as pulling from the other end of things."

I narrowed my eyes.

"They say it hovers over the divine line."

My temples were pounding. "Look, just because I know darkness doesn't mean I play with the devil. Can you say the same?"

She remained quiet. When she blinked, it reminded me of a lizard.

"There is no devil. But you and I may have danced together once upon a time. Most old souls have." Before I had even the slightest chance to respond, she continued. "Never mind. You wouldn't have the capacity to think that far back— you don't have the strength."

My mouth was unhinged by the time she finally stood.

"*Who are you*? Because I *know* you're not Cee-Cee."

"Listen, pet, that pretty-faced bovine mess of a girl you first met—*that* was the imposter." She pointed a sharp fingernail down at the maps. "She wouldn't have been able to help you find your way into your precious Raton; she didn't even know who she was."

By now the sides of my head were pulsating, and the more this creature in front of me spoke, the sicker I felt.

She smirked and bit her lip, taking small but well thought out steps towards me, her faery prey. "Let's be clear. I don't give a lick about you undoing the King of Garlandia—"

"You don't give a lick?" What the actual—

She shook her head carelessly. "Listen to me faery. The king will be your last venture, your last victory. For what lurks in the shadows is growing, and once all that is lost is found, there will be nothing that can stand in our way."

Again, I found my jaw coming unhinged. *What in the world* was going on here? *Listen to me faery.* But then—wait. There was something else. There had been since the moment she opened her eyes and stared down at me, and if I hadn't been so astute at observations, I may have missed it.

"You're wearing a shield."

She let up on her guard only for long enough to cross her brows for a split second. "Excuse me?"

I'd had a shield up nearly all my life before I figured out my true identity. It was part of my coping mechanism, for I knew I was missing the greatest part of me.

I took a half step in her direction. "I'm not speaking literally. What I mean is you're protecting yourself." I bit down over my lip, and in an instant, I knew I had my finger directly over her hot little red button. If I listened hard enough to her soul, I could even hear a little snake-like voice searching for pieces of her story that had been lost. "You lied to me a little bit ago." Her expression got even harder. "You've got your magic back, but here's the hitch—you don't remember exactly who you are. You don't know any more than Cee-Cee did, other than some immoral incantations that might help you intimidate a few unfortunate souls."

She narrowed her eyes into thin slits.

Bingo.

I dragged my back foot forward. "Gloria buried you and Dora brought you back, but somewhere along the way you hit your evil little head and now you have amnesia. That's why you have to find what is lost."

Her head twitched too quickly to the left to have been considered a natural reaction. When she faced me again, she shot daggers into my skull with her beady little eyes. "I hope you've enjoyed your time with your precious Toby, *queenie*, because what you have—it's not going to last. You're not the only one who can dig into souls."

I had to stop myself from snapping back with something juvenile. "Enough," I said instead. "I am done with these empty threats."

"Oh honey, they aren't empty."

I had to wiggle my jaw to loosen it enough to speak again. "Cee-Cee's still in there. I know she is."

The wicked witch wearing my friend's face squinted her eyes. "Does it matter?"

My legs were going numb from standing so still. After another moment, filled with enough electricity to shock someone's heart back into rhythm, I loosed a breath before picking up a blood colored velvet jacket that matched the dress she was wearing. Walking over to the door and holding it open, I said, "I think you should go."

She chuckled dismissively but didn't argue. She did, however, turn back around once she'd gotten outside. "I see you're no longer afraid to send me off to Dora."

I instantly snapped back, "I'm not afraid to send you,

because whoever you are can probably plant seeds into *her* head, instead of the other way around."

The imposter flicked her tongue up behind her teeth. Holding out her hand, she said, "I'll take the jacket now please."

I looked down at my aunt's old wrap, and then back up at her. Then thinking back to what I knew about my house, and who it would or would not let in, I said, "Why don't you just come back inside and get it yourself?"

She chuckled. "Games are what you seek. Is that it, Makayla Wood?"

"I just want to see the truth for myself."

She glared at me for another moment before taking a step closer, but as soon as she came to the threshold her toes came to a quick halt. She either couldn't move forward or was refusing to let me see if the barrier was going to let her in or not.

"I've got other ways of keeping myself warm," she said, before backing away. "Keep it." She had started to walk away when she paused and turned around. "Oh, and take care of yourself, faery queen. I'll be seeing you around, I'm sure."

And then she was off, moving at an inhuman speed.

Whoever that was, she was completely uncrossed from her mother's magic. She had the power of Hecate at her disposal, and I knew very much that it wasn't from the light she reached to gather the energy for her spells.

"And you're still inside there, Cee-Cee—a prisoner," I muttered.

I closed the door and laid the jacket down over the sofa before settling my gaze down over the maps. It was obvious from what the witch had said that she was my enemy. She had roots, that much was clear. Yet she'd helped me to understand the hidden clue in the map. Of course, she *had* said that she didn't care if I took down King Loral. Why was that, I wondered? Were they two different forms of evil, or did she simply not care about him either way?

After only a few more minutes of scattered thinking, I gathered my things together and readied myself to get out of that house. The energy was stagnant, and I couldn't be in there another second without suffocating.

Unfortunately, I didn't have time to deal with this new roadblock. I still had a rune to find, Toby to worry about, and I hadn't yet heard back from Adlar. I would simply have to tackle my problems one thing at a time. For the time being, I just had to get out of that house.

"Don't worry, I'll bring you back," I whispered in promise, staring at the space where I'd last seen my friend the night before. Just before Cee-Cee had walked away from me and broken the wicked out from the cave it had been sealed into.

❧ 19 ❧

When I arrived at 17 Serendipity Lane, Contessa was sitting next to the statue of Herbert the frog. Her head had fallen between her shoulders and her beautiful orange wings looked almost soggy.

"Hey," I said, sitting next to her. "What's wrong?"

She sniffled, wiping her nose with the back of her hand. Looking away, she said in a voice that sounded as though it were covered in scars, "They took Owen."

"What? When?"

"Last night. They stood outside our tree for an entire day, but neither one of us had been summoned. I thought maybe they'd found out about the two of us, but in the end, they were just trying to scare us. I told him not to open the door— that—that they were just trying to get us to come out so that they could—" Unable to finish, she started sobbing, her wings shaking.

"Oh Contessa, I'm so sorry . . ." I took the orange wing closest to me and pulled it over my lap, smoothing it over my leg. "Breathe, just breathe."

"It was a trick!" she shouted out into the woods. "As soon as he came outside, they bound his hands and wings!"

"Shhhh," I said, moving my arm up to rub her shoulder.

Lowering her voice, it deepened. "They said they were taking him away because it was suspicious that he hadn't come out when they'd first arrived. That they were leaving me in kindness."

"They can't do that," I whispered.

"They can't do any of this." She squeezed my hand into hers and then looked at me for the first time. I gasped. Her eyes weren't just gold like they'd been last I'd seen her, but shimmering. "We have to get him back. *We* need him."

It was then I realized that even though she'd been emotionally gutted, she was glowing, and that there was a slight golden dust emanating from every part of her body. I was still learning about what it meant to be a faery, but there were some things that seemed to translate over between the worlds.

"Contessa," I whispered very softly. "What did you mean you worried they'd found out about the two of you?"

She looked down again and placed a hand over her stomach and sighed.

Drawing a hand over my mouth, I pulled away just enough to take in what I was looking at. It was impossible . . . wasn't it? Or was it? I was proof that the king's spell against the Erwain race wasn't fool proof. Apparently, I'd wanted to be born so badly no one could stop me. It didn't appear that I was the only one anymore.

"Are you?"

She nodded.

"How far along are you? Is it the same as humans?"

"The goddess spins in months of nine. It's still very early, but like witches, we tend to show evidence of our situation earlier than humans. This happened shortly after I met you for the first time." Wiping away a tear with the edge of her finger, she continued, "And it gets harder and harder to hide every day."

The sound of pinecones crunching under someone's feet caused us to hush up and watch for who was nearing us. A few seconds later Adlar appeared. I heaved a sigh of relief as soon as I saw his face.

"Contessa," he said, his tone devastated. "I heard about Owen. They did fourteen raids yesterday—only four of the residents had been summoned."

Contessa cried out, "I don't know what to do—where to go!"

I stared up at Adlar, trying to decipher whether he knew. His next words assured me that he was wise of the situation. "We need to get you someplace safe. If they take you, you are as good as dead, and if they take Owen's dust they will know."

I didn't hesitate to say what I was thinking, what I knew we had to do. "She will come with me."

They both looked at me in question.

"I've found it, Adlar. The place we were talking about yesterday."

His back seemed to lengthen. "The safe place."

"Yes."

"But what of the key?" he asked.

"I'm guessing that question means you didn't get any closer to it yourself?"

"Unfortunately, no. I persuaded Teagan to come with me after we couldn't find it in his stash; we went to every gnome's dwelling along the borders of this land. None of them have it."

"Are you sure?" My eyebrows were crossed. "What if the symbol etched into the rune we are looking for is some kind of riddle—what if we aren't looking hard enough?"

"Not one of them was the stone, I can be sure of that."

"Shit," I cursed, biting the tip of my finger. "Have you heard from your cousin?"

"No. I'm sorry." He fidgeted with the ring on his finger. "It's been silent on that front as well." He took a step back and peered into the woods. Like all the other days since I'd been back, it was too quiet. Before long there would be no one left at all. "I need to go. I suggest the two of you get out of here. I will alert my cousin as to where you have gone."

Contessa had stood up and was pacing. As Adlar tried to comfort her one last time I stared over at Herbert.

"He knew all of this," I muttered. "Before this shit storm rolled in, Herbert, like, hinted that it was coming . . . the way he looked at me before he said that name out loud" —I scooted closer to his statue— "it was like he was sure he'd see me again."

"Makayla," Adlar said, peering down over my shoulders. "You should step away from him, and you and Contessa should be on your way. I will alert my cousin, and the two of you shall wait until there is word of the key being found. Only then—"

"No," I shook my head. "One thing I have never been very good at is waiting. I will take Contessa, but I'm returning as soon as I see to it that she is safe. And as for Loral, I want that scab to have no misunderstanding of who he's dealing with. That I'm not afraid of him." I turned towards Contessa. "Get ready to fly."

She paused from where she'd been fluttering back and forth between a ninny flower and a decorative rock. And then, before either of them could stop me, I brushed my fingers over the top of Herbert's stony head.

I'm not sure what I was expecting, but I knew I was taking a gamble. I was prepared for an instantaneous stampede of knights in blue, all of them with their wands pointed down at me, but it didn't happen like that. Instead, the air around us remained at a steady graveyard silence, Adlar and Contessa frozen in shock . . . Until that deathly quiet was cut by one of the biggest belches I'd ever heard in any life. Immediately, all three of our heads fell down upon the frog, who was very much alive.

"Oh my, been holding that in, for what, over a month then? BURP. BURP."

None of us budged, not even to breathe, standing before the creature who had been turned to stone just weeks ago. An intellectual frog who was now back to his old self. One who I'd thought had been murdered by the king's spell, but whose life was now a whole new kind of revelation. None of us could speak, not soon enough anyway.

Almost immediately there was the sound of a horn in the distance, and the trees around us began to sway, some of them even lifting their roots from the earth and clearing the grounds.

"Well then—sounds like the gig's up. You'd better go," Herbert said, giving a bit of a jump from the steps, preparing to make his own run for it. "They'll be here any moment, I expect."

An intellectual rabbit who had been taking refuge under a boulder that had just rolled away, screamed and took off as fast as she could over the hill.

"What—how—you're alive?" It was all I could get out.

"I told you, didn't I?" he answered. "Creation, at the end of your fingertips." He looked up at me as though it was the simplest thing in the world, and then he burped. "Well, what are you all waiting for? You have saved me, but unfortunately I can't do the same for you." He shouted the rest as he disappeared into the brush, "This is what he's been waiting for —proof! For you to reveal yourself to him! They'll be here any minute! Go—GO!"

Contessa grabbed my arm and Adlar pulled the two of us

away from the house. We paused, listening for any signs of movement—all three of our heads lowered. The earth was beginning to shake.

"He's right, you need to go!" Adlar shouted, pushing the two of us into the forest. "What about you—they'll get you!" I shouted, Contessa's wings already lifting her into the air, the grip of her hand on my arm lifting my feet about an inch off the ground.

"I can hold my own—just go! Makayla Wood—*go now*!"

There wasn't time for good-bye, just a fleeting last look down at Toby's cousin before Contessa pulled me completely from the ground, my own wings now beating hard behind my shoulders.

"Where are we going?" Contessa blurted out, hooves pounding the earth as the knights grew closer. "If you can promise we are close, we can go above the treetops in order to get there faster."

"We are headed for Nightingale and Blackberry. But stay low, they'll have a harder time seeing us this way, and I don't want to risk one of us getting shot. There's a tree that should be marked with some sort of heart—" My voice trailed off as I tried to catch my breath. Both my heartbeats were pounding, and Toby's seemed to be getting louder and louder, until— "Oh my god!" I exclaimed, my gaze shifting to directly below where we flew.

An explosion of snowflakes appeared over my vision and it was all I could do to remain steady. I was born focused, and with everything before me (and behind me) and all these puzzles I'd been working to string together, I'd become distracted. But as soon as I saw the vision of a white horse racing along beneath us, and Toby, dirty and rather beat down looking riding on its back, the stitching I'd been keeping in place around my heart fell to loose strings and red dust began to flow outwardly from all parts of my being. For just a second all I was was a teenage girl in love.

Just for that second though. Future queens of Garlandia didn't have the luxury of swooning.

I yelled down to him the name of the crossroads in which we were headed and saw him nod his head. I glanced over my shoulder, a hurricane blowing through my insides as the army materialized below. Seven knights in tow, led by my least favorite elf, and they were closer than I imagined. There wasn't a single second to waste.

Contessa pointed a painted red nail down at a sign. "That's Nightingale!" she shouted.

"Land—now!" I yelled back, and as soon as our feet touched the ground, we started running, Toby directly at our sides.

I knew the tree immediately. In the map I could clearly see that its trunk grew unevenly, setting it apart.

"We're looking for a heart!" I exclaimed, running around the trunk as Contessa and Toby did the same. The earth was shaking, the branches of the trees dancing—the knights were so close.

"Here!" Petal exclaimed. "I have a heart right here!"

Toby jumped down and gathered both I and Contessa into his arms as the three of us stared at it along with the horse. It was a heart carved into the trunk; inside it were a pair of initials I didn't recognize. Without any time to spare, and the faces of the knights close enough to decipher—Rally's teeth bared—I yelled at everyone to grab onto each other before I hastily whispered into the heart my grandmother's name. As soon as I said it, we were gone.

20

At first there was nothing but darkness. The air was a few degrees below chilly and it smelled faintly of rot and dank wood.

"Wh—Where are we?" Contessa asked, her voice echoing down an unseen tunnel.

I waded through the blackness until I reached a thin, warm arm. Taking it into my hands, I replied to her. "We are inside the tree."

"Right," she answered, the shake still heavy in her voice. "Can they hear us—the knights?"

"No," Petal affirmed, her hooves clomping against the hard ground. "Sir Toby and I have used these before."

"Shhhh," I said, letting go of Contessa's arm and pressing my ear to the tree. "I can hear them."

There were several muffled voices shouting out at one another.

"They don't have a clue where we've gone," Toby said, lighting the end of his wand so we had light, "and the tree's enchantment allows us to hear them, but they can't hear us."

"Finally, something has gone right," I began, but quickly

lost that thought, suddenly struck by Toby's appearance. His skin looked torn—stained from mud, dirt, and blood. His pale blond hair was now tarnished in a dark brown. "What happened to you?" I gasped, bringing light to the end of my own wand in order to see him better, Titania's mark shining brighter than ever.

Toby pulled me into his chest, resting his chin over the top of my head. "It is a long story. I am just relieved that you are safe."

"Our story is one I believe we shall have time for, Sir Toby," Petal said, scoping out what was waiting for us in the dark. "This tunnel feels long; it may take us days to get to where we are going."

I pulled away from Toby just enough to look up at Petal. "Days?"

"Possibly," she answered. "There really is no way to know. These tunnels are ancient and that which has been left alone too long grows a mildewed sort of magic. We must be on guard."

Toby took my chin in his hand so that I would be forced to look at him again. "Why were they after you? Had they found something?"

I nodded, but I was still in shock. I hadn't had time to digest what had just happened.

"Makayla can bring the statues back to life," Contessa offered in an airy voice. After she said it, she centered her gaze over mine, as if in instant realization.

"What?" Toby asked. Petal moved back into our circle.

"She simply tickled the top of the frog's head and he returned instantly to life. It was as though he'd never been frozen to begin with." With a hand over her belly, Contessa repeated Herbert's words, "Titania was rumored to have creation at her fingertips."

Though her maternal passageway to life was right there on

the surface, all Toby seemed to have heard was the part about awakening Herbert's statue.

"Is this true?" he asked.

My voice barely more than a whisper, I replied, "Yes."

The inside of the tree became quiet once more as everyone stared at the star encased in the diamond that was illuminating our cave.

"By the gods," Toby whispered. "Well, if my uncle wasn't sure before of your situation, he is now." Returning his attention to Contessa, he asked, "What remains of your kind?"

Her lips trembled. "It's not good."

"They took her husband last night," I said.

Contessa loosed a small cry at the reminder of Owen's arrest and Toby wasted no time reaching for her arm. "We will get him back. Up until recently they've been reforming the fugitive elves into the king's guard, while throwing the faeries into special cells that bind their magic. They haven't been forcing the dust from all of them; the process takes time and there are too many. Last I heard most of the newest captures have been thrown together in a single holding cell until they can make more room for them elsewhere."

Contessa gritted her teeth and pulled Toby closer. "He's the husband of a council member who has fled. We both know they won't waste any time with him. If they expel his dust, he is as good as dead. We have to get to him before they do."

"He is strong, Contessa. I have no doubt he will hold out as long as he can."

Her wings lifted her from the ground, and she lit her wand so that she was illuminated as she shouted, "Look at me, Sir Toby! Makayla's touch—creation! They *will* kill him!"

Finally, Toby saw what he had been missing. His jaw came unhinged and Petal took a step forward, both of them assessing Contessa's golden eyes and the soft glow emanating from her body.

"It is happening," said Petal, in a voice that sounded wiser than time.

"What's happening, Petal?" I asked.

The horse looked at me. "If the spirits are starting to come back down from where they have been waiting, then they must know his power is about to crumble. The Erwain is not mistaken," she said of Contessa, "for it is your touch, Makayla Wood, that has the potential to tell them it is okay to return."

I quietly ingested her words. Somewhere in the deep recesses of my mind, what she was saying made sense. But the answers were so far below the surface, several layers were going to have to be pulled away before I could find them.

"Come," Petal continued, "we must move. Let us get to the safe land, regroup, and then return to unfasten the cords from around King Loral. Let us defeat him once and for all."

No one argued. Together, we lit our wands and walked forward into what looked like nothing more than a dark, endless hole. But even in the dreariness of it all, it was still less foreboding than the place we had just come from.

21

The tunnel we were carving ourselves through proved much like an opening of trees over a frozen stream at midnight. A stale dampness hung in the air like spiderwebs; one could almost chew on it.

Contessa had conjured a brightly lit hologram of a butterfly to illuminate our path, much like the one I'd used to lead Cee-Cee and I into the forest. Cee-Cee, or the witch inside her body, was probably settled in as Dora's new roommate by now. I held strongly to my conviction that my friend was still in there somewhere—that I would return to fish her out. But unfortunately, that was going to have to wait.

As if reading my mind, Contessa glanced over her wing, back to where Toby and I were walking beside Petal, hands clasped together. "Hey Makayla, where's that witchy friend of yours?"

A forced breath escaped my lungs. "It doesn't matter right now." But it would. If what she'd been insinuating that morning was true, then King Loral was just the tip of the iceberg. In hindsight, his evil, compared to what I'd seen in those witchy eyes, seemed as if it had been bred from a kitten.

Toby peered down at me. "What witchy friend?"

Petal turned her head my way and blinked, showing interest.

"It doesn't matter. She's gone now."

Toby nearly halted us. "It matters to me. Now is not the time to be making new friendships in a land where half the troops are against you."

"It wasn't a new friendship," I snapped. "It was Cee-Cee, and it's a long story that to be perfectly honest, I don't have the energy right now to tell."

The air around us grew even thicker, the metaphorical spiderwebs—electric. But no one chose to speak, not even Toby. Contessa turned around long enough to shoot me a look, but she held her tongue.

"That's fine," he snipped. "For now."

I took the offer.

We continued to march on through the damp tunnel in silence. I suppose each one of us had enough to think about that we could have made it all the way to Raton without speaking out loud.

Eventually, though, I needed to hear why my future king appeared as though he'd dug himself out of an early grave. After many hours of walking, we took a rest near a trickling bit of water that looked more like a wall crying than a small waterfall. We had nothing with us but a few rations Toby had left in his satchel, but it was enough to get us by, and the water tasted clean and fresh. Sharing a handful of berries between the three of us, Petal chewing on what looked like bark, we listened as Toby relayed his story.

"I'd been in Anemone for weeks," he began. "King Tathaln had requested a new army, sending his old guard into Bathar in exchange for a new one."

"What is Bathar?" I questioned.

"One of the worlds." He assessed my confusion. "Every

planet has more than one realm. For instance, you lived in a sphere most refer to as the human world for most of your life. Garlandia is part of a world where our kind, primarily elves and fey, prefer to live, but there are many more places of existence within this planet."

I bit my lip, chewing back words of confusion.

A step ahead of my constant queries, he added, "The Earth has one mother. The human world and the world in which Garlandia resides are her children, but they have many more brothers and sisters. Does this make more sense to you?"

Not really. "I'll try to understand all of that later. For right now, I just need the basics; like how does one travel from one world to the other?"

"How do you get from your adopted parents' home to Tanker and Maude's?" Toby asked.

"I don't know. I've never done it on my own."

"You must have," Contessa said. "How else would you have arrived? The gnomes have been shut down since shortly before you left—or is that why Mort was taken?"

I contorted my face. "I surely hope that's not why they took Mort. Toby brought us here."

"No, I didn't," he answered quickly.

"What? Yes, you did. The night we spoke last, inside my father's memory, you had to leave abruptly and when I opened my eyes Jeremy, Cee-Cee, and I were in my bedroom at Tanker and Maude's."

"Makayla, to take you from one place to the other we would have to be physically together. As you'll soon learn, there are portals everywhere, doorways. Faeries can move from one realm to the other easily enough, that is if you know how to POP. The rest of us have our own sort of magic, but if you don't know where you are going, then you need to find a portal, or something, an object perhaps, that will lead you to where you need to go. I could have, I suppose, gotten you to

Maude and Tanker's, but never your friends. They weren't with us in that memory." He crossed his brow before cupping a hand around his chin. "Somebody else was responsible for that."

"Like who?" I asked, mimicking Toby's expression as I touched my face.

Contessa rinsed her berry-stained hands in the water. "Most likely someone who wanted to get you in trouble. Someone affiliated with the king. Otherwise, I don't know how you, and your friends especially, would have gotten in at all with the walls he's secured to keep creatures both in and out of Garlandia."

My forehead throbbed as the truth came to me. "Rally. Of course!" It was completely plausible that the shady elf had arrived while I'd been with Toby, then moved the three of us while we were sleeping, or in my case he could have stunned me as soon as I arrived while simultaneously wiping my memory of the disruption. I turned towards Toby. "So much for him not being a problem."

Toby shook his head. "He's not a problem, I assure you."

"Yes, he is. He tried to get my friends killed!" I thought back to when Cee-Cee and I met with him in the place of reckoning. Even with the charm Heime had used to replace Jeremy's identity, Rally seemed to have been reminded that there was someone else. Somebody he'd wanted to use against me.

"But it didn't work, and it wouldn't have." Toby placed his hand over mine. "Trust me. Now, if I may return to what I was saying."

I made as though to jump back in, to continue the argument, but what was the point? Rally was foul; that was not new information. I was actually fairly surprised that even a desperate creature the likes of Princess Louisa was willing to put up with that. I think I would rather be alone forever than have his slimy hands all over me.

"Fine," I snorted, letting up on my frustrations just enough to listen to what my future king had to say.

"Like I said, King Tathaln was trading his army for a new one, out of Bathar—the world of Minx dragons." He assessed my mixed reaction. "Minx aren't telepathic like many of the dragons one finds in every other world. They are ruthless, cunning, and survive from the energies battle provides. No one goes to Bathar except to train. It is the worst of the worlds and survival is but a teasing notion. There is no adapting to the terrain; death is imminent, which is why training is swift when in Bathar."

"How long can someone like you or I last in a place like that?" I asked.

"Days, sometimes weeks. However, even if one survives the world, his, her, or their lives will be shortened by the experience. The elements take an unforgiving toll over the body, and many who return do so with unhinged minds." Toby hesitated a beat before going on, letting the heavy sink in. "King Tathaln was growing weary of his knights, and he'd communicated with King Loral that the reformation he'd been practicing didn't seem to be taking. His elves didn't appear as 'hard' as he'd hoped." Toby looked down at his hands, they were rough and discolored. "And he was right to assume this, but in sending his old army to Bathar—a tactic King Loral has used many times over the years, which has made my job less than easy—I was left with no other choice than to start over with a brand new set of elves, and at the end of a ticking bomb no less."

I shook my head. "I'm not following you."

"He's talking about *your* army, Makayla," Contessa said, her golden eyes fully on mine. "Every army built under King Loral's new laws of reformation is but a shield for the true fight. Shields with your face in the reflection of their swords. Guards who made artificial oaths under their kings, saving their true words for she who would lead the real fight. You."

My chest fluttered like it had its own pair of wings. "This is why they say this, that I have their sword."

Toby tucked his chin into his chest. "I told you it would begin to make sense."

"And you've been organizing this for how long?"

"My entire life. But it wasn't until most recently that your face appeared in mine and every other knight's sword who has sworn in under the new queen. I'm assuming your realization of your true identity brought the oath full circle."

"Can't Loral see this?" I questioned.

Toby shook his head. "Only the sons of Lanake."

"Right," I muttered.

After a moment, Toby went on with his narrative. "When we received word that we would be sent to train the new order, I knew it would be trivial. We needed all the sons and daughters of Lanake that we could get—elves who originated from pure light. There are fewer and fewer of us now," he explained. "These are the souls who can be turned from my uncle's virus, who willingly step from his side to ours. They hold the sword of their new queen, and only pretend to fight for the new regime of making the world of faeries and elves into a predominantly Aeronian world.

"But with the knowledge that the army had been traded, I had no other choice than to set out and pretend to act with King Loral's guard, to train King Tathaln's army, or brainwash them more like, to fight in honor of a label. To be Aeronian and only that. To view those who didn't share that title as less than worthy, as potential threats. But if I could find just one son or daughter of Lanake, which was going to be a trial in itself, then I could count on at least one to stifle this new army when the time came."

"And did you find one?" I asked, my eyes beginning to dry out from my lack of blinking.

"One. There was but one."

"One knight, the only she-elf in their legion, and the only descendant of the great Lanake to redirect an entire army filled with Dankas," Petal muttered, spitting out her bark. "Do we have any carrots left?"

Toby dug into his dirty sack and pulled out a sickly-looking orange vegetable.

"In any case, we found her just in time, because as I was about to find out, my uncle had decided the time had come to do away with me completely. He sent word to have one of his guards lead me back to the castle, but insisted we take a different route. He claimed it was faster and he needed to see me right away. I, of course, knew what he was up to as soon as I saw the route he intended for us to take. Unfortunately for Willem, the chosen knight my uncle must have presumed disposable, he hadn't grown up hearing the tales of the Easternly Witches."

Toby rattled off the legend, also referred to as The Undead Sisters. As he told the story, he made sure to clarify that it wasn't because these four former sisters were wicked to the core that their souls were stolen—swept under the veil to be kept and used as the underworld saw fit. It was because their spirits had been claimed by the light, and that was what made them so tasty to those who kept to the shadows. When the four of them split apart from the rest of their coven and decided to practice a newfound spell under the sky where the moon had been rumored never to shine, they were taken. Bodies and all.

"They are death," Toby explained. "You smell them in the air before you see them, rotted flesh and intestinal breath. They come from the ground and they take what they find with them. There is no escaping them unless you can get above their heads." He looked at Petal who nodded back at him. "And so, we did just that; waiting them out until they grew impatient and sank back into the earth. When the coast was clear we found a cave and waited."

"For what?" I asked. "Why wouldn't you just come back the second you were free of them?"

"My uncle sent us there to be killed, and I needed him to think we had been. The second we left Breya's Pass he would know that his plan had failed, and I couldn't allow that until the moment was exactly right."

"Until you could get close to me again, you mean?" I asked.

"Yes."

"But how did you know—" I cut myself off. "Never mind, don't answer that." If I knew all the ways Toby was able to know where I was and what was happening to me, it might make me crazy. "The important part is that you did find us just in time."

"And the shitty part is that King Loral now knows you've gone against him," added Contessa.

Toby immediately started shaking his head. "He's known that forever. He's just decided it's no longer safe to pretend that he doesn't fear me, or what I stand for. The same goes for Makayla. If you hadn't done what you had," he said, referring to waking up Herbert, "I would bet that he would have found cause to bring you in soon enough. The only reason, I believe, that you've been safe from him thus far is because he believed you couldn't leave, not with the travel ban set in place. That and he most likely wanted to deplete the faery count—take down as much of a guard as he could. He knows not of what is coming for him."

Petal had finished chewing on her carrot. Eyeing Toby carefully, she asked, "Are you going to tell her about Breya? Of her warning?"

"Breya," I asked, as I slowly got back to my feet, preparing to rinse my hands in the water, but before I could stand all the way up, I felt a sharp pinch at my ankle. "Ouch!" I exclaimed, immediately falling against the wall and lifting my leg. It was so dark, I had to light the end of my wand to see what it was.

"What's wrong?" Toby asked, promptly coming to my aid and lifting the hem of my purple dress so that he could get a better look.

"It felt like something bit me. Are there mosquitos down here?"

"What are mosquitos?" Contessa asked, shedding her own wand light down towards my leg.

"Blood-sucking bugs—disregard, it must be only in the human world."

"Oh no," Contessa said, covering her mouth and taking a quick step back as soon as she saw my ankle. Then looking up at Toby, she asked, "Is it?"

He'd pulled my ankle closer to his eyes, trying to get a better look. I still couldn't see the bite, but I could *feel* it. It stung like mad, and the skin around it felt tight; it was already throbbing.

Toby looked up at Contessa, a grim expression on his face.

"Dragon dung," she cursed, her eyes widening as she held out her wand for light, scanning the walls.

"What is it?" I was beginning to feel anxious. "Let me see."

"No," Toby said, pulling me immediately up into his arms. "It will only frighten you. We need to go—we need to get to the safe land."

"She can ride on my back, Sir Toby," Petal offered.

"You will carry us both," he replied while scanning every last inch of our surroundings.

"Will somebody please—" I began but was quickly silenced by the strange hissing of an unfamiliar sound. As we stood there, the hissing grew like a sick snake, choking on its own venom.

"Where is it!" Contessa shouted, swiping her lit wand through the air like a knife.

"Contessa, get going!" Toby ordered, swinging his leg up and around his horse. "Petal, run!"

"What's going on?" I asked, fearing the unknown and struggling to keep feeling in my toes. A burning sensation was beginning to creep up and down my leg.

Contessa, her giant orange wings flapping like mad in front of us, shouted back our way, "It will die soon, will it not?"

"Yes! But it's confused and will think it needs more blood. We can't risk it biting her again, nor you! Not to mention" – he choked on his breath as he held tightly to Petal's mane— "where there is one Morcai, there are many!"

"Toby!" I yelled at his face, my wings cramping behind me from where they were crushed against his arms.

"Hang tight, Makayla!"

"No—Toby—what the *hell* is that!" I exclaimed, staring at something that was staring right back at me, just inches from my face. I couldn't take my eyes away from it, this creature who I could only describe as an Ardeen faery dipped in tar. It was slippery black in appearance, with a large set of fangs, and wings like a bat . . . its eyes far too big for its tiny head. As I continued to stare at it, I saw three more fly up around it.

"There's more!" he shouted ahead. "Go faster!"

Petal began pounding her hooves harder into the ground as Contessa flipped around so that she was facing us. She was flying backwards at an incredible speed, pointing her wand at the tiny blood-sucking faeries, and shooting what looked like white bullets out into the air. The world began to turn blurry as small explosions began to erupt all around us.

That continued on for what felt like forever, but in reality, it couldn't have been that long at all. Eventually Toby shouted and Petal came to a halt. Still on her back and with me in his arms, he turned around and pointed his own wand out to whatever was coming for us, chanting in elvish until a very bright light flared out into the distance. Dozens of tiny brittle screams screeched back at us as their burning bodies hit the ground . . . and then I blacked out.

❧

Morcai, also known as a way less fabulous breed of faeries. Apparently they originated in an underground forest that most fey didn't speak about for fear of bringing its dodgy energy closer to the surface.

The one that bit me, along with its friends, I was told, must have escaped from another world. Apparently, these tunnels had more than a mildewed sort of magic in them, they also had the potential of drawing in creatures who didn't belong. The Morcai had either entered because they'd gotten lost or smelled fey and couldn't resist searching them out.

They fed on blood, but ironically, feeding on other fey killed them. It was a catch 22—the meal they so desired would inevitably be their last. It was like a bee losing its stinger. Evidently, they weren't all that bright, and bit whenever given the option, no matter what sort of blood was living in the veins of their victims.

I learned all of this once I woke up to Toby sucking at my ankle. Contessa and Petal filled me in as he attempted to pull out the venom.

"What's going to happen to me?" I asked, when enough of the venom had been taken out that the walls had stopped spinning around my head.

"Toby has gotten a great portion of it out of your system, so hopefully nothing," Contessa answered, wiping away beads of sweat from my forehead. "As soon as we can, we will start moving again. The safe land should have remedies."

"Raton."

"What?" she asked.

"That's what it's called," I answered, her face blurring in and out. "Raton."

"Makayla?" I heard her say, worry thick in her voice. "How many fingers am I holding up, love?"

I squinted, her red fingernails were meshing together. "Two—three—one. One?" The edges sharpened and the fingers spread out. "Four! There are four—" and then it went blurry again, but not before I saw the fear in her eyes.

She turned to Toby. "Move faster. We need to get her there as soon as possible."

But just then, a voice belonging to none of us cut through the shadows. "I'm afraid, cousin, that you and your troop aren't going anywhere."

Everyone froze, and the sound of a foot being dragged across the ground caused me to twitch my head to the side. There still wasn't a ton of light and my vision was wavering, but I could have sworn it was the figure of a man, or *some* kind of creature.

❧ 22 ❧

Contessa's body lifted from where it had been rested next to mine, and my head throbbed as she screeched. "NO! Toby, get up! Get up now!"

I was a rag doll, at the mercy of others, and whatever had found us seemed to be more of a threat than the winged asshole who had bitten me. Even with my waning vision, I'd caught a glimpse of it, and it wasn't something I wanted to get a better look at.

My body rose into Toby's arms instantly, and Contessa lifted the two of us back onto Petal's back with a single flick of her wand. A second later we were galloping through the skimpy tunnel.

"Was that a jester?" I asked, as Toby wrapped a hand around my head, holding tight to Petal with the other.

"It used to be. It's something else now, and he's not alone."

"No . . ." Contessa seconded. The sound of her wings beating quieted, and there was a thump as her feet hit the ground. We came to an abrupt halt. "He's definitely not alone."

"Gods be with us," Petal said.

I lifted my head out from Toby's stiff embrace, my vision clearing just enough for me to cringe before shrinking back down. We were surrounded. There must have been at least fifteen or more of them—elfin court jesters. Their costumes were frayed and worn, their skin pale—white and blue—and their mouths open, salivating with fangs as long as saber-toothed tigers. The tunnel hadn't been built tall enough for Contessa to fly over the creatures. None of us were safe.

Toby tightened his grip around me and sat up taller. Whether he was afraid or not, he put on as though he wasn't at all.

"You will let us pass," he demanded, sounding like a true heir to the throne.

The one closest to us, a dark-haired creature wearing a blue and red outfit, stepped forward. "I have family members who haven't fed for years, cousin. You understand, it is nothing personal."

"I am sorry this has happened to you," Toby continued in an authoritative voice. "May I presume you were all servants of King Loral?"

The jester with whom we were speaking twitched and hissed at the name like a demon would a man of the cross.

"I am sorry, friends," Toby repeated, releasing one of his hands from me only to pull Contessa towards us. "I assure you, King Loral is no ally of ours."

The jester's eyes flew open, and he pointed a claw-like finger at us. "He threw us to the dungeons! Locked us away! Left us for dead!"

His screeching voice made me cringe, causing my wings to become unsettled; before long they began trying to lift me from Toby's arms. Toby maintained his composure, while holding me down and ignoring the steady inching forward of every one of the creatures.

"May I ask how you escaped?"

The leader of jesters snickered. "There is a door in one of the cells . . . a door no one but us has been able to see. I was the first, the chosen one. The rest of these" —he spread his arms wide— "are now my family."

"You were bit by the Morcai?" Toby asked.

"I was the chosen one, yes. The rest of these were made by me. And now we feed. We feed on those who find us here, letting those who are worthy pass; but I am afraid it has been some time since we have come across any blood vessels at all. We are starving, cousin, and we cannot get through the doors that lead to the other worlds. I am sorry, but we need all of you." He licked the tip of his fang with his tongue, his gaze digging hardest into Petal. "We are just so hungry."

"Wait," Toby said, as he pulled on Petal's mane and she took a hesitant step back. The jesters paused. "What if I could offer you not only your freedom from these walls, but the blood of the one who took away your lives."

The jester's lips curled to the side in a sickening manner. "You mean King Loral? How say you?" He proceeded to narrow his eyes as he scoffed. "This is just a final attempt to save yourself."

"No, it is not. Unfortunately, my ties to him are personal, as are they for she who I hold in my arms. That is if you allow us to move on before the Morcai venom in her system takes hold of her. She alone has the power to defeat him. Think about it, will you? Would you rather enjoy this *one* meal, or would you hunger for just a few days longer at the prospect of having the freedom to feed whenever you like?"

A jester in the middle of the group crept forward, wheezing. His eyes were unfocused, and his lips were curled around his fangs. Their leader watched him creep towards us, keeping a steady eye on the hungry vampire jester. Just before the creature got close enough to sink his fangs into Contessa's neck, however, the leader stepped forward and pulled him away.

"Our kind," he said, lifting a hand figuratively into the air, "the players we used to be before we were this—we knew how to read others well. It is a trait found in most performers." He took a step forward and cupped his chin with his hand, studying the three of us hunkered over Petal. "You have honesty in your soul, cousin, so allow me to ask you this: why do you want the king dead? Who is he to you?"

"He is my uncle," Toby answered, causing the jesters to hiss. "And he is no more an elf any more than a groundling. I believe he's traded part of himself for the protection of the darkness, and what is left of him no longer knows what it means to stand in the light."

"One may assume to argue the same of us," argued the jester. "How do I know you will not hunt me and my kin if I allow you to pass?"

"You don't. But we can act as reasonable folk. You let us pass, we free you. In exchange for my uncle's blood, you agree to move on from Garlandia, to anywhere far away. From that point on, god save he who crosses your path, for it will no longer be any of my concern."

Trembling in Toby's arms, I dared to peek in Contessa's direction. Her glow had dulled, and she was holding her breath.

"And how do you suppose you will get us this feast?"

Toby answered without pause. "The Door of Rastovier, the same one you used to enter. Return to its backside and when the time comes, it will open."

"He lies!" hissed a jester in pale blue attire, the leg of his right legging torn off, revealing skin the same color as his wardrobe.

"The door hasn't opened in years!" shouted another one from the crowd.

The leader lifted his hand in the air, stopping an inevitable uproar. "Quiet, my children. Let me consider what our cousin is saying."

"May I ask your name, jester," Toby asked. If nothing else, to buy us more time.

The jester curled its fingers into its palm and lifted his chin. "They used to call me Levelathon, or L for short."

"Levelathon, you may call me Tobias Koehaias, or Toby for short. Now that we are more than strangers, please consider faster. The future queen of Garlandia requires a healer, or it will not matter to me whether you get your blood, as the world will end as a result of her death."

The jester stared uncomfortably at Toby for longer than I would have liked. As he did, I felt the numbness in my foot reaching further up my leg—my vision continuing to waver.

"She will not turn," L said after the moment had passed. "Faeries are immune to the virus . . . but she may go blind. That is if she survives."

My heart skipped a beat. "Toby," I whispered. It was as if my veins were filling in with black tar.

"What will it be?" he asked the jester. "If you are to kill us, do it now. Otherwise, let us be on our way and I will make sure the door opens when the time comes."

L took another frustrating moment to contemplate his choices. Finally, he took a step back and ordered his family to do the same, waving us forward. They parted unhappily, their desire to drain each of us dry dancing around our shoulders as Petal clomped through the slim opening that they afforded us. Every one of us was holding what potentially could have been our last breath, deep inside our chests, as we passed through the wheezing creatures.

Just as we cleared the last one, L shouted back to us, "Why do they call it the Door of Rastovier?"

Toby carefully turned his head back towards the leader, his

glass blue eyes matching the blood thirsty ones of his opponent. "It was named after an elf whose heart knew freedom more so than death. He heard the whispers telling him that if he could unlock a secret then he would live to breathe in the scent of the lover waiting for him in the hills. So, he listened for years to the walls of his prison, until one day he heard them calling to him, and when he placed his hand on the wall a door appeared. He found the tunnel and escaped to where the second half of his heart beat."

The jester placed a hand on his hip. "And how do you know this to be true?"

"Because Rastovier Koehaias was my father, and the whispers came from that of my mother. A princess of the castle, who knew this imprisoned elf was to one day be her husband."

And though my vision was only getting worse, I could still make it out as L formed his lips into an interesting smile, his eyes traveling down to the vial hanging around Toby's neck. He lifted his nose into the air, as though he were sniffing out whatever spell could possibly be contained inside it. Lowering his gaze, he said, "I see. Go, Toby of the hills. That is unless you would like me to pierce your skin and leave some of my venom in your veins. You could save the vial for another time."

Without hesitation, Toby shook his head. "I thank you, Levelathon, but it is not what I desire.'"

"So be it," answered L. "The door you seek is but a few feet away. I have no doubt it will open for you, just as I know your father's door will indeed open for us when the time comes."

Toby nodded his head curtly, and then waved a final good-bye as he asked Petal to move on with soft words and a firm jaw.

L was right, the door we'd been traveling towards was just around the corner. If they hadn't spared us, we would have been just heartbeats away from our freedom as our vessels closed from lack of blood.

"Hold on, my queen," Toby whispered into my ear, as Contessa clasped the golden doorknob in her hands.

"Are you ready?" she asked, turning to look up at Toby.

"Yes," he replied, and as he did, she pulled open the door, light infiltrating the darkness as the vampire jesters scampered away into the shadows.

Raton. And I'd thought Garlandia was magical. This place was like a flowered cherry blossom branch, so intertwined in a grouping of dead and broken brothers and sisters that no one even knew it was there.

I woke up to butterfly kisses and to the fluttering of purple wings. I wiggled my toes; I had feeling again.

"Lala?" said a familiar female voice.

I moved my tongue around in my mouth . . . it tasted of blood and something sweet.

"She's moving! Tank, get Toby! She's waking!"

"THE BRAT'S BACK! SHE'S AWAKE! THE BRAT'S BACK! SHE'S AWAKE!"

My eyes flickered all the way open and light filtered into my soul. The blurriness began to seep away and the faces hovering over me began to come into focus. Kevin, along with a gruff looking faery with leathery skin and large purple wings was studying me, and the purple butterfly I'd seen back in Garlandia was circulating around his head. As soon as my eyes adjusted to the light and I could keep them open, Maude shoved him away and pounced all over me—her wings flapping violently behind her. Kevin began to whine.

I'd never been happier to be somewhere so chaotic.

The voice of my birth mother filled my ears like exploding confetti. "Get out of the way, let me see her! Lala! Lala, can you see us?"

"Of course I can," I answered groggily. Shielding the setting sun with the palm of my hand, I stared up at Maude's purple and red hair. It appeared on fire as the light filtered through it. "How long have I been out?" I tried to sit up, but a wave of dizziness upset me, laying me back down.

"Don't try to get up just yet," she cooed. "And it's been three days. I was so worried the remedies wouldn't work."

"Almighty! Let her breathe, woman!" growled the large faery, who I had to assume was Allender Voss. My grandfather.

Suddenly I remembered what had happened before I closed my eyes. The tunnel, the jester vampires. Levelathon, and his warning of what might happen to me.

"I was bitten," I murmured.

"Yes," Maude said, while caressing my forehead with one hand and holding one of my wings in the other. "The Morcai. They must have been awakened from their slumber when the keeper and his family came through. They were waiting." Snapping her head in Allender's direction, she questioned angrily, "Why wouldn't you alert us to the fact that they could have been in there?"

Unfazed by her anger, my grandfather simply continued to look down at me. "How was I to know what was in there? It has been years since I've come out from this place." Inhaling a thick breath through his large nose, he said specifically to me, "Let me see it."

I frowned up at him, hard. I was about to ask exactly what 'it' was, when a warm wind blew to the sides and a pair of blue wings flashed before me—Tanker landing swiftly by my side.

He was wearing a red evening dress and had a turban wrapped around his head. A grin immediately found my face and my veins filled with hot cocoa. I was welcomed by my birth father's embrace like a ray of sunshine on a chilly day and when my grandfather repeated himself, I chose to ignore him.

"Al," Tanker warned, keeping me safe in his arms. "Let her be. She needs to regain her strength."

"You all wouldn't be here if it weren't for me. I believe I've earned the right to see what everyone is whispering about. Proof that my granddaughter carries the mark of Titania— more so than what is on her wing, as that is nothing more than a birth translation."

I peered at him in a way that I'd seen prisoners do in the movies, like I was egging him on from across the yard. I held onto Tanker's arm as I steadied myself, moving slowly to ward off the spins as I squared my shoulders with the faery named Allender. I was big on first impressions. This wasn't how I imagined greeting my long-lost grandfather.

"First, *I* think I deserve to know what's happened to me." I blinked, waiting for him to give me a reply. But before he could, footsteps came running up behind me and a moment later Toby was there. In a matter of seconds, I forgot about Allender Voss and embraced my future king.

He was in a change of clothes, and clean, his hair back to its usual bleached blond. Immediately he took my face into his hands and studied me, diving deep into my pupils.

"Can you see?" The necklace he always wore was swinging between our chests.

"Yes, and I have the feeling back in my legs. Does this mean I won't go blind?"

He pulled back and strummed my chin with his thumb. "It means the remedy Maude made for you works."

"So, I'm good, then? The venom is out of my body?"

Maude let out a small cry, and I shot her a worried look.

"We got as much of it out as we could," Toby clarified. "But unfortunately, enough of it leached into your heart. There will be permanent side effects, I am afraid."

I furrowed my brow, taking his hand in mine and lowering it down from my chin. "Permanent?"

"You must take the remedy regularly to ward off the blindness."

"The remedy?"

Toby gestured to my birth mother. "Lucky she's a witch with potions." And then he slipped a vial attached to a chain around my neck. It wasn't very big, but one look at it and I knew it contained blood. "One drop in each eye and one on the tongue every morning. If you miss it your vision will slowly start to fade. The good news is that it doesn't need to stay in your system to work, so if you happen to miss several days in a row, you can always take it and it will bring back your sight."

I uncorked the vial and sniffed its contents. "And the bad news is that it can only be made from my mother's blood . . . so if something happens to her, I will never see again."

"How can you tell that?" Toby asked.

Looking at my birth mother, her eyes rather wet, I answered, "Because it smells of her."

She wiped her eyes and sniffed. "It can be made from either one of us." She grappled for Tanker's arm. "Don't worry, Lala, now that we know it works, we will begin making enough vials to last you well past the end of our days."

"Well this is all very touching, isn't it?" Allender scowled, bringing the attention back to him. "But in case you've all forgotten, faeries are becoming extinct, and we are forever losing our home to the elves." He peered at Toby and growled. "Before we go any further, I demand to see the wand."

"It's very nice to meet you, too, Grandpa," I grumbled,

allowing Toby to help me to stand all the way up, groaning from the stiffness in my back.

Tanker and Maude backed away as Toby continued to steady me with his hand, and without retracting my gaze from Allender, I pulled out my wand. "Before I show you this, I would like to know, how are you so sure I carry the mark at its tip? *They* haven't even seen it." I gestured towards Tanker and Maude. "And I can't imagine that the two of you have sat down and shared a cup of tea." I nodded towards Toby. Even if he was no longer using his organization to try and make the elves bow before faeries, from what I'd learned of Allender Voss, he did not care for the creatures.

Allender remained stiff. "Helene managed to get her last words sent off to Midnight before she was stoned."

I rolled my shoulders back. "Midnight?"

"Her butterfly, dear," Maude clarified.

"I don't understand."

Allender placed his vibrating energy over Maude. "My god, woman. Did you teach her nothing whilst you had her in your possession?"

Maude averted her eyes to the ground. "There wasn't time, Fath—"

"From my understanding you had days—weeks! You should have had her properly trained within the first few hours of getting her back!"

"Quit yelling at her!" I shouted, feeling a bit light-headed from exhorting my energy. I wanted nothing more than to smack him with the back of my wing. "She wanted to teach me everything. I wasn't having it! Leave her be!" I fell back into Toby's arms and he pleaded with me to calm down. "I'm fine," I muttered through clenched teeth. "Now," returning my attention back to my grandfather, I said, "explain this butterfly phenomenon to me. I already know we can communicate through them. I've put that much together."

Allender, rather grim-faced, still hadn't moved a muscle. He took his time responding, as though he were weighing out whether or not to pound my face in with the back of his hand. I gathered, just by looking at him, that my birth mother knew what that sensation felt like.

"The fey have an affiliation with the butterflies. We can speak telepathically with them, some fey more than others. I possess strong telepathy, as did your aunt; therefore, I was able to not just call on the butterflies, but to take one into my possession." He snapped his fingers and immediately the same purple butterfly I'd seen more than once now came fluttering over. "This is Magillian, she's been with me for over three hundred years. When our kind calls on the butterflies, we must call to the one who is nearest ourselves. However, fey like myself have the ability to call on one particular butterfly, no matter how far away it is. Helene did this just before you had her killed."

"I didn't have her killed. *She* tried to kill *me*!" My blood immediately began to boil, and I found myself declaring to my stony grandmother, wherever her soul truly was, that she was not missing anything. Or perhaps she was the one thing that had kept this faery tame.

"Allender," Tanker warned, holding Maude in his arms.

Allender restructured his feet into the ground and continued to stand strong and tall. "Are you finished?" His question was directed at me.

"Ass," I murmured. I could tell where I'd received my stubbornness, but I would like to think that even I was more forgiving than this hunk of hardened faery.

"*You* asked *me* a question. I'm trying to answer it. What Helene saw moments before her death was enough to cause her to reach for Midnight, who was still in this realm with me. The butterfly heard her message and delivered it. Soon after that I sent Magillian into Garlandia, but it was too late. Helene was already gone."

"Your precious Helene tried to kill me," I repeated. "You get that, right?"

He simply blinked. I shouldn't have been surprised, because from what I'd read of Maude's diary, her father had always favored Helene. My aunt had been the studious one, the sharp one, whereas my mother had longed to know love more than anything. One wasn't better than the other, the world needed both. But it seemed fairly obvious that my grandfather didn't see things that way.

I jerked my head to the side. "Just so you know, *Grandpa*, I told them not to do it. Not to turn her into stone."

Toby gripped my elbow harder, as he pulled my back into his chest. "You want someone to blame, Allender Voss, then blame me. Leave Makayla out of this. What she had to see completely broke her into pieces."

My grandfather's eyes, level with mine, slid over towards Toby's. "Don't worry, elf, I blame you more than you know."

Toby's grip over me tightened.

"Fine," I said after a long stare off between the three of us. "This is what you want, right?" I held up my wand. "You need proof that she exists, here it is." I pulled from the energy surrounding my wand, which had become quite heated, and allowed it to enter. I didn't even really need to think about it anymore, it just happened. As soon as it was felt, the star and diamond appeared at the end.

Maude yelped and Tanker had to hold onto her as her knees unbuckled, his own eyes larger than I'd ever seen them. Allender, though, he didn't budge, not an inch. He waited until I let the light go out and then looked up at Toby.

"Your mother, they called her Daphne?"

Toby's jaw tightened. "Yes. How do you know that?"

"I know many things. Have met many travelers who have needed to find refuge here."

"And what is it you presume to know?"

"Your mother was Titania's keeper, was she not?"

Toby remained guarded, but eventually he answered very softly. "This is true."

Maude clenched a fist to her chest, as did Tanker.

"Since she no longer breathes the gods given air, this means that she had to have passed her mission on to someone." His gaze fell to the vial hanging around Toby's neck. "May I assume this chosen elf was you?"

"Yes."

"It is strange that a faery would call on an elf to carry his or her secrets . . . it is something that isn't done. The creatures of this land, we've always proceeded with like for like."

"Forgive me, Allender," replied Toby stiffly, "but isn't that why things are falling apart as we speak? Titania chose her form; she could have been anything she wanted. She did not see elves and faeries, intellectuals or ninnies, she saw souls. My mother was like a daughter to her, and Titania cared very much for her."

Allender, his strong jaw chiseled as though it was stone, finally seemed to let up a little as he stared at Toby. "You plan on marrying my granddaughter, is this correct?"

"Yes sir."

"Fine. You will do it here, before you return to Garlandia."

My stomach fell, and my jaw deviated to the side in discontent. Not because I didn't want to marry Toby, of course I did. But when *I* wanted to, not when this arrogant biker faery said it was time.

"We can't do it now," I protested. "My other parents are in some oddball place or another—probably drunk on blueberry vodka!"

"You will do it now."

I bit down over the tip of my tongue, a vibration coursing through my body with enough current to shove someone down without lifting a finger. My grandfather said nothing more, instead all four of his wings lifted as he prepared to fly away. But before he could leave us, I pulled away from Toby and proceeded to regain his attention.

"Allender wait!" He paused, levitating a foot from the ground. "How come you are so willing and eager for this union, when you can't even address Toby by his name?"

He retorted without pause. "*Toby* knows as well as I do. You may love each other to the end of the worlds and back, but that is not what this is about."

My tongue dragged along the back of my teeth. "Then what is this about?"

"Retracing lost steps. Putting that back together which was once severed."

Suddenly I was right back at the beginning of things— right back where I'd been when I'd first arrived in Garlandia. In the dark.

"Speak plainly, would you?" I said to him.

His large wings beating just enough to keep him hovering over the earth, he said, "You need your other half to be bound to you. You need that strength for what you're up against. We mate for life because once we are tethered to another, we may share our spirits. Our magic, our strength."

Oh, okay. That made sense. Why wouldn't they all just tell me that from the get-go?

Allender continued to peer at me as if my face repulsed him. "That is all I am willing to say to you right now." He quickly began to lift away.

Maddened by his abruptness, I shouted up at him. "Wait!" He came to a slow halt, and spun around, sneering down at me. "I get it, you're an ass, it's your thing." He grunted. "But we're all in this together now, because if I fail, we all lose everything. Now, these secrets Toby inherited, the ones that are to pave the way to taking down Loral, they are covered up with clues. At this point, we've uncovered the first one."

Allender lowered back to the ground. "You said nothing of this," he spit out towards Toby.

"We've been a little busy nursing Makayla back to health," Toby retorted.

"Stop it," I said to Allender. "Stop berating everyone. What matters is what lies before us. Unfortunately, what we've come up against is as foreign as the idea of you wearing flowers in your hair."

He narrowed his eyes at me but said nothing in his defense.

"Whatever we are seeking, whether it is the first or final component to this puzzle, it's in something referred to as the Pool of Aeslin. Does this mean anything to you?"

His wings lowered. "What did you just say?"

The dizziness I had been feeling since I woke had finally begun to dissipate, so I stood taller. "The Pool of Aeslin."

For the first time his demeanor softened. "Yes," he said, the edges of his voice sinking back into his thoughts. "Aeslin. Her I've heard of."

24

I 'd woken just as day was turning to night, and apparently my grandfather was a stickler about what time he had his meals. Allender demanded food before any further explanation.

The blue and purple sunset was still lit enough above our heads as we sat in a circle around a campfire. The smells pouring out from all sides of the camp were more than mouthwatering. The rebel faeries of Raton—and a few elves as well—had set up dinner in a buffet along the edge of the lake. Not all the rebels were from Garlandia. That much, I was sure. For some of the species had subtle differences that set them apart from the homeland I'd just been getting to know. Some with a sparkle of the skin that didn't exist in any faery I'd seen yet, and a couple of fey who looked like Erwains, but with pointy ears, like elves.

Everyone but me balanced dinner plates over their knees and laps as we waited for Allender to suck down his meal so we could get to the center of the lollipop. Maude and Contessa kept pushing plates of leafy greens and glazed meat in my face, but even though my stomach was jumping around in search of food, I was far too anxious to eat. However, my grandfather's appetite didn't seem to be affected. I chewed on the side of my cheek as I peered over the fire at him, as he used his teeth to rip apart chunks of roasted bird.

"What made you change your mind about the elves?" I asked, after I couldn't take it any longer.

He grunted as he tossed a bone into the fire and grabbed another drumstick from his plate. "There has always only been one elf who I was ever really after. The idea of taking them all down was nothing more than a reaction birthed from outrage."

"But you never thought to change your mission statement?"

He grimaced. "I will take anyone on my side who is willing to aid in the fight. I will take wings, fangs, broomsticks, and pointy ears—anyone who wants to drown Sebastian Loral in the flood of his own tears."

"Sebastian?" I questioned the name out loud. "I thought Loral was his first name."

Allender shook his head, throwing another bone into the fire. "Loral is the surname of King Mikel, an ancient elfin ruler who had the ability to breathe fire." He assessed my reaction, then clarified, "King Mikel was rumored to have been in relations with a witch who only spun from the other side of things. The two of them were known as The Destroyers, because everything within their reach either crumbled or burned. It was rumored that this witch gifted him with dragon's breath so that he could easily kill those who he despised." He took a gulp from a leather mug; a concoction that smelled of cinnamon, oranges, and hops. "The day he was crowned, Sebastian renamed himself after this ruler. It was his way of making a statement, I gather, and if causing uproar was his intention, it worked. For the same day he renamed himself, he put out the order that fey and elves were no longer allowed to intermingle any further than business matters.

"As you might imagine, shortly after his coronation there was a rebellion. The Bahidicaras had just up and disappeared after having been rumored to have been on their way to the Garlandian castle—our people were not about to have their home threatened by madness a second time. Nearly everyone stood up and prepared to fight, minus the witches who chose to keep their heads down and away."

"Why were the witches hunkering down?" I asked.

Allender shot Toby a questionable look. "Have you not given her a proper history lesson by now?"

Toby, who was much better than me at handling his emotions, didn't seem fazed by my grandfather's assuming glare. Instead, he answered cordially. "I have told her how the destruction known as the Bahidicaras began, but our time together has been limited. I've only been able to outline the course; it has yet to be colored in."

Allender grunted before returning his gaze to mine. "The Bahidicaras began in a faraway land, and it began with witches."

"Yes," I answered. "I understand that. But from there the cult spread out to include all creatures."

Allender gave a curt shake of his head. "Even though their leader was of Hecate, witches with or without the mark of the dark one running through their veins, feared the world would turn against them after the cult was slaughtered."

I went temporarily deaf. The leader of the Bahidicaras was of Hecate . . . the same as Cee-Cee's heritage.

"My point is," my grandfather rattled on, "most of the witches chose to lay low for a few years after the cult was terminated. But everyone else, fey and elves, and even a few brave intellectual creatures, came to the castle with the intent of taking Loral's organs straight from his body. They stormed into the castle and marched right up to his throne. Arrows, daggers, and wands all pointed directly at his smug face."

Wiping my hands down my cheeks, I said through waves of exhaustion, "Please don't tell me he killed them with fire breath."

"No," my grandfather assured. "He told them plainly that they had this one moment to get it out of their systems, to try and kill him—save for one. To shoot their arrows, their spells, and their daggers, and that he wouldn't budge or duck from their blows. But he required that one of them hand over his or her weapon to the guards and simply stand back and watch. And so, one soldier was chosen and stood back as the rest of the small army did as King Loral had said to do. When they were done, the king sat taller than he had minutes before the attack, blood wounds healing within seconds. And then it began.

"The chosen bystander watched in horror as his friends from the forest began to melt like candle wax, their screams sucked into their chests as their bodies puddled against the marble floor, sinking into the cracks made between the stone. After it was all said and done, King Loral looked down at the last one standing and stated very simply, 'You've been spared so that you may return to the forest and spread word of what will happen to those who try and spear my heart. I have been touched by an unbreakable force. For better or worse, I am the new ruler of this land.'"

"For better or worse?" I whispered.

Tanker, who was sitting with his legs crossed on the log to my right—now dressed in Levi's and a fluffy pirate shirt—piped up, "Theo was his name, the Wood elf who got away. Before he fled the kingdom, he returned to the forest to give us the news, just as King Loral had demanded. He said the look on the king's face wasn't justified . . . that he spoke without emotion. As though he was soulless. The deaths of those who he murdered didn't appear to make him happy or sad—it was almost as though he just didn't care."

I stared up at the sky as I pondered back upon the one time I had even the slightest glance at Toby's despicable uncle. He'd been shrouded in his blue robe, and his face turned away. It was possible, had I been afforded an actual look into his eyes, that I might have seen an expression fitted to what Tanker had just described.

"He is like this for a reason," I stated.

"What was that, Makayla?" Contessa asked, her hand resting protectively over her stomach.

I returned my gaze down to those who shared my circle. "He chose a name he believed would send a message of destruction, and he made himself immortal. One might grow into this role if they were seeking power, but if strength and defiance was what his heart beat for, why would he appear so careless? It doesn't match up . . . not unless something caused him to be this way. Something that, if surfaced, could undo him all over again."

Caressing my hand with his own, Toby said, "My uncle has never shown the slightest regard towards any emotion, and one needs to *feel* to have the ability to come undone. However he got his power, he traded his soul for it. His love."

"Exactly," I replied. "And no one seems to know Loral well enough to understand where his love might have resided before he gave it away." I stared across the flames into my grandfather's eyes, the fire beginning to glow more orange as the stars above our heads grew brighter. "Though someone who used to know him by his real name might have a better idea of who he used to be."

Allender cleared his throat, taking another swig from his mug. When he was done, he set it down and wiped his mouth with the back of his arm. "He was a nobody, a chameleon. He rode in his brother Anthony's army on a tan horse who often stopped to take a piss at the most inappropriate of times. They called her Mitzy, short for Misty Waterfalls." For the first time since I'd met Allender Voss, he chuckled. "She was an intellectual, and despised being ridden at all. She once bucked Sebastian from her back during a routine stroll through the market." Once again, he stifled an amused laugh. "The old prat used to survive by keeping his eyes to the ground as he reluctantly climbed back on top of her. It was clear who the boss was between the two of them. But as far as what could have caused him to turn into King Loral, I couldn't tell you. All I know is what he did to my Cecilia the day after word came into the forest that he had massacred all our friends and neighbors. She brought no weapon to his throne, only conversation. Still, he froze her heart." His face grew fierce again. "He is not the monster he claims to be, but a fearful elf who has danced in the dark forest and is using un-enchanted magic to burn down our home."

"Why did my grandmother go to the castle?" I questioned without pause. "Why, after all that he'd done, did she take it upon herself to face him?"

Allender's face came close to softening, but he was careful to keep his edge. "Because she was someone who made you look like a lamb, granddaughter. She was as fierce as a bear with a cub on the loose. And" —he took a deep breath in through his nose— "there was a time when we were all equals. Just children playing together in a forest that knew no boundaries."

My jaw nearly unhinged. "Are you saying you were *friends* with him? With Loral?"

The look he gave me said it all. Even he couldn't believe it.

Everyone was silent for a moment, pondering over their own thoughts. I wanted to hear more, more about who King Loral used to be—to whom he could've found to trade his soul for his brutality. But our time was running short, and we still had other mysteries to solve. A key to find.

"Tell me about Aeslin," I said. "You said you knew her."

"No," Allender corrected, "I said I knew *of* her."

Toby and I shared a look and then returned our attention back to my grandfather. "Elaborate," Toby said.

Allender's great chest filled. "The story of the two sisters is long, so I will try to shorten it as much as I can. It started before I came to this place. You see, after Cecilia was turned to stone, I didn't care what happened to me. I went to Loral's throne with the knowledge that he would most likely free the soul from my body. But he didn't. Instead, he simply stared down at me, his eyes darker than I remembered, shallower. I shouted at him for what must have been hours, trying to get him to stand and fight, but he refused. He only sat there, looking down at me. That was when I cursed him, pointing my wand towards him and vowing that I would be back the day he could be killed. I headed for the tunnel, an old family secret—to the tree that would lead me to Raton.

"When I arrived here it was empty, save for a witch, and a fairly young thing she was. Forty or fifty if I had to guess, practically a newborn. She was waiting for her sister to return, and she was worried beyond worry that she wasn't going to. Both her and her sister had witnessed the beginning of those who referred to themselves as the Bahidicaras. The dark mass had originated in a coven inside their homeland, from a group of witches intent on finding power reminiscent of the gods. These two sisters had gone to only one of the meetings before turning their back on the coven. They sensed something was off about the leader . . . They couldn't put their fingers on it, but it just felt wrong.

"Later they would hear snippets from those who had stayed within bounds of the coven. The followers were expected to increase their strength by growing their circle to include all races of creatures, and once they'd grown to the suitable size, they would be asked to deposit offerings into one single vessel."

"Offerings?" I lifted a brow.

Allender simply returned my question with an identical gesture.

"All right . . . So tell me this, what kind of vessel are we talking about?" I asked, sidling my elbows together over my knees.

"She didn't say. Could've been flesh, could've been glass. Anyway, as the coven grew, they began to sweep through the lands, and just as the legend states, they fed upon not only the souls of whoever they encountered, but the essence of the earth." He paused, letting his prose settle before clarifying. "The essence of any world is a reflection of the hands that carved it."

Remembering what Toby had told me in that eighties dive bar, I repeated the words. "They began to feed from the gods."

Allender dipped his forehead forward. "As it goes, the creatures began to transform into beastly things. Bones began to twist and become gnarly like the branches of a tree. The stain of dark magic was all around them—karma wrapped into their cells like a deadly virus."

"Why would they continue to go on as they were if this was the result?"

"Dependance," Allender stated. "Except the drug of choice was consuming raw energy."

I had to roll his words around in my head for a long minute, and still, it did not resonate. "How does one even do that? What you're talking about sounds like vampirism?"

"It is at its heart quite similar; except that when one is infected by a vampire, their body transforms into a new breed —they feed to sustain themselves. Whereas the Bahidicaras fed to feel something unearthly. The cult members weren't predators chasing after dinner; no, they were just a group of creatures out to escalate their power until it was a replica of the gods."

"Okay . . ." I started. "So, the two sisters who had seen the beginning of, well let's just say the end, followed this group of power-hungry *things*, and that's how they ended up here? How does this relate to Loral?"

"I'm getting there," Allender stated impatiently. "Avalon, the daughter of the sea—offspring of the gods, the same as Titania—was rumored to have been killed, and there was much chatter going on that the Bahidicaras had something to do with it. The witch informed me that before her and her sister came to Raton, they had heard that the cult was after the sword that Avalon had carried before her death—"

"The same sword that killed Anthony and Titania," I whispered.

Allender nodded. "The gods had not only sent their children to spare this world from the bad village but the only weapon that could kill a deity. Since the Bahidicaras had been feeding from the gods, this was rumored to have been the only way to end them. This is why they were supposedly on their way into Garlandia. For they had it on good authority that the sword had traveled from Avalon to the next daughter sent by the gods."

I released the hold my teeth had over my bottom lip. "They came to Garlandia specifically to kill Titania . . . and to take the sword."

Allender nodded.

"Okay . . ." Things were starting to line up. "What happened next?"

"The witch I met here was stowed away by her sister. Hunting that closely behind that group of soldiers or cult followers, or whatever you'd like to call them, it was not safe. The sisters had made sure to keep their distance ever since shying away from the coven and its leader, but they weren't ignorant. If they got caught trying to meddle in Bahidicara business, they wouldn't just be killed, their souls would be sucked from their bodies like marrow. Aeslin insisted her younger sister hold tight and stay in this safe land until she came back for her."

"I take it Aeslin's sister, the witch you met here in Raton, never saw her sister again?" Toby asked.

Allender shook his head. "I must assume she didn't, but then again—well, let me finish my story. The witch told me that she'd received word from her sister that Aeslin had witnessed an exchange between an elf and a witch somewhere in the woods. The scene she witnessed was a war zone. Around this witch and elf, creatures laid like burn victims, their features unrecognizable. The head priestess was dead. It was the remains of the Bahidicaras. The bad village had been ravaged, but something was still terribly off.

"Aeslin, unable to get a good look at the last remaining cult member—this lone witch laden with Hecate blood— witnessed the witch disappear from thin air, from where she and the elf had been conversing. With no other path to the witch, she followed the elf back to where he took up residence in the castle. Unwilling to let this elf out of her sight, as she was sure he would lead her once again to this mysterious witch in the woods, she accepted a job inside the castle walls. As you may very well guess, she witnessed the rise of Sebastian Loral—"

"By the gods," Toby whispered, his eyes widening as though he'd just remembered his own name after being burdened by years of dementia. "Aeslin . . . I *have* heard this witch's name."

Allender used the interruption to place a hand over his mouth as he stifled a burp.

Toby looked at me, his eyes electric as he spiraled through

his lost memories. "Titania told my mother many tales, many secrets." His gaze rose to the stars. "It was a dark tale the faery queen told my mother one night, except it wasn't a tale at all, but a premonition. One she knew she must share, for if it came true, she would need to pass on the information that could undo the spell. The story was about a good witch who had been crossed by vengeance, cursed to live amongst the sparkling waters. Only she with the right key would be able to unlock the secrets inside the Pool of Aeslin."

He lowered his gaze back down and let out a breath.

"Holy shit," I muttered. "Why have you only just remembered this now?"

Toby looked up at me, shaking his head. "I—I was just a little elf. Barely three years of age when my mother told me that story."

Allender had come forward in his seat. "She actually said these words?"

"Yes," Toby's voice was wavering in and out as he tried to remember his mother's tale. "Titania saw it all before it happened . . . she saw it in a dream. It was why she had the key made and sent my mother off into the hills."

Allender grunted. "This information only collaborates what others have speculated. That Aeslin caught Sebastian doing something illegal with a very shady witch who was most likely a survivor of the cult, and that Aeslin herself was caught sleuthing. But, of course, if what you are saying is credible, elf, then not only was she caught, but she was murdered."

I arched my brow. "Aeslin died knowing Loral's secrets."

Allender moved his stony gaze to rest over my shoulders. "Most likely."

"So then where is this pool?" I questioned. "Is it a river, a lake, an ocean—"

"There are stories," Allender said, "woven from those who have been inside those marble walls for days on end, that

Aeslin's spirit is somewhere within the confines of the castle. Either her spirit or her memories. My guess is that the pool is near Sebastian. Close enough so that he may always keep watch."

I chewed over his assumption for a moment, before returning to a lost bit of detail that had been nagging at me like an insect swarming around my eyes. "You never said what happened to Aeslin's sister. Surely she went after her once it appeared she wasn't coming back."

"She did," Allender assured. "She left as soon as she felt a tear in her heart. She called it an echo; for her sister and her had been close, and what one felt so did the other. She left in search of her, and years later I finally received word from her that she was working in the castle. That she believed she was getting closer to uncovering the truth about what happened to Aeslin."

By this point, all of us with wings had them extended up well past our shoulders, and Toby's ears were sticking up straighter than usual. The stars were fully out and the lake beside our campfire was reflecting all the tiny lights strewn from the branches of the trees. The shimmer of lights made the lake look alive.

"Is this witch still living?" Toby asked.

"She's still alive, in theory. From my understanding she was very good at gaining the king's trust, and he seemed to have an affinity for her, which was very noticeable seeing as he didn't like anyone. My correspondence with her was very light, seeing as it was too risky for both of us if he found out we knew one another; but when I didn't hear from her for over a year, I had a feeling something had gone sour. And sure enough, as I would find out, it had."

"What happened?" I asked.

"Like I've said, we are all living on assumptions, but one can surmise that my friend found what she was looking for.

That she found out what happened to her sister but didn't get away in time."

"But she's still alive?" Contessa questioned.

"Do we know of her?" Maude asked.

Allender looked around the circle. "You all do. He didn't kill her, but he made damn sure she wouldn't remember what she saw; in fact, he made sure she would never remember anything ever again. The witch I met when I first came here, her name was Castonia. But when she headed out to find her sister, she altered it slightly in case the king had already heard of her name. You all know her as Cathy."

25

It took both Toby and Tanker, as well as Maude's glowing wand pointed down at me, to keep me from running back to the tree that would lead me into Garlandia.

"Calm down!" Allender shouted over the fire. "What are you thinking you're going to do, Makayla? Even if you manage to survive the tunnel again, you still wouldn't be able to get anything out of that poor old soul. She's permanently damaged, don't you see?"

I didn't care—all I could think about was taking action. "Has anyone even tried to get the truth out of her? Maybe all it will take is the mention of her sister's name!"

Allender placed a hand in the air, and a thick purple wand filled his palm. "Have a sit. I'd rather not have to jolt you."

I stared him down, trying to wiggle free of my captors. Once I'd agreed to chill out, my grandfather's wand disappeared, and I was reluctantly freed.

Allender continued with his speech. "She's not just been tampered with, but what she hears the king seems to also hear.

Anyone who has been sent to jog her memory is then 'taken care of.'"

"But she knows! Somewhere in that clouded brain of hers, she knows the truth!"

Contessa, who was biting her red fingernails, stared into the fire. "That cunning bastard. Planting her in the heart of the forest." She looked up at Tanker. "It's how he's been bringing us in—he's been using her to listen to our conversations."

"Good thing we never spoke too loud in there, then," Tanker stated, his jaw as tight as Toby's had been since the day I'd first met him.

"So, what are we supposed to do?" I looked around the circle. "Just sit here in this paradise with all this information and do nothing!"

"Of course not," Toby said. "We will do what we first set out to do. But we have to make sure you are strong enough before we can head out again."

I spoke through a rigged jaw. "I am plenty strong enough right now. And once we bind our souls together, I will be even stronger."

The circle we sat in became saturated in silence. I sucked in a ragged breath and stood.

Most kids my age were just getting ready to go to college—growing into their own and making mistakes. But me, I was getting married; and not just that, but to someone who I'd loved before in another body, in another life. Someone whose soul I'd known for ages. And as far as mistakes went, I couldn't afford them. I guess it was a good thing I wasn't very good at making them then.

I lifted my wings and temporarily departed from the circle, hovering over the edge of the lake. It was so dark I had to shake out my wand to see my reflection in the waters. If I looked close enough, I could make out my twisted thoughts rising to the surface of the lake like a herd of hungry piranhas. My head felt as though it needed to depressurize. A slight wind blew over the water, transforming my reflection into nothing more than a sparkling of dancing colors. It reminded me of something, something I'd seen not so long ago. Something that I'd found peculiar . . . and then it hit me.

"Oh my god," the words left my lips in an air of disbelief. My grandfather had been right—Loral *had* been keeping his secrets close!

I spun around and flew back to the fire circle. "I've seen it! The Pool of Aeslin—I know where it is!"

Toby stood. "What do you mean? How could you—"

"You've seen it, too! All your life!" I was practically panting, the memory of the long rectangular pool invading my mind. "There is a reason he hardly ever leaves his throne; it's because he's guarding it."

Suddenly Toby's expression fell, as he, too, saw the answer. "The Pool of Aeslin," he whispered.

"It sits before his throne! The secrets have been there in front of our faces this entire time—right there out in the open!"

Allender stood like a bear in the dark. "So, it *is* in the castle." He cupped his chin with one hand as he stared off into the lake. "This makes things more difficult."

"Getting into the castle will be the easy part," Toby said. "It's finding the key to unlocking those secrets that puts a damper on things."

Allender glanced at Toby. "What *is* this key you've been speaking about?"

"A rune given to my mother by Titania herself. And it is proving as easy to find as the tip of an Ardeen's wand against the starlit sky. I don't suppose you've ever had any travelers speak to you of such a thing, perhaps as they are passing through this safe land?"

"No," Allender said, his expression as stone-cold as ever. "I am afraid not. But I must believe that it will find you. The faery queen is with us even as we speak. She will not let us fail."

I knew he meant Titania, but it was *my* identity fated to rise to the occasion. If my destiny was to wear a crown, then I was damn well going to earn it. Titania was but a ghost, a traveler. It was by the strength of my own will that this foul illness that had spread through Sebastian and whoever else it had touched, would be turned to dust, then thrown in the wind. Mine and mine alone.

26

A tent made of woven tapestries surrounded us as we pretended to sleep. My head rested over Toby's bare chest as my finger traced circles over his skin. We hadn't yet succumbed to our one overwhelming desire, but to be truthful, even if he would have allowed it before tomorrow's ceremony, we had way too much on our minds to focus on our own needs.

On the other side of one of the thin sheets of fabric I saw the outline of a horse laying down, a soft grunt as Petal settled into the ground to rest her eyes. She'd been stomping around in the water all day, whinnying and tossing her nose into the air. She was just as exhausted as the rest of us.

"Toby?" I asked, checking to see if he was still awake.

Very softly, he answered, "Yes."

"How are we getting back into Garlandia? I assume we can't take the tunnel again—and will the ban even allow us back in?"

"We've got someone on the inside, literally within the castle walls who has already lifted the ban without the king knowing. As for our transport, Petal will take us back. It is easier to get from one place to the other when one knows where they are going. We had to travel through the tunnel because none of us had been here before."

Who did we have on the inside?

"As for the rebels, the faeries will POP, and the elves will hitch a ride or find another way back into the kingdom."

My thoughts suddenly stopped shifting around and hung in the air around the one skill I desperately needed to add to my repertoire. "I really must learn how to do that—to POP."

"From what I know, one doesn't learn how to POP. It must come to you naturally."

I pressed up from his chest and rested on my elbows, giving him an exasperated look. "Really?"

"What?" He'd brought his hands up underneath his white hair and was returning the look.

I shook my head, a tired smile finding its way onto my face. "Nothing. I just—I just wish one thing could be explained to me without someone telling me that I had to search inside myself to find it."

Toby reached for my cheek, and I folded into it.

"Makayla, you didn't come here for things to be easy."

"What do you mean by that?"

"You might've followed my soul down into this world, but that wasn't the only reason you came here. The both of us—we came here to make a change. No one forced you, there was no prophecy. We simply saw something that needed mending and took the plunge."

"It's still so much for me to comprehend . . . the workings of the afterlife. Or the beforelife, or whatever. Before I knew I was a faery, I kind of just thought the lights went out when we died."

"Our bodies are but vessels, Makayla, our spirits never die. And your spirit is very old and very wise. It's why Titania clung to you. You can see that now, can't you?" He stroked my chin with his thumb. "She waited two hundred years, watching countless souls enter the system, but it wasn't until yours came through that she saw true strength of character."

"It's just crazy for me to think that we choose our bodies, our parents even." Which would mean that I'd most likely chosen all four of mine. At least that made sense; I'd learned so much from all of them.

Toby dropped his hand from my face and pulled my head back down to rest against his chest. "Close your eyes, Miss Wood. Tomorrow is for us. The rest of our days, for them."

I let his words be the last before morning.

⚜

Before my wings returned, I hadn't given a second thought to what lay on the other side of human, and now faery, existence. The way Toby and everyone else in Garlandia spoke, it was as though they each had manuals to the after and before life inside their bedside tables. It was this idea that we chose our bodies that got me, and not because it didn't make sense, but because it did. I was baffled that I could live my life for so many years and not even give notice to what was swarming all around me. These thoughts continued to fill my head until I drifted away. When I woke, I could tell it was late morning by the way the tent was heated from the sun.

I reached for Toby, patting the area where he'd been sleeping next to me, but he wasn't there. I blinked my eyes and noticed that the edges of the tent were blurrier than they should've been. I reached for the vial around my neck and sighed. It was the beginning of a never-ending cycle. I placed a red drop in each of my eyes and then one on my tongue; as soon as I did, the edges straightened out.

Returning the vial to where it had been hanging down by my chest, I wondered, was this similar to what Toby had hanging around his own neck? A remedy? But I didn't have long to think on it, for a second later a mess of female voices crowding up around my bohemian dwelling interrupted my last few moments alone; and before I could sit up, a flap swung open, and three rebel faeries were staring down at me. Two Erwains and a Sheridan—panic in their eyes.

"Have you been sleeping all morning?"

My heart rate immediately picked up.

"No one woke me—is everything okay?"

"NO!" screeched the one in front. She bore a striking resemblance to Helene but was dressed like a gypsy.

"I'm so sorry." I climbed clumsily to my feet. "What's happened? Is everyone all right?" I was suddenly quite worried about Toby's whereabouts. Could Rally have somehow figured out where we disappeared to and gotten through the tunnel? Worse yet, had the Morcai figured a way out of it?

The Erwain in front gasped and grabbed my arm, pulling me from the tent. "We have exactly five hours before the festivities begin, and we have yet to start your baths."

"My what?" I asked, all three faeries now had hold of me and were yanking me through the camp.

It looked nothing like it had the day before. Ardeens were flying around with streamers coming from their wands, tying colorful ribbons from tree to tree. Elves were pulling together seating, and Erwains and Sheridans were working in an assembly line, cooking up more food than I'd probably ever seen in one place in my entire life.

"What's going on?" I asked, as they dragged me through the camp and over a group of rocks to where I noticed quite a bit of steam rising into the air. Before any of them could answer, two sets of wings came rushing towards us and stole off with me in a whirlwind of orange and purple.

My heartbeats fluttered as Contessa pulled me to the top of a gray boulder, just as Maude pointed her wand at my stomach and all my clothes disappeared. I took one look down at my bare body and shrieked, my wings instantly wrapping around my naked curves.

"What did you do that for!" I was not a confident nude.

The three faeries who had pulled me from the tent continued to flap their wings and swarm around me, calling to a group of Ardeens who were splashing in the springs below.

"Get up here *now*! Today is not for playing!" the Helene-look-alike yelled, while placing a crystal hanging from a golden chain around my neck.

Maude flew over and pulled my wings away from my body and I instantly wrapped them back around.

"Now stop that, Lala!" she scolded, hurriedly signaling Contessa to help her. "Hold still!"

"Here, why don't I—" Contessa pointed her orange wand at my wings and paralyzed them, so they stuck straight out.

"Hey!"

But no one seemed to be hearing anything I was saying.

"Where are the oils!" screamed the gypsy Helene.

Maude looked at her. "I believe they are down there, Penelope." She pointed to a rock ledge.

The gypsy faery rolled her eyes and flew away, muttering something about having to do everything for the little ones. "This is not a daycare!" she shouted down to them again.

"Louise! Judy! Henrietta!" Maude shouted down to the splashing faeries. "Up here now!"

A second later an eruption of tiny laughter and multiple colors flew up from below, and almost immediately multicolored dust began trailing around my body. Contessa and Maude stepped away and watched as the three small faeries circled around me until I could hardly see out from their enchantments.

"Excuse me!" I shouted after a few more dumbfounded moments. When no one answered, I parted the cocoon of dust that had been spun around my body and peeked out. "Would anyone fancy telling me what the *hell* is going on?"

Penelope landed right in front of me, her striking eyes level with my own. Throwing the bottles she'd collected into the air and flicking her wand at them, they came uncorked, and their contents fell into the bubbling springs below.

"It's your wedding day, what do you think is going on?"

Using my wand to undo the freeze Contessa had used on my wings, I waved away the Ardeen dust and wrapped my wings around my body like a robe. "I have no idea. I don't even know what happens in *my* world when someone gets married."

Penelope smirked. "Oh honey, *this is* your world. And when one of our own gets married, we fluff her first."

"Fluff?"

She grinned an evil grin and then pushed me off the rock, my wings extending to ease my fall, but still I found myself immersed in near boiling water that smelled of herbs and flowers. When I came back up for air, all the she-faeries were around me again, scrubbing my skin and hair with pinecones and flower petals.

"Don't fight it," Contessa whispered into my ear. "We've all had to do it." She pulled away, a smile lining her face. If nothing else, at least one good thing had come from my 'fluffing.' Contessa seemed to have temporarily let go of her anxiety over Owen's whereabouts. She was glowing more than ever.

Hours later, my skin pink from exfoliation, and my hair braided and filled with flowers, the final touches were being sewn into and around me. Maude was pulling at the bottom of my hem, a needle sticking out from her lip as she asked Contessa for a bit of thread.

I had on a simple, strappy, white layered dress. Maude had put it together from silk, and there were three very exhausted intellectual silkworms passed out by her feet.

"It's so beautiful," I observed, feeling the fabric between my finger and thumb. I was calmer than I should've been, seeing as I was getting married in a few minutes. *Married.* Then again, I'd already graduated college, owned a company, and was now entrusted by an entire population of creatures to save their world. I suppose I was mature enough.

Maude shot me an annoyed look and swatted my hand away from the dress. "Don't mess with it."

The Ardeen named Judy flew up around my face and crossed her arms. "You're pretty."

"Thank you." I smiled.

"You're missing something, though." Her eyes drifted to the top of my head. "Isn't this supposed to be a royal wedding?"

I felt my cheeks color. Technically, I suppose, it would have been if we weren't all fugitives.

The faery shrugged. "Oh well, someday." She flew down by the other two female Ardeens and began messing with the small train beneath my large wings.

Maude leaned in and whispered in my ear. "You can wear a crown for the next wedding day—the one where your other parents will be present."

There was a tug on my heart as she stepped back, and I did my best to choke down the emotion trying to rise in the back of my throat.

The day continued as a blur, and it didn't for a second slow down. As we got closer to the final moments before the ceremony, I found myself alone for the first time all day, but it didn't last for long.

A strong whoosh of air came down around my shoulders, causing my train to lift and ripple, and I looked over just in time to find Tanker walking towards me. I couldn't believe what he was wearing.

"Why Tanker, you look smashing."

He pulled on the collar of the pressed white dress shirt under the tux he was sporting.

"Isn't it lovely? A bit restricting though."

It was too difficult to hide my surprise. "And here I was, worried that you would show up in a fancier dress than me."

"No, not today." He smirked, but as he lifted his hand to straighten his bow tie, I spied a diamond bracelet dangling from his wrist, and a little blue key dangling from the end. Well, I couldn't expect him to leave off his icing, now could I. And if he was going to do it, he sure knew how to do it right.

The dimples of my cheek deepened. "Well, there's already been talk of a second ceremony so that my other parents can have a part in this. When the time comes, you can wear whatever you like."

He beamed. "You can count on that."

Toby spied the small family from behind the trunk of a tree. He wasn't supposed to be there, but the elf who was supposed to be keeping watch over him had gone off temporarily to help with the crab mafia who had crawled out from the lake and was attempting to steal food from the buffet.

A wet nose sniffed his ear, and he turned to find Petal spying on him, her neck strewn with wildflowers.

"You know, some say it is bad luck to see the bride before the ceremony."

"You know as well as I, that hokey superstition is but that."

Petal gazed towards the faeries. "It is unfolding without a hitch."

Keeping his eyes glued to his queen, he stroked Petal's mane. "I wouldn't say without a hitch—she got bit. That wound will never heal."

"She's been remedied."

"Yes, but the venom remains in her blood. It could affect certain *things*."

Petal's eyes softened. "Sir Toby, what are you insinuating?"

But he never answered her.

As the keeper of Titania's secrets, he had been given certain abilities. The future was a movie he'd seen playing over in his dreams ever since the day his mother died. It wasn't for the faint of heart—knowing one's destiny.

Clasping the silver vial around his neck, he tucked it under his dress shirt. "Nothing. Nothing that means anything right at this moment." He stared out at Makayla once more before backing away, watching as her and her parents wrapped their arms around one another, their wings hugging them together. "Makayla will be okay. Her strength is about to double, and no matter what anyone does—no matter what happens to me —that power will stay with her for the rest of her faery days. Love will be with her. That is all that matters."

Petal's long lashes fluttered. "I hate to ask on this day of all days, but I need to know—did you tell her what the ghost of Breya told us?"

He remained still. "Not yet."

"She needs to know. If Hecate herself has turned from the darkness that looms inside that girl, then Makayla Wood has a lot more to worry about than just destroying King Loral. The Crone—"

"One thing at a time, Petal. I've met Anastacia Montgomery; she wouldn't harm a spider."

"Anastacia might not, but it does not sound as though

that girl still exists. The girl's own mother had to go into hiding—"

"Not right now, Petal. Please. Today . . . let us just have this one day."

Hurried footsteps rushed up behind the two of them, and Cleo, the elf who was supposed to be watching him, snagged his arm and began pulling him away.

"Sir, what are you doing here? Everyone's waiting! The ceremony is about to begin."

"Right," Toby said. "Where to, then?"

The elf, a stern look upon his face, peeked around Toby's shoulders and saw what the heir had been up to. Shaking his head, he muttered something about disobedient royalty and continued to drag Toby through the camp towards the lake, to where the entire population of Raton was waiting to witness a marriage that had been in the works for many, many years.

27

A melody played from a guitar and cello, their strings plucked and played by a rebel elf and faerie duo. It was almost as though one could see the notes dancing up into the clouds where Tanker and I floated in waiting. As I looked down into the rows of wings and pointy ears, I could have made believe that there was no such place as Garlandia, that this was the only place in existence. Because here, it was happy. Just . . . happy.

Maude had just been seated by a male faery who shared Helene's features. Another cousin, no doubt, and as soon as he sat himself Tanker's arm linked with mine and we floated down from the sky. My bare feet met the thick green grass and my gaze found Toby's on the other side of the aisle.

"Is it what you imagined your wedding day to be?" my faery birth father asked.

My purple and blue wings fluttered softly behind my shoulders as Tanker began to walk me down the aisle. "Not at all."

In fact, I'd never really pictured this day. I'd been too busy growing up too fast.

"Is it fit for a queen?" Tanker asked, his warm hand over my arm.

"It's fit for anyone in love," I answered, batting my extra-long lashes.

All too quickly we were at the beginning of the end, standing just inches from my grandfather and my soon to be king. My womanhood had found me, and my youth—what there had been of it—was about to completely fade away.

My grandfather was in line with Toby, Petal to the side as though she'd been the chosen Mare of Honor, or I guess in Toby's case, Best Mare. She whinnied appreciatively as Tanker and I paused before my future king and officiant.

Allender hadn't changed his clothes for the affair—dressed in black leather pants accompanied by a matching vest. But he had made an attempt to clean up, and his peppered black and purple hair was slicked back with gel. He also smelled of cedar, which I assumed meant he'd bathed in cologne.

He nodded towards Tanker, before speaking, "Are her wings freed?"

"Yes," Tanker answered solidly. "Her mother and I, as well as Philip and Naomi Wood, place her in the hands of Tobias Koehaias of the Aeronian descent."

"Mote it be," Allender said.

Tanker bowed his head towards Toby and kissed my cheek before backing away to sit next to Maude, who was already sobbing into a mound of pink tissues. She had an Ardeen faery on each shoulder. Toby held out his hand, and I took it. The crystal around my neck was glowing.

Allender motioned for us to kneel, and so we did. "Wands together," he said, and so we each pulled out our wands and crossed them like opposing swords. "We are here today to witness the coming together of two souls who have been parted along their journey. Having already been one, and having found one another again, we will put them back together." He stared down at Toby. "Do you, one son of Lanake, take this daughter of Gaia?"

"I do." As he said it, a bit of light began to seep from his mouth, swimming up into the air and then back down into our crossed wands.

"And do you, young Erwain, daughter of Gaia, take this son of Lanake?"

I nodded, answering, "Yes, I do." Immediately there was a warmth in my heart that began to bleed through my skin. The same yellow light I'd seen coming from Toby began to radiate away from my body and into our wands; the star that usually took up residence at the tip of my wand, grew larger than life.

The audience gasped, but Allender didn't falter for a second. "Our journeys out of the body are just as trivial as those inside them. May this blessing keep you bound whether you live out the rest of these lives together or not. With this new blessing, no evil, no torment, not even bodily death can part you." He leaned forward and took each of our hands, placing them together. "By the gods and by the magic of the earth, I bind you, heart and soul. May you always trust your heartbeats, and may you love even when the cut runs deep."

The star at the tip of my wand began shining brighter, and the light that had come from each of us was tying a knot around our wands. The heat coming from the magic intensified; it was nearly overwhelming. I had to remind myself to breathe.

When it was over, Allender motioned for us to stand.

Toby, a handsome smile on his face, pulled me to his chest and kissed me differently than he ever had. Passionately, and like a kiss we'd been sharing for ages.

"Your future king and queen of Garlandia!" Allender shouted, the faeries shooting up from their seats, exploding with dust like fireworks, and the elves standing and cheering.

Toby grabbed my waist and motioned for me to fly us up

to Petal's back. I lifted my wings and set us on top of her as requested, then whispered into my love's ear, "Was that it?"

He smirked. "Yes, my queen, it was."

"We are married?"

"We are bound."

I bit my lip, memorizing this moment—this feeling. I knew for a fact that this happiness and euphoria was a once in a lifetime experience.

Toby's lips curled up at the side. "Don't you feel them?"

"What?"

"Our stitches. We've been sewn back together."

I stared solemnly into his eyes for another second before bursting into laughter. Yes, as a matter of fact. I could feel it.

And just like that, I was Makayla Wood Koehaias, also known as Lala Abberwockey Koehaias of the Erwain descent.

☙❦❧

This is what I had always imagined fairy tale weddings to be like.

The forest was our frame, the lake and camp our playground. The food was endless and tasted like the world, and the dancing and flying into the fireworks lasted the whole night through. Sometime after dark, and about five or six of Monica the elf's cinnamon whiskeys later, I was ready to lower my wings and fold them around my husband.

"Maybe don't sleep so close to the tent tonight!" Toby hollered at Petal who was keeping a close watch on us as we clumsily held each other up on our way back to our honeymoon suite under the stars.

The old girl grunted behind us and we laughed heartily, my head resting on Toby's shoulder as he pulled me in closer. I sighed as I looked up at the sky.

"Tell me, Toby, are those stars the same in every world?"

He brought my knuckles up to his lips and kissed them. "For this planet, they remain the same for every world. But once you leave this planet, the moon changes. As do the gods and goddesses."

"I think for now, the idea of various worlds contained in this one planet is enough to make my head explode." I let my words fade into a hum, gazing up to where the moon should've been. "Look at that," I pointed to the sky. "The moon looks only but an outline. It is full, but black."

"It's a New Moon. It is a cause for new beginnings."

Finding ourselves back at our tent, Toby lifted one of the tapestries away, allowing me to step inside first. Once inside, he turned his attention on me fully, surveying my body as though it was a gift he'd never expected to actually receive.

I was glad for the whiskey; my nerves were satiated by its warmth as it ran through my veins. Not that I should've been nervous. From the moment I'd seen Toby for the first time— staring back at me from where Helene had made us invisible in the forest—and that day in the woods, the second he'd first pulled me into his body to hush me from saying the queen's name out loud—I knew. I knew my body needed to lie against his, that it had already many times before in previous lives; and even though that concept hadn't really made sense to me at the time, it did now.

"We are each other's forever," I said, pulling the silken straps of my dress away from my shoulders.

Toby stood across from me for a second longer before slowly moving in. With one easy move, he unzipped the back of my dress and it fell to the ground. Placing his thumb and forefinger around my chin, he lifted my eyes to meet his.

"When you feel lost, my queen, look into her ocean eyes— that is where we will always find the dance. Where you will hear our song."

I wasn't sure if it was the alcohol buzz running through

my faery veins, but his words confused me. I cracked a smile. "What does that mean?"

Placing a hand against my lower back he leaned his lips next to my ear and began to hum. As he did, he began to move his feet, taking me with him. "It sounds like this . . ." He reached down with his free hand and wrapped it around mine. ". . . and it feels like this. You will close your eyes and we will be right here. On this perfect night, in this perfect place, with each other. This is our forever."

I don't know why, but as he spoke a hot tear ran down my cheek.

He continued to hum, and we danced for a long while. Eventually our lips found one another, and as they did, they dove deeper and closer together than they'd ever been. I tasted his soul more so than I ever had, and my heart began to beat in an identical rhythm to his.

When he laid me down, it felt like we were floating into the ocean, and when we came together, I realized what it felt like to really breathe for the first time.

I heard the music—our song. I felt it in every cell of my body, and my wings lifted, pulling our bodies into the air until I brought Toby's backside against the ground.

"Did you hear that?" Toby gasped, my hips rocking over his, my hands over his chest.

"Hear what?" My words were so thick.

"Neptune has set free one of its greatest instruments."

I threw back my red and purple hair and gazed up at the sky through a break in the tent. It's possible it was just the magic we were making with our love, but I did perhaps see a bright light moving in the sky that night—an old tune that had been waiting for centuries to be played again.

❧ 28 ❧

The next day the sun shone just the same as it did any other ordinary day, except now I was married. A truth that greeted me with lips of ginger when I rolled over and met Toby's eyes.

"You really are a goddess," he said, stroking my hair.

"And you really are mine."

He grabbed my hand and I stared down at where our fingers were entangled, it was a bit fuzzy. I deposited my remedy and took another look.

"We don't have wedding rings." It was the first time the thought had even crossed my mind. For a moment I entertained the idea that faeries and elves didn't have them, but Maude and Tanker had them, as did Contessa and Owen.

"Royalty don't wear rings," Toby answered. "We wear crowns."

"Oh . . . right. So, your uncle is wearing yours and—"

"And yours is in a glass case next to his bed. But I wouldn't be discouraged from having new ones forged. I think an update is warranted."

"I wouldn't complain."

Suddenly he retrieved his hand from mine and sat up. "Speaking of rings." He pulled off the simple gold band around his finger and peeked inside.

"What is it?" I asked.

The lines of his face stiffened, and his energy shifted to stormy. "It's Adlar—he's been taken."

My wings extended so fast that I was on my feet before I could even get the words out of my mouth.

"Where is he?"

Toby whispered something into the ring and slipped it back onto his finger. "The castle—they've taken him to the training ground. They intend to make him fight against his peers."

"Can they do that?"

He began dressing quickly, pulling on a pair of weathered leather boots over some clothes he'd been given by one of the rebel elves. He grabbed the purple dress I'd been wearing, the one Esmerelda had given to me in the forest, and tossed it my way.

"They will try to brainwash him, but he is a son of Lanake. As long as he can see into the swords of those like him, he will remember who he truly is. He's going to have to bury the ring, though, just in case he loses himself."

I pulled the dress over my head and slipped on a pair of black flats, reaching for my bag and slinging it around my neck so it hung across my body. Toby opened the tent's flap and motioned for me to go first.

"They must be starting to pull all the citizens from their homes," he said, as we trekked quickly through our secluded area in the forest towards the camp.

There were Ardeens and Sheridans passed out on the ground (sleeping off the celebration from the night before) as we made our way through. A male Erwain who I recognized as one of Maude's cousins waved a lazy hand in the air as he passed us. "Great party, guys. Congrats." He bent over and threw up.

I made a face as we continued towards the smell of breakfast being cooked up near the lake's edge. "I guess this means the honeymoon is over."

Toby didn't answer, instead he just kept marching until we found Maude and Tanker. They were sitting at a table with Contessa and Penelope, each of them eating a healthy helping of sausage, pancakes, and eggs. Large cups of piping hot licorice root in front of each of their plates.

The female faeries eyed the two of us mischievously as we walked up, snickering to themselves about my deflowering. But Tanker seemed to only see the restlessness in my husband's eyes. Standing, my birth father asked, "What's wrong?"

"They have Adlar, and from what I suspect, anyone who hasn't found a place to hide."

My grandfather walked up, a greasy plate in his hands. "A place to hide—there isn't one. This is it."

Contessa stared down mournfully at her half-eaten food. "It's happening. He's finishing what he's started, and he's not going to rest until all the riff-raff is taken care of."

I crossed my brows. "What do you mean by that?"

She looked up at me. "Until all the faeries are gone, and all the elves he feels he cannot trust. Until he is the only one with unrivaled magic."

I stepped forward. "That will never happen. Magic cannot be challenged, not really. It is energy, it grows and weakens—"

"Exactly Makayla," Contessa said, her hand tightening around her mug. "It weakens under fear. Those who are left have nothing but fear in their hearts; they've watched countless friends and family taken in and not returned. This is the time for him to strike."

A giant splash sounded near the lake and I turned to find Petal shaking the water from her back. Sauntering over to where we stood, she spoke as though she'd heard every word. "We must return, now. They are afraid, let us remind them that they have no reason to be. They have a new queen—she needs only to get her hands on the crown."

"As easy as you make it sound," I retorted, "there is still the small matter of finding a single rune in a very large kingdom. We cannot rid Loral of the crown he still falsely wears until we have that."

Maude stood, her fists balled up by her sides. Nearing me, she placed them around my shoulders. "Carry no doubt, daughter of mine. We are stronger than that." Her eyes traveling to Toby's, she continued, "Daphne was Titania's keeper before this burden was handed to you. As a mother, I know that she wouldn't have left something for you that you couldn't find. She may have been small when she planted it, but somewhere deep inside, she left it where her future son would have no problem reaching for it. You must go—go forward as though you have what you need, and it will find you. I promise it will."

Maude's hands fell away from my shoulders just as Allender walked up behind her. There was a heavy thud as he dropped his very full plate onto the table. "Well, this is all very touching, but if this is going on right now then we don't have any more time to waste." He eyed Toby. "I need to round everyone up, and it won't be easy as most of these assholes still have whiskey on their breath. Will you be able to get a head start safely?"

Toby took my hand. "Of course. There are many Garlandian shields with swords sworn under the queen. They will be ready to cross over when that time comes, but once they do there will be no turning back. As soon as they turn, the king will know his trust has been usurped."

By now everyone was standing. "I'll go start rounding them up," Tanker said.

"Wait!"

He turned and faced me. I took a deep breath and then shook my head. "I can't do what I need to do unless I know you all will be safe." My gaze traveled from Maude and Tanker and then to Contessa. "I'm sorry, but I can't leave unless you promise to stay here."

Tanker frowned. "Makayla, forgive me, but Garlandia needs all the help it can get—"

"No," Allender stated. "She's right. You should stay here. We can use it as a place to bring the wounded, to nurse them back to health and send them back. We will need someone here and Maude is a demon with remedies. And, of course, Contessa cannot fight, not in her condition."

"I'm not going to sit around here like some nurse!" Tanker shouted.

I lunged forward, taking his hands in mine. "Please," I pleaded. "When this is over, and it *will* be over some day, I need to know that I still have a family. I just got you back— please, Dad. Please."

His shoulders and wings fell. The lines of his forehead disappeared, and he looked deeper into my eyes than he ever had. Another minute passed before he nodded his head. "Fine." He lowered down into the seat next to Maude.

"Good, it's settled." Allender took two large steps over to where Toby and I were standing. "After you get whatever you get from that pool, before he goes, tell that poor excuse of an elf that Reign said the knight in gray only slayed the beast before his feet out of pity."

Toby crossed his brow, as did I. But there was no time for questions. I didn't even get the chance to lift my wings before Toby picked me up and placed me on Petal's back, jumping up and landing behind me.

"You will move forward cautiously," he said down to my grandfather. "If you fight with hatred, you are no better than he. Defend our country with honor—we will move as quickly as we can to find the key."

Allender didn't move, but he didn't argue. Instead he simply stood there as Petal began to pick up her feet, affording me only a quick second to wave good-bye to those who I loved.

I barely got to mouth the words I love you to my faery parents before Petal started galloping, and the trees began blurring past us, and eventually the world faded to white.

29

The throne room was cold, the energy stiff. King Loral's hands were folded over one another on top of his pale blue robes and his jaw was set tightly together. One wouldn't know there was a war readying outside those marble walls. Not from the silence hovering over the sparkling waters that rested just under his feet.

When he'd commissioned the pool, it hadn't drawn even a single eye. It wasn't unusual for a new owner of the crown to add their own flair to the setting that was to be their official place of business. It was no different than having the furniture updated in an office one might call oval. Only *he* knew the importance of this 'decorative pool,' and the secrets it contained. Anyone who thought they'd heard the voice of the deceased trying to break through had been taken care of.

His attention was immediately drawn away from the sparkling waters as a pair of double doors flew open and a shrouded figure with a cloth bag over its head was ushered in by two of his guards. Through their porcelain masks, he noticed the elf on the left had harder eyes than the one on the right, and upon a second glance, the king noted that the guard on the right seemed anxious, agitated.

The bag of bones was deposited in front of the pool.

"Remove your porcelains," the king ordered. As soon as they did, he motioned to the irritated knight. "You seem displeased. May I assume you have an affinity for a certain spiced dish?" The elf refused to meet his eyes.

King Loral lifted his chin and snapped. "I am speaking to you, Marilyn!"

The elf locked his gaze onto his king's. There wasn't a hint of remorse. "How would you like me to answer, sir?"

"Excuse me?"

"You heard me. Shall I repeat myself? Or shall I just simply walk myself down to the dungeons. There are plenty of cells left empty now that you've sent most of the fey into Bathar without their dust."

The king's legs began to twitch as though he was holding himself back from lunging forward and strangling the insolent knight himself. "What cause be for this behavior?" he bellowed. A twinge of sharpness ran through his chest, and he reached for the robes over his heart. *What was that?* He'd been immune from pain for so long he'd almost forgotten what it felt like. And was that rage running through his veins? No, it couldn't be.

Just then the double doors swung open once more, distracting him from his thoughts for the second time. Princess Louisa came rushing in, holding a black lab puppy in her arms. The king grumbled—*couldn't Rally keep his dog on a leash?* It was bad enough he'd gotten her a pet.

The girl stumbled forward once she saw he was engaged with the knights. "Oh dear," she gasped, landing next to Marilyn while bowing gently towards the king. "I am so sorry, your highness. I thought you were alone."

"What is it, Louisa?" he snapped, removing his fist from his chest.

"I was just wondering if you'd seen my beating heart?"

"Your what?"

The other guard, the one who seemed ready to take a blade anywhere on his body for his liege, stifled a laugh. King Loral shot him a look of warning.

"My Rally bear. Have you seen him? Lancelot needs more diapers."

The king looked somewhere between repulsed and ticked off. "Don't you see, Louisa, that we are in the middle of an important meeting?"

Her face grew red. "Oh my, I've done it again, haven't I? Always messing up—oh blast! She threw the dog into Marilyn's arms and held out her dress. "And he's done it again, hasn't he! He's peed on me. Bad boy!" She pointed a shaking finger at the pup. "Very bad indeed!"

Growing impatient, the king stammered out, "I've never heard of a dog wearing diapers. Why are you not training it outside?"

She appeared aghast. "Why King Loral, what kind of mum would I be to allow my pup out of doors when there are swords everywhere!" She stared at the floor and shook her head violently. "No. Lancelot will be using diapers until it is safe for him to use nature's toilet."

"Arrggh!" Marilyn shouted, holding the pup away from his body, a steady stream of urine marking his uniform with its stench.

"Bad boy!" Louisa scolded but didn't make any effort to take the pup back into her arms.

"That is enough of this!" King Loral exclaimed. "Get it out of here! And go change your uniform, Marilyn!"

"Yes sir," the elf grumbled.

Louisa smiled a crooked toothed smile at the king and curtsied. "My apologies, your highness."

"Marilyn," the king said stiffly, causing the elf to turn around from where he was already on his way out. "She might have just saved you, you know. Next time hold your tongue or prepare for it to be cut out."

The knight just stared back at his king, his features sewn together in hatred.

When they were gone, King Loral returned his gaze to the other knight. "Do you have anything to say to me?"

The knight rolled his shoulders back. "I am your servant, sir. You have my sword."

King Loral sat back against his throne, inhaling deeply through his nose. "Very well, remove that sack from over her face."

The knight did as he was told, revealing Cajun Cathy to her lord.

The witch hadn't needed to be sedated. In her rearranged mind she thought nothing more of being beckoned. She was quick to believe the knights when they told her she would be heading off to meet up with an old friend. Never mind the sack over her head.

"Sebastian," she said. "Had I known this was where I was going, I would have prepared a less spicy dish just how you like it. How is the indigestion these days?"

He had to keep his eyes steady, pretend as though his heart wasn't racing. He liked very few souls roaming this earth. But it had to be done—the Crone had left him no other choice.

Clenching his robes, he averted his eyes to the knight standing next to her. "Do it."

The knight gave a quick nod of his head before pulling out his sword, which seemed to reflect a certain kind of darkness, then sliced the witch's head from her body. The glass eye the king had replaced the old one with—the one that had witnessed the truth inside the pool—rolled out of its socket and spun in place over the ground. As soon as it stopped, there was a loud crack; and the knight standing before Cathy's dead body practically fell over, as Dora and a young girl with dark skin and pink hair appeared from out of nowhere.

Dora took one look at the dead witch and then at the knight, his sword still drawn.

"By your hands?" she asked the elf.

"On his orders," the knight replied.

"Give me your sword."

The knight looked offended, his eyes searching his king's person for advice. King Loral nodded in approval.

Dora accepted the heavy blade, and as soon as it was in her hands, she shoved the tip of it through the knight's chest. Immediately he fell backwards, holding the handle with both hands. Staring at his king with wide eyes, he muttered a single word. "Why?" And then his body fell dead to the ground.

Dora wiped her hands clean of the deed and turned to the king. "We had a deal."

"You wouldn't return my requests to see you."

"I've been busy. I have a student," she motioned to the girl.

King Loral inspected Dora's protégé. Rally's warning from the other day echoed in his ear. Could this be her? The descendant of the dark goddess.

"The Robes of Lorelei have crossed into this world," he stated firmly. "They are on their way to the castle as we speak."

Dora raised a brow, a sparkle to her eye that gave King Loral pause. "What has attracted them to this institution, I wonder?"

Loral sneered. "You know as well as I the answer to that question." He was in possession of their leader's son. "What I desire to know is what their first move is going to be." His gaze moved steadily from Dora to the girl. The girl simply stared back at him with cold, *ancient* eyes.

"The robes care not about you or your company, Sebastian." Dora continued to stare into him in a way that made his stomach queasy . . . another lost sensation he should not have had the misfortune of experiencing anymore. "If I were you, I would think more about my own situation and less about the affairs of witches. They are not after you. That is unless they find out about this." She stepped to the side and kicked Cathy's headless body. "Or any other missteps you might have made since our agreement."

King Loral hadn't lowered his wand in respect of another for a very long time, and he wasn't about to start now; even if he had broken their agreement nearly as soon as they'd completed his transaction. Dora had never made any mention that she'd been wise to any other witch's blood he might have had on his hands. Her new associate, however, didn't seem to trust him for a second.

"The Lantern's Edge is offering niceties that most of our kind wouldn't think to allocate to crocodiles such as yourself. You should bow to my teacher, for you are on thin ice, Sebastian."

The king's gaze moved quickly to the girl. Only Dora and Cathy had ever been allowed to address him as such. But Dora shared a special relationship with him, and Cathy had been his frien— In any case, it mattered not. He would not be disrespected in his own throne.

"Who are you to speak to me that way?"

"Oh, dearest king," the girl answered without an ounce of remorse. "I don't think you want to find out."

An aghast expression that hadn't graced his face for more years than there were to count washed over him as he turned his attention back to Dora. He then stated with a flippancy he would soon learn to regret, "I care not for this student of yours, Dora. If the witches are to meet at my castle, then so be it; your business—their business—is yours alone. What I do care about is that my nephew managed to get through the pass, and he and Makayla Wood are no longer in Garlandia. Our deal was supposed to provide me with ultimate protection and authority." He assessed the way the faerie's name affected the girl who Dora had brought with her. How she looked away the second he'd said it, her eyes transforming from dark, to light, then back to dark. "My confidence is growing shaky."

"Our deal was based on you leaving my family alone," Dora stated plainly.

The king scoffed. "Are we still on this? Your sisters and brothers have been splitting apart like weathered hairs for centuries. Can you tell me that *this* witch," —he pointed carelessly towards Cathy's remains— "when she first landed on my doorstep, would have been your friend? And in any case, the faery and my nephew crossed out of the land days before this happened."

Dora's eyes fell upon the dark blood pooling around the witch's severed head. "It matters not whether this witch was my foe. You and I had a deal that you would leave the witches alone. 'Tis bad enough that you've recently been pulling some of them away from their homes for questioning."

"It would have looked suspicious if I hadn't."

"You've crossed the line, Sebastian!"

The king pounded a fist over the arm of his throne. "You gave me no choice, Dora! If you had answered me promptly this wouldn't have happened!"

The witch stepped forward, pulling one of the glass vials from her leather belt. Holding it up so he could see it clearly, she seethed through a clenched jaw, "I don't think you want to piss me off any more than you already have."

The king's expression remained hard to the core. "I have half a mind to believe you've already tampered with it."

Dora looked pensive. "And why do you say that? Are you *feeling* something, Sebastian?"

The king growled, and as he did, he noted how the girl's expression changed—as though she was scrutinizing Dora's statement. It was curious enough for him to question her.

"What is it that you know, girl?"

She sneered at him. "What did you just call me?"

He said nothing. Instead, he narrowed his eyes and dove into her soul. However, as soon as he began searching through her spirit as though it contained files he could easily skim through, he felt an icy hand reaching down his throat. The girl's pupils darkened as she continued reaching, reaching—he took a deep breath and his veins turned to ice.

"Anastacia!" Dora scolded, turning around to face the young girl.

Ever so slowly, the girl removed her frozen stare from the king and relaxed her shoulders.

His heart thawed and his blood began to pump once more. "What is she?" he asked as soon as he could form his mouth around the words, sitting up on his throne as if gasping for air. No one should have been able to touch his heart . . . no one. "What are you two up to, Dora of Lantern's Edge?"

Dora faced him again, this time with a crooked smile. "You leave my witches alone, and you won't have to find out. How about that?"

The king brought a hand up to his throat, as if shielding himself from whatever powers lay dormant inside that being. "Where is Makayla Wood—where is my nephew? You owe me that much."

Dora swept an arm over the remains of Cajun Cathy. "None of this was necessary. Had you just waited a few more minutes you would have had your answer." King Loral dropped his hand and jutted out his chin. "They are here, Sebastian. In your kingdom."

"Impossible. They outsmarted my knights and freed themselves from this place, but there is no way they could possibly get back—"

"Have you not realized, Sebastian, that your weak little travel ban has been lifted?"

The king froze like one of his statues.

Who was it? Who had outsmarted him?

With a shaking voice, he bellowed, "Who has betrayed me!"

Dora and the girl simply stood there, watching while his stitching came apart.

"You know nothing about loyalty, Sebastian," Dora said. "'Tis a pity . . . I doubt you'll get the chance to learn." The king's chin quivered as his head ticked to the side. However, Dora wasn't going to let him speak over her and she wasn't done with what she'd come to say. "Makayla Wood and your nephew returned while you were slitting the throat of the one friend you had left. But really, she was never even that. She only pretended to like you because she could tell you trusted her. Trusted her enough to get close to that." She pointed a finger down at the pool. "Witches with blood ties, we hear each other even when one of us has passed. In your defense, how were you to know they were sisters? That Cathy would hear Aeslin's secrets in the water."

"You—You knew about her? About Aeslin . . ."

Dora grinned, and the king winced as bile crept up his throat.

"I know everything, Sebastian."

"You wicked crone," he stammered out through a shaking jaw. "What is happening to me? Why am I starting to come apart!" Dora continued to stand there with that insolent expression on her face. He hadn't meant to admit to that much out loud. His expression firmed back up as he retorted, "You never wanted me to win this fight."

"I don't take sides. I'm a businesswoman. I take only payment. Besides, I have much bigger fish to fry now. I will leave you with one simple warning: do not touch any more of my sisters or brothers; if you do, there will be consequences. Believe it or not, I haven't messed with your offering. Anything you're experiencing is on you." Then, with her gaze still locked onto his, she said to the girl, "Come Anastacia. We are done here."

The witches vanished before he could say another word, leaving the throne room as quiet as it had been moments before the guards had ushered Cathy up to her dead sister's grave. The king was still for a moment, going through the last few minutes over and over. He couldn't get those raw, frigid eyes out of his head. Had that girl—Anastacia was her name—had she truly done what he thought she'd done? Reached into his throat and clasped his heart. If she had, then she had power like he'd never seen . . . at least in over two hundred years. But even the Bahidicaras, some of the most wicked creatures ever formed—their power was summoned between many souls. This girl had it all contained in one.

The king stood, wrapping his robes around his body as he exited the throne. Walking around the pool, he lifted each foot carefully over the remains of Cathy the witch.

He placed his hand on the handle of one of the double doors that would lead him out of the room, and he hesitated only a second before pulling it open. Immediately the sound of swords clashing and bodies slicing entered his ears—cries of pain. Blood filled his vision. A war had erupted, and it had entered the castle. But it wasn't the villagers his knights were fighting—the knights, they were fighting each other.

He stood frozen in the doorway, watching the unspeakable unfold. One of his knights spied him and shouted, "Gain shelter, my lord! Get away from here!" As he shouted this, another elf wearing the Garlandian shield came upon him, his sword pulled from his side.

"You can run, *sir*," Marilyn said as he slit the other knight's throat, "but she will find you. You cannot hide, not forever, for my queen has arrived."

30

Traveling between the worlds was fuzzy—like flying through a storm cloud.

When the fog began to lift and it became apparent that we were getting closer, Toby shouted through the haze, "You are no longer to hide who you are! As soon as we land, pull out your wand!"

Almost as soon as the words were out of his mouth, the scenery around us sharpened, and Petal's hooves slowed to a trot. We came through a patch of trees and entered into a clearing. I did as I was told and reached for my wand, pulling from the energy around us to activate the star and diamond at the tip.

I'd been preparing to gallop through the king's men once we arrived, but this was clearly the opposite of that. Although it was anything but peaceful to the knowing eye, it was quiet. Petal slowed to a walk past the first place where Toby and I had kissed. Helene and Peter's gazebo.

She came to a stop and lifted her nose in the air, as if sniffing for signs of life. As she did, a heaviness laid over my heart, like gray smog.

"It is dormant," she said.

Toby loosened his grip from around my waist and jumped from her back. I lifted my wings and got myself down.

"It's already started," Toby said, staring out into the trees.

"What's started?" I asked.

"Lanakes versus Dankas . . . it has been a long time coming."

Toby then explained that all his work had been set to lead up to one of two conclusions. One, that the knights who had taken an oath under my name would keep their heads down until I was in immediate peril, and then and only then they would strike against the others. The second one being that the sons of Lanake would no longer be able to watch the injustice of what was happening, and with their numbers grown to the hundreds they would simply strike when they'd had enough.

"So, they blew a gasket," I said.

"They what?" Toby looked confused.

"It is a human expression, Sir Toby," Petal explained, strutting over towards the path and looking around. "It is utterly empty here."

"What of the fey? And the other creatures? Shouldn't *somebody* be here?" I asked.

"My guess is that they are in and around the castle—aiding in the fight against the enemy. Either that or tucked away in their homes. If the fight has begun, then there will be no more king's men to come and strip Garlandian's from this forest." Toby walked up behind Petal. "It will make things easier for those who are still here and don't want to fight. I heard some of the rebels speaking in Raton, they're planning on rescuing as many souls as they can who don't feel up to fighting. Anybody who wants to go will be taken to Raton until this war is over."

I turned towards the statue of Peter Kiln. His eyes still

seemed to be looking directly at me, willing me to free him . . . and I had creation at my fingertips.

"Toby."

He turned and looked at me.

"Are you positive that the king's guard is tied up right now?"

"Quite. They are using all their strength to ward off your army, my queen. By now the king *must* know where we are headed anyhow; he'll be expecting us to arrive at the castle."

"Good." And then, without hesitating a second more, I ran over and placed my hands over Peter Kiln's cheeks, praying to Gaia that he was still in there.

Immediately, Toby rushed over and pulled me away from the statue, guarding me as though I'd just released a monster. "What are you doing? He might be vengeful!"

I scowled at Toby. "I am rescuing him!"

But either way it was done, and within seconds the statue seemed to relax, letting out a breath that had been held for probably many more years than I had time to count.

As his color was returned to him, I whispered, "You're alive." This, the elf, who my aunt had killed so many for. I thought briefly what this meant for Helene, but even in that moment, I was fairly positive her soul was completely gone. The expression left on her statue's face was all one needed to see to know that.

Returned to life, Peter immediately gasped, taking a step forward only to come to a full halt. Bending over, he wrenched in pain, reaching for his back. "How long has it been? And where is Helene? I know she got away, she visits me often—well, until recently."

I couldn't take my eyes away from him, but at the same time I couldn't form my lips around the words I needed to say.

Toby stepped forward, keeping me locked away behind

him. "I hate to be the one to tell you this, cousin, but a lot has happened since you've been away."

"Away? I haven't been away! I've been right here. Frozen. I've seen everything; in fact, I've seen the two of you sneaking around when no one else was looking." He raised his eyebrows and cleared his throat.

"Right. Well, I wish there was time to explain, but—"

"Wait." I walked around Toby. "He deserves to know the truth."

"Fine," Toby snipped, before returning his attention to Peter. "Your beloved tried to kill my wife."

Peter looked taken aback. "No. She wouldn't harm a soul. Sure, she admitted to my statue that she danced with the dragons to try and get the breath to undo this spell, but she wouldn't have ever—"

"She killed two hundred Ardeens trying to bring you back," I said. "And she was about to kill me, but the king's guard got to her first."

Peter nearly fell over. "What?"

Petal, who had been ignoring our conversation, stepped away from the path. "I hate to break up this welcome wagon, but we really must be going."

Toby wrapped his hand around my wrist and began pulling me towards Petal. "I am sorry, cousin, that this happened to you. The truth is madness took Helene Voss. A madness that was driven into her by the king and his company. I fear there is no time for mourning, but if you want the heads of those who put you there, *the heads of those who eventually took her life*, then come with us to the castle."

For the first time Peter noticed the star at the end of my wand. As soon as he saw it, he fell to his knees. "Is that . . . No. H—Helene said it was just a myth." His gaze reached for mine.

"Helene said a lot of things," I answered, catching sight of three pairs of wings stepping out from behind some nearby trees. Two Sheridens and an Ardeen. Soon after that, five more Garlandians stepped out from where they had been hiding. Two male witches, a female witch, an intellectual fox, and a Wood elf. They were all staring at my wand.

Before long we were in the center of a large circle of magical folk, of all shapes and sizes—including Jeremy Love, or Bally, as was his new name. It didn't take me long to realize what they were there for, and there was no denying it as soon as the witch nearest us lifted her broom in the air.

"We have no swords, but we have fight, and spells unlike the castle has ever seen. We've lasted this long for a reason, and we want to take back our home!"

Her statement was soon followed by cheers.

I looked to my new husband, and asked, "Is this all that is left?"

"It is all we need," he said, staring around at our circle of mismatched warriors.

A haggard witch stepped forward, the desire to fight was swimming in her veins—it was palpable. "I have it on good authority, from the spirits who have visited me from the castle walls, that many of the elves have been reprogrammed, and the fey sent to the dragons without their ability to leave that world. If I die fighting, I die happy knowing that I did all I could to end that hapless beast who calls himself Loral."

Toby tilted his chin up to the witch. "What do your spirits say of my uncle? Is he prepared for this fight?"

The witch smirked. "They say that he knows not of what is coming for him."

Toby took a moment, staring out at those who had survived only to step directly into the line of fire. "All right, then. From this point, you are all my cousins. I ask of you, my family, are you ready to save Garlandia?"

The ground literally shook. The trees' roots came up from

the ground in preparation to move, as wands, broomsticks, arrows, and the like, all of them lifted into the air. The entire forest answered him in the name of Garlandia. As the energy continued to grow, Toby jumped onto Petal's back, pulling me up along his side. Petal picked up her front hooves and whinnied, before lunging forward, leading us to the castle.

As we galloped through the forest, the faeries who had joined our cause lifted their wings and flew over the tops of the moving trees, gaining speed. It didn't matter if it was against the law, there would be arrows flying our way no matter what we did—and the law, it was about to be reformed. As we moved swiftly through the trees, more and more Garlandians came through the brush—faeries POPPING from out of nowhere—and without hesitation, every species with a glowing heart began flying or running at our sides. The king may have skimmed through the forest with a fine-tooth comb, but either he could still be outsmarted or his comb had been missing bristles, for by the time we were near the edge of the forest, there must have been at least a hundred or so more creatures ready to fight for what was left of Garlandia.

Before long, Bernice and Edmond loomed before our army, the two trees who guarded the area between the forest and the valley. We didn't know for sure what destruction was waiting for us past their entangled branches, but the smell of blood was in the air, so the battle couldn't be all that far.

As if reading my thoughts, Toby shouted past the wind in our faces, "If we are met with too many swords to wrangle, leave us and fly as high as you can! We will meet you at the castle!"

I shook my head violently. "I'm not leaving you—" But my words drifted away as we passed a frozen creature who I'd seen once before.

Maude's words echoed in my head . . . that Daphne would never have hidden the key where we wouldn't have been able to find it. So far, we'd gone forward as if we had what we needed, just as she'd instructed; and if I wasn't mistaken, my birth mother had been correct.

She'd said the key would find us.

I rammed my heels into Petal's sides.

"Almighty!" she screeched.

"Makayla! What are you doing?" Toby questioned.

Petal slowed so abruptly that I thought she might take us with her on a somersault, but as usual she held her own.

"I'm sorry, Petal," I said, flying down from the horse and running for what it was that had caught my attention—the statue of the gnome who I'd passed more than a couple times whilst on this path. I'd never thought much about the statue before, other than that its presence bothered me. But there was something about it *now* that I could not look away from. The small creature seemed to have been trying to pay for her freedom . . . Or was it something else? Could she have been trying to reach out to someone who was seeking the very thing she was holding. Just like the Pool of Aeslin, was the answer to everything right there in plain sight?

"Makayla! We cannot do this right now!" Toby jumped from Petal's back and was running after me. "I understand that you want to help them all, but there just isn't time!"

"I understand, but this one—this one is different." I was standing before the gnome, my hands on *her* hands before Toby had a chance to say another word. The crowd that had grown into a small army, had also come to a halt behind Petal and was watching my every move. As soon as I touched the gnome there was an outbreak of shocked reactions, and my chest heaved as I waited for her to open her eyes.

The ground around the statue began to shake and the marble began to crumble.

I gasped, a hand coming up to cover my mouth, but before

Toby or I could say anything, a very light blue outline of the gnome that used to be escaped from the rubble.

My wand was clasped in my hand, and as the spirit lifted, she looked down at it and bowed. "For you, my queen."

Toby and I watched as the soul faded away into what my future king would call the ether. I reached down and picked up the rune stone, before handing it to Toby. "What does it say?"

He accepted it into his palm, his eyes grazing the symbol etched over the rock. His expression didn't waver.

"Well?" I asked.

His lips closed and he exhaled through his nose. "What was it that Maude said just before we left?" A hot tear sprang from my right eye. "Something about a mother making sure she followed through." His fingers closed around the stone and his eyes lifted to meet mine.

"She was right, wasn't she? Is it—is that the stone?"

He smiled, then turned the rock around so that I could read the symbol.

"I can't read that language."

"It's your name, my queen. It is marked with your name."

How it was Titania had known my actual name, one would never know. What I was positive of, however, was that now I was ready for the fight. Before I hadn't been sure, but that was because we hadn't had all that we needed. Now we did.

There was an army waiting for us past the trampled tulips and out of the forest. Those we came upon were only the faces bred from hatred and authority, led by the king's own poster boy.

Rally sat tall on his tan horse, his sword in one hand and his shield in the other. Those around us slowed their pace as we came upon the king's guard.

"Oi! Stand back!" Toby yelled over his shoulders as he held out an arm. He retrieved his wand, and as he shook it out before him, it became a sword. In it, I saw myself.

Petal moved towards Rally; we were like two pyramids coming together, our armies staying behind us.

"How's the honeymoon going thus far?" Rally asked as soon as Petal was nose to nose with his horse. It was the first time I'd heard Petal growl.

Toby spoke first. "And how do you know we are married?"

Rally scoffed. "I'm not stupid, and neither is your uncle." His eyes shifted down to my wand, to what was glowing at the end of it. "I see you've uncovered that moth your people refer to as a faery."

I gritted my teeth. "Why are you so foul?"

"Why are you so stupid?" he retorted. "You're not going to win—my king is immortal."

"No," I corrected, "he's enchanted. There's a difference."

"And who, may I ask, is your source of information?"

I opened my mouth to retort, but was cut off by a familiar voice, as smooth to the ears as fresh gravel is to uncalloused feet. "I am." Just mere feet behind us, my grandfather stepped out from the crowd. As soon as he did, all the swords behind Rally lifted.

Rally's expression fixed itself tighter as his eyes scraped those of Allender Voss. "Who are you?"

The elf just behind Rally and to the right of him leaned forward. "That is the leader of the rebels, sir."

Allender reached up and pulled down the collar of his shirt, revealing the same mark I'd seen on Helene's skin just before they turned her to stone.

Rally's eyes, twisted and dark, returned to mine and then directed themselves at Toby. "You really think this old man and your rebel misfits can defend your honor? You're making a very big mistake, Sir Toby. May I remind you that the crown would have been yours next."

"The crown was stolen. I was born to help bring it back to its rightful owner."

"And I was born to make sure that didn't happen."

Toby narrowed his eyes on Rally. "And how do you know that, exactly?"

Rally moved his gaze to meet mine long enough to say,

"*My* queen has also returned. It won't be long now. The robes have already arrived."

Cee-Cee . . . or that twisted witch who now wore her face. I knew without asking that this was his queen. "What do you mean," I asked, "when you say, *the robes have already arrived.*"

With his gaze now firmly set over Toby's, Rally said to my king, "I think she knows what I mean, as do you, cousin."

Speaking for the both of us, Toby replied, "I'm afraid we *don't* know what you mean."

My jaw was deviated to the left as I tried to make sense of what this rotten elf was getting at. "Who is my friend to you, Rally? Who is this witch whose blood was handed down from Hecate?"

But he wasn't about to answer me, not with words anyway. Instead, he curled his top lip up into a fowl grin and chuckled softly to himself. I could feel his energy twisting inside of that body like a snake. He had secrets . . . and there wasn't an ounce of good in any of them.

Rally's gaze fell upon my wand before he looked back up at me. "Go ahead then, kill the king if you must—appease the ghost of Titania. Now that he's disowned you, Sir Toby, I'm next in line for the throne. You'd be doing me a favor, really."

"Not if my uncle is found guilty of treason," Toby snapped back. "You'll be guilty by association."

"In the new Garlandia, it will not matter, cousin."

I studied the rotten elf in front of me. "What do you seek to gain from this source of power?"

Rally looked at me as if he were preparing to spit at my feet. It wouldn't be the first time. "It isn't about gaining power. It is about taking it back."

A thick line was appearing between my brows. He didn't wait for me to ask any more questions. Instead, he looked at Toby and repeated something in a language I didn't know.

When he was finished, he returned his attention to me. "Are you prepared to die, again, *faery queen*."

I raised my wand in the air, seeing out of the corners of my eyes that behind us, our army was following suit—wands turning to swords and reflecting my likeness back at our enemy.

"I'm prepared to do what it takes to take back the freedom that was stolen from this kingdom and to appease the ghost of Titania."

Rally's irises darkened even more than I thought possible, and as he lifted his sword into the air, he shouted, "For the Aeronian Way—for purity!" And then, focusing his eyes back on my king, he stated so quietly that only Toby and I could hear him. "And for Hecate, and the reclamation of the lost village."

I narrowed my eyes at his distinctly brave and rotten statement, but there was no time for speculation.

"Now!" Toby yelled, and as Rally made to sweep his sword across my neck, those behind us lunged forward to block his blade just as Petal whinnied so loud the vibrations could've cut through the air like glass, and we *lifted* above the clashing armies.

For a second I was madly confused, thinking Toby had bewitched my wings to lift us all from the ground—but then I caught sight of the large, white feathered wings beating to our sides, and my jaw came unhinged as we flew over the masses. Rally's frustrated features sank into the outline of a small dark dot as we took off for the castle.

"Petal's a Pegasus?" I mused.

"Of course she is," Toby said, his arms hugging me tight. "How do you think I made it this far into my journey?"

"How come I've never seen her wings?" I asked in awe.

"They come when needed," Petal answered, steering her

nose in my direction for a half second. Long enough for me to catch the twinkle in her eye.

"Right." The word rode on the wisps of my breath as my heart pounded fiercely in my chest. I stared back and down at the clashing swords that we were quickly departing from. "Will they be able to defeat him, you think?"

"He will get away." The way Toby stated it, it was as if he knew this for sure. "It isn't just any blood he wants lining the edges of his sword. It's yours and mine."

"Well, he can't have it, can he?"

Toby hugged me tighter. "You're a true warrior, Queen Koehaias."

I smiled, even though it felt strange to do so. Because within minutes we would be landing somewhere near, or on that castle, and I would be face to face with my worst enemy for the first time.

"I love you, Tobias Koehaias. Don't ever leave me."

"I won't," he whispered, if not just a little too softly.

32

The grounds had become a sea of blood. I had to shield my eyes as we flew over them, close enough to the earth to see the bodies of the dead. Blue costumes lay stained and covered with the stench of death and faeries were stomped to the ground like dead butterflies. Their eyes permanently open, watching us as we flew over the killing ground to a landing on the castle that seemed void yet of any fighting.

"Where are we?" I asked, as Toby pulled me down from Petal's back.

He patted her side and reached for her nose. Petting her face, he spoke to her, "You know where to go, when to come."

She nodded, before turning to face me. "Be safe, my queen." And then, after one last look into Toby's eyes, she was gone.

Toby grabbed my hand and began pulling me with him, past a thick red curtain and into what appeared to be a bedroom. It was oddly bare, minus a chest of drawers, a basin, and a broken mirror laying in pieces on the floor.

"Toby?" I questioned, staring at an empty glass case next to the bed.

"This is my uncle's room." Speaking over my horrified expression, he explained, "I knew he wouldn't hide in here, just as I knew it would be empty of either friends or foe." He grabbed my hands and forced me to look at him. "Are you ready?"

I took a large gulp of air and nodded.

"So mote it be," he whispered, placing the rune into my palms. "We must get to the throne room. My guess is, wherever my uncle is, he is lurking somewhere near there. He will know what we are coming for." He waited for me to acknowledge his direction. Sifting through the fury of static clogging my ears, I nodded. He squeezed my wrist before backing away towards the door. "I am going to check the hallway, keep quiet."

I nodded again, gripping the key to the Pool of Aeslin so tightly in my hand that it made my palm itch. I listened, as Toby ever so carefully, pulled on the heavy bedroom door, and peeked out.

"It looks clear," he whispered back to me, "but I'm going to sneak out just a little further to make sure."

"Be careful," I whispered.

I hardly took a single breath. My jaw was locked firmly together, and my stomach felt as though it was filled with broken glass as the sound of fighting inside and outside the castle walls grew louder.

When Toby had been gone for more than a minute, I poked my head out from the doorway and saw him dredging away along the stony corridor with his sword held out before him. Other than the echoes of swords clashing together and the occasional bellowing from what one had to assume was an impaled knight, the hallway appeared clear.

With predator-like reflexes Toby snapped his head in my direction and shooed me away. I gulped and slipped back into the room, my shoulders ramming into the back of a curtained wall. I stifled a cry as my wings crunched against something sharp on the other side. The rune stone fell from my grip, and I yelped.

I hastily dropped to the ground and reached for the key, dropping it into my satchel. When I turned to find what I'd smashed my wings against, I frowned. It was nothing more than a single drape hanging in one sheet along the wall, and it was sorely out of place. Without much thought, I pulled it away, revealing a cluster of portraits. Toby's family tree.

In the middle of them all hung a picture of a family, much like I would expect the royal British family portrait to appear. The oldest male elf with a large crown upon his head, seated in a plush chair and surrounded by what had to have been his three kids. I knew right away that I was looking at the faces of Anthony, Daphne, and Sebastian. There was no mother because she had died when Daphne was very young. I knew that much. I noted, as I peered into the portrait, that everyone was smiling—except young Sebastian. His expression was flat, and the longer I stared at it the creepier it became. Like he was staring back at me.

I shivered and moved my gaze to a different picture. King Anthony and Queen Titania. Their wedding portrait. Daphne was to the side, probably only a girl of about thirteen or so, and Sebastian was missing from the photo.

I was just about to go back and check on Toby when one of the framed photographs caught my attention—it wasn't hanging quite right. I reached for it, because these things still had a habit of growing nails under my skin, but the more I messed with it the more crooked it became. Eventually, I pulled the picture from the wall to investigate, and as soon as I did, I saw the problem. One of the bricks was sticking out too far from the wall. The mortar must've come loose over the years. Without giving it a second thought, I pushed it in, and as soon as I did, the ground moved and spun me around so quickly that I didn't have a chance to get off the ride.

"Shit!" I cursed under my breath, staring at the same wall, but looking down at a very steep set of stairs.

A secret passageway. Of course, it was a creepy castle. What was I thinking? Messing with silly things like pictures and out of place bricks?

I stared down the dimly lit stairs; my chest constricted, and my air stilled. I stood perfectly frozen for the count of ten before immediately flipping around and pressing my body up against the wall of pictures. Rapping on the wall, I shouted quietly into it, "Toby! Can you hear me?" But there was nothing.

I cursed again.

Laying the picture down on the stair, I reached for the brick and tried to move it, thinking it would turn me and this wall back around, but it was immobile.

"What the hell?" I murmured, beginning to feel real panic set in.

I pulled out my wand and lit the end, trying to draw a keyhole like I'd done when I'd found the map to Raton, but the only thing that came from that was a bunch of purple sparks. I had to jump around on the skinny stone step to avoid getting burned as the bits of fire fell towards my feet.

Once my sparkler on steroids had gone out, I lit the end of my wand and searched the wall for a lever, or anything that would turn this ride back around, but still, there was nothing. I had no idea what to do.

I reached inside to where my heart beat, trying to send some sort of message to Toby, as though he could somehow hear me telepathically; but after several minutes passed, I had to believe he wasn't going to find me. Supposedly, now that we'd been married, our strength was doubled; but just then, I was feeling pretty damn defenseless.

Very reluctantly, I turned around and faced the stairs. They were anything but inviting, and I had a sick feeling about what might be at the bottom. Still, the clock was ticking and every moment that passed us by was another gained by the king to try and figure out a way to keep us from getting to the truth.

Hesitantly, and with my wand out before me, I began descending the stone stairs one at a time. I clung to the wall; my wings lifted. I would have saved some time and balance issues by flying straight down, but I was not in a hurry to see what was waiting for me.

About two-thirds into the descent, I began to hear voices. Soft chatter, like a classroom full of scorned students who were on guard, waiting for their teacher to stick her head back into the room. Pressing my palm harder into the wall, I paused, trying to extend my ears to hear what was being said. A few more steps downward and I could sort of make one of them out.

It sounded like a male voice, and he was frantic. "There's a door in here—I know it for a fact! It leads to a safe land."

"How does it open, then?" another male voice replied.

"I haven't the faintest idea, you twit! Don't you think if I did, that I would have used it already! I've been here for days! I swear I hear someone breathing through this wall, though. It's got to be here somewhere."

"Breathing? Well, get it open, then!"

"I don't know how, you daft monkey!"

My face was burning. Prisoners . . . These had to be the voices of Loral's captives, which would mean that he was keeping them just steps away from where he slept at night. Ew. What a vile beast.

"Sounds like wheezing, doesn't it? Maybe whoever's on the other side can't breathe? They might be suffocating."

And then it hit me like a violent wave. The Door of Rastovier. The door Toby had promised Levelathon would open when the time was right. This stairwell led down into the dungeons, and those prisoners were about to open a tunnel filled with hungry vampire jesters.

Suddenly, I realized I needed to get down there as fast as possible. I lifted my wings and prepared to fly the rest of the way down, but the stairwell was so narrow that flying wasn't as easy as it sounded. My wings expanded only to retract as if they were in control of their own decisions. I tried again, but as my wings crippled for the second time my feet slipped and I ended up falling very ungracefully and skidding down five or six steps in a row on my rump. I clumsily gathered myself back up, ensuring that the rune hadn't slipped out of my satchel, then recovered my balance and stood once more on the stone steps. This time I resigned myself to getting down the stairs the old-fashioned way. I cursed Loral's name as I carefully, but briskly skimmed down the rest of the stairs, all the while keeping my ears open to the conversation below.

"Try knocking on the wall," a female voice said over the beating of my heart.

"Knocking? Seriously? You really are a nutter."

"Well it's worth a try, ain't it?" That voice I recognized. It was Mort.

"Don't knock!" I shouted down the stairs, half running, half flying down.

"You 'ear somethin'?" someone asked.

"Quiet you," said the voice of an annoyed elf from the sound of it. "You have been asking that over and over for five days."

"Whatever, I'm just going to do it," someone else said.

"No—don't!" I shouted, but if they'd heard me, it was too late. For a second later I heard the sound of someone knocking against a wall three times. My heart dropped to the stony stairs, and I cursed. But I was too late, and it was done. Immediately, the dungeon solicitor was rewarded with three more knocks coming from the other side.

"Did you hear it?" someone shrieked. "They knocked back, they did!"

"Course I heard it. You think I'm deaf?"

"Me thinks I hear voices on the other side," Mort said. Knock again.

The light from the dungeon finally appeared, so I wasted little time wiping at my sweaty brow as I all but dove towards the landing.

"STOP!" I screeched, out of breath and my chest heaving. Face to face with at least fifty caged Garlandians, I shouted, "Do NOT open that door!"

My wand unlit and by my side, I surveyed the group, all of them packed into one long cell: a large piece of glass separating them from freedom. They were dirty, and from the looks of things had not been fed for days.

Mort, hunched over the shoulder of an Erwain faery, was the first to speak. "Miss Makayla? What's you doin' here?"

I peeked around the corner, on the lookout for guards, but it seemed the place was empty, save for this cell. "Is there anyone else down here?" I huffed.

Mort shook his head. "We's all that's left. They's taken all the faery dust from the fey and alls the goodness out of the elves." He turned and motioned to the faeries, elves, and other creatures around him. "They's kept the rest of us here to starve to death."

I pushed a hand against the glass. "What is this? Some kind of enchantment?"

"It's Pluto's glass—there's no way outta here. It's practically fool proof," said the gnome.

I backed away from it, trying to assess what to do next. As my mind continued to race, I heard a scraping coming from the wall inside the cell.

"You hear that!" a female Wood elf exclaimed. "They are trying to open the door for us!"

"No!" I shouted. "You must not open that door! I will get you out of here another way."

"Why can't we open it?" Mort asked. "No offense, Miss Makayla, but this glass can't be cut by nothin' we gots. We ain't got diamonds in Garlandia, 'cept for what the king has. He ain't gonna open this until we's all dead, you see."

"You'll be dead if that door opens, trust me—wait, what did you just say?"

"That's we's gonna all die in here unless—"

"No, the part about diamonds."

The gnome frowned. "Pluto's glass comes from the underworld. There is only one material strong enough to—"

"She has a diamond. In fact, she has more than that." A familiar faery pushed his way through the creatures and stepped up to the glass. As soon as I saw his face, my shoulders lowered in relief.

"Owen?"

He nodded, solemnly. "How is Contessa? Is she okay?"

I muttered out a breathy, "Yes, they all are. They are in Raton."

"Is Toby with you?"

I gestured to the stairs. "We got separated. I must get to the throne room. Do you know how to get there from here?"

A male Wood elf with his arms crossed, said impatiently, "Why don't you show us that you can get us out of here first, and then he'll answer you."

"Oh, right," I said, my eyes scanning all those on the other side of the glass; and then I pulled out my wand and activated it. Immediately an uproar sounded from the cell.

A portly Sheridan faery wearing a bright blue tutu pushed her way through the crowd of the wrongly accused and pasted her hand against the glass. "It's true, then . . . you've got *her* inside you." Her eyes grew as she stared into the glowing star at the end of my wand.

"Yes. Well, I don't know that she's inside me exactly," I explained. That part still didn't make a lot of sense. It was more like she was haunting my soul, and she wasn't going to leave until I finished her story. "But her influence most definitely is."

Laying the tip of my wand against the glass, I traced a line across, testing the waters. Sure enough, it cut into it. The creatures inside the cell gasped.

I smiled happily. Finally, something was going right. I was about to lay into it again when I heard one of the creatures scream out, "I've got it! It opens right here!" And then before I or anyone else could say another word, there was the sickening sound of stone sliding against stone.

"Shit," I muttered, staring over the heads of the prisoners and choking back the bile that had crept up into the back of my throat.

It took only seconds for what erupted next to happen. The cell was quickly filled with the sound of several screams as elves and faeries began getting pulled down. This wasn't a cell anymore; it was a feeding cage.

"What's going on?" Owen asked, a grim look on his face.

"I've got to get you out of here," I said, hastily laying into the glass and tracing the outline of a door. As soon as it was finished, I shouted, "Push it open!"

Owen, along with Mort, who had pushed his way to the front, pushed on it with their hands, and it miraculously fell.

Those trapped inside didn't hesitate to run forward, Owen taking my arm in his and ushering me to the side.

"We have to close it back up as soon as they are all out," I explained. "There're vampires in there. We can't let them out!"

"Vampires?" he questioned.

"There's no time to explain."

"Makayla" —Owen shook his head— "once the glass is cut there is no way to put it back together."

"What?" The realization of what was about to escape into this world swallowed my courage and replaced it with a sluggish mass of tar.

"We have to go," Owen said, grabbing my wrist and pushing us through the crowd.

I stared into the cell. It had emptied enough that we could see crimson puddles spread out all over the floor, and just before Owen pulled me completely away, I saw a vampire jester's sickening face lift from the neck of a Wood elf. Blood trickling down his chin, and a most wicked grin spread upon his face.

"Everyone—run!" I shouted, just as Owen pulled harder on my arm, flinging me through the crowd.

"Let us through!" he growled, steering us through the freed prisoners, past the many empty cells that made up the rest of the dungeons, and towards a dark hallway.

"Do you know where you're going?" I asked, my chest heaving. I was constantly looking over my shoulders, listening for the bells that were sewn into the jesters' costumes.

He didn't answer, instead he kept pulling me along until we found ourselves at the bottom of yet another windy staircase. There wasn't time to think, only to flee. He pushed me up and I didn't fight. The cries coming from those who hadn't made it away from the blood thirsty jesters were echoing against the stone walls, causing us to move faster up the stairs.

"Here!" Owen shouted, pulling me to the side after what felt like at least three floors of stairs. Before I had a chance to ask what was happening, he leaned back against one side of the wall and then pushed forward, kicking at a small wooden door embedded into the stone.

"How do you know where that goes?"

"I don't." He kicked harder and the door flew open. Immediately we were greeted with sunlight and the sound of war.

Before we could crawl through the window, an unwelcome hissing and scraping snuck up on us, causing each of us to turn towards the shadows, just in time to see the pale skin of a jester's arm reaching for my hand. Owen shifted his weight and sun filtered in over the stairs, touching the jester's exposed hand. He shrieked, cursed the light, and then sank away—his yellow eyes marking us, a warning that he would be waiting for us yet again when it became dark.

"There's no time," Owen said, pushing me out of the window. "Fly upwards as fast as you can. If you keep to the side of the castle, they may not see you."

There was no arguing. We couldn't go down, and who knew what was waiting for us at the top of this staircase. So, without hesitation, I jumped from the window and allowed my wings to extend, flapping like mad.

There was nothing but metal grinding beneath the flapping of my wings, as swords clashed, and arrows broke the flesh of all who fought for either side. There was a flash of green as Owen escaped the castle tower and flew around me, shouting back down for me to follow his lead.

We stayed close to the castle wall, flying up the side to the top of the tower. There was a single knight up top, and as we were about to find out, he was no son of Lanake.

The second he saw our wings appear before him, he pulled

out his sword. "Well, well, well, isn't it my lucky day?" he said through gritted teeth.

Owen didn't hesitate. "Not so, sir." And he pulled out his wand and stunned the cocky knight, who then fell flat on his face.

"Come on!" Owen shouted, lifting from the tower and flying to the next landing just a few feet away. "There's an entrance over here!"

I looked down at the knight as I raised my wings. "What about this guy?"

"Leave him. He'll come to in a few hours!"

"Sh—Shouldn't we maybe kill him?" I hated that I'd even asked it, but as far as wars went, I was sort of a rookie.

`His answer was stern. "I don't kill unless I have to."

I walked around the stunned son of Danka, then flew up to meet Owen. Landing next to him, I shot him a discerning look. "But they are trying to kill us."

"I can stop them from doing so without brutally harming them—you can choose to do whatever you like." He turned away before I could answer and pulled at a wooden door on the side of the castle wall. Peering his head inside, he turned back to me and lifted his chin. "Stay close. We move swiftly, but quietly, do you understand?"

I nodded, following his lead, allowing the darkness to swallow us up once more. The hallway was lit by fire lamps but that was all. Judging by where we'd entered, I had to guess we were on the opposite side of the building from where Toby had left me in the king's bedroom. At this point, Toby could be anywhere, but he was most likely far away from where Owen and I were slowly making our way into what felt like purgatory.

We turned a corner into another deserted hall, passing over the body of a knight with his throat slit. There was no way to know whose side he'd been on before his soul departed; at this point it seemed safer to err on the side of distrust.

Keeping to the shadows, our wands out before us, we steered towards the middle of the castle. The more into its heart we ventured, the more bodies we came upon. An elf here, a witch there . . . a faery with its wings pinned to the ground and its soul departed. An innocent gnome whose only crime was supporting me. It was all I could do not to scream. My lips trembled, and I couldn't keep from whimpering.

"Keep it together," Owen whispered over his shoulder.

The hand I was using to cover my mouth was shaking; I needed to be stronger than this. Lowering my hand, I jerked my head up and down, taking a deep breath as we crept past three knights stacked on top of one another. Before this day, I'd never seen a dead body. In a matter of seconds that had changed. I'd now seen enough death to last one hundred lifetimes.

A loud clatter from up ahead caused us both to stop in our tracks, and Owen swung an arm my way, plastering me against the wall.

"Oi! Deralique! Let's be on with it, there's nothing left up here!"

"Hang tight, I just want to double check," someone answered, as the sound of boots pounding against the marble floor grew closer.

Owen stared at me, his eyes wide. "Don't breathe," he mouthed, and then shoved me down onto the ground, falling immediately on top of me.

I thanked the gods that he wasn't a huge faery. I held my breath and prayed that the knight coming upon us was hard of hearing, because as we laid there, my heart was thumping louder than Petal's hooves in an empty stadium. Owen's green wings were splayed over my body, so all that we appeared to be were a couple of dead rebel Erwains.

I was afforded a tiny gap to look through and watched in horror as a pair of white boots walked past us and stopped. I could hear him breathing, clicking his tongue. And then something crackled, and the sword I'd seen hanging by his side shrunk, turning back into a wand. He lifted it and flicked it in the air.

"What is it, sir?"

A bead of sweat rolled down my nose as I tried to remain still, a hologram of Rally's face appearing before the knight.

"She's in the castle. She was seen with another Erwain, flying up to the fifth tower. What's your position?"

The knight turned around in a circle. "The Hades wing . . . just off the fifth tower."

It was too quiet. Was he looking at us? I crammed my eyes shut and continued to do my best to play dead.

"What color wings did the insect with her have?" His tone was strangely inquisitive. I felt one of Owen's wings move just a pinch.

"Green."

"Thank you, sir. I'll keep my eyes out for them."

The hologram evaporated and the sword grew back in place of the wand, the knight's breathing was audible. He took only two steps forward, closer to where we were holding our breath. It was too quiet. Far too quiet. Until—

"You're not fooling anyone," the knight hissed just before Owen's body tightened over mine.

The next ten seconds were a blur.

Owen jumped away from me and waved his wand at the knight, and before he could even blink, a stream of purple goo slammed the guard against the stone wall, encasing him in what looked like Jell-O.

Frozen inside the mold, he attempted to move but with no avail. Owen gestured to the hall before us, and said, "Come on, he's not going anywhere."

"How'd you do that?" I asked.

"No time, come on, there's still the matter of his friend."

He pulled me along, creeping over more bodies as we prepared to meet the other knight's killing buddy. But when we turned the corner to the next hallway it appeared empty, save for about a dozen bodies. That was until a small jingle sounded a few yards ahead, and a pair of fangs lifted from the neck of a Garlandian knight, blood falling from his opened mouth like rubies.

33

The jester smiled as soon as he laid its wicked eyes on us, licking the fresh blood from his fangs. He stood from his most recent feed and wiped a gangly hand across his mouth. When he spoke, his voice was like a velvety liquid, partially strained. The blood was rehydrating his sandpaper windpipes.

"I remember you. The young fey from the tunnels—the one we let pass."

Owen held his wand further out, standing before me protectively. Stepping to the side, so that the jester could see me fully, I answered, as I repeated a mantra inside my head to appear courageous. "Yes."

"Is it true? That you can save this world?"

"If I can get down to the throne before I am eaten or killed, then yes. I may have a shot."

"You'd save it from what? Monsters?" His eyes were twinkling with mischief. When I didn't answer right away, his eyes danced from mine to Owen's. "And what is your role, *faery?*"

"I am making sure she gets where she is needed."

By this point, both Owen and I were breathing heavily through our noses, our hands out to the sides, our wings extended. The rune key in my bag felt like a glowing piece of kryptonite. We didn't dare move an inch, for fear of the jester jumping into action. We may have had the power of flight, but the ceilings were low, and the jester no doubt had speed on his side.

"Levelathon has said that we must respect you and your elf," he said to me. "He says you're off limits."

"So?" I asked, trying to keep the shake from my voice. "Will you obey your father?"

"That's an interesting question. You see, we are no longer locked in a tunnel. We are free. We must obey only the rules of the sun and moon."

"But you could have killed us in that tunnel. There were more of you than him, you didn't have to listen to L then, either. Not really."

"True." His eyes widened then returned to normal.

Pressing my luck, I stood taller and rolled my shoulders back. "Speaking of agreements, you weren't to come out until it was time. The only blood you were offered was King Loral's."

"The door opened, we took that as a sign; and in all fairness, we never agreed to anything."

The sound of more footsteps came upon us, and my heart sank as two more jesters walked up next to the one with whom we were speaking. One of them was L.

"My my, Makayla Wood. In the flesh." He licked his lips. They were glistening from his most recent feed.

"You know my name now?" My breath was heavy in my voice.

Levelathon lifted a hand and peered at his fingernails, long and yellow. "I like to play with my food before I eat it. I learned your story just before I tasted my last knight."

I waited for him to go on, but he only just stood there, like a tattered old horror story bound in paperback. Owen hadn't moved an inch.

"Have you picked a side, or are you just going to kill us all?" I asked.

Levelathon moved only his eyes in my direction. "I can't tell if you're extremely brave or utterly witless."

"Both." I volunteered.

"Where's your elfin plaything? He saved you once, can he not do it again?"

"I don't know where he is. I'm trying to find him, as well as slay the king. If you let us go, I can do both."

No one said anything for a moment, and as we all stood there, the knight lying on the floor began to gurgle and shake. The jester who'd been feeding from him leaned down and began to pick him up.

Levelathon immediately shot his protégé a stern look. "What are you doing?"

"I was going to move him somewhere with roots. Allow him to change."

"Why?"

"You said it yourself; this is our opportunity to grow ourselves."

"Yes, but was this knight one of the king's men, or was he one of the queen's?"

"There is no queen." The jester looked truly confused.

Levelathon, his eyes landing on mine once more, said very clearly, "Yes there is. That's her right there." Pulling the knight from the other jester's arms, L pulled a sword from where it was lying on the floor, covered in blood, and decapitated the infected knight.

Keeping the sword, he turned to his children. "We bring back only those who fight for *her*, do we understand one another?"

"Yes sir," the one who I'd thought was about to drain us a moment ago answered, followed by the other one nodding his head. Apparently, though lippy, the jester still followed orders.

I bit my lip and clenched my fist tighter around my wand, but Owen beat me to what I couldn't stop myself from needing to know.

"You are infecting the elves with your virus?"

"We don't think of it as a virus, but the beginning of a new life after death," said the jester who had shown up with L.

Levelathon kept a neutral expression on his rehydrated face as he casually rested his gaze over Owen's shoulders. "I'm curious, who are you?"

"A defender of this land, and an Erwain faery who has lived here for over four hundred years. So, forgive me, stranger, for questioning what you may be bringing into the only place I've ever called home."

Levelathon's gaze continued to dig into Owen's as he digested his words. Finally, he answered him. "We can only recreate ourselves from elves, your kind cannot be changed."

"I figured as much," said Owen, "but that doesn't mean you cannot feed from us. It also doesn't confirm our safety if you decided to stay or left some of yourselves here."

L sneered. "One is always in danger. Even after the king is wasted, there will inevitably be something else that Miss Wood—"

"It's Koehaias now." I corrected.

They all took turns giving me sordid looks before L continued with his speech. "As I was saying, there will always be something for Miss—for Queen Koehaias to battle." Goosebumps spread up and down my arm when next he looked at me. "Fear not, Mr. Erwain, for we are only biding our time until we get what we've been promised. But it seems the king is crossed by a spell, and until that is removed, we cannot take what was offered to us willingly. Besides, we have much to offer. We can bring back those who are too injured to fight, those who are dying in the name of your queen."

Owen and I shared a look. It wasn't a terrible justification, but the idea of having a virus like this one, regardless of what they called it, spreading like wildfire wasn't anything to take lightly. Still, it wasn't as though we could really stop them.

Finally, I spoke. "Once King Loral's defenses are down, once you've gotten what was promised to you, you *will* be leaving. Correct?"

The head jester's eyes narrowed and rested on mine for a lengthy minute. "We no longer have wands, and therefore we have no swords. I cannot swear under your name, but my lady, I promise you this much, you have our word." He paused. "That is, if when this is all over, you still want us to leave."

My chest was too full, but still, I could not bring myself to empty it out. Could one trust a vampire? Or more than that—could one trust a herd of vampire jesters? In the end, what choice did I have?

"Fine. I accept this. But I cannot promise the king's blood this very second. As it is, I have only a clue to go on as to how to begin to undo this creature."

"Forgive me, your future highness, but we have lived in the tunnels for many years. Long before your soul ventured anywhere near this planet. Patience, we have."

Very slowly, I turned and looked at Owen, pleading with him to give me a sign of what to do next. Still holding his wand out as a weapon, he gave a very quick nod of his head. Copying the action, I looked back over to the jesters.

"Very well." I lowered my wand and began to walk towards them, Owen directly behind me. Holding out my hand, forgetting all about the false handshake I'd introduced to this world, I held out my hand to Levelathon. "Let us shake on it."

"Makayla," Owen whispered hastily behind me.

"No," L said, "it is okay, I will not harm her."

Taking my hand in his, he lowered his ruby colored lips and brushed them over my skin. Then, before he uttered a single word, he closed his eyes and sniffed my hand, long and slow. When he looked at me again, he seemed contemplative.

"You smell . . . interesting."

Owen clenched up beside me, but I made sure I neither faltered, nor stuttered when next I spoke. I didn't want this vampire catching a whiff of fear.

"I've recently just reattached the other half of my soul. I've been told it should make me stronger."

L smiled and moved with an achy, restricted movement, before releasing my hand. "Yes," was all he said.

"Well then," I offered, "we ought to be on our way. We have a king to slay."

"Wait." L motioned to his followers. "Allow us to take you to him."

Owen frowned. "You know where he is?"

"We can smell him from here, but I guarantee he will have lodged himself in some hideous hiding quarters. We can get Makayla as close to him as possible, while ensuring that she is safe on her journey to find him."

I shook my head. "I don't even need him at the moment. In fact, what I have to do will be easier if he is not there to block me."

"Where do you need to go, then, Miss Koehaias?" asked the jester who had entered the scene behind Levelathon.

"To his throne. To the pool that sits before it."

L gave a quick nod of his head. "That's easy enough. Come, stay between myself and my children. We will get you there."

"Thank you," I said, lowering my chin in Owen's direction, giving him an assured look.

We made our way through the cold, stone walls of the

castle, Owen stalking behind me, with two vampire jesters behind him, and Levelathon leading the way. Bodies littered the corridor and my shoes quickly filled with the blood of the fallen.

At the end of a very long hall we came upon an elevator; though it was more like a dumbwaiter, but large enough to fit many men, or many pairs of wings. As we stepped up to it, L grabbed a wand from the hand of a dead knight.

"Do you really think it wise to box ourselves in?" Owen asked, as soon as L began shuffling us inside.

L simply lifted the corners of his upper lips and slowly bared his fangs. "We've got three sets of these in here and move a bit faster than the sons of Danka. But if our venom frightens you so much and you would like to take the windy stairs full of clashing swords and magic wands filled with hexes, then Mr. Erwain, your wish is our command. I can assure you, though, that of all the places in the castle, this is the least traveled at the moment."

Owen simply bent his head down and entered the elevator. I was already on board, for it seemed fairly obvious, that as far as bodyguards go, we had the pick of the litter.

Once we were all inside, L took the end of the wand—a bit of white marble now a stained rouge from elfin blood—and pressed it into a hole in the side of the stone wall. Immediately the ground began to shake, and my wings lifted, keeping me steady as the dodgy contraption began to move around like a creature made from rocks. Like a boulder inching its way downward before picking up speed, the floor creaked down, inch by inch, then fell about twenty feet all at once before coming to a halt. From there it descended unsteadily like a tower made of sticks that could collapse any second.

Owen shouted at L as he and I stood strapped together in a full embrace, our eyes popping out of our skulls.

"Are you crazy? You're going to get us killed in this thing!"

"It's a lift made from stone," L replied calmly, once more inspecting his disgusting claws. "What do you expect—the Skyway Manor?"

"What the hell is that?" I questioned, my fingernails digging into Owen's arms, his green wings wrapped around the two of us.

L gave me an aghast look. "It's only the most prestigious hotel in all of the land. Why, I used to do shows there during Samhain. Perhaps one day I will again, if you can make it so."

I waited until I caught my breath. "Perhaps," I answered, simply. And then the elevator fell another twenty feet. This time, instead of continuing to inch downwards, it came to an abrupt stop, causing L to signal to his goonies to be on guard.

"What's happening?" I asked.

"Someone stopped it from the other side." L turned to Owen. "You two, stand to the very back."

Owen did as he was told and pulled me against the back wall. A moment later, the stone wall, serving as the elevator door, shook violently and slid open with a sickening, scraping sound. Standing on the other side was a middle-aged wizard (or at least that was what I assumed he was), wearing a dark green cloak and holding a large stick—gnarled and twisted like the root of a tree. He had but a few sprigs of dark brown hair left on his head and his skin was the color of a sick whale. His bone structure was also strange—as if his bones had learned to grow like the staff he clung to. He stared blankly at L, and then past the others directly towards me.

"I have a message for you, Lala Abberwockey of the Erwain descent." The way he said it reminded me one hundred percent of Rally. "Pack up and leave this place. Return to the life you thought was yours. Never come back."

I fought against Owen's hold and took a step forward. The witch, or wizard, at first glimpse had a considerable presence; but the longer I studied him, the more I realized his essence was lacking any amount of substantial girth. It was as if he was operating on an artificial source of power.

"Who are you?" I asked as I narrowed my eyes.

"Do what you will with Loral if you must, he means nothing to us. But in the interest of keeping your life, finish what you've started and go."

"And who are you, exactly?" I asked.

"We are the Robes of Lorelei, and we will keep to the deep end of the forest no more."

A slow trickle of a high-pitched breath escaped Levelathon's slightly parted mouth, his lips only separated by a single fang.

My gaze shot from the wizard to the leader of the vampire jesters. "Do you know what that means, L?"

"Unfortunately, I do. This man is no friend of mine, or of yours or of anyone in your future kingdom." The jester cocked his head to the side and stated to the robed man, "Tread wisely, traveler of the dead lands, for I have it on good authority that your army of robes is quite small these days."

"The magnitude of our circle matters not," replied the wizard. "Not when our priestess has been returned."

Cee-Cee . . .

I tried to ignore the pinch near my heart as he said this— the picture of my once friend that flashed before my eyes. "And this priestess of yours, is she the one who has told you to seek me out?"

The wizard didn't answer, but his eyes said it all. All I could think to save myself from falling to my knees was that there had to be a part of my old friend still hanging on inside the body of Anastacia Montgomery. Why else would she bother with a warning at all?

Poison continued to fall as words from the wizard's tongue. "The Crone will receive us and pay homage to our many years of fruitful labor. We will be rewarded."

I couldn't stand it. "What the hell?" Owen reached for my arm as I took yet another step towards the delusional sorcerer. "You sound like just another cult follower. You're brainwashed. Don't you see?"

"Not brainwashed. Chosen."

Those of us residing inside the elevator stood still, the twisted words of this strange wizard befalling our shoulders.

"You've completely lost your marbles." L stated. "I am of half a mind to let you go, for I almost feel sorry for you, but you've made the dire mistake of threatening my queen." He took a step forward and revealed his fangs.

The wizard moved his gaze to L's, studying the creature. "This isn't only a warning for the ex-future queen of Garlandia. It is for you as well. Actually," the wizard said, appearing to reevaluate his last speech, "*your kind* could be very beneficial to our cause. I daresay, you're on the wrong side, jester."

Levelathon hissed. "I am as good as sworn into my lady, and I will not let anyone threaten her—" But he never got to finish what he was saying, for just then, his words were cut short and the nauseating sound of something warm and wet being impaled filled the lift.

As soon as I realized what had happened, why it was L had become suddenly silent, I pulled free of Owen's strong hold and lunged forward to catch L's crumpling body. It wasn't until his knees hit the stone that I saw it . . . the end of the wizard's walking stick, still hanging in the air, Levelathon's heart scored around it.

"NO!" I screamed, my arms around the dying vampire. His face was frozen in shock, his eyes turning a deeper blue as they rolled over to meet mine. A hot tear rolled down my face. "No, Levelathon!"

"I have failed you, my queen . . . I—"

"No," I repeated, shaking my head. "You can't die—you are immortal."

"His heart the ticking clock," Owen whispered from behind.

"NO!" I screamed. "I'm sorry I didn't trust you, please don't go!" But it was too late, he was gone. In his death, I was positive I had lost one of my greatest allies.

I stared up at the wizard, and he returned my glare. Shaking away the heart from his stick, the organ falling into a heap on the elevator floor, he cleaned the blood off with the ends of his robes and then stood tall again, just as L's body and heart turned to dust.

"I should kill you," I growled through gritted teeth.

"You don't know how," he said, his face expressionless. Then, looking at the two jesters left, he asked dryly, "Who will join us? And who will stay with her and die the same death as your father?"

Owen's hands laid down over my shoulders, and I could see the glow from his wand out of the corner of my eye. The two jesters looked at one another. The one who had threatened Owen and me just before L showed up, didn't hesitate. He barely even looked down at what was left of his dead maker before crossing the elevator's threshold and standing next to the wizard.

"Clarence?" The jester who was left with us questioned.

The one standing next to the wizard narrowed his eyes. "Levelathon is gone. We have no one to answer to anymore."

"Yes, you do." His eyes shifted to the wizard. "He's just claimed you."

The jester named Clarence simply looked away.

"May I assume, then," asked the wizard of the jester still by our sides, "that you have chosen death?"

The jester took a step back further into the elevator. Leaning down to the dust of his fallen leader, he took the wand from the ground that had been in Levelathon's grip just seconds ago. "Assume away, but death will not find me. I may have been infected, but I was never cursed. You, however, seemed to have been." And then, before the wizard could say another word, he stuck the wand into the hole in the wall, causing the stone door to close the gap between good and evil. "I've sworn myself to the queen!" he announced, as the ground began to shake. The wand, still in his hand, turned into a sword. It was as if it had claimed him.

Once the elevator began moving downward again, the jester took a deep breath and turned to us. "Do not worry, I will get you to where you need to go." He was careful not to look at Levelathon's remains.

"Here cousin," Owen said. He pointed his wand at the dust covering the floor until it swirled together, then became what looked like a coin.

The jester held out his hand and received it. He appeared completely in shock.

"Thank you, Erwain. That was very kind."

"You may call me Owen, and it was the right thing to do. He obviously meant very much to you."

The jester pocketed the coin, and I reached for his hand. Again, he seemed confused about the kind gesture. His expression was one of dulled pain. Like a soldier who had just seen his father's head decapitated, but knew the fight was far from over. One who knew there was no time to mourn.

"What is your name?" I asked.

He stalled before answering. "They call me Foxfire."

I held out my hand for the sword in Foxfire's hand. At first, he was reluctant, but eventually he handed it over.

"Makayla?" Owen questioned.

I held out a hand. "It's okay. I just—I feel like we need to make things right." I looked at the vampire jester. "Can I trust you the same as I trusted Levelathon?"

"He was my father, I loved him. He believed that you were the answer, and so I believe that you are the answer."

"That's not what I asked?"

He bowed his head. "Yes, my queen, you can trust me."

"Kneel."

He looked back up at me, and his bloodshot eyes widened. I remained still, waiting for him to do as I ordered, and eventually, even though the jostling movements of the stone elevator made it difficult, he lowered to one knee.

"I'm not going to pretend as though I know what I'm doing, or that I have the actual authority to do this, but I believe that if you believe I do, then this is real." I lowered the sword, quite a bit heavier than I'd intended for it to be, carefully over one of his shoulders. "Firefox" —I paused— "do you have a last name?" He shook his head. "Fine. Firefox, I knight you in the name of Garlandia, and I swear you under my own name, Makayla Wood Koehaias, also known as Lala Abberwockey Koehaias of the Erwain descent. Do you swear to protect this land as well as your future queen?"

He lifted his eyes to meet mine. "I swear."

The lift came to an abrupt stop, and I looked up to the stone door. I knew that in less than a minute it would open into a full-on battle.

"Then it is so. I declare you a knight under the queen. Stand and take your sword."

"Can she do that?" the jester asked Owen.

"She just did," he answered. "And I believe she can do whatever she bloody well wants."

But there was no more time for chit chat. The door began to shake and scrape along the edges, revealing a curtain of fighting on the other side. Firefox didn't hesitate to take the sword a second time, and as he lifted it into his hands, I saw my eyes blinking back at me, as a white light enveloped the jester before sinking into his soul. It had worked . . . I'd actually created a knight of my very own. If only I still had a list somewhere to write that one down.

"Stay behind me," he ordered, the scent of blood on his breath, holding the sword in one hand, while cupping the other one around my body—Owen taking guard over my other side. "They are too involved with their own fight. If we do this right, we can get you through their swords unnoticed."

With no time to argue, I allowed them to lead me into the throng of knights, witches, gnomes, and fey. We'd entered another hallway, except this one was made of white marble, or at least it *had* been white. I could only guess we were feet from the room that held the throne. Staying in a stiff line, Firefox led us through the fighting creatures—our faces getting splattered with blood confetti as we skimmed through, completely unseen. He was right, they were too busy killing each other to notice us.

Once we turned the corner at the end of the hall, we came upon a very tall wooden door tucked into the stone. "This is it," Firefox said.

"No," I shook my head, "I need to get to his throne." I'd only been here once, but I remembered the large double doors leading into the vast room.

"Yes, this is the back way. This is how I was led in once upon a time. Back when I was to perform for the king."

I hesitated before nodding. "Right. Of course." Firefox ushered me forward as he pulled on the door. It might as well have led into a black hole.

"This will lead you to the backside of the throne. There's a curtain separating this space from the throne itself. Be quick, for I can smell his foul highness—he is near."

I thanked him as he backed away. I was just about to walk through the door before I made a snap decision and turned back to face Owen. "You saved me today, thank you."

He reached for me. "I should come with you; ensure you get to where you are going."

I immediately shook my head. "No, I have to do this on my own. If you want to help, find Toby. Find my husband, tell him where I am, and then get yourself to Raton." I looked down at my wand, suddenly realizing I could give him the secret of how to get there with but a flick of my soul. "Here," I said, gesturing to his wand. He appeared confused at first, but then did as I said.

Concentrating on the memory of the map that had led us to Raton, and infusing it with a navigation spell, I pointed my wand at his—a yellow butterfly flying from the tip of my star into his wand. "When the time comes, if no one comes for you, then let this butterfly lead you to the tree, then whisper Cecilia into the heart. Move fast through the tunnel, for there are Morcai, but at its end you will find Raton. You will find Contessa."

He allowed the information to soak in before nodding his head in agreement. "Thank you." And then he tucked his chin and bowed slightly.

"Now go!" I shouted at them over the war cries ensuing just feet behind them, as I tucked myself behind the door and closed it.

The dark tunnel of an unknown future wrapped around me like a sheer blanket, and from there I began to walk towards my destiny. . . in silence.

34

I was captured in darkness.

Backstage, my slippered feet began to tread softly over a wooden floor where hundreds, if not thousands, of various souls had come before me and stood in waiting. But it wasn't as it should've been, instead he who had been taking up residence out beyond the curtains—on center stage—for the past two hundred years had become the audience. The audience, the play. It was time to change things up.

I skulked forward cautiously. For all I knew, King Loral could be but a breath away from where I came walking. A shudder of a breath left my lips as I dug out the key from where it had found the bottom of my satchel, next to the only other stone I'd kept. The one with Toby's secret.

As I tip-toed over the stage, I held out my runeless hand and felt my way around. Finally, taking deep, heated breaths through my nose, I felt the weighted fabric of the curtain. With only a second's hesitation and a heavy heartbeat, I pulled it to the side. Immediately, sunlight infiltrated the space around me. I saw nothing but an empty throne room, but I knew better than to trust the assumption, so I pulled out my wand and gripped it tightly in my hand.

My bloodied shoes slid across the floor. This seemed to be the only part of the castle untouched by blood. As I left red streaks from those who had sacrificed their lives for a better Garlandia, I traveled towards the edge of the stage on which the throne sat. All I could see was the back of the chair, but I knew it was empty.

The last time I'd been in this room, I'd entered from the opposite side. How different it looked up here, yet it was the same. Like a graveyard. And as soon as I reached the throne, empty of his *highness*, I saw that it was more than a metaphorical feeling this time. Lying on the floor were two dead bodies: one of the king's guards and Cajun Cathy. Her head separated from her body.

Sickened by the portrait of murder that had been painted over the marble canvas, I froze. My gaze lifted and met the double doors, aware that just on the other side of them elves, faeries, witches, and creatures of all shapes and sizes were taking their last breaths. They were fighting in my name . . . fighting to get back what was rightfully theirs.

The wand in my hand warmed and the star grew from the diamond, larger than I'd ever seen it. She was anxious— Titania. She felt how close we were, and that the sparkling waters were just below my feet.

Moving steadily, but not too quickly, I climbed down the stairs from the stage to the marble floor—my eyes scraping the ground where Cathy laid in pieces. I came to a halt just in front of her cloudy eye, which must've rolled out of her decapitated head once it hit the ground. I bent down and reached for it. It was cold, heavy. I felt a shiver run through my spine and dropped it back to the floor—my gaze lifting and settling on what was directly in front of me. The Pool of Aeslin.

It was just as mysterious as the first time I'd come upon it. How had I not thought of this from the start? The longer I peered into it, the more I saw the colors twisting inside it as actual whispers . . . secrets.

I hesitated for a second, long enough to look over my shoulders—to see if the sadistic King Loral had decided to finally show his face—which of course, he had not. And then I held my hand defiantly over the pool, before letting the rune with my name etched into its surface fall into the sparkling waters.

Like a bath bomb, the rune began fizzing. The water, bubbling. I took several steps back, watching in awe as the colors flashed and the bubbles grew, like a jacuzzi tub set to its highest setting. Eventually, the stone encasing the pool disappeared and the water began to crawl upwards, taking form. Still glistening, the water took the outline of a woman; her features evening out enough to observe that she bore a striking resemblance to a younger version of Cathy.

The form looked to the windows lining the walls near the ceiling, and in a heart's beat, she blinked and they shattered. As the glass fell, she returned her gaze to rest over my shoulders, and as she spoke, her voice boomed and echoed. Her speech, loud enough to be heard in a distant land, halted the war cries outside these walls, and as if I could see through the castle, I just knew—everyone, regardless of which side they fought for, had frozen in their tracks.

"My name is Aeslin, descendant of Athena. I came to Garlandia in search of darkness, which I found. Unfortunately, it also found me.

"The elf who has risen to power in this land, traded not just a piece of his soul, but *all* his love, to get the crown which sits on his head. He cut a deal with a witch, and it was she who provided him with the crossed magic he's used for years as protection. The same magic he used to possess *my* soul.

"King Loral used me; he possessed my body with darkened magic, then forced me to infiltrate the queen with his twisted enchantment. Queen Titania did not commit those acts of murder; it was from my hijacked wand that she was forced to impale the chest of he who she so loved, King Anthony; and to write a false note in her lover's blood before slitting her own throat. When it was done, the magic forced me to take the queen's sword and drive it through my heart. I have since been buried with Avalon's blade in the waters that sparkle before the throne. This is the work of the elf who you've been taught to bow to. He only allows you to see what he wants you to see. You've all been ruled by a criminal. The crown was never meant for his head, and justice will find him."

Only once she had finished speaking did her transparency fade. She became whole again, walking towards me as though she was as real as she had been two hundred years ago.

"You now know the truth, Makayla of the Erwain descent. The elf named Sebastian killed them . . . he killed us all."

I was practically speechless, but somehow, I still found the words. "How do I return the favor?"

"You must first terminate the unnatural energy that is responsible for dealing Sebastian his power—"

"Dora." That much was more than obvious by now.

Aeslin tilted her head to the side. "Do not look only at the surface, Makayla Wood. You are smarter than that, girl."

"But I know she's the one. She has my friend."

Aeslin stepped in closer to me by an inch. "Listen to me now. You must return the sword of Avalon to its home. From there, the sea will move you in the right direction to where it is you must go. Do not stray from this path. The Crone of Light's End has no home, she lives in the past. You must find where it began. Only then may it end, and once the spirits are put to rest only then can you undo the king."

The Crone of Light's End? I'd never heard of her or him or whoever . . . but something about that seemed familiar.

I released the hold I had over my tongue, tasting blood as I did so. "Okay . . . If I do as you have said and I finish off this crone, then how do I end Loral?"

"'Tis simple. Return the love he lost."

My head started shaking as my chest filled. "I—I don't see how that's simple."

She brought her hands up to my cheeks and held them there. They were surprisingly warm. "'Tis as simple as this."

My heart warmed as her eyes peered into mine. I was just about to ask what 'this' was, but I never got the chance. Her hands slipped from my face and her body fell to the floor. A white light lifted from her dead body and a sword stuck out from her chest.

I looked up at the shards of glass now taking up residence all over the marble floor, then shifted my gaze to the windows now void of any protection. It was so quiet one could hear an Ardeen sneeze, but I knew it wouldn't last long. Aeslin had spoken and now every man, woman, and child—wings or no —would be out for blood. Perhaps even some of Loral's own knights would turn now that they knew the truth. Could Dankas transform into Lanakes?

As I moved towards the hilt of the blade that killed Aeslin, the star at the end of my wand growing brighter by the second, I could feel her beside me, *Titania*, reaching for the sword that had once been in her possession. But just as I was about to reach for it, a sudden burst of light from across the room forced me to halt before the sword.

I flinched as I listened to the fizzle of a dying firework and clenched the space over my heart as King Loral stepped out of a glowing sphere. I froze in terror as he stood, still as one of his terrible statues, his eyes on me as the sphere behind him shrunk back down into an identical replica of what lay on the floor. Cathy's eye—it belonged to a pair. Grabbing the glass ball from where it floated midair into his hands, he faced me, head on, for the very first time.

I took a quick inhale, surveying his appearance. He was smaller than Toby, and his features were stern, but there were most definitely similarities. Tinted skin, blue eyes—light hair.

"I suppose you think you can stop me," was all he said.

I remained frozen, just inches before the sword stuck in Aeslin's chest. "I could say the same to you." My voice was shakier than I had intended it to be.

"I don't have to stop you; you'll manage that on your own. You're but a human who thinks she's a faery."

Suddenly, my racing heart came to an abrupt stop before picking back up at a leisurely pace. I felt the glow inside me, the one that had grown when Toby and I had been stitched back together again, begin to warm.

Shaking my head, I retrained my breath. "You know nothing about what it is to be me. And for your information, I am a faery who once thought she was a human. It isn't a weakness, however, but a strength. The magic that should have been as easy to spin from my soul as the blood pumping through my heart, I had to dig inside to find again. And do you know what I came to understand?"

He didn't give me the satisfaction of a reaction.

"That love and magic go hand in hand. That they are the same thing."

His lip curled up into an unsavory expression. "Then you and I shall be on the same playing field soon enough, I think."

I scowled. "What is that supposed to mean?"

"That once love is gone, you must find an artificial sort of magic."

"Is that a threat?"

He just blinked and turned his chin to the side.

As I stood there, staring at this despicable elf, at his smug face and twisted heart, I relayed to him a truth he could never understand. "Toby and I have been married." He didn't flinch. "But all we did was retie that which had been pulled apart once upon a time, for when we met weeks ago, it wasn't *for* the first time. We were already married, you see; because in another life, we'd already bound our souls for eternity." I thought of the words Allender had recited during our ceremony. "We are bound together, even in death."

The king squinted his eyes and took a step towards me, as he did the overwhelming scent of cloves wafted over my nostrils. "You say that now, but you have not yet experienced heartache in that shell of a body. You were torn apart once before—that is why your side had to be restitched. And if I recall, the last you roamed this world was hundreds of years ago. Can you tell me where your soul has been since then?" He waited and I said nothing. "That's right, Ms. Wood. Your soul knows what it is to be lost more than it knows love."

I turned my cheek to him in question as a sinister laugh escaped his parted lips.

"You think that I am blind. That is where you are wrong —I am shut off. A quality that makes it easy for me to evaluate my enemy's weaknesses."

Practically spitting at his smug face, I asked, "What could have possibly made you this way?"

He juggled the glass ball still in his hands, jostling his jaw from side to side. "You assume that one *must* know tragedy to live a certain way?"

"I believe something happened to make you so terrible, yes." He clenched the ball tighter in his hand, and for some reason I was suddenly reminded of Allender, and the strange last words he'd said to Toby and me before we left. Deviating my jaw to the right, I asked, "Who is the gray knight, Sebastian? What does he mean to you?"

His dark eyes froze.

As the seconds ticked by, I pointed a finger at his chest. "You and Allender Voss know one another, don't you? More so than meets the eye."

He chose not to answer, but I couldn't help but feel as though I'd hit the nail on the head.

"All I have to do is wait." he seethed. "For you are as easy to read as the books you cling to. When your love is strong, you feel invincible, but your heart tends to beat slower when that same emotion disappears."

"Good thing then, that I have an extraordinary memory, and if anything were to happen to anyone I love, I would rise above the sickness you've allowed to infiltrate your being. Only a fool would give away his love—his essence. You are powered by an artificial source of energy, and for your information, its batteries are about to wear out." I reached forward and pulled the sword from Aeslin's body—the power surging through it was electric. "Enjoy your next few breaths, *king*, for they will soon be your last."

"Go ahead, run the blade through my chest. Slit my throat."

Chuckling softly to myself, I tucked my chin. "You underestimate me, and it will catch up with you very soon. I *know* what will happen if I try to kill you before reaching the Crone of Light's End." His eyes grew. "That's right. *She* told me, and everyone else in the kingdom, everything." I motioned to Aeslin's body. "It's finally time that you get yours."

The king didn't even have time to react. As soon as the words had exited my mouth, both sets of double doors flew open, and within seconds the space before us was permeated with swords reflecting my face, and creatures ready to fight in my honor.

Voices of outrage filled the gaps between them and us.

"You killed the king and queen!"

"Murderer!"

"Witch slayer!"

"Take his head!"

With fists in the air, wands and swords crossed before their chests, they all swarmed in and around the king, caring not about the curse he carried in his blood. They'd heard Aeslin's account, and they weren't going to stop until the king was dead.

My wings lifted, sweeping me up and over the heads of those hungry for justice—Avalon's sword heavy in my hand, and Titania's mark glowing in the other. I glanced over my shoulder just before exiting the room, watching as the king retrieved Cathy's glass eye from the floor then threw the ball he'd been holding into the air. It grew quickly, and as soon as it was large enough for him to slip inside, he disappeared into its void.

"Coward," I muttered.

As soon as I was on the other side of the doors I came to my feet. The halls were empty, save for the dead and abandoned weapons; everyone had penetrated the king's throne, and they were now discovering the pair of sisters he had killed to rise above them all.

At first, I ran, my head jerking from left to right in search of Toby, finding nothing but more dead bodies. It was like the halls had been carpeted by flesh, battered shields, and wasted weapons. My lungs were burning as I turned a corner, leading to the castle's main entryway. Just as I opened my mouth and prepared to use my lungs to call out the name of my future king, a cluster of stars exploded in my face as I slammed into someone coming just as quickly my way. Immediately I was overcome by a wave of dizziness as I recognized not only the eyes of the guard, but the face of my enemy.

🦎 35 🦎

"Lala," Rally hissed.

I lifted Avalon's sword, backing away just enough so that its tip, along with my wand, was pointed at his chest. "You have something to say to me?"

A detestable grin lined his face. "I've been waiting to get you alone for a long time so that I can personally remove those wings of yours."

I was about to strike, when a strong arm wrapped itself around my center and pulled me back; my heart warmed at the overwhelming scent of ginger.

"Step away, my queen," Toby whispered into my ear, before pressing me into the wall and marking Rally as his own.

With my chest heaving, I pushed away from the marble wall and leaned on the sword of Avalon for support. "Toby—no!" I shouted. "He's not worth it! Just leave him—I'm sure the others will be out to tear him apart any moment now!"

His eyes pierced the enemy like blue ice as he replied, "He'll be long gone by the time those creatures leave that room." The two elves faced one another, circling each other with their swords pointed at each other's hearts. "If anyone's going to take him, it must be now."

"You should listen to your *faery* and leave now," Rally spat out.

"You mean my wife, and your future queen. That is if you were even going to be alive to witness the coronation."

"No, but I'll be alive for her termination." He lunged forward and jabbed his sword at Toby. I yelped as Toby veered to the side, just nearly missing the blade.

Rally's first strike spurred a full-on duel between the two, no longer just stalking one another, but striking freely. It was all I could do to just stand there, holding onto the sword, defenseless against their skill level. It was a dance, and they were perfectly matched partners; but then again, they'd been raised together, fought together their entire lives.

"Remember the proper way to strike?" Rally questioned, through gritted teeth.

"One must use patience," Toby answered, his posture perfect as he skirted away from the tip of Rally's blade.

"Yes. And envision the end. Your enemy's blood dripping from your wand." As he said it, Rally's sword indeed changed back into a wand, and he shot a curse at Toby.

I lunged forward only to be pushed back into the wall with a flick of Toby's wand. As I grunted, stuck to the wall like glue, the sword fight quickly changed to a battle of hexes. Flashes of bright pink, green, and blue striking the air. I had a feeling they had practiced this routine many times. Now, during the real thing, I couldn't help but wonder who usually won.

"I understand my uncle has given away his soul, but why are you so foul, Rally?" Toby asked, a green flare aimed at the elf's heart, deterred by a counter curse.

"I am only being true to he who I swore to protect."

"Give it up, you've already admitted you're after the

crown. And from the sound of it, you just as falsely swore under the king as I did."

Rally winked at Toby. "Nailed that one."

Without a chance to question the comment, Toby jumped over a lizard with canines the size of its long tail that had erupted from Rally's wand. "Relative of yours?" Toby zapped it with his wand and transformed it into a miniature dragon, who flew immediately towards Rally, unlimited rounds of fire erupting from its mouth. Blue light sprayed from Rally's wand, enveloping the creature before the entire thing blew up and fizzled to the ground.

With his wand at attention, Toby said, "How about a little story, Ral? Why *did* you swear under the king?"

"Who cares where my motivation lies, Sir Toby? All that matters, is that in a brief moment you and your bride will be of no more concern to me, and the crown will be mine."

"How do you plan on doing that? You will need to kill the king to get the precious crown, and there is but one soul who has the ability to send him to his grave."

"We're under strict orders not to harm your sparkly little butterfly, but that doesn't mean I have to play nice nice."

We?

Toby was in the middle of questioning Rally's statement when out of nowhere a pink light flew towards my heart, causing me to shriek, but as it turned out it was only meant to free me from where I'd been strapped to the wall. I stepped away, looking for the source. Creeping nearer to where the hexes continued to fly back and forth, I spotted a tall, thin character creeping out from the opposite wall. It was Firefox —three more of his kind just behind him.

Catching my eye, he lifted a finger to his mouth, and in one swift movement, he was standing just behind Rally. Toby fell back as soon as he saw him, Firefox curling a lip around his fang, lifting the sword I'd gifted him into the air.

Rally, a queer expression sewn into his face, continued to glare at Toby, as he lowered his wand and it turned back into a sword. He carefully turned and faced the vampire jester, and his cowardly nature showed as his eyes widened in fear. Firefox's fangs were dripping with a contagion that could either kill you or make you stronger.

Rally turned to run, but even though he was fast, he wasn't as fast as the undead. Within another second, Foxfire had lunged forward and sank his teeth into Rally's jugular, the elf's body crumpling down into a pained position.

Toby, his sword lowered, began moving closer to his fallen enemy. Avalon's sword lowered in my grip as I inched closer as well. Toby stepped into a sunbeam, standing over Rally's near bloodless body. I stood there, shaking, watching as Firefox fed with the intention of draining my enemy dry—when suddenly, a black puppy came running up to my feet. Confused by the interruption, I lifted him into my arms, and then all our attention was stolen by a voice as sickly as a demon crying out from an innocent host.

"If you want her out of this alive, then unhand him."

The jesters, Toby, and I all jumped in the direction of the voice, while Firefox lifted his fangs from Rally's neck, his gaze centering in on the intruder.

"Clarence?"

As soon as Firefox spoke the traitor's name, he appeared from the shadows with Princess Louisa in his arms. She had a sword dangling from a thick, leather belt strung around her middle, and as the light hit it, it reflected a pair of female eyes . . . but they were not mine.

"Let her go," Toby stated firmly.

I couldn't keep my gaze centered. It bounced from Toby, to Louisa, to the lunatic look on Clarence's face, and finally down to where Firefox had Rally in the shadows. My enemy was still too weak to move, but he was conscious and had taken notice of everything that was happening.

"An even trade, I think," Clarence said. "One of yours for one of ours."

Firefox stood; his followers ready to strike.

"What's going on?" Toby asked, staring from one vampire to the other. "Where is your leader? Where is Levelathon?"

"He is dead," Clarence repeated. "We answer to no one now."

"That is a lie!" Firefox shouted. "*You* answer to the other side of things now!" Lifting his new sword, he continued to rant, "*I* am the new leader of this nest, and *we* serve the queen!"

Clarence scowled. "You've chosen the weaker side, brother. Regardless, I've come here for *him*." He averted his eyes to Rally, whose chest was rising further up into the air as he struggled to breathe. "He is protected by the Robes."

Firefox, careful to stay clear of the sunbeam reaching through the shadows, took a step closer to where Louisa was being held hostage. "Why would I willingly hand over King Loral's first knight, especially now that he's been infected? What is *she* to us?"

"Why don't you ask him?" Clarence jerked his head in Toby's direction.

Toby stared from the horrible jester to the she-elf in his arms. Her chin quivering, the vein in her neck throbbing, she nodded her head. Toby's shoulders shrunk down as he relayed the truth. "King Afron is dead. Louisa is the Queen of Lauslin. She has been ever since she arrived here."

The air in my chest left all at once as the puppy in my arms struggled against my grip. Rally let out a small cry of outrage.

"Do her people know?" I gasped.

"Of course not; she would not have been able to leave her

land otherwise," Toby stated. "She was supposed to take back her land and reform her army so they could aid in *our* fight." He shot her an aggrieved look. "She was supposed to be gone by now—she was to leave as soon as she lifted the king's travel ban."

"He's been practicing witchcraft!" Louisa blurted out, her gaze on Rally. "I had to know his business before I could go."

Toby looked down at Rally. "What would an elf need of a sorcerer's magic?"

Rally's expression stiffened, and he spoke with a weak voice. "I am only part elf." And then everything happened at once.

Using whatever strength was left in him, Rally turned on Firefox, sending a bolt of electricity through him before muttering a strange curse under his breath. He was too weak, as was his magic, to do any real damage, but it stunned Firefox momentarily, long enough for Rally to escape him and retrieve something from his pocket and chuck it against the marble so hard it shattered.

After that there was a blur of colors as the jesters moved in on each other. Firefox lunged for Clarence, as the 'good' jesters reached for Princess Louisa, pulling her to safety—and then there was a loud crash near the front doors as they flew open and the sound of fighting from outside entered in, as the war was far from over. Hooves pounded so hard against the marble floor that it began to shatter.

"Toby!" I shouted over the chaos. "We must go—now!"

But even as I said the words, as I watched Louisa pull out her sword and prepare to defend herself, a darkness crept from the broken vial Rally had thrown, it crept along the floor— black smoke attempting to make itself into a form. Before I could whisper another word, it sank into Rally. As soon as it did, a palpable strength seemed to infiltrate his body, making him strong enough to fight.

"Toby, my old friend, I've not yet finished what I set out to do." His voice was thick with malevolence.

Toby, who had been reaching towards Louisa, motioned for her to come with us. He then turned to face Rally at the exact same time Rally lifted his sword. The timing of it all, just as Toby turned and Rally's sword sliced through the air . . . it was as if it had been written from the words of a depressed poet.

The way my king's eyes looked at me just as the blade sliced through his—

It was a nightmare I would never unsee.

"NO!" I screamed, the puppy in my arms falling to the floor as my knees unbuckled and I began to fall, the sword toppling from my grip . . . but I never made it to the ground.

My body was scooped up by a swift force, and though I wanted to refuse this service, I was incapable of fighting. I was too horrified, too pained by what I had just seen to even grasp how Petal had gotten into the castle. She whinnied then bit down over Avalon's sword, lifting her front hooves from the ground, before spinning and galloping away—too quickly for me to get a second look at the terror I'd just witnessed.

After we'd exited the castle and were on its grounds, I tried to sit up. To fight.

"STOP!" I screeched, yanking on her mane. But she wouldn't listen.

I tried to lift my wings and fly from her back, but her own wings had reappeared and were strapping me down as she made her way swiftly over the grounds.

"I have to go back to him!" I protested, turning around, spotting Louisa racing behind us. A look of devastation coloring her face.

The world blurred beside my cries, my ignored protests that I be released. All I could think was that I needed to get back to him, that maybe my eyes had played tricks on me. Rally's sword . . . it couldn't have done what I thought it did.

Petal cantered through the fighting that continued to rage. Her hooves kicked up grass as dirt and blood grazed every inch of me—sticking to my tear-stricken face. My head was pounding, my voice was beginning to crack, and my vocal cords were giving out.

Finally, she steered us away into a bit of land still untouched by blood, and within seconds we had disappeared into the thick of the forest. As soon as she lessened her pace down to a trot, I let go of her mane and jumped from her back; the sword of Avalon releasing from her jaw as I immediately began pounding my fists into her side.

Attempting to shout at her with my wasted voice, my throat still coated in mucus and tears, I cried out, "Why did you tear me from that place! You *made* me leave him! You made me—"

"Makayla, stop. She only did as she was told."

My fists, embedded in Petal's white mane, clenched up.

"That's not real," I whispered, my eyes closed. But then a hand, *a warm hand*, touched my shoulder and pulled me away.

A fresh tear leapt from my eyes, and I reopened them, my body squaring itself with Toby's. "This can't be." My hand reached for his cheek, his hair—his everything. "He killed you. I saw . . . I saw his sword cut off your head."

"I am here with you, Makayla," he said, his hand reaching to grab mine.

"But if you are real, then how did you get from there to here so quickly?" My weak voice trembling, my hand in his, I searched his features for any discrepancies. For any evidence that this was a false character only playing the part of my dead king so that it could get close enough to slay me. Rally had been playing with dark magic; it was completely feasible that he could be using Toby's image to get to me.

"I have magic of my own, you know. Just because elves can't fly doesn't mean we can't get somewhere in a hurry."

I continued to peruse his likeness. My mind was reeling, jumping to every conclusion. I looked to Petal, who had taken to grooming herself. If this had been an imposter, she, if anyone, would have known.

"I don't understand. I saw what I saw . . . but you are fine. In fact, you look better than ever—" Suddenly, I jumped away, jolted by a thought. We'd been separated for a long time in that castle. In that castle full of creatures infected with a catching virus. "Toby, tell me you didn't let them, that you didn't become a . . ." I couldn't finish the sentence.

Toby calmly reached forward and grabbed my hands. "Makayla, what are you trying to say?"

"Did they turn you into a vampire?"

His expression softened and he smiled. "No, my queen. I believe it takes days to transform into one of those things."

I felt a tiny wave of relief, but not enough to cancel out the rest of my perturbation. "Then what the hell? I saw what I saw! I saw that dark cloud climb into Rally and give him the strength to lift that sword off the ground and take your head. Toby, I saw it! I'm not crazy!"

Toby waited a second for me to calm down. "No Makayla, you're not crazy."

I cocked a brow, freezing where I stood as I tried to catch my breath. And then it hit me. The necklace he'd been wearing since the moment I'd first met him; it was no longer around his neck. He followed my eyes to his chest and then looked back up at me.

"I may have known death was coming for me."

"That vial—it was—it—"

The smile on Toby's face widened as he pulled me into his

chest and placed his lips against mine, muting my jumbled thoughts. "I am here with you now," he said between breaths. "Rest your beating heart, save it for what is next."

When he pulled away, he bent down and picked up the Sword of Avalon, sticking it in between the leather belt that hung around my hips and my purple dress. "Come," he held out his hand for me to take, then helped me mount Petal.

"To where?" I asked, dizzied from all that had just occurred.

"To wherever it is *that* is to lead us." He gestured to the sword.

As he climbed up behind me, I glanced back at him. "But what about Louisa? We can't just leave her back there."

Petal began to trot, the trees beginning to speed by us more quickly as she picked up her pace.

"Do not worry about Louisa. She is strong. Besides, we need her to get back to her land so that she may redirect her army."

"What happened to her father—the king of Lauslin?"

"He saw what he shouldn't have been able to see, he saw your face in her sword. Soon after that he threatened to kill her. So, she beat him to the task."

"But my eyes don't reflect in her sword, I've seen it."

"Not *anymore*." Toby's arms grew tighter around my waist as the woods surrounding us began to blur into a mashed-up color of brown and green. "As soon as her sword slit his throat and she became queen, it reflected her own strength, for she fights in her own honor. After we win the fight against King Loral, the Knights of Lauslin who have sworn under your name, they will return their swords to her. For she is not a threat, but an ally."

"An ally," I repeated the words. Finally, in this nonsensical world, there was hope. "What about Rally, though. What will become of him?"

"I cannot say," Toby said. "He's been infected with more than one kind of venom now. If he survives the vampire transition, which not all do, then he will have to be dealt with."

"He's not the only one."

"What do you mean?"

An exasperated breath fell from my lips as I thought of Cee-Cee and the witch that now shared her body. The Crone of Light's End . . . She had no true body, no true home. And I was destined to not only take out Loral, but this witch.

I blinked away a tear. "I'm too exhausted to broach that subject right now—Toby, where are we?"

Petal had slowed her cadence enough for us to see that the trees we sped by were no longer trees, but bushes. The ground was purple, and we were climbing a steady hill. As Toby leaned in, placing his cheek against mine, he murmured, "I'm not sure, but I think it's safe to assume we are no longer in our own world."

I listened to the passing wind as it whistled into my ears. The sky was no longer blue; instead, the sun shining through thick gray clouds reflected the purple land. I inhaled the humid air into my nostrils, thick with sea salt—and then I heard them. Waves crashing in the distance.

"Toby."

"Yes."

"Who was it that Avalon was again?"

"Titania's cousin, a daughter of the sea."

I exhaled through my parted lips, cracked and stained with dried blood. "Right. Well, I hope someone here knows how to swim."

Toby shifted behind me, sitting taller. As soon as I said the words Petal reached the top of the hill, or mountain more like. Slowing her pace to a complete stop, she caught her breath while taking it all in. There was probably at least five miles of purple terrain between us and what lay below, but it was so vast we couldn't help but see it. The ocean.

"How are we supposed to find where we are supposed to go?" I gasped.

Petal shook her head and flipped her ears back and forth. Finally, for the first time since she'd picked me up back at the castle, she spoke. "I don't think one finds a child of a goddess; I think that child finds us."

"But from what I've heard, she was killed," I argued.

"So was Titania. That hasn't stopped her," Toby jested.

"Right. Well, what form did she take while she was alive? Perhaps we can find her people and go from there."

Petal looked back at me and then to Toby. "She was of the sea. What else would she have been?"

I nearly choked. A mermaid. Of course.

Just perfect.

It had been but a couple days since Makayla Wood had fled the land. Since that time, Dora had been keeping a keen eye on the boundaries of Lantern's Edge. The Robes desired for their priestess to join them at the castle, however Dora had kept them at bay, demanding that the girl needed more time to come back into her power. So far, they hadn't pushed. Still, Dora and her crew would need to get moving soon. The plan hindered over several glass pillars and the witch couldn't afford a single one to fall out of place. *The worlds* couldn't afford for a single one to fall out of place. If any one of those mindless drones—if just one single *robe*—mentioned anything from the past, it could shred all of her carefully constructed blueprints.

Outside the memory Dora inhabited, the entire forest was empty, save for a few less than courageous souls who had sunken into the shadows. The war was raging. Dankas versus Lanakes, good old fashioned good versus evil. Even the witches had come out from their quarters, and just as expected, they had taken sides. This part of the forest, however, was always desolate. Cold and unforgiving. Dora knew it well, for though the entrance to her inhabitance moved now and again, she had lived over this frozen ground and in the memory of Lantern's Edge for over two-hundred years.

"Where are you going?"

Dora looked down at the girl splayed arrogantly over the ancient furniture, her eyes the same in this body as they were in her last. Black. Did she recognize her yet, Dora wondered for the hundredth time? Messing with memories was tricky, the magic could fade anytime.

Dora had obviously set up insurance policies. She'd long ago disguised her likeness, altering her features so that she appeared much different from the witch born hundreds of years ago. But someone as powerful as *this* . . . No, she couldn't have recognized her; for if she had, it would have been obvious. And if the priestess figured out that the Robes desired her company because she was their long-lost savior, well, that would have been obvious too.

No way would Dora have let something of this proportion out from that binding unless it was still mostly chained down. The entity inside of Anastacia Montgomery's body was still missing a portion of her power, and Dora was the only witch to know where that portion existed. As far as the girl knew, it was now Dora's job to make her remember her past, and Dora *was* helping her . . . in Dora's way.

"I have some correspondence to tend to," Dora said in answer to the inquiry.

The girl's expression remained stiff. "I'm not yet finished with this lesson. You should stay in case I have questions."

Scoffing, Dora snapped back at her. "There are other things going on in this world right now besides your rise to power. You are not the only dog I have on a leash." She half expected the girl to rage at her comparison, but instead she came at her with a retort that fit the young face of the body she wore more easily than her ancient soul.

"I care not for this faery business. It does not matter who wears the crown, I can infiltrate any of them. What I'd like to know is what value there is in that sword . . ."

Dora's spine stiffened. Aeslin's speech had reached far and wide the day Makayla Wood followed her destiny and released the ghost from the king's pool. Dora had been ready for anything, and she'd been able to dull the vibrations that had seeped up against Lantern's Edge, shaking the memory that her and the girl had been inside of. But still, parts of the message got through, and now the girl was aware that the sword existed.

"'Tis but a status symbol," Dora had proclaimed. So far, the girl hadn't fought her on the subject, but Dora wasn't mindless—she continued to tread carefully.

Since that day, the Robes of Lorelei had taken charge of the castle. *Their huntress*, though removed from the earth's surface years ago after trying to infiltrate Avalon's people in search of her blade, had planted roots. And if the claims were correct, roots had been needed; for even though the huntress had been sent to her grave, she'd raised her son to take over the family business, if and when, the time came. But poor Rally had been bitten. Any day now, any hour, the half elf half wizard born of the huntress, would either show his face under the light of the moon or shrivel into the dirt and become nothing more than worm food.

Either way, the Robes now knew who had the Sword of Avalon, and so did the girl, but so far Dora had been able to keep the absolute truth about the sword's power away from her. It was the same sword the Bahidicaras had been searching for before they were taken out the first time. The robes, that copycat cult, had their assumptions as to where Makayla Wood had gone, but even if Dora and her new associate hadn't proclaimed that the faery was to remain alive *no matter what*, escaping back into their homeland would be suicide. To avoid death, they'd need their new priestess, and she wasn't ready.

"You say you don't care about Makayla Wood," Dora replied, "but even though you desire to know more about the sword she now carries, you refuse to let anyone hurt your old friend."

"She's not my friend," the girl barked back.

Dora simply raised a brow. It was true, she wasn't her friend, but the other soul who shared that body was, and that tiny little hold that Cee-Cee had over the priestess's speech was enough to let that faery get the head start she needed.

"Start over."

"What?"

Dora pointed to the dusty old grimoire in the girl's hands. "You heard me. Start over. You're not taking your lessons seriously. You browse over them as if you are above them. Magic will work differently in each body you take. Not to mention that it has been many years since you've taken one."

"That wasn't my fault. I may not remember who I used to be, but I know I was great." She raised an arm and pointed out into the forest. "I have *followers*." It was all Dora could do not to roll her eyes. Though Dora tread carefully around them, the fact remained that there were but a handful of witches who called themselves the Robes of Lorelei. True, witches were taking sides and some of them were standing with the Robes, but not a one of them knew what was coming. Oblivious to her teacher's musings, the girl continued. "Something, or some*one* took me down in my last life and that same someone kept me from reincarnating." Dora watched as the name 'Gloria' seeped from the girl's mouth before she bit the tip of her fingernail and stared out before her. "It's all there, in my dreams. I just—I can't remember the details when I wake."

Dora remained still, taking steadied breaths through her flared nostrils.

Eventually, the girl looked back up at her. "I need lemon."

Dora narrowed her eyes. "Why."

"I need to clear out some of this unwanted energy. It is crowding my memories."

"'Tis not around you, 'tis inside you," Dora clarified. "You were absent for a long time. Cee-Cee is as real as you or I. You can't *clear* her out."

She deviated her chin to the side. "I can try. She bothers me. Get me some lemon."

Dora looked at the ceiling and exhaled. "I have told you already, the market is shut down—everyone is fighting. No one is selling anything."

"Then go steal one off somebody's tree. Just get me some."

Dora's hands found her hips and the bottles around her waist shook. She didn't have to act this time; she was truly peeved. "You have hands. If you want the fruit so bad, *you* go steal it." And with that she turned and exited the space.

She didn't exhale again until she closed and sealed the door of the storage closet, collapsing her back against it and wiping her hands down the front of her face. Taking a deep breath, steadying herself and regaining her composure, she neared the large smoky quartz crystal ball that stood upon the same gold stand as it had when the scrying tool had belonged to her mother.

She centered herself, kicking the flats from her feet and scrunching her toes into the floorboards. After a few deep breaths, in through her nose and out through her mouth, she opened her eyes and allowed them to glow as green fire. When she was ready, she connected the pads of her fingers to the orb and waited as the smoke came alive inside the ball and began to swirl.

Only a minute after she'd made the call, he picked up.

"Sebastian," she said, her voice sounding anything but her own.

"Crone?"

"You've escaped," she said into the ball.

He nodded, then quickly shot a glance over his shoulder.

"You are right. No one seems to know of this place." His voice was tender, shaken—might one even daresay mortal. "I've heard the castle has been overtaken, that my once protégé—"

"*I* called *you*, Sebastian."

He froze on the other end of the call, then after a long moment, nodded his head. "Of course. What is it?"

"The Enclave Mountains."

His likeness didn't move, as if he was waiting for more. When she didn't offer more, he raised his brows. "What about them?"

"Could a descendant of Hecate be safe there?"

For years the bloodline had been hunted by what villagers and country people referred to as a single witch hunter. No one had ever seen a face, or even a glimpse of the shrouded figure who was rumored to have scraped and pawed through the worlds since the end of the Bahidicaras—ravaging through sand and forests to get to every last possible Hecate descendant. Still, as it stood, there were exactly three bodies left on the earth belonging to the goddess.

"I suppose. To be honest, I don't know that much about the place, other than getting to it is nearly impossible."

"And why is that?"

A wave of King Loral's royal temperament washed over his face. "Well, because of Breya's Pass of course."

Dora's thoughts centered over the name. *Breya* . . . Oh yes, she thought.

With but a quick blink of her glaring green eyes, she spat out, "Thank you, Sebastian. That will be all." And prepared to sign off.

"Wait!" She turned her cheek back towards the ball. The

arrogance he'd allowed to settle over his face for that brief moment had all but evaporated. "What happens now? I—I can't stay here."

Dora stared back at him with a practiced vacant expression. "Oh? And why not?"

"It's—It's a cave. There are ninny bears and other predators."

It was all she could do to keep herself from hexing him from afar. "You're an elf, Sebastian. Use your magic to protect yourself."

"There's no food!"

This time, Dora couldn't help it. Narrowing her eyes, she stated plainly, "Then maybe you shouldn't have taken out the one person in this world deranged enough to like you."

The king appeared aghast. "Killing Cathy was simply an act of—"

"I do not mean the kitchen witch, Sebastian." Dora took a moment to let the message sink in, and when the moment felt right, pulled her fingers from the ball, allowing the smoke to still inside the crystal.

She backed away from the pedestal and her eyes returned to normal. As if she'd done nothing more than come into the closet to check on her Rosemary supply, she exited the space. She pulled her black shawl over her shoulders as she neared the main living area. Ever since the girl had come here, it had gotten colder.

Dora rested her eyes over the evil who shared her space; the girl looked up from her reading.

"What were you doing?"

Her armor back in place, thick as steel, she replied, "I took a moment. Is that okay with you, Anastacia?"

"I told you not to call me that."

"I will call you by your true name when you earn it."

The girl continued to stare her down.

"Whatever," she rolled her eyes. "I'm hungry. Make me some food."

Dora scoffed. "You can feed yourself. I have things to tend to." She turned and made as if to walk away, but before she left the room completely, she heard the girl whisper very quietly over the pages of the book.

"Be careful."

Dora turned back towards the girl and narrowed her eyes like a mother would to her insolent daughter. "Excuse me?"

"You heard me," she said without lifting her eyes. "I said, be careful, witch."

Dora relaxed the muscles around her eyes, as well as her shoulders. But she didn't reply. Instead, she continued her way out of the room and didn't stop until she got to the back door, strutting ever so quickly to the stream that ran behind the house.

Sinking her fingers into the trickling water, she let out a ragged breath. She could do this. She'd come this far. And in the end, she had no choice.

Suddenly a chill overcame her, one that had nothing to do with the forest. Looking over her shoulder, she saw her. The girl. She couldn't get away from her no matter where she went.

As she prepared for another round of uneasy conversation, a yellow butterfly that didn't belong to this memory fluttered around her head.

Wait . . . Dora instructed.

The butterfly danced around her for a second longer then flew over towards the branch of a tree.

The girl strutted over to the creek and Dora stood.

"I am tired of these lessons. I know you are plotting our next steps; I demand to know what they are."

Dora smoothed out her skirt and ensured all her glass bottles were secured in place around her leather belt. "Your tea leaves, we've read them three times now. I have seen where we need to go. 'Tis treacherous."

The girl's black eyes squinted back at Dora. "I'll be the judge of that. Where are we going?"

"The Enclave Mountains. To get there we must first pass by the sisters of the undead. I shall need time alone, to secure offerings to the goddess. We will need all the help we can get to receive safe passage."

The girl's expression didn't budge, nor did she. "Shall we call on the Robes?"

"No. I've already taken care of our guard."

"Fine. When do we leave?"

Dora sighed. "The journey is a rough one. We will head for the pass tomorrow."

The girl very slowly let up on her guard and gave a curt nod to her teacher as she started to turn away. Dora began to let the air she'd coupled into her chest seep out from her lips, but before she could completely let her shoulders relax, the girl swung halfway around and looked back at her while pointing a finger at the house.

"Didn't there at one point used to be a lake in front of this cottage?"

It was all Dora could do to remain fixed in her position. The spirit inside the girl had not yet figured out how to read minds as she had in her previous life, but Dora had no choice but to pretend as though she could. It would be more than unwise to underestimate the volume of evil that stood before her.

Dora casually placed a hand in the pocket of her skirt and gazed at the house as if she was looking through it. "There may have been." Lightly. She had to tread lightly. "A lot has changed since you've last walked the earth." And the longer she could keep the priestess ignorant the better.

The girl pushed a finger into her cheek while placing her

attention wholly over Dora. "You know I have all these memories in here . . . from *her*." She spoke of the other spirit in her body as if it were an infestation. "Shortly before I was released, Cee-Cee was accosted by a couple of witches who looked rather worse for the wear. They spoke of the lost child . . . they mentioned the name Malina."

Dora had to refrain from tightening her fist. "Oh?"

"Do you know anything about any of that?"

Dora sighed as if there weren't ten thousand pounds raining over her chest and shoulders. "Haven't you heard a single thing I've told you about this world we're in right now? 'Tis under attack. The king has turned all the creatures against one another, including our brothers and sisters." She shook her head. "What Cee-Cee most likely encountered was a couple of deranged witches, their minds scrambled from the wand of Sebastian Loral."

Dora continued to steady her nerves as the girl soaked in her explanation. *Take the bait,* she pleaded.

"Huh," the girl mused. "That elf really is a piece of work, isn't he? Are we sure we can't just end him and get him out of the way?"

"Like I've said, there is only one with the touch to make that happen. We must continue on our own path, Anastacia."

The girl's eyes dimmed, and her head shook as if a bee had flown into her ear. "I really don't want you to call me that."

Dora folded her hands together before her stomach. "Fine. What would you like to be called then?"

"Priestess will do until I can get my memories back."

"As you wish," Dora said, thanking Hecate that her communication had come out so smoothly.

Finally, the girl turned and began trekking back to the house. Without turning back to face Dora, she added, "We will leave first thing. I am done sitting here like a duck waiting to be roasted." Then she aimed her wand at the branch of a tree, watched as a yellow fruit blossomed to life, and plucked it. Only then did she turn around and shoot the nastiest glimmer of a smile she could muster in Dora's direction. "For the riff raff."

Dora waited until the girl was back indoors to deflate. Careful to keep her back to the windows but her ears open, she sat back down before the creek, dipping her fingers into the stream.

Before long the butterfly was back.

Dora listened to its message, which by all accounts was quite bizarre. When it was done with its recording it simply hovered by Dora's ear.

Flutter around, Dora insisted of the insect. It did as it was told as she rolled around the thoughts she couldn't quite lasso together. After several hurried calculated moments, she sent her reply.

I'll meet you as you wish. At the sacred grounds once the sun has found its coffin.

She then dipped her forehead towards the butterfly, acknowledging that she was finished. A second later, it flew away. The sacred grounds . . . Dora hadn't walked that bit of earth since the day she'd arrived in Garlandia.

The witch sighed. It was just Dora, her belt full of empty jars, the memory of the stream she'd played in as a child, and the ghost of more than one of the persons from her past living inside that body of a girl.

The lake. The girl had remembered the lake. However, she truly hadn't seemed to have evoked more than that memory. No, so far so good. The girl didn't know who she was, only that she had been someone of great importance. She did not know that before she rose to power all those years ago, she had in fact lived in this house, and that the lake she could somewhat remember was the turning point in all their lives. For it was in that lake that she had tried to drown her daughter, and it was in that lake that Dora had been reborn.

Dora pulled a blade of grass between her fingers as she rocked back and forth. "'Tis time now, Mother, time for you to finally be forever gone."

This time there would be no hiccup. This time, Dora would finish what she'd set out to do. And this time, she wasn't about to let anyone get in the way.

ACKNOWLEDGMENTS

A huge shout out to my publisher, Creative James Media. Thank you once again for taking a shot on this new author. Also, thank you to all my street team members and readers who have already begun to follow Makayla's journey. You are bringing her to life.

Thank you to my little family—my husband who doesn't know how to not support me anymore than I don't know how to live life without stories pouring out of me. And to my beautiful daughter. Liv, you're my muse, my heart, and my forever.

Thank you to my sister and mom for always seeding my creativity with talk of faeries and sprites, and to all of the vibrant personalities and wonderful weirdos who have helped shape me over the years. We are all connected. I found Garlandia through all of you.

Thank you.

ABOUT THE AUTHOR

Mariah Stillbrook, originally from Iowa, lives in Colorado with her white German shepherd, husband, and little girl. She graduated from the University of Colorado at Colorado Springs. She spends most of her days writing, reading, and enjoying the occasional hike. In her late twenties she realized that her writing was missing something, magic. She now focuses her writing on horror and urban fantasy in both adult and young adult genres.

www.ingramcontent.com/pod-product-compliance
Lightning Source LLC
Chambersburg PA
CBHW061630190726
48289CB00006B/1553